Other works by M.J. Stewart

Kingdom of Lorr series (Epic Fantasy)

WorldGate Crossing

The Return

Demon of Lorr

Key Quest

Displacement

Displacement: The Long Sleep

Heralds of the Culling series (Vampire action/horror)

Heir of Darkness

Blood of the Third

Previews and purchasing information at:

https://majorstewart.com/

The Kingdom of Lorr:
The Return

M.J. Stewart

M.J. STEWART

Paperback
ISBN-13: 978-0-9889158-2-4

ISBN-10: 0988915820

Ebook
ISBN: 978-0-9889158-0-0

This is a work of fiction. Names, characters, places and incidents either are the product of the author's imagination or are used fictitiously, and any resemblance to any actual persons, living or dead, events, or locales is entirely coincidental.

Dedications

Dr. Denise, I love you for your patience, your eyes, your smile, and for completing me.

To Major II (aka “Super”), I love you for being the perfect combination of Dr. Denise and me. You got the best parts of both of us, and a little bit of my crazy.

Mom and Dad (may he rest in comfort), I love you both for raising me to be confident, determined, and respectful to those who deserve respect.

Can’t forget Veloria and Billie. Thanks for being the best sisters a little brother could have. Love y’all!

PROLOGUE

Joel gave the steering wheel an affectionate squeeze as he drove up the highway, his shiny brown leather gloves crunching against the rubber-coated steering wheel. He smiled inwardly and considered himself blessed. He did not think he would ever return to the town he called home, at least not to stay. The people at the Catholic church-sponsored group home where he grew up told him that he was actually from the east coast, but he had no memory of that. They said a Catholic priest visiting Maryland found him as a homeless toddler near the harbor. The priest, a middle aged Irish-American named Father O'Shea, took an instant liking to the young boy and could not let such a young, imperiled child fend for himself on the mean streets of Baltimore. Without Father O'Shea, there was no telling what kind of life – assuming he would have survived – Joel would have had.

Many of his peers at the orphanage and group home in Chicago drifted away from the church as they grew older, swallowed up by the myriad dangers in the rough neighborhoods on the South Side. Gangs, drugs, and other forms of shady endeavors claimed most of his childhood friends. Joel, on the other hand, had always had a knack for staying out of trouble. And on the few occasions he could not avoid trouble, he wasted no time getting the hell away from it. With the exception of a particularly traumatic experience with a fellow eighth grade student, he did not have any problems out of the ordinary during his years in the group home and Catholic school.

The home and school were his refuge from the streets. The priests and nuns were glad to have him, proud, in fact. When he reached the legal working age he immediately went to work at the group home. He did well in the Catholic high school he attended while earning his keep as a counselor's assistant until he eventually became a junior counselor himself. By the time he finished high school, he had earned several scholarship offers to both big and small universities. He chose to become a vocational education major at a historically Black university in Montgomery, Alabama.

Father O'Shea urged him to attend Notre Dame, but Joel chose a different direction. After attending Catholic school his entire life, and enjoying the experience, Joel felt he had missed out on a lot of his African American culture. There was no bitterness about it. But when he had the chance to learn more about his heritage he decided to seize it. The decision turned out to be a good one. The historically black university experience fulfilled him in a way that he knew no other school could have.

And, best of all, he met the love of his life there. During his junior year at Alabama State he met Lisa, the woman who would eventually become his wife, while partying at Tuskegee University with classmates. Lisa was in the pre-veterinary medicine program and planned to go to Tuskegee's School of Veterinary Medicine. She was two years behind him and Joel initially thought their relationship would last only until he graduated. He was wrong.

There was something different about her from the very beginning. Something special. It took him a while to figure out what it was. She was pretty, no doubt. Not in that artificial, superficial, cover-girl way, but more in a girl-next-door kind of way. She was petite and slim, with a figure blessed with soft curves that were easily hidden in loose, unassuming clothes but surprisingly fetching on the few occasions when she chose to wear something form-fitting. There was a refreshing sincerity in her big brown eyes and bright smile. And, somehow, she managed to be both shy and confident at the same time.

All of these things were more than enough to attract him to her, but none of those things were what really set her apart from other women. When he finally realized what did, he thought he might have been going crazy. What set her apart from other women, what captivated him more than anything else, was...well... She smelled good. All the time. It had nothing to do with perfume or soap or deodorant or hairspray.

It was simply *her*. One of his favorite things to do was to stand near her or lie next to her and just breathe the air around her. Joel never told anyone – not even her – for fear that people would think he was weird.

Even though her scent captivated him and she was pleasing to behold, what made him fall in love was the way they fit. They were like puzzle pieces: he was strong where she was weak and where he was weak she was strong. Her laid-back attitude perfectly complimented his quicker temper. Her somewhat skittish nature toward everything except animals was bolstered by his boldness. And they genuinely liked each other. They enjoyed many of the same things and had a similar sense of humor. They recognized that had there never been a romantic attraction between them, they could have easily been best friends. He fell more deeply in love than he had ever thought possible, and apparently, so had she.

Instead of returning to Chicago after he graduated, as he planned before falling for her, he went to graduate school at Tuskegee so that they could be together. They were married shortly after her graduation and he worked to support them while she attended vet school. He quickly found out that the job market in the small college town of Tuskegee was almost nonexistent. The few job offerings at the university did not pay enough to support them adequately so he found work in Montgomery, AL. forty miles away.

It was a stressful time financially but their love served as their anchor. It took him a while to find a decent job as a computer-aided drafting teacher at a private technical high school in Montgomery. In the interim, with the expenses of life in general and vet school in particular, as well as a job that barely paid enough to cover the two, they had substantial financial struggles and accrued a great deal of debt. He had no family to lend support and her family could afford to help only so much. For the most part, they were on their own. People often told Joel that better paying jobs could be found in different parts of the country; that he should go east to Atlanta and work while his wife finished school in Tuskegee, which was only a couple of hours away.

Joel would not hear of it. He was Lisa's support system and she was his. There was no way he would leave her side. Not even a distance of less than two hundred miles was tolerable. They struggled together through four years of veterinary school and one year of an internship before all of their hard work and struggle finally paid off.

Lisa was offered a position at a veterinary hospital in Chicago that was to begin at the start of the next year. Joel was elated. He would get to go home after thinking he would spend the rest of his life in the south. He did not have anything against the south. The winters were obviously much better if one preferred sun to snow, which he did, but the south simply was not his home. He was more concerned about his wife, who was born and raised in Louisiana and had never seriously considered leaving the south. But the job offer was too good to refuse. Joel tendered his resignation at the end of the fall semester. The school administration hated to see him go but they wished him well.

Now he was driving them home…to *his* home. The Mason Dixon line was miles behind them and so was the relative warmth of the southern winter. They were far enough into Illinois that snow blanketed the ground and they had to crank the heat up higher to keep their breath from turning to vapor within their double-cab pickup truck.

Joel was startled out of his reverie by the roar of an engine growing louder behind him. A green, late model Honda Civic came up in a hurry, driving way too fast for the sleet-streaked two-lane highway. The driver darted into the southbound lane to pass them. Both the male driver and the man riding in the passenger seat had their heads turned in his direction as they shot past. Both African American men were wearing sunglasses that hid their eyes. Joel could only assume they were looking at him, though it was quite possible that they were looking past him at his wife where she sat sleeping on the passenger side.

They jumped back into the correct lane too soon. Joel had to break to keep them from clipping the front of his truck but he was not quite successful. The other car's passenger side taillight hit the driver side corner of the truck bumper. The sudden deceleration and the sound of the impact woke Lisa with a small yelp. The car skid to a halt ahead of them and Joel pumped his breaks frantically to keep from making contact with the car a second time. Mercifully, the truck came to a stop less than ten yards away.

Both the driver and the passenger of the other car threw their doors open violently and got out of their vehicles. Joel, more composed than the two strangers, climbed down out of the truck.

"Be careful," he heard Lisa say. He turned and smiled at her. Her face was creased with worry and she gave her husband a concerned look. "People are crazy nowadays."

"Don't worry, baby," Joel assured.

He inspected the front end of his truck. The damage was minimal, the bumper having absorbed the impact. The other car, however, had a dented rear fender and smashed tail light.

"You hit me in the back," the driver accused. He stepped closer as he ranted. "Where the hell did you learn to drive?"

Joel was tempted to match the other's attitude but thought better of it. "You cut in front of me a little too soon," he countered in a calm voice. "But it's not that serious."

"Not that serious?" the other echoed, coming to a stop barely an arm's reach away from Joel. "Look at my shit! Somebody's paying for that!"

"Let's just exchange insurance information," Joel soothed. "Then we can – "

"Here's my insurance, nigga!" The driver pulled a pistol from the pocket of his bomber jacket and let it hang at his hip. "It insures that you're going to give us whatever the hell we want."

Joel stepped back and brought his arms up in a defensive posture. His heart raced and fear turned his pulse to thunder in his ears. He knew this was no empty threat. It was like he could smell the stranger's dark intentions.

"This ain't necessary, man," Joel sputtered. "We can work something out."

The thug brought up his right hand to level his pistol at Joel's head and took another step forward. Joel chanced a look back at his wife. Lisa's eyes were wide with fear and her eyebrows knitted with worry. The gunman looked over Joel's shoulder and noticed Lisa.

"Hmmm. Maybe we *can* work something out." The gunman agreed with a leer and a wolfish grin. "Now I know what we gonna do when we're done with you."

The hungry smile on the gunmen's faces left no doubt about their intentions. Joel could feel his heart rate rev so high that it sounded like a low hum. Sharp scarlet suddenly rimmed his vision. An unexplainable inner heat erupted around the base of his neck and rushed into his skull. He went light-headed, and for an instant all he saw was crimson darkness. He thought he would stagger from the sudden rush of anger but he was still standing when his vision cleared only a moment later.

His assailants were not.

The gunman lay at Joel's feet, with the right side of his face resting in the slush on the pavement. His dead eyes bulged with fear; his mouth frozen in a silent scream. A round crimson cavity dotted his temple and a dark red puddle crept out ominously from under his head, mixing with the soot-gray slush.

His companion lay sprawled beside the passenger side of the car, his head propped up on the curb. The middle of his forehead was adorned with a ruby-red hole identical to the one in the gunman's temple. Blood ran down the curb from behind his head. A gun lay on the wet ground just a few inches away from his limp right hand. He looked down at his own right hand to see the gunman's pistol locked in his fist. The heat from its nose warmed his thigh.

He heard a vaguely familiar voice.

"Joel...baby?"

He turned to see his wife standing outside of their truck with a fearful look on her face. The pistol slipped out of his gloved hand. Lisa's lips moved again. An instant later her voice was in his ears.

"Let's go, baby." She tried unsuccessfully to mask the fear in her quivering voice. "It's time for us to leave."

Joel looked back at the dead men and at the gun now lying by his foot. He turned back to Lisa.

"I did that...didn't I?"

"Let's talk about it in the car, Joel."

She calmly beckoned to him as she made her way around the front of the vehicle to the driver's side.

"I don't remember..." He said it so quietly that his wife could barely make out the words. "Everything went black – or red. I don't..."

"I'll drive," she said in as comforting a voice as she could manage. "Just sit down and relax."

Her husband took two hesitant steps to the passenger side door and then stopped. "No," he began. "I can't...we can't leave like this. We gotta call the police or something. This was self-defense, so..." his hand went toward the cell phone hooked onto his belt.

"I don't think that's a good idea," Lisa warned. "Do you even know where we are? We've been on this stretch of highway for hours and I haven't seen anything but snow and gray sky," she spread her arms and turned to emphasize how barren their surroundings actually were. "I can't remember how long ago we passed the nearest town. Who knows how long it'll take for the police to get here."

Joel looked over at the dead men. "But we can't..."

"This could be mistaken for road rage," she argued. "The police may think we skid into them and then had a shootout. I'm about to start a new job and you're about to start looking for one. We don't need this. Let's just get out of here."

"Can you live with this on your conscience, Lisa?"

"I'm damn sure willing to find out," she answered nervously. "I don't think I'll feel all that guilty."

Joel glared at her. "You didn't pull the trigger."

Lisa put a hand on her hip the way she did when she was about to make a point. Joel never knew if she was bracing herself or signaling for him to brace himself. She met her husband's glare and spoke.

"These motherfuckers were going to *kill* you," the nervousness in her voice was replaced by icy seriousness. "They were probably gonna rape me before they killed me, too. You shouldn't give a damn if they rot out here!"

Joel finally remembered what the man said before everything went red and black. The memory dulled the pangs of fear and guilt. They were dulled but not dismissed.

Lisa's gaze softened. "I just don't want to lose you." She patted her stomach. "*We* don't want to lose you."

Joel lifted an eyebrow suspiciously. "Now you wanna play the baby card?"

"I'm not playing, Joel. This might be Illinois, but we're closer to Kentucky than Chicago. This is redneck country and I'm scared things could go bad for us."

Joel exhaled sharply before climbing into the car and slamming the door. Lisa hurried and followed suit on the driver's side. She fired up the truck and drove away, tossing one more frightful look at her husband's handiwork as she steered around the carnage. And then she looked at him. He was staring straight ahead with a blank expression.

As she drove, Lisa rubbed her forehead with her right hand the way one would wipe away sweat, even though her forehead was cool and dry. Joel noticed the movement and recognized his wife's nervous tick. Lisa wondered what was going through Joel's mind. She wondered what he had been thinking – or better yet, *if* he had been thinking – when he killed their would-be assailants.

He told her that he did not remember doing it.

She remembered.

"I was afraid of this," Joel finally said. "I've always been of afraid this."

"You mean fighting," Lisa realized. "You once told me that your last fight was in the eighth grade. And you lost it. Not the fight, but the memory of it. After that you were afraid to fight."

Joel did not respond, so Lisa looked at the road ahead. The sky was a vast expanse of gray. Thick, dirty clouds stretched across the northern horizon ahead of her, as well the horizon to her left and right, blotting out the morning sun. The clouds were saturated with the same sooty grayness as the slush and snow that was pushed up into mounds on both sides of the road. The day, just starting, already seemed worn and tired.

The dreariness was reflected in her husband's eyes as he recalled a memory that he never completely shared with her. He would only say that he had "lost it" and it frightened him.

Lisa never pressed the issue because of the mood that enveloped him whenever he spoke of it. Her curiosity was piqued now, and more importantly, her husband's silence worried her. She knew it was unsafe to bottle up troublesome emotions. As his wife, she believed she should share his burden. She hoped that talking about it aloud might allow him to let some of the hurt go.

"What happened back then?" she asked.

Joel took a deep breath. He started to speak but he paused, clearly considering whether he should or not.

"It's probably nothing," he said quietly. "Not even worth talking about."

"What happened?" she pressed. Her voice was soft and gentle, yet laced with a firmness that made it clear that she would brook no refusal. "Why was that fight so traumatic? How did you lose it?"

Joel exhaled and surrendered. "I almost killed the kid," he said quickly, as if saying it fast would somehow lessen the pain of the admission.

Lisa glanced at him with concern, waiting for him continue. After another few breaths, he did.

"The cause of the fight was silly," Joel began. "We'd been playing touch football during recess at the catholic group home. I was on the kickoff team and we were going after the returner. The blockers had lined up and were coming at us. I ended up squaring off with this guy named Finley. I knew I was quicker than him so I gave a little fake and spun right around him and got to the kickoff returner for an easy two-handed tag. Everybody saw it. Finley was embarrassed."

Joel smiled at the memory, but the smile was a brief one.

"I teased him real good about it all through recess, talking trash about how he was 'too slow to mess with the kid.' After a while I could tell it got under his skin and that just egged me on."

"Kids can be pretty cruel," Lisa noted.

"I was no different," Joel confirmed. "I kept after him after the bell rung, following him back into the school building. Some of my homeboys who saw the play had joined in the teasing and we could see he was getting pissed."

"So you kept at it?" Lisa asked.

"Of course. We were going up an enclosed outdoor stairway leading to the side entrance. I was a couple of stairs behind him and teasing him constantly. When Finley reached the top of stairs, I guess he got good and fed up. He turned around and shoved me with both hands. I was a bony little boy and he was taller and a lot heavier than me, so of course I went down."

"Did you get hurt?" Lisa asked, caught up in the story. The way he told it caught her attention more than the facts themselves.

"Two of my friends caught me before I hit the stairs. I regained my balance and I thought about how badly I could've been hurt. All I could think of was my head being cracked open on those concrete stairs. For a second I really thought that boy was trying to kill me and a second was all it took. That was when I lost it. I literally saw red and rushed back up the stairs at him. He took a swing, I ducked and the next thing I knew..." he fell silent again, recalling the moment internally before speaking of it aloud.

"The next thing you knew…" Lisa urged.

"I jumped up, grabbed his head and pulled him to the brick wall of the enclosure. I was gonna bash his head against that wall as hard as I could and as many times as I could."

"But you stopped yourself, right?"

"Just barely," Joel told her. "But that's not the scariest part. After the other kids broke us up and Sister Mary gave us a paddling, I found out from one of my friends that there was a lot more to the fight than I remembered."

They said I that after I ducked that right hook, I just unloaded on him. They told me I hit him close to ten times, in the stomach, the head, the chest, wherever I could find an opening. I didn't remember any of it and I still don't."

"You blacked out," Lisa said. "I've heard of that happening to lots of people."

"But I remember the last part," Joel pressed. "I wanted to kill him. I was *trying* to kill him. If I had been out of it for a couple more seconds, I probably *would've* killed him. Who knows where I'd be right now?"

Lisa glanced over at him. He clutched the cross-strap of his seatbelt with a white-knuckled grip.

"That's why I never let myself get into another fight," he continued. "How can I trust myself if I black out that way but keep on fighting? My greatest fear is that I wouldn't come to in time and I'd end up getting myself killed without even realizing it. Or..." he trailed off.

Doing what you just did back there, Lisa concluded to herself. Joel glanced back over his shoulder as if he could still see the bodies on the slushy concrete now miles away.

"It's like I turned into a different person," Joel went on, "like a wild animal or something."

Lisa was quiet for a moment, as if measuring her words. Joel gave her a curious look until she responded.

"You weren't like a wild animal," she corrected.

Joel continued to look at her questioningly, his eyes asking her to continue even though he could not bring himself to say the words.

"You weren't wild at all, Joel. What you did back there looked," she tried to find the words. "It looked smooth," she decided. "It looked like a rehearsed move, something you might have been trained to do."

Joel leaned in as close as his seatbelt would allow. "What did it look like exactly?"

Lisa told him, reliving the disturbing incident in her mind as she spoke:

> *Lisa's heart almost stopped when she saw the guns. Firearms had always terrified her, and suddenly, for no good reason, a gun was pointed at her husband. She did not hear what the gunman said but his leer at her, followed by a nervous glance from her husband, had given her a pretty good indication that more than her life was in danger.*
>
> *The chill of fear eased up her spine. After the quick look over his shoulder, Joel's back was to her the whole time – as short as it was – so that she never got to look into his eyes*

during the events that followed. For some reason, however, she was glad for that. There was no telling what she might have seen there.

What she did see shocked her. The whole thing happened in just a few seconds but Lisa remembered every bit of it. She saw her husband's hands flash up and out and she just knew he was a dead man. His right hand locked onto the gunman's right wrist. The heel of his left palm simultaneously struck the back of the gunman's elbow. With the wrist held firmly, the blow to the elbow caused the gunman's arm to bend the wrong way with a loud snap that Lisa could hear from the car. The pain sent the attacker to his knees and the gun slipped from his hand. Joel released the man's wrist and his right hand darted toward the falling pistol.

The man at the passenger side of the car reached toward the pistol tucked into his belt. Lisa barely had time to gasp.

By the time the other's hand closed on the handle of his pistol, Joel had snatched the falling gun right out of the air. When the man at the passenger side of the car had cleared his own gun from his belt, Joel was pointing the retrieved firearm. By the time the gunman had his weapon in firing position Joel had already squeezed off a shot.

The gunman at the passenger side of the car never got off a shot of his own. His head snapped back as a dark red cavity appeared in his forehead and a spray of blood and chunks of brain burst from the back of his head. Lisa watched in terrified awe as the man crumpled to the ground.

She returned her focused to husband. He was calmly stepping forward, toward the man whose arm he had just broken. The would-be assassin was using his functional arm to drag himself back toward his open car door.

Joel was having none of it. He took one more step closer, aimed, and fired. The man fell still with a steaming hole in his temple.

Lisa looked back over to the first man who was shot. One last exhalation turned into vapor as it touched the icy winter air before he went completely limp.

Her husband just stood there. She could see his head move slowly from side to side as he coldly inspected the dead bodies. He did not move again until she called his name.

"But they were going to kill us," she finished, reiterating the justification she used earlier. "You did the only thing you could do."

"You said I shot one in the temple and one in the middle of the forehead," Joel argued, turning to look out of the passenger side window as if he too ashamed to look his wife in the eye. "I executed them! If I was so smooth and precise, why didn't I just injure them enough for us to get away?"

As Joel expected, Lisa had no answer for that. Joel shook his head, trying in vain to jar his own memory, to get some inkling as to how and why he could do what his wife described. The semi-passive man who, since that fight in the eighth grade had always been able to talk, walk, or run his way out of physical confrontations had transformed into an efficient, heartless killing machine in a matter of seconds.

He tried to use his wife's argument on himself: There was no reasoning his way out of that confrontation. He knew he could not plead or bullshit the men out of their deadly plans. James had always had a knack for reading people's intentions in their eyes no matter what words came out of their mouths. In this case their would-be assailants' intentions and words matched perfectly. They had no intention of letting him and his wife live.

But the loss of memory and the loss of control still frightened him. It was like he had turned into a completely different person. What if that person – for some ungodly reason – was ever to turn against someone he cared about?

Fat snowflakes began to fall softly from the gray clouds. Both Joel and Lisa hoped the snowfall would conceal forever the death they left in their wake.

Both of them knew they hoped in vain.

PART I

PREDATORS AND PREY

Chapter 1: Eight Kings

The great citadel stood at the crest of the lone mountain that formed the island. In actuality, the island was only the top quarter of a massive mountain that rose from the depths of the Ocean Crystalline. The mountain isle was all that was left of a continent that had been submerged below miles of salt water. The citadel had at one time stood commandingly above an entire continent and had been the earth-bound home of the first generation of Leader Children.

But that was before Heaven's War. Rather than cede the land to the descendants of the victorious Protector Children, the Leaders unleashed a power that shook the foundation of the continent to its very core, causing the great landmass to disappear into the ocean and all but fade from memory.

Much of the great citadel had fallen into ruin. It survived Heaven's War with more than a few blemishes but time had ravaged it far worse than even the devastating war. Most of the outer walls had crumbled. The ones that survived stood as a powerful testament to the citadel's past greatness. Some of the surviving outer walls climbed hundreds of feet into the air before ending in rough edges that were jagged and, in some cases, singed to blackness. A few of the surviving wall segments soared to their full height. Those walls were so high that the battlements were obscured in the low-hanging cloud mist that perpetually hovered over the island.

The citadel had once been a symbol of divine inspiration and awe. War, time, and neglect, however, had reduced it to a symbol of decay and the methodical, inexorable corruption of purity. In hindsight, that was an accurate reflection of what the world had become once the terrible war ended.

Prior to the war, the walls of the citadel were a pristine ivory that seemed right at home with the gleaming clouds floating in the heavens. On clear days, the mountaintop could be seen from halfway across the now-submerged continent. Now, the stone that formed the soaring walls were dark gray and imposing.

The high turrets, the sprawling battlements and ramparts, and the lofty towers with climbing spires that disappeared into the clouds had once seemed to form a physical link between heaven and earth. Now, those same structures resembled cursed monoliths being pushed slowly from grace into the bowels of the ocean.

Most of the inner walls had crumbled as severely as the outer ones, as had the peripheral structures of the castle proper. Unbeknownst to all but a very small few, however, the heart of the citadel stood nearly whole. Though it had been almost completely vacant for over two thousand years, the weatherworn walls that formed the central structures were, with the exception of some visible cracking, intact. The heart of the citadel remained almost as awesome as it had been two thousand years earlier.

From the outside of the citadel, the surviving outer walls were tall enough to effectively conceal the structures within. However, a bird's eye view – if unobstructed by the heavy, low-hanging cloud cover – revealed a palatial construction at the exact geographical center of the mountain crest. When the stronghold was whole the rest of the citadel had dwarfed the central structure. But even now, despite the decay of the surrounding citadel, the central palace was still larger than any other man-made structure in the Known Lands.

The central structure consisted of a massive set of walls that connected six soaring towers arranged to form the points of an equilateral hexagon. A series of multi-storied catwalks, supported by massive columns with footings anchored hundreds of feet deep beneath the dense earth of the mountaintop, stretched two hundred feet inward from each tower to the corners of the inner walls. The inner walls were over fifty feet higher than the outer walls, and were roughly two hundred feet outside of the walls of the main keep.

Sailors and sky sleigh pilots alike never ventured out far enough on – or over – the Ocean Crystalline to know the island and citadel existed, out of fear that their vessels would be claimed by the nightmares that patrolled the far-flung expanses of the ocean. The deep, foreboding waters surrounding the all-but-submerged mountain formed the extreme outer edge of one of the natural and impassible borders separating the Known Lands from the Unknown

Lands. These waters were known to contain creatures so gargantuan that they could reach high enough above the surface to pluck the highest-flying sky sleigh out of the air without ever completely emerging from the sea.

There were also sea-creatures that could glide high above the surface of the ocean. They could only glide for distances relatively short for their incredible size, but that was more than far enough and fast enough to catch the avicaws that bore sky sleighs – or any other bird that dared to fly over the treacherous region.

Despite the dangers surrounding the island citadel, eight small but well guarded sky sleigh crews were camped at various locations just outside of those high walls. They were able to reach the island because every sleigh carried a sovereign of one of the kingdoms of the Known Lands.

Each sitting king or queen of the Known Lands was bequeathed with the knowledge of the whereabouts of the remote citadel and the ability to reach it safely. Without that enchantment, the location of the island would disappear from one's memory like a light puff of smoke in a strong breeze. The sovereigns were the only ones who knew the way, and as such, they had to act as navigator on every trip. If their reign as king or queen ended while they yet lived, the memory of the island's whereabouts fled them as surely as every other person the moment the new sovereign took the throne.

This knowledge was a legacy of magic created by the Children of the Old Ones after the citadel was conquered. This legacy passed from sovereign to sovereign without fail and without any ritual or talisman needed to facilitate the transfer. It allowed a sovereign to travel on or above these waters without their vessels attracting the attention of the leviathans swimming beneath them. Sky sleighs, however, were always the vessel of choice. While the kings and queens of the Known Lands believed and trusted in the magic, they did not dare making the trip in a ship. They did not want to chance brushing up against a creature that might be swimming near the surface. For all they knew, such a physical encounter with one of the great beasts might very well circumvent the protective magic.

The men and women that comprised the crews of the eight royal sky sleighs eyed each other warily but did not communicate. While none of the kingdoms were at war at the moment, there were still simmering disagreements between several of them as well as lingering hostilities from past conflicts. The island was established as a neutral zone, a place of peaceful negotiation and discussion where absolutely no fighting was to take place. So while the sky sleigh crews would not engage each other, they would certainly not let down their guard as they kept watch around the citadel's main keep.

The keep was a monstrous, hexagonal edifice that claimed over a square mile of the land at the center of the vast mountaintop. The central spire of its cathedral roof disappeared into the clouds. A tower pierced the sky at each corner of the keep. The spires atop each reached half the height of the great central spire.

Within the easternmost tower, eight kings and queens sat around a large, decagonal conference table in an ornate meeting room. Raised voices echoed through the large chamber, the sound traveling up and around the high domed ceiling as the sovereigns held several different arguments simultaneously.

The conference table was made of a thick slab of stone that bore a strong resemblance to marble. The stone was carved into a perfect equal-sided decagon. Elaborate geometrical designs were etched flawlessly into the smooth, shining tabletop. Gleaming gems of various hues were inlaid into some of the etchings as well as other parts of the stone to form beautiful glyphs and runes that radiated outwards from the center of the table in patterns that were at once chaotic, symmetrical, mathematical and beautiful.

No one seated at the table knew what those symbols and images meant, and neither had any sovereign before them. They did know that the First Generation of Children created the table. That was all they needed to know.

Two sides of the ten-sided marble table stood conspicuously empty, but the men and women occupying the other eight sides paid no heed to the unoccupied places nor made any mention of those to whom those places belonged.

One of the empty spaces faced the north wall. The other was parallel to and facing away from the east wall, into which was built a grand arched window that displayed a beautifully panoramic view of the Ocean Crystalline. When the two suns rose in the morning, the sovereign that sat in that space was framed by a one of the most breathtaking sights in creation. The sweeping crystal-blue ocean and the magnificent azure sky, streaked with the myriad shades of light beaming from the dawn suns, made the sovereign look more like a deity than royalty.

At that place, the tabletop bore a gem-inlaid engraving of the crest of the Kingdom of Lorr.

The crest was outlined in gold in the shape of a shield. Inside the shield outline was an image of the two suns, the smaller sun was near the left edge and roughly at the shield's vertical middle. The larger sun was on the right side of the shield and near the top. An ornate broadsword was superimposed over the suns, tilted at an angle that placed the sword's pommel inside the lower sun and the tip of the wide blade at the center of the larger sun. Below the sword, in the lower half of the shield outline, was the image of a mountain range set on the horizon behind a calm ocean. Floating just above the ocean, and just below the tilted broadsword, was an open, gilded tome with words spelled with crimson letters of an ancient, unknown language.

The larger, higher sun represented the Lord Ascendant's light, which also represented life in all of its forms. The lower sun represented fire and the sky represented air. The mountains and oceans represented earth and water. The book represented knowledge, and the broadsword represented the divine protection of every other aspect of the crest. The gems that comprised the artwork were smaller than an infant's fingertip, and were placed so intricately that the crest almost resembled the painting of a master artist.

All of the rulers present wished that it were their crest branded in the table at that exact spot. Any one of them would have happily sanded the surface smooth in order to replace the Kingdom of Lorr's insignia with their own.

They could have sanded the table from its current eight-inch thickness to an inch, and the crest would still be engraved in its surface. It was placed there by ancient magic and could not be removed or replaced by any means other than the magic that had placed it there. And there the crest of the Kingdom of Lorr would remain, as it had for nearly two centuries, until another kingdom grew strong enough to eclipse Lorr as the most powerful in the Known Lands.

The table itself was created over two thousand years earlier, in the wake of Heaven's War and shortly after the great continent was reduced to an island. While elves, dwarves, Minotaur, and non-neutral creatures of faerie fought exclusively on the side of the Protectors, the human race was divided. There were some human kingdoms with rulers who believed the Leaders would win, so that was with whom they allied themselves. One kingdom remained neutral.

There were also beings of several races, from trolls to goblins, vampires to were-beasts, who derived pleasure from victimizing the other races. They joined eagerly when they found that the Leaders endorsed and even encouraged them to express themselves in any dark and twisted way they desired – as long as it was in the advancement of the Leaders' quest for domination.

When the war ended, and all of the Old Ones had destroyed one another the Children of the Protectors were the victors. The Leader Children had been wiped out completely and only three Children survived, each from a different family of Protectors: the Lorr lineage, the Saiil-dah lineage, and the lineage of Shanderah's ancestry: Afenrhena.

Instead of outright punishing the humans who followed the Leader faction, the Protector Children gave them the choice of joining the Council of Sovereignty or banishment to the uninhabited – and nearly uninhabitable – regions of the planet that would come to be called the Unknown Lands.

Ten of the fourteen kingdoms of the human race agreed – some reluctantly. The other four were banished along with the non-human races that supported the Leaders. Some were banished to regions to the extreme north and south of the Known Lands, beyond impassable frozen wastelands of ice-strewn oceans where the very air would freeze solid the insides of any living creature to breathe it.

Others were sent to a land somewhere beyond the extreme west of the Known Lands. God's Gate Ocean, so named because it seemingly stretched out to the west forever, was for all practical purposes the end of the world. According to all available historical record, the ocean had never been crossed successfully since Heaven's War. During the millennia since the War many had set sail with the intent to cross it. A few returned months or years later barely alive, none of them reached another continent. The rest had never returned at all.

To the extreme east of the Known Lands was the Ocean Crystalline, another incredibly vast ocean that, thousands of miles beyond the border waters of the Citadel Island, eventually became an oceanic region of unnatural heat and constant, searing rains. In the midst of that region rested a hellish borderland of volcanic mountains fraught with vast rivers of lava so hot that it caused the very air to burn.

And then there was the magic. Wards of the most awesome and terrible divine magic lurked in these regions as a reinforcement should the natural barriers fail to stop intruders. Very few, and none in recent history, had ever tried – and none succeeded – to cross any of the barriers. And no one from any race had been known to successfully cross over into the Known Lands from the other side.

The ten human kingdoms that remained did so under the strict condition that their leaders join the Council of Sovereignty. The surviving Children of the Old Ones forged the Council of Sovereignty in order to foster a workable balance among the human kingdoms to ensure that they dealt fairly with one another and to form a common voice when dealing with other races.

The ruler of the most powerful kingdom served as the Council chair. "Powerful" was defined in terms of not only monetary wealth and military might, but also the wellbeing of the citizens within the kingdom. This wellbeing was defined by the fairness with which the kingdom's subjects were treated and the harmony the people of the kingdom formed with the land on which they lived.

As one would expect, the Council did not always see eye-to-eye, which resulted in the occasional war between two of the member kingdoms. By the first of the Great Directives laid down at the formation of the Council of Sovereignty, the other sovereigns would not actively side with either of the warring nations. They would let the two kingdoms war with each other without interference, and, under certain specific conditions the victor might replace the loser on the hierarchy of the Council of Sovereignty. The purpose of the Council of Sovereignty was not to give one kingdom dominion over the others, but to maintain as much of a balance as possible between the kingdoms of humans.

The Children who created the Council were not so naive as to give the kingdoms a directive to never go to war. They understood full well that conflict was part of the nature of man, and all forms of nature have to be allowed to run their course. Attempts to repress or control it too acutely would serve to disrupt that balance, and when nature is forced to restore balance on her own, the consequences are almost always catastrophic to all forms of life in her path.

The table was created by the combined magic of the surviving Children to serve as an icon for the Council. They gave every last bit of their magic, their will, and even their blood, to craft its complex magic. They gave their earthly lives to ensure their realm would never succumb to the dark desires that caused their ancestors to nearly destroy it, leaving their progeny to decide their own paths.

The side of the table that was closest and parallel to the large arched window was the Seat of Power belonging to the Council chair. In cases where the votes of the ten members were split down the middle on any issue, the Council chair's vote counted twice, preventing any draws.

The Council chair was not an elected position voted upon by the members. It was not a reward won in a tournament nor was it automatically conferred as one of the spoils of war. The Council chair was an appointment.

The Children that created it imbued it with a magic that surveyed the ten kingdoms of the Known Lands on a perpetual basis to identify the most powerful kingdom based on the prescribed criteria. If there were any changes, the magic would adjust the order of royal crests accordingly. It would engrave the most powerful kingdom's crest into the table at the Seat of Power. The second most powerful kingdom was immediately to the right, and then the third most powerful, and so the decreasing hierarchy continued in a counter-clockwise order around the table.

The Council met once every five years to discuss political matters and to check the table to see which kingdom's crest was emblazoned onto the smooth finish of the thick marble slab. For nearly the last two hundred years, the Kingdom of Lorr was the holder of the Council chair.

Most of the other sovereigns attributed that holding to preferential treatment. At the end of Heaven's War, while the descendants of Saiil-dah and Afenrhena chose not to involve themselves in the politics of any of the intelligent races, the Lorr progeny pledged their direct and lasting protection to the kingdom that bore their name. All of the kingdoms employed powerful Head Mages, but the Lorr Head Mages were of divine lineage and easily the most powerful.

All of the kings and queens knew the history. In the time before Heaven's War, the Kingdom of Lorr was a cultural, artistic, and educational Mecca. It was a gathering place for all who came in peace. The kingdom was a gift to all the races of the world from the Old Ones themselves and entrusted solely to the Old One called Lorr and his progeny for its protection. That trust was to extend beyond the War and it was to endure as long as the Lorr line existed.

Most of the current rulers did not care about why the Lorr lineage chose to lend their protection to their kingdom over the course of millennia. They would only acknowledge that their presence gave the Kingdom of Lorr an unfair advantage over the others, and that was the only reason they had held the Council chair for so long.

That belief blatantly disregarded the fact that during the eighteen hundred and more years prior to Lorr's extended reign, the chair had rotated regularly among most of the kingdoms every one hundred to one hundred and fifty years, despite the fact that a Child of the Old Ones had always served as Head Mage in the Kingdom of Lorr. There were times in the Kingdom of Lorr's history when a sitting Lorrian king was not as effective as a counterpart in another kingdom. There were other times when agricultural failings due to unfavorable atmospheric conditions resulted in Lorr losing the Council chair.

The jealousy of the sovereigns meeting this night did not allow them to care about what to them was ancient history. It was that jealousy that brought eight of the ten rulers together. They felt that it was time for the reign of the Kingdom of Lorr to end.

They would not, however, break the First Great Directive and join forces to wage open war against Lorr. If they did, according to the Directive, the magic contained in the Table of Sovereigns would be released to "throw the Known Lands into dire chaos." The threat was severe, yet vague. While there were different theories as to exactly what was being threatened, most agreed that if Children almost as powerful as the Old Ones themselves gave their very lives to create the Table of Sovereigns, it would be foolish to risk its wrath. They did, however, hope to find other methods to bring Lorr closer to the pack in order to give the rest of the rulers what they felt was a fair chance at the Seat of Power.

The king immediately to the right of the Seat of Power surveyed the seven others at the table. All of them were having heated debates with the person to either side. Seated only one seat to the right of the empty Seat of Power made him the highest-ranking sovereign present, which made him the acting Council chair. He cleared his throat loudly to get the others' attention.

The arguing kings and queens ignored him as they continued to snipe at one another, so the acting chair slammed a large, heavily ringed fist down on the table with enough force get their attention. The heavy marble absorbed and muffled the blow from the king's fist, but his many bejeweled rings rang above the din. The arguments abruptly ceased and the others turned to him with looks of annoyance.

"May we call this meeting to order?" the acting chair asked in a booming baritone voice.

"Parliamentary procedure?" asked the woman sitting opposite him across the table. "Let us not pretend this is an *official* meeting. We are still a year away from the scheduled gathering and two kingdoms are not represented, one of them purposely excluded. There is no need for formalities."

"If not formalities," the acting chair allowed, "then certainly *some* semblance of order is necessary."

"Yes," said a king who sat directly opposite the seat of power. He spoke with a deep resounding voice that was out of character with his relatively small stature. Despite his narrow shoulders and thin face, bolstered slightly by a full and neatly trimmed light brown beard, his voice and his hard blue eyes lent him a commanding air. "And our first order of business should be an explanation of why we were all summoned here at such an inconvenient time."

The acting chair leveled a blank stare at the one who had just spoken. "Do not feign innocence or ignorance. We all know the *why* of it."

"Of course," the queen immediately to his right concurred. "Just as you know that what he really meant was *how*." Her wide eyes, a shade of gray so pale they were nearly silver, bore into him accusingly. She lifted one of her pencil-thin eyebrows of the same color as her eyes. "Let us be blunt. We all agree that we want Lorr to falter if not fall completely. You have obviously come up with some plot to achieve that end."

"We 'all' do not necessarily agree," amended the king opposite the seat of power. "I have not made up my mind one way or the other. I am here merely out of curiosity."

"On the fence as ever, eh, *king*?" rumbled a king seated three seats to the left of the seat of power. He was the least adorned of the rulers seated, but what he lacked in glitter he more than made up for with his intimidating size.

Instead of the regal travelling tunic and breeches worn by his male peers, he wore an unadorned vest over an otherwise bare chest. He was more muscle than fat, and looked more like a soldier than a king. A small golden headband was the only thing he wore to indicate his station, and even it resembled a utilitarian headband to hold back his long, thick, gray-streaked hair. His stressing of the word "king" was an open insult that brought a sneer from the man to whom it was directed. The big man ignored the sneer and continued.

"I am certain of this: we should forget about any trickery or shadowy dealings and simply unite in open warfare against Lorr. They cannot hope to defeat our combined forces."

"Are you *that* eager to test the power behind the First Great Directive?" asked the king seated to the right of the battle-hungry ruler.

"Myths and fairytales," the large king dismissed with a wave of his beefy hand. "And unclear, as well. What is 'dire chaos?' This is a world of dire chaos already. Better to be seated at the top of that chaos than be overrun by it."

"That 'chaos' you so nonchalantly refer to could come in any form," said the king seated to the immediate left of the seat of power. "Must I remind you that the First Directive is a divine edict? I, for one, am not willing to risk the wrath of the Old Ones on my kingdom and my people. In fact, I am not very comfortable even speaking of such things at this Council table."

"The Gods are dead," countered the queen seated three seats to the right of the acting chair. She was a heavyset woman, though not obese, and plain in every sense of the word. To compensate – many would say "overcompensate", though not in her presence – she wore so much jewelry that even the smallest movement sounded out like wind chimes.

"And if there was anyone I would expect to hold no belief in them, it would be you," she continued.

"The Old Ones are *not* gods," the king corrected. "There is only one God, and that is the Lord Ascendant. That is one of the problems with so many of you sovereigns. You either refuse to understand or refuse to care about the difference."

The queen rolled her eyes. "Call them what you want. The fact remains that you have little reason to have faith in them. It is your kingdom and you whom they seem to have forsaken."

"That has not always been the case," the slighted king reminded. "We were the ones who held the seat of power before Lorr took hold after the Dragon War. And all we need to do to regain it is to prove our mettle to the Old Ones, who are certainly *not* dead." He glared at the queen who had uttered the blasphemy. "They are simply on another plane, watching as they always have."

"The Old Ones may be dead or otherwise absent," the acting chair said, subtly regaining control of the conversation by lending credence to both sides of the current debate. "But I submit to you that it does not matter. They have long since left us to our own devices. Their spawn created this table and this Council, and it is their descendants who would try to bring to bear any punishment for breaking the directive."

"Are we to assume you have found a way to dispose of the Children?" asked the queen to his right. "For I fear we would have to in order to bring down the Kingdom of Lorr."

"We know they can be killed," the acting chair offered. "The death of the old witch Shanderah is proof of that, as is the death of the wizard Mar-dah."

"So you agree that we should all form against Lorr?" demanded the king two seats to the left of the acting chair. "Why? Is it because, out of all of us, it is you who have the most to gain?"

"Not at all," the acting chair assured. "I have no desire to break the First Great Directive, and I do not believe the death of the Children must be our primary aim. As our colleague pointed out, others have held the seat of power while a Child of Lorr protected his or her kingdom. We need merely weaken them sufficiently."

"You have not *sufficiently* addressed the latter question," noted the king seated opposite the seat of power. "Of all of us here, you certainly have the most to gain from the fall of Lorr. Why should we support any scheme to lift you to the Seat of Power?"

The acting chair affected an injured frown. "I merely wish to bring true balance back to this Council. Yes, it is true that I am the closest to Seat of Power, but if Lorr is brought low, all of you would be that much closer, as well." The king gave a knowing smile. "And then you could go about the business of hatching your own little schemes to wrest the seat from me."

No one could argue his logic, but several were visibly surprised that he would voice aloud what all of them were thinking. With the group now thoroughly attentive, the king quickly pressed on.

"Some of the pieces are already in place and alliances have been formed." He turned pointedly to the king seated four places to his right, the one who had stated that his mind was not made up. "But I will not elaborate until I have your oaths that you are committed to bringing down Lorr."

"You said it may not be necessary to dispose of the Children of the Old Ones," recalled the queen who sat at the acting chair's immediate right. "How can it not be when they clearly favor the Kingdom of Lorr? Mar-dah and Shanderah are gone, but there is still the offworlder. They even say his Child grandfather resides with him across the WorldGate."

"And they are a danger to us all!" added the warrior king. "Can we chance another of them going bad?" He pulled his decorative – yet very deadly – dagger from his belt and waved it for emphasis. "I say they are a menace lying in wait. The lot of them should be scourged."

"That is ambitious indeed, and probably necessary, but your enthusiasm gives me pause," said the queen three seats to the right of the acting chair. "Would you then go after all of the other magic workers that you consider a threat?"

"Mar-dah loosed *demons* upon our world, woman," the warrior king argued in an exasperated tone. "Demons! A mere human mage, no matter how learned or powerful, would not be able to accomplish such a feat. As long as a Child of the Old Ones lives, so does the threat that demons can be loosed once more. How can we possibly abide that?"

"I agree," said the king to the right of the warrior king. "He is not talking about mere wizards, witches and warlocks. We can control them. He is talking about the Children of the Divine. Heaven's War wiped out and banished entire species, entire races, even the Gods themselves, all because the Children of the Old Ones could not decide what to do with us…as if we were pets of some sort. Mar-dah's actions could very well be the beginnings of the cycle repeating itself. I say that if the opportunity presents itself to reduce their number, we take it."

That was what the acting chair was waiting to hear. He would not bring it up himself for fear of seeming too ambitious, but knowing the people around the table the way he did, he knew someone would broach that topic.

"So," the warrior king started, his voice like distant thunder. "How do you expect us to assist you without breaking the Directive you all fear so much?"

The acting chair's aquiline nose wrinkled just a bit as he smiled and turned to the warrior king. "I'd rather not go into too much detail, you understand. But I will say this: no direct cooperation will be asked for or expected. There may be an occasion where certain parties will need to cross various lands or waterways unmolested. The need may arise to hire specialized craftsmen from different kingdoms, and some relaxation of certain tariffs would be greatly appreciated. I'll be more than happy to elaborate in a much more specific manner once I have firm agreements from everyone here."

He fell silent and listened intently to the murmurs buzzing around the table. After a few minutes, the king opposite the Seat of Power gestured for the acting chair's attention. When he gained it, he asked another question.

"And what of the one kingdom that refused your invitation? How would you propose to respond to their neutrality?"

The acting chair expected that particular sovereign to ask that particular question. He was the one who expressed uncertainty earlier. It was only obvious that he would want to know the consequences of refusal.

"We don't respond," the acting chair said. "As long as they do not ally themselves with Lorr, we will respect their neutrality."

A look of relief passed through his eyes so quickly that only someone with the sharp mind and observant nature of the acting chair would notice. He decided, however, not to let the undecided king completely off the hook.

"Of course," the acting chair continued, "I expect that might affect their overall influence on Council matters after the reorganization of the hierarchy."

Nods of agreement followed as the acting chair continued, intending to get the most out of this veiled impromptu campaign session.

"But no sanctions would be imposed. After all, this is still the Council of Sovereignty. Trivial retribution and petty vendettas have no place at this table or among our kingdoms. We only wish to restore the balance that has been tilted toward the Kingdom of Lorr for far too long because of their unfair favor. After that, things will commence as usual."

"And what is your stance on how to handle the Children of the Old Ones?" asked the queen who sat directly across the table from him.

The acting chair feigned a thoughtful expression while smiling on the inside. The fact that she was asking his opinion was an indication that she was already in agreement. She was only questioning him to see if she could get a little of his plan from him before she voiced her inclusion.

"While I don't think it is absolutely necessary to kill the Children, I do agree with our colleague that if an opportunity presents itself to reduce their number, we should take advantage of it. And with the help of everyone here, that could prove to be very likely." He took in each facial expression, every gesture, and knew that the majority of the people around the table were of a like mind.

There remained a couple that seemed undecided, but he would give them no more time to ponder. He came slowly to his feet. The deliberateness with which he stood to his full, impressive height pulled all eyes to him. He raised his long arms in welcome and spoke, projecting his baritone voice across the room.

"So are we in agreement then?" He stood tall at the table and took turns meeting the gaze of each king and queen. "Anyone that does not wish to participate can leave now without reprisal. If you choose to stay, together we will map out the future of our world."

He still saw hesitancy in a few eyes but he did not expect anyone to leave. They all knew that just by coming here this evening they had admitted to their desire to see Lorr fall.

They were not here by "invitation," as the undecided king stated. During the Cursed Opening, as the Kingdom of Lorr battled demons from five of the seven levels of hell, an underground association was formed that quietly protested what was perceived as preferential treatment to the Kingdom of Lorr by the dangerous and powerful Children.

An undercurrent of resentment and jealousy had existed for years, but the king acting as Council chair made the decision to organize those ill feelings into a quiet movement. Vague rumors of the movement spread to all of the human-ruled kingdoms, as well as the dwarven and elven kingdoms, in the Known Lands. As expected, elves and dwarves dismissed the rumors, wanting nothing to do with humans beyond fair trade. The other kingdoms were a different story.

The movement was covert but carefully seeded only throughout the most influential circles so that it was sure to eventually reach the ears of royalty. It was well known that the rulers of the other kingdoms envied Lorr, but the depth of their envy would be exposed by their reaction to their discovery of the movement's possible existence. How would they respond when they discovered that there were others beside themselves that might actually be willing to actively participate in bringing about the fall of the envied kingdom?

In order to arrive at tonight's meeting, the rulers had to first be intrigued enough to desire more details. From there, they had to make the effort of assigning their best spies to get more information. And the king made sure that details were hard to come by, for the other rulers would bolt in an instant if they had the faintest suspicion that they were being led.

In most cases, lives were lost or taken in route to getting to the heart of the rumored movement. In the end, any of them that went through the trouble of finding out about and secretly attending this meeting made it crystal clear that they had deadly serious interest in the rumors.

The acting chair was sure several of the rulers would lose interest or their nerve along the way and ultimately either ignore the movement or acknowledge it as nothing more than a passing fancy, so a unanimous showing was neither expected nor needed. A slight majority would have been sufficient, but when he saw eight of the nine other kingdoms represented at the unofficial meeting, he knew providence was smiling upon him.

Chapter 2: The Gatekeeper's Hounds

2.1

"This is the place," the youngster informed his comrades. A dark gray cloth mantle concealed all of his face with the exception of two eyeholes cut into the front of it, but his age was betrayed by a voice that was barely past puberty.

The light of the three moons, filtered through the still branches and leaves of the forest, revealed blonde eyebrows knitted over dark blue eyes as he gazed closely at the small crimson orb he held between his thumb and forefinger. The orb was barely larger in diameter than the width of his thumbnail and there were two slightly overlapping dots within it. One was black and the other gold, and both were virtually invisible to all save those with the sharpest vision. The golden pinpoint of light was to the left of and slightly higher than the black dot residing at the core of the bauble.

An older, taller man leaned over the younger man's shoulder to peer just as intently through his own shroud and then slowly shook his head. "Are you sure?" he questioned. "How can you tell? I can barely see anything. Why could he not have given us a larger piece?"

"It is somewhere to the northwest," the youngster continued, ignoring the annoying questions. His commander had asked those same questions at least once during every hunt. More often than not, though, he would ask those questions several times during the course of a trek. It had become something like a superstitious mantra or a nervous tick of the commander's. Everyone knew the young man's eyes were almost as sharp as an elf's. That was why he was entrusted with the orb in the first place.

Perhaps the commander used the mantra as a good luck charm, because he had repeated the mantra on each of their fourteen hunts even though the youngster had never been wrong. The young hunter knew he should have gotten used to his commander's questions by now but they remained as annoying as ever.

"The sphere will not get any more specific than this," the commander whispered to the eleven other hooded people huddled around them. He was more than familiar with the properties of the orb and its handler by now. If his young, sharp-eyed scout was certain, then the commander was certain.

"From here we must track by conventional methods," the commander went on. He turned to the handler of the orb. "Lead the way, Eagle Eye."

Eagle Eye crouched low to the ground and looked for the tracks that he knew should be there. He did not know what kind of tracks he would find, but he expected to find something. At times, the tracks he would find on their hunts resembled the paws of a cat or canine, with slight variations to betray their true nature. At other times the tracks were from hooves, either split or whole and occasionally a weird combination of the two. Sometimes the tracks revealed the splayed, webbed characteristics of an amphibian creature. One thing was always common, though: no matter how much the track might resemble something natural, there was always something – whether it was the size of the tracks, the number of digits, or a slight difference in the shape – that marked them otherwise.

There were even times when the tracks were uncomfortably similar to human tracks. And then there were times when the tracks resembled nothing that he had ever seen, but the pattern of depressed grasses or broken twigs or crushed leaves or overturned stones made them stand out nonetheless. Those were the most disturbing, for then they had no idea what they would discover. Their prey took many forms, but they were usually discernable by this point of the hunt.

Eagle Eye was troubled by the absence of telltale traces of their prey. There were plenty of tracks around, but they were the common tracks of human traffic: boot prints of varying, yet normal sizes; thin grooves caused by wagon wheels; horse, goat, and cattle hooves as well as other domesticated animals that strayed from the wide and worn main trail that cut a northwest/southeast swath through the forest less than twenty yards to the west. There were also the signs of nocturnal animals, both large and small, that walked these woods during the still night hours when humans usually did not.

They were just to the south of the town of Tohrfell's Valley, so the high amount of traffic was anticipated. But where was the slightly unusual trail? The proximity of the golden pinpoint to the black core of the crimson orb suggested that they were very close, within an eighth of a mile away from their prey. Eagle Eye had been leading the others on a search covering an area of almost a quarter mile in diameter but the out-of-the-ordinary tracks that usually gave away the presence of their prey continued to elude him.

"Eagle Eye?" the commander asked, noticing the youngster's hesitation. "Is there something wrong?"

"The trail seems to be obscured," Eagle Eye admitted. "But I'll find it."

He ignored a chill autumn breeze that swept sharply through the trees and concentrated. His father taught him that it took more than keen vision to make a good tracker. The best trackers searched with more than their eyes. It was not always what one could see before him that revealed a trail, but what one could piece together from the sum of his knowledge. A broken twig revealed that something had stepped on it, but the number of pieces into which it was broken and the depth to which it was pushed into the soil could sometimes allow for an accurate estimate of the size or weight of the creature that had stepped on it.

Eagle Eye applied that lesson to his current situation. While he could not find any revealing tracks, he knew their prey was close. He also knew from monitoring the blood-red orb over the course of several days that at one time their prey had moved about in varying directions, as if wandering aimlessly. Eagle Eye, the commander, and the others had found partially eaten carcasses of both man and beast along that meandering trail but they found no unusual tracks. On a couple of occasions, they were even able to find trace evidence that some tracks had been purposely obscured in those areas.

And then the golden point of light suddenly began to move at a faster pace and in a more direct path along a northwestern direction parallel to the main trail. It moved in that way for nearly two days, stopping for several hours both nights before finally stopping for good less than a day earlier. And there it remained until this very night. The new path, the pace and the times it stopped were reminiscent of the movements of a horse or borough-drawn wagon. It seemed unlikely that the kind of prey they hunted had been captured and transported in that fashion, but he had to consider the possibility.

Unfortunately, he had counted at least a half dozen wagon tracks that were fresh enough to have passed that way in the last few days. He needed more information so that he could narrow his search. Eagle Eye and his companions questioned citizens of farming communities as they passed near them. One such community was in an uproar about a missing infant, and Eagle Eye prayed it had nothing to do with their quarry, but no one could remember seeing anything other than the ordinary traffic that passed so frequently through the area.

He thought again about the state of the corpses they had found in their prey's wake while the trail was still meandering. The fact that they found no remains of an infant somewhat calmed their fears that the infant had been taken by their target. The way the victims had been slaughtered indicated that something large, possibly as heavy as an adolescent tygra, had ravaged them. Something that heavy, if captured, would most likely be loaded onto a large wagon. A wagon that large and hauling that kind of weight would leave deep tracks and be pulled by boroughs, which were stronger and more durable than horses. Out of the multiple wagon tracks he spied, he picked the one heading northwest that best fit this profile and led the team in that direction.

It took them less than an hour of cautious travel before they could smell the smoke of a campfire. Eagle Eye stopped and the commander signaled for the rest of the team to stop as well. The young scout examined the ground for a moment before he slipped the orb into a pouch on his belt and used his free, gloved hands to grasp the thick trunk of a tree just beside him. The others watched as Eagle Eye climbed the tree with the dexterity of a squirrel. He did not stop until the lower limbs of the tree concealed him. After crawling several feet out on a broad branch, he surveyed as much of the area as he could through the filtered moons' light.

The rest of the team waited until Eagle Eye climbed down out of the tree. The watchful hunters once again huddled in close around him and the commander.

"I have not found any direct signs of our prey," Eagle Eye began, "But there are sentries to the west, sentries near the main road, another group seventy yards northeast, and one lone sentry due north. Each group is a team of five heavily armed men."

"Sentries?" asked the commander. "What do we care about sentries? They are not our prey."

"I believe they guard our prey," Eagle Eye explained.

"They *guard* it?" came a female voice from beneath a dark hood to his right. "Are you sure?"

"I cannot be absolutely positive from here, Cobra," Eagle Eye answered honestly, "But I am very sure. The campfire we smell is coming from a clearing just to the north and roughly fifty yards further east of the main road than where we are now. From this distance, the clearing is somewhat obscured by the trees, but it is in the path of our search. There are probably more sentries closer to the clearing."

"Why would they go through the trouble of catching and guarding such a thing so far out in the middle of nowhere?" the commander questioned.

"I wish I knew," Eagle Eye returned. "And I am anxious to find out."

"We will investigate," declared the commander. "You three," he went on, pointing at the one called Cobra and two others. "Cover the sentries near the road." He pointed to two others. "I want you two to cover the sentry due north. You three," he gestured toward Eagle Eye and two others to his left. "Eagle Eye, you, Hammer and Arrowhead will cover the sentries to the northeast. The rest of us will make our way to the clearing. Do not engage any of them unless you hear the signal, and when you do, strike quickly and get to us as fast as you can."

Eagle Eye smiled briefly beneath his mantle. He was always pleased when he was teamed with Arrowhead. She was all business, she was a great fighter, and she was pretty. She had never shown any romantic interest in him, unfortunately, but she treated him more like peer than any of the other Hounds. The others treated him like a child, and in some cases, like a burden. Arrowhead's company somewhat eased his frustration at always being relegated to perimeter guard duty when the Hounds ran down their prey, but only somewhat.

"I should be a part of the group that goes to the clearing," Eagle Eye suggested. "I can help to track--"

"Thanks to you, we know where the clearing is," the commander interrupted. "Everyone has their job, and that was yours. Now follow orders." He turned a stern gaze onto Eagle Eye. "I sincerely hope you are right, young one. We will lose valuable time if you are not."

"I almost hope I'm not," Eagle Eye told him, struggling to keep the timbre of frustration from his tone. "I do not know which is worse: our prey, or those insane enough to capture and protect it."

"We're about to find out," the commander assured. "Hounds, let us hunt!" he ordered in a harsh whisper.

The group split into four teams and moved stealthily through the forest. Their dark gray cowls and cloaks blended in well with the shadows, making them virtually invisible.

Eagle Eye and his group were still far enough away from their destination for verbal communication, but the young hunter kept his aggravation to himself. They were perilously close to dragon country, and even though the dragons had stayed true to their agreement not to attack humans, all of the Keeper's Hounds felt safer if they kept noise to a minimum. With the exception of the great battle at the Tyne during the Cursed Opening, none of them had even seen a dragon in their lifetimes. But why tempt fate? Besides, he knew the man and woman accompanying him had no interest in his complaints.

All of the Hounds knew that besides his unusually keen eyesight and tracking skills, Eagle Eye was the most skilled fighter among them…with a sword, at least. But he was also the youngest. He was all but unrivaled as a tracker and swordsman and was indispensable to the team. Thanks to his natural ability and his father's tutoring, which began the moment Eagle Eye could walk, he completed the four-year curriculum at the military academy in only two years. Yet several members openly objected to his membership in the Keeper's Hounds because of his age. The commander was among them. As a result, in an attempt to keep him as safe as possible, Eagle Eye was always relegated to the periphery when the Hounds attacked.

Because of the nature of their missions he still saw his share of action, but that was not the point as far as he was concerned. The point was that he was treated like the weakest member of the team even though he was one of the most formidable, simply because the others had seen a few more years.

The trio crept to within twenty yards of the five sentries, taking care to stay low behind concealing brush and thick tree trunks and keeping to the shadows between the pale beams of moons' light that penetrated the leafy limbs above them. Eagle Eye wrapped is right hand around the hilt of his beloved broadsword. The feel of its wide, leather-wrapped handle gave him confidence. He ran the fingertips of his left hand over the coiled lasso hanging from his right shoulder for extra reassurance. He then knelt and peeked through a break in the low brush at the two large, heavily armed men standing alertly on each side of a small, barely visible trail that led to the clearing where their prey most likely resided.

The woman carefully and quietly loaded her one-handed crossbow. The third member of their detachment, a broad, muscle-bound man two hands taller than Eagle Eye, unhooked a long handled war hammer from a thick strap on his back and rested the heavy weapon on his broad thighs as he crouched behind a thick tree trunk. The three of them settled in and waited patiently for the signal.

The commander and the four men accompanying him crept easily past the lone sentry while the two other Hounds took their positions watching the heavily armed and wary man. The sentry was fully alert, but the Hounds were adept at staying concealed from both man and beast. Their dark clothing was perfect camouflage during the night. They were trained to move as silently as shadows and to stay upwind of their target. By the time their presence was detected, if they were detected at all, it was usually too late.

As Eagle Eye had predicted, there were several more sentries near the clearing, but the Hounds easily avoided them as they moved closer to the edge of the tree line. The clearing opened onto a decline that dropped softly down into a small meadow. The moons' light revealed a narrow, burbling stream rushing across the meadow at its lowest point. The scene would have been beautiful if the commander had not been so shocked and sickened by what he saw and heard down there.

2.2

"Can we hurry this along, wizard?" asked the big man, one of several men standing around the meadow. A heavy, fancy cloak hung over his broad shoulders. The cloak's hood was pulled down to reveal long dark hair, its color obscured by the reddish firelight and the dancing shadows they cast, hanging sloppily from the bottom of the armored bascinet that concealed most of his face. Only his shadowed eyes and the bottom of his bearded chin were visible beneath the helmet. The cloak's cape was pulled back to display an intricately fashioned muscled cuirass with segmented spaulders protecting his bulging deltoids.

His thick wrists and big hands were protected by fingered gauntlets attached to wristbands that reached as high as his forearm. The metal headpiece and armor gleamed in a menacing hue of crimson in the firelight. He did not wear all of the lower part of what was almost certainly a full suit of armor. Instead, he wore heavy, loose-fitting leather breeches tucked into knee-high armored boots that matched the hue and polish of the armor covering his upper body.

"This is bad business," he continued. "Best to be done with it as soon as possible." His deep voice was tinged with something akin to dread.

A hooded, black-cloaked figure stood to the right of big man. The firelight could not penetrate the shadows of the hood, leaving the face within it completely hidden. The figure was not as tall as the huge armored man, but he was tall nonetheless and as narrow at the shoulders as his armored companion was wide. The cloak was cinched at the throat but billowed open just below the neck, fluttering in the stiff breezes that rushed through the clearing. A body length robe the same color as the cloak concealed every part of the wearer's body. Even the hands were concealed, tucked within the robe's draping sleeves while the figure's arms were crossed.

The hood turned slowly and tilted up toward the big soldier to its left. A cold, barely audible male voice that seemed to drift from some distant void within the blackness of the hood echoed in reply:

"You knew this was bad business when you signed on, Baron Dirk. But this *is* part of your agreement, and the master would not be pleased if you broke it."

"The *master*," Baron Dirk spat. "How do I know this master you speak of truly exists? I have only spoken to you. For all I know, you could be fabricating this entire story. I'd like to meet this master of yours."

An icy chuckle escaped the shadows of the dark hood. "No. You really would not. And what does it matter to you if the master exists or not? This partnership has brought you fortune and power you would never have obtained on your own. Is that not enough?"

"It was," Baron Dirk said darkly. "Until this. I've done my part. I've given you the access you requested. Why did I have to be the one to do *this*?"

"The spell requires the cutter and the server to be untouched by magic." The hood tilted to the side. "And the master likes to know the depths of his partners' dedication."

The baron's doubtful frown made it clear that he was unconvinced. The cloaked wizard regarded him for a moment before continuing. "Think of what you have been given, and then tell me whether or not you would complete this task again if presented with the same opportunity."

Baron Dirk recalled who and where he was before this strange, shadowy wizard slithered into his life. He was not a baron, not even close. He was just another peasant scraping together a meager living before he became a fugitive soldier of a soon-to-be vanquished army. He thought fortune had finally smiled upon him when he was lucky enough to be away on a special assignment for the Legion Midnight when his army was routed. The special assignment ended in utter failure, but even then he was lucky enough to have stumbled upon a fortune in plundered gold, silver, and precious gems.

What he thought was good luck, however, quickly turned sour when he realized that he was stranded with that treasure. He had no way to take a significant amount of it away with him and there was no one he trusted enough to help him transport it back to his homeland. As it turned out, fortune was not smiling on him at all. It was laughing at him. Mocking him. It was as if the gods, if there even *were* any gods, were having a great deal of amusement at his expense.

And then he thought about who and where he was now: A powerful baron with wealth he had only dreamed of.

His current good fortune had nothing to do with his considerable muscle or fighting skill. Instead, it was a result of the counsel from – and influence of – this wizard and the wizard's so-called master.

The baron looked at the object that sat in the back of the large, horseless wagon before him, at what he knew to be an iron cage hidden beneath a thick woolen blanket that visually concealed its contents. The cage moved as soon as the baron looked at it, as if the captive within could feel his gaze and was enraged by it. The movement, accompanied by the sounds of rattling chains, was a quick and violent one that shook the wagon and caused the baron to jump involuntarily.

He looked at the heavy block of stone, as wide his broad shoulders, as high as his ample waist, and the still body of an infant whose blood from her slit throat had just finished draining into a funneled hole drilled into the stone just under her neck. The crimson fluid ran through a conduit that had been drilled through the makeshift altar and it dripped from a small tube protruding from just above the base of the stone into a large copper bowl.

The baron grimaced and looked down at the bloody knife in his hand. He turned to the wizard nodded his head.

"I would," he admitted. "I would do it as many times as necessary to make and to keep my fortune."

2.3

The commander swallowed back the bile that rose to the back of his throat and shivered with rage, disgust, and fear. The rage and disgust were generated by the disturbing sight of the murdered infant; the fear, by a spell that would require such a horrific act of violence and cold-heartedness for its casting. When they heard of the infant's disappearance, the Hounds had hoped the baby had not been devoured by the nightmare hidden beneath the filthy blanket on the back of the wagon. Now they almost wished she had, having seen the manner – and especially the reason – for the abduction and murder. The commander was not a conjurer of any sort, but he knew he was not witnessing any ordinary or trivial conjuring. This was a conjuring of profound wickedness.

The soldier to the commander's left tensed as he prepared to attack. The commander stopped him with a quick, firm grasp of the other's shoulder and a stern but understanding stare. It was too late to save the infant and they did not yet know what they were facing. He was determined to stop them from completing whatever evil task they were about, but to attack without some measure of their enemy was potentially suicidal. A wizard of unknown power was down there, along with their prey, which was dangerous enough by itself. Caution and diligence had to overrule passion.

The commander was positive their prey was in the covered cage, but being sure was not enough. He had to know. The cage was closely guarded, so when his team made its move there would be no turning back. They would have to kill people to complete their mission. That was something they preferred not to do. It was, however, something they were definitely prepared to do. Especially under these circumstances.

Unfortunately, they had been forced to kill people on a few of their earlier hunts. Sometimes they had to battle competing hunters who hunted the same prey not to kill, but to exhibit, which was both dangerous and foolish. At other times their prey wandered onto the private property of landowners both within and outside of the Kingdom of Lorr.

Some of the landowners simply refused to respect the team's authority despite the document of authorization the Keeper's Hounds always carried. The document consisted of a letter signed by the king and stamped with the royal seal, explaining the nature of the Hounds' mission and an order to allow them safe passage on any property within the Kingdom of Lorr in order to complete their mission. On the few occasions when some of the more stubborn landowners ignored the letter, the commander had little difficulty bringing them to task.

Some landowners, on the other hand, simply were not familiar with the kingdom's documents of authorization and were afraid that thugs carrying forged documents were attempting to swindle them. Those were the worst cases. Because of the nature of their prey and the danger it posed to the community at large, the team could not take the time to go through official channels to confirm their identity and authority. In order to complete their mission they sometimes had to physically engage – and sometimes kill – people who believed themselves to be protecting their land.

So before the commander committed himself and his men to such a grim path as attacking fellow humans, he had to *know*.

The commander heard the cloaked wizard speak once more:

"Now finish it, baron."

The big man walked slowly and reluctantly to the makeshift altar on which the tiny body was placed, picked up the copper bowl, and walked over to the covered cage on the back of the wagon. Two of the six armed and armored men that accompanied the wizard and the baron warily made their way to the other side of the wagon.

Whatever was in the cage could obviously sense their approach, for as the men neared, unnerving snarls and sounds somewhere between coughs and barks boomed from beneath the heavy blanket that shrouded the cage. The rattling of chains and the banging of something hard against the cage bars accompanied those sounds. The noise and jostling grew more intense as the men came nearer, causing the cage to literally bounce off of the floor of the wagon.

The baron placed the copper bowl a foot away from the cage and quickly backed away. The blood inside of the bowl sloshed around but did not spill as the hidden creature went berserk. The two armored men that approached from the other side of the cage went to opposite corners, carefully grasped the edges of the concealing blanket, and pulled it away to reveal what was hidden within the cage.

With the heavy blanket pulled away, the creature's stink spread quickly through and beyond the meadow. The commander and his charges had to stifle a collective gag to keep from giving themselves away. The ruffians down in the clearing coughed while some even wretched from the olfactory assault.

At first glance, the creature resembled an immature tygra, the sky-blue, long-limbed cat that, when it reached full maturity, stood roughly two and a half times as tall as full-grown man. However, this creature's ears were longer and more pointed than a tygra's, and its fur was short and bristly where a tygra's was long and smooth. The color of the creature's fur was not discernable in the glow of the firelight but it was definitely darker than a tygra's, and it was a third of the height of the full-grown great cat.

Like a tygra, it was broad across the shoulders and densely muscled. But unlike a tygra, its forelegs were disproportionately long compared to the rest of its body. Instead of paws, the forelegs ended in long primate-like hands with wickedly pointed claws protruding from its fingers. The feline creature's hind end was narrow and much lower to the ground than its shoulders, giving the impression of a perpetual, threatening crouch. Its hind legs were short but incredibly muscled and ended in the same evil long-fingered hands as its forelegs.

As fierce as its body was, its face was its most intimidating feature. For the most part, the cat-thing's face was feline. There were, however, some very significant differences. Aside from the long pointed ears flaring out to either side, the creature's head was abnormally wide and boxy. Its whiskers were more like jutting spikes that were so hard they made sharp "ting" sounds as they knocked against the cage bars. A mess of long, curved teeth, each with needle-tip points, protruded from its upper and lower jaws while the dark, twisted lines that were its lips were pulled back into a terrifying and permanent snarl.

Its rough fur wrinkled tightly on the bridge of its nose beneath and between large triangular eyes that glowed yellow in the firelight. Those eyes immediately fell upon the copper bowl of blood. It tilted its wide head slightly to thrust it through the gap in the bars. As it attacked the bowl, its eyes burned brighter still, easily outshining the firelight and marking the beast for what it truly was.

2.4

Demon!

No matter how many times the commander encountered demons, the moment of recognition was always startling. The commander was almost relieved, however, to see the yellow glow of its eyes as opposed to an orange or – worse yet – a red glow.

They had no way of knowing exactly which level of the seven hells the beast was pulled from, but they knew a yellow glow signified a lower level demon, one that could most certainly be killed by conventional weapons. The illumination trended toward red for demons from the higher levels. The closest he and the Hounds had ever faced was a very light, very pale orange. It killed three of the Hounds and nearly a fourth before they finally took it down.

This one was not likely to be that formidable. But it was still hell-spawn. If they were careless it would kill them just as dead. And it had humans fighting to protect it. All of this flashed through One-Shot's mind in the second it took for him to cringe, take a deep breath and let loose a loud canine howl that echoed through the night.

One-Shot and his Hounds burst from hiding and rushed into the clearing.

To the northeast of the commander's position, all five sentries turned at the strange howl, but four of them turned back quickly as the fifth went down from an arrow to the neck. The other four ducked low and scrambled to hide themselves from the unseen shooter. As they reached the cover of trees and bushes, one of the remaining four was struck down by a huge war hammer that arced from behind a broad tree trunk, crushing his skull and killing him instantly. A lasso dropped around the shoulders of one of the remaining three and snatched him backwards as the last two disappeared into the shadows.

Arrowhead dashed out from the opposite side of the clearing while Eagle Eye towed in the captured sentry. "Hammer and I will stop the last two and meet with the commander," she said as she ran past. She called back over her shoulder: "Catch up with us when you are done here!"

Hammer spared a moment to cast a curious glance at the sprinting Arrowhead and then another at Eagle Eye before taking off after his teammate.

Eagle Eye paused in surprise and then quickly continued to tow his captive in as he pondered what to do. He had never been left alone in a combat situation. The commander always had him flanked with at least two others and always tried to keep him as far away from the real action as possible. This, he understood, was Arrowhead's way of letting him know that she thought he was ready. It was either that or a dangerous test to determine whether or not he really was.

And now he had to quickly determine a course of action. On past hunts when they had to battle humans, they used non-lethal force to subdue their opponents whenever possible. In those instances he and his chaperones were usually able to easily overcome and incapacitate their enemies. But this time he was alone. And the commander howled his signal instead of using his usual night bird call. The howl was a signal to take out their targets with quickness and finality and to form up with the commander at the attack sight as soon as possible. Simply put, it was the signal to use deadly force.

But Eagle Eye could not kill an incapacitated opponent. His father had instilled in him a sense of honor that would not allow him to execute a man in cold blood. Without hesitation, he tied his rope to a nearby tree. As he did so he saw the man successfully struggling to work his way free of the lasso. By the time the knot was tied the captive was tossing the rope away and rising to his feet, his short sword raised for attack.

Eagle Eye wished he had his crossbow. He did not mind using deadly force now that the man was attacking, and a crossbow would have been the perfect weapon to achieve that end quickly and efficiently. But because they had to travel light on their hunts, each team member was allowed to carry only two primary weapons along with any smaller weapons that were unobtrusive and easy to conceal. So his weapons were his lasso and his broadsword. He owned a masterfully crafted javelin in addition to his crossbow and would have chosen to carry all of them. All of his weapons were passed down to him from his father and he hated having to leave any of them behind. They were his most prized possessions, and the fact that he left them for his service to the crown was a testament to how much that service meant to him.

In any other circumstance he would never have left any of his weapons behind. Unfortunately, no more than two teammates were allowed to carry the same type of weapon. This ensured that the team had a wide variety of weapons at their disposal, which would prepare them for almost any eventuality. In addition, it was hard to move fast and silently with an arsenal of large weapons strapped to one's person. Unfortunately for him the crossbow had been claimed by Arrowhead and One-Shot, who was also the commander of the Hounds, before Eagle Eye had joined. Their seniority took precedence over the fact that Eagle Eye was probably a better archer than both of them.

As a result, Eagle Eye would have to face this opponent in close quarters combat. He slid his beloved broadsword from the baldric on his back and dropped into a defensive crouch. This, he knew, would only take a couple of seconds longer than his crossbow would have.

2.5

"We are the Keepers' Hounds!" the commander cried as he and his warriors charged. "By the authority of the Sovereign Kingdom of Lorr, we have come to slay the demon!"

"Keep them at bay!" the wizard ordered in a harsh whisper. He immediately started gesturing and mumbling in tones too low for the baron to decipher.

The six armored men in the clearing were already charging to meet the intruders. The baron reached out for the shoulder of one of them, yanking him to an abrupt and jarring halt.

"Leesil, stay here and guard the wizard," the baron ordered.

"And what will *you* be doing, *baron*?" Leesil questioned, stressing the word "baron" with noticeable sarcasm.

"Covering our flank," the baron snapped. "The Keeper's Hounds run in larger numbers than this. Our surrounding sentries will need assistance." He wrapped his hand around the hilt of the sheathed sword at his hip, leaned close, and growled: "You are the only man that can talk to me so and keep his teeth in his fool head. But don't press your luck." He turned and ran to the far side of the clearing, disappearing into the forest.

Leesil drew his own sword and stood near the wizard, who was so busy murmuring and gesturing that he seemed not to notice the exchange with the baron. That barb used to draw a chuckle, not a threat. But Leesil could only spare a brief moment to wonder at old his friend's gradual but noticeable change. His attention was torn between the mysterious wizard and the battle between the Keeper's Hounds and his company. They were even in number, but not even close in skill. The Keeper's Hounds had already cut down two of their five combatants, and if not for the five nearby sentries who heard the commotion and rushed into the fray, the Hounds would already be victorious.

After a few seconds of battle Leesil wondered why the other sentries scattered around their camp had not yet returned to assist them. He decided that the baron was right about other Hounds being in the vicinity. But he still had doubts that the baron was actually assisting them. It just did not fit with what he knew of the man. The baron was more likely fleeing to protect his own skin. Leesil knew the baron was not a coward, but he also knew that self-preservation was the big warrior's highest priority.

And then the captured demon commanded Leesil's full attention. The creature, having licked clean the bowl of blood, raged ferociously in its cage. The bars began to visibly bend at its assault and the chain creaked from the demon's powerful straining against it. The cage bounced ever more violently with enough force to cause the wagon, which had the breaks engaged and was also anchored by a chain fastened to a thick stake driven into the forest floor, to skid slightly as the stake yielded a few inches.

Fearful now and fighting the urge to bolt, Leesil chanced a look at the wizard, who was astoundingly unmoved by the demon's weakening restraints. The wizard calmly continued to weave his unknown spell. When Leesil looked back at the demon he saw two people emerge from the opposite side of the clearing. They were dressed in the same shadowy garments as the other intruders.

One of them was a man that, from a distance, looked at least as big as the baron. He held a large war hammer that a smaller person would not have been able to lift, let alone wield effectively. The person accompanying him was clearly a woman. Her disguise hid her facial features but her size, shape, and graceful movements could not be mistaken. And neither could the crossbow she raised and aimed in his direction.

Leesil threw himself to the ground. He expected the wizard to do the same and was surprised that he did not. His surprise was short-lived, however, when he saw the arrow strike the raging demon in the back of its neck just at the base of its skull.

The arrow sent the demon into an even more violent frenzy, causing the cage to bounce to the very edge of the wagon bed where it began to teeter and tilt. Leesil knew what was coming and scrambled as quickly as he could in a low crouch to the west edge of the clearing. He heard the cage fall from the wagon bed and crash to the ground and, against his will, looked over his shoulder. There he saw the cage in several pieces surrounding the emancipated demon. He turned away, rose to his full height and fled as quickly as he could into the shadows. This time he did not look back.

Several arrows protruded from the demon's thick hide in areas that would have proven fatal to a natural beast. The demon raged on as if the bolts were minor irritants. It shook itself with enough force to toss the bloody arrows from its hide, causing the loud clanging from the thick chains hanging from its neck to echo through the night. It turned to face its attacker and lunged.

Arrowhead drew her straight sword while Hammer stepped between her and the approaching demon with his war hammer hefted and ready to swing. The demon easily soared thirty feet across the meadow with the heavy chains trailing out behind it as if they were weightless. It had not yet reached the apex of it bound before it stopped abruptly in the air as if it had hit an invisible wall.

To Hammer's and Arrowhead's surprise, the creature smoothly floated away from them, clawing and snapping at the air all the while. They looked past the demon to see the wizard gesturing with one hand in a motion that made it obvious that he was controlling the demon. With a slow wave of his arm, the wizard ushered the demon across the meadow until it hovered over the stream. It promptly exploded into cloud of dark mist and a spray of wet chunks of flesh that rained down into the rushing water.

By that time, the commander and his group, as well as the other two groups of Hounds that had burst into the clearing during the battle, had either killed or incapacitated all of the sentries. Even though the wizard stood alone, surrounded by the Keeper's Hounds, nothing in his posture suggested even the slightest hint of concern.

"I know not what transpired here, wizard," One-Shot called out, "but we will take you into custody to answer to the King of Lorr and the Head Mage for your role in harboring this demon and using it to cast whatever wicked spell you have just cast!"

The wizard made no attempt to hide the amusement in the chilling voice that drifted from the shadows of his hood.

"I neither recognize nor respect the authority you claim. And I certainly will not be taken into custody on this or any night. Had I not more important matters to attend, I would kill the lot of you."

The commander's response was a dead sprint toward the wizard, which his charges mimicked without hesitation. The wizard waved a hand and brought a strong wind howling through the clearing. When the gale settled, the wizard and the surviving guards were gone.

The Hounds clumsily broke off their charge. The commander turned in a slow circle to survey the meadow. He quickly noticed bits of demon flesh and blood on either side of the creek. Most of the destroyed demon had fallen into the water and, thanks to the current, had been carried away. He remembered how the toxic remains of the demons had poisoned the Tyne River and left it barren for over a year.

"You four," the commander barked, pointing at the four men who rushed the clearing with him, "You know the procedure."

Two of the Hounds pulled six inch vials filled with clear liquid from small satchels attached to their weapons belts. The liquid could easily be mistaken for water but it was actually a compound developed by the Head Mage and a team of Echelon One mages and master alchemists. They pulled the stoppers from the vials and sprinkled the liquid over the bloodied area. The liquid hissed where it came into contact with demon blood, sterilizing the area by quickly searing away all traces of the demon blood and whatever it rested upon.

The other two pulled thick gloves and a folded leather pouch from their pouches. They donned the gloves and unfolded the pouches with a flick of the wrist and commenced to gathering as many bits of demon flesh as they could. They would take it to the conjurers at the capital city for proper disposal.

"I hate this part of the job," one of the men grumbled, but not silently enough.

"Would you rather leave it here to eventually turn to ash?" the commander challenged. "Have you forgotten how long it takes the dead flesh for lower level demons to completely disintegrate? Or perhaps you'd like to burn it yourself and risk inhaling its vile smoke. You know what it did to the poor bastards who tried that right after the war. The lucky ones died quickly."

The grumbler glanced over at the stream before he looked back to the commander. "Actually, sir, why don't we just – "

The commander cut him off. "If you suggest tossing it into the creek, I'll toss *you* in. It's been contaminated enough. We'll not be responsible for adding to it. Just be happy we don't have to haul a heavy demon carcass."

His exasperation turned into worry when his gaze fell upon Hammer and Arrowhead.

"Where is the youngling?" he demanded.

"We left him to secure the remaining sentry," Arrowhead answered.

"You left him alone?" the commander questioned harshly. "He was your responsibility. He was not to be left alone!"

Arrowhead flushed beneath her cowl. "I believe he was ready –"

"The rest of us will stay here to be sure there are no signs left of the demon's remains. You and Hammer find him!" the commander snapped.

"NOW!"

2.6

Eagle Eye saw that familiar spark of overconfidence in his attacker's eyes as he charged. As usual, when his opponents noticed his relatively smaller stature and the lack of an elfish slant to his eyes, they assumed he was either a stout female or an adolescent male and therefore an easy kill. And as always, he used that misconception to his full advantage.

He remained in his defensive crouch, which in most cases was a mistake against oncoming assailants because it gave them the advantage of momentum. It was a mistake that was common to inexperienced fighters. Eagle Eye, however, was not inexperienced. He had been trained by some of the best swordsmen in the Known Lands. His attacker had no way of knowing this, so his overconfidence rose higher still.

When he was within a few yards of Eagle Eye, he brought his short sword around with his right hand in a powerful sideways arc meant to behead his target or knock him off balance if he parried. Instead, the youngster exploded into motion, catching his attacker off-guard by stepping into the arc of blade and thrusting his broadsword forward.

Eagle Eye stepped forward so quickly that the short sword missed him completely and only the attacker's wrist struck the adolescent's shoulder. The force of the blow sent Eagle Eye stumbling to his right, but not before his broadsword plunged through the other's chain mail vest and leather cuirass just beneath his chest.

The attacker went into a staggering spin that sent him crashing to the forest floor. Breathless and bleeding, he tried unsuccessfully to regain his footing. He got to as far as a kneeling position before looking up at the youngster in pain, shock, and confusion. He mouthed a gurgling curse that even Eagle Eye's sharp hearing could not perceive, and then he fell dead.

Eagle Eye spared a moment to check the fallen man's pulse and breath. Once satisfied that he was dead, the youngster sprinted quickly and quietly and warily toward the battle site, determined not to be left out of the kill nor ambushed on the way. He had run for several seconds before he detected the sounds of someone else running through the forest toward him, coming from the direction of the meadow.

He stopped and hid behind a tree, not knowing if the person coming his way was friend or foe. A quick peek revealed a man roughly the same height and width as Hammer. But the long, poorly groomed hair hanging from beneath his helmet and his gleaming armor, along with the gem-studded cloak flowing behind him made it obvious that this was no Hound.

Assuming he was a member of the party that was holding the demon, Eagle Eye considered confronting the man. And then he noticed the man's gaudy attire, seemingly more for show than utility. That and the fact that he was fleeing led Eagle Eye to conclude that he was no threat. He decided to let him pass without confrontation so that he could resume his cautious dash to the meadow. But instead of continuing his escape, the large man pulled to a stop a few feet away from Eagle Eye's hiding place.

Eagle Eye watched warily as the flamboyantly dressed escapee drew his sword from its sheath. What he drew forth was no ordinary weapon. It appeared to be the bottom half of a broken broadsword. What made it even more unusual was its size. Even though it looked as if it was broken, it was still nearly as long as Eagle Eye's average-sized broadsword. He would have thought it was merely some weirdly designed, jagged yet deadly sharp double-edged broadsword that was fully intact. But the exaggerated width of the blade and the overly large pommel, grip, and cross guard made it obvious that the blade was broken. If the weapon had been whole, it would have been at least a third longer than Eagle Eye's broadsword.

The other thing that made it unusual was its color. Although all colors were distorted in the darkness of night, the broken broadsword appeared to have been carved from some ivory-like material as opposed to being forged from metal. It did not reflect the moons' light the way metal would. Eagle Eye knew he had never seen the broadsword before. He would surely remember if he had. Yet there was something at once familiar and sinister about the weapon.

Before he could figure out what that something was, the stranger growled into the darkness. "I heard you as surely as you heard me, and I know there is only one of you. Come out of hiding and face me or be hunted down like the coward you are."

Eagle Eye had assumed the man was some over-fed, ostentatious noble from the Kingdom of Darshay. The fact that he had heard Eagle Eye despite his attempt at stealth, and furthermore, the fact that he was able to determine from the sound that Eagle Eye was alone, led the youngster to quickly re-assess the man as a definite threat. Strangely intimidating broadsword or not, Eagle Eye knew he had to face the stranger. If he did not, he ran the deadly risk of being trailed and attacked from behind.

"My intention was to let you escape," Eagle Eye said as he stepped out from his hiding place. "But if you are so eager to die, then I will oblige you."

The baron laughed heartily. "Come kill me, youngling!"

They approached one another cautiously. Eagle Eye could see the overconfidence, but he could also see that this one did not allow it to make him careless…at least not yet. Eagle Eye did not depend on an overconfident adversary to be victorious, but it did make for a quicker fight.

The baron circled for a moment, sizing up the adolescent, and then he attacked. He struck three quick blows, each one powerful yet controlled and in a different area. Eagle Eye blocked each one with more than a small amount of effort, surprised by the quickness the man displayed. His size and the size of his broadsword did not give the impression of speed and balance, but he had both in abundance, along with bullish power.

After deflecting the third blow, Eagle Eye went on the attack, striking a quick two-handed thrust at the other's chest. To his surprise, his blade tip rebounded violently from the contact, not even chipping the armor, and sending a painful jolt up his arms. He shuffled away to give his arms a chance to recover from the jarring blow but the stranger would not allow that opportunity. He moved smoothly in pursuit, almost appearing to glide with more grace than a man his size should have displayed. Eagle Eye stayed out of reach though, skipping back and away from every thrust and quick stroke.

The baron launched a wild jab at the youngster's midsection, forcing him to back away more quickly than he wanted, and making him trip over a thick root running along the top of the forest floor. Instead of falling, Eagle Eye stumbled and rapidly regained his footing. The baron was on him the very next instant. He feinted a high crossways stroke to the chest, and when Eagle Eye leaned away, the baron thrust his forward leg out and delivered a powerful, steel-booted kick just below the teen's left knee.

Eagle Eye faltered but did not fall, shifting his weight to right leg and bringing up his blade to deflect a two-handed thrust of the jagged-tipped broadsword. He was just barely able to bring it back in a vertical position to block a forceful roundhouse backhanded strike. The teen allowed the momentum of the blow to throw him backwards and away from his attacker. He had to concentrate to keep from going down, a feat made that much harder by his damaged leg, and then prepare himself for another rush with the hope that the big warrior would become careless. But the baron did not charge. In fact, he paused, and his mouth twisted into a curious frown beneath the rim of his helmet.

"I know that blade," the baron said. "It has been repaired, the chink that nearly broke it two has been removed and the nicks have been smoothed, but I know that blade." He leveled a malevolent gaze on the younger warrior's blue eyes. "And I know those eyes." His frown turned into an evil smile.

"You are the eldest Sureblade whelp," the baron concluded. "It seems, Ethan, that the gods love coincidence." He hefted his unique sword with flair. "This is Dragon-fang, the blade that made necessary those repairs to your sword, the blade that took your father's useless life."

"Who are you?" Eagle Eye snarled, dropping to a fighting stance. "Come closer so that I can cut out your lying tongue."

"You have your father's confidence, but not even a quarter of his strength and skill," the baron guffawed. "I am Baron Dirk Tauran, and it will be a pleasure to send you to your father's side! But only in the afterlife, though, because the vultures, worms and other carrion eaters did not leave enough of him to bury!"

Eagle Eye, or Ethan, cried out in rage and rushed Tauran despite his painful limp. Tauran cried out in return and rushed to meet him. As the distance closed between them, Tauran caught a glimpse of something speeding toward him from his left. He had just enough time to realize it was an arrow before a flash of silver streaked down from above and cut the bolt in half, sending the pieces spinning in different directions. He looked up and saw a familiar shape dropping out of the trees just as two Keeper's Hounds, a man as big him and a petite woman rushed into view.

Tauran may have been distracted, but his adversary was not. Eagle Eye was nearly upon him, but Tauran was able to swing Dragon-fang up just in time to knock the arcing broadsword aside while the teen was still more than an arm's length away. In the same motion, the baron snapped his right foot up and out with surprising quickness, delivering a heavy kick to the youngster's stomach that sent him hurtling backward.

Arrowhead and Hammer pulled up short as the dark figure landed softly from the shadows of the high canopy. He landed a few feet in front of Tauran and next to the dagger he had used to stop the arrow. Its blade was halfway submerged in the earth and the handle faced skyward. The man's hand moved so smoothly and quickly that they almost missed it when he retrieved the dagger and hid it somewhere behind his back.

When he stood to his full height, both of the Hounds had to make an effort to keep their eyes from widening. He stood a full head higher than Hammer and the fancy dressed warrior and was just as broad-shouldered, but otherwise much leaner than the other two large warriors.

His clothes were very similar to the Hounds'. In the moons' light, the short-tailed tunic and leggings appeared to be dull greens and soft grays, allowing them to blend into the forest even more so than the Hounds' clothing. The clothes fitted closely without appearing to be tight, and he did not wear a cloak or a cowl. A scarf was wrapped tightly around his head with the hanging corners tucked under the scarf. His face was wide with a sharply angled jaw line that sloped down to a protruding square chin. His nose was long and straight with a flat bridge and a straight brow that, from a distance, cast a shadow over his eyes.

Arrowhead could see dagger handles lining the sash that cinched the newcomer's tunic to his narrow waist. He held a short sword in one hand and a short, spiked club in the other. His bearing gave every indication that he was proficient in the use of both.

The baron sneered at Arrowhead and Hammer. "I think we can take the three them, T'cheln. What say you?"

"Of course we can," T'cheln answered in a matter of fact tone. "But not before the rest of the Hounds arrive. And even with *my* assistance, those odds would be too much to overcome."

"I sincerely hope we meet again, young Sureblade," Tauran taunted before he and his tall companion raced into the darkness.

"We must go after them!" Ethan said, using his broadsword to balance himself on his damaged leg as he struggled to his feet.

"Not unless One-Shot commands it," Arrowhead ordered. "And you are in no condition to pursue anyone."

They could hear the sound of some big and quick animal moving away from them in the darkness. The sound came from the direction in which the two huge warriors escaped.

One-Shot and the rest of the Hounds began filtering into view. One-Shot surveyed the area, from the two halves of the arrow to the trampled foliage and scuffed roots, to the sorry condition of Eagle Eye. He shook his head in disappointment even as something resembling relief flashed across his face.

"I take it the baron escaped," the commander observed.

"He had assistance," Ethan said, voice trembling with anger, "But we could have bested them."

"I have my doubts," Arrowhead countered. "What little of the fight I saw revealed that the baron is no ordinary swordsman. He used his feet almost as deftly as his blade, and he looked as strong as Hammer."

"And his friend looked even more formidable," Hammer added.

The commander gave Ethan another appraising look. "Your determination is appreciated, Eagle Eye, but any *one* man capable of doing this to a fighter of your caliber is someone to pursue very cautiously, let alone two of them." He paused and looked to the three moons through breaks in the thick canopy as if searching the heavens for an unanswered question. He shook his head again.

"Something both significant and sinister has transpired in this wood. But we have no evidence as to what and no prisoners to question."

"At least the wizard did us a favor by destroying the demon," Cobra said.

"He destroyed the demon," One-Shot conceded, "but I seriously doubt that he did us any favors."

Ethan stared into the darkness in the direction that the two men had fled. Beneath his cowl his lips were pursed in frustration. He knew Tauran was not lying. He recognized Dragon-fang from his friend's description. He had also heard the reports of the Finder's defeat at the hands of Raxe, the Child of the Old Ones and direct descendant of the Gatekeeper. But that was no excuse. Ethan had allowed the man to anger him to the point of distraction…and he almost lost his life for it.

The young Sureblade knew that the Finder, not Tauran, had killed his father. It was Tauran, though, who possessed the Finder's weapon. He was there to witness the murder, probably cheering on the murderer, who had defeated his father only because of his enchanted broadsword and dwarf-forged armor that was even denser than the Legion Midnight armor Tauran wore. Tauran taunted Ethan in a coward's attempt to gain an advantage by making him lose control.

For all of these things, Ethan promised himself and the Lord Ascendant, he would make Tauran pay with his life.

Chapter 3: Weapons

3.1

Ryan stood naked in front of the bathroom mirror, waiting for the steam to dissipate so he could inspect himself. The full-length mirror was on the back of the door, and Ryan could see his reflection from the top of his ankles to the top of his head.

His torso, arms and knees were marked with hardened scar tissue. There was a long thin scar across his chest from a bullet that had grazed him while he was in the Special Forces. A toughened puckered scar on the right side of his waist marked the entry point of a bullet he caught while in service to the Cutters. A jagged, vertical scar line over his left rib cage evidenced a knife wound he sustained during hand-to-hand combat on one of his first missions for the organization.

Each of those scars represented more than physical trauma. They represented just a few of the many lives that he had taken. So many scars, so many kills, and he was barely in his thirties.

Then he looked at the newer scars, the ones he attained during his stay in the Kingdom of Lorr. If not for the talented healers of the Kingdom – especially Catherine, the half-elf-half-human wife of the Head Mage – there would be even more scars. There was virtually no evidence of the broken bones and deep lacerations from his many battles during his time across the WorldGate. There were, however, other far more telling scars that not even the most talented healers could remove.

His arms, the backs of his knees and his upper calves, the areas that were not covered by Raxe's armor – were pocked with lumps of dark scar tissue. He still had nightmares about the origins of those scars. Being chewed up and swallowed by a demonic sea monster was not something easily forgotten, no matter how much he wanted to.

To this day he was amazed that even the massive, powerful teeth of that creature could not penetrate his enchanted armor to puncture his vital organs. Even still, the creature's teeth dripped with foul toxins and poisons that would have killed him if Sabrina, the Mistress of the Sea, had not saved his life. But not even her magic or the mysterious healing creatures beneath the surface of Lake Onyx could rid him of the scars.

And then there was the most significant scar of them all: the nasty exit wound on his throat from the knife that the Finder threw at him. The scar looked like the remnants of a tracheotomy gone awry. There was a matching scar on the back of his neck that marked the entry point of the blade. That was the blow that should have sent him to his death; that should have eternally submerged him in the fires of the Hell that awaited him for the evil he had done during his lifetime.

Instead of dying, he had been given another chance. Instead of damning him for eternity, the fires baptized him and sent his soul back into his body. His voice was still a hoarse rasp, having never fully recovered from the wound.

For the first two years after his return from the Kingdom of Lorr, he held out hope that the harsh edges of the memories of the sea demon and his brief glimpse of hell would dull over time. He hoped that they would fade to the level of remembered nightmares, recollections that were unpleasant but no longer caused fear or pain.

That was not to be. The sound of his damaged voice was still alien to his own ears, a constant reminder of his death and second chance. The puckered scars still flared with pain, not constantly, but frequently and randomly enough to assure him that every snap of the sea demon's giant reptilian jaws would forever be emblazoned in his mind.

But he was alive.

The marks on his neck, along with his voice, told him every day that he had been spared for a reason. There was much for which he had to atone. He wondered how much he had to do to save his soul. He wondered if he even could.

A sultry female voice floated to him from behind the shower curtain. "I didn't notice all those scars last night."

Ryan turned to watch the tall, buxom woman step out of the shower and reach for the towel hanging from a bar next to the shower.

"Nasty, ain't it, Synn?" Ryan asked.

"Not at all," Synn returned. "They make those muscles look even sexier. They make you look dangerous."

"So…" Ryan began, preparing to do a little bartering as he enjoyed the spectacle of her slowly and softly padding the moisture from her tawny skin and her short black hair. "The shower action was cool, but how much extra is it?"

"Oh, that was for me, baby," she assured. "No extra charge."

"Thanks," Ryan said with genuine surprise. Her services were expensive to begin with, and when she stayed the whole night and took a shower with him this morning, he was expecting her to charge him double…and she would have been well worth it. "That's mighty generous of you."

"A little something for you to remember me by, sweetie," she gave him a well-practiced and well-executed sexy smile.

"You've been in there for damn near an hour!" Dan called from outside of the bathroom. "Bring your ass on so we can take a ride."

Synn twirled the towel around her damp hair and opened the bathroom door. Dan whistled as she winked and tiptoed past. He twirled his wheelchair around to watch her quickly dress, scoop up her purse and the wad of money beside it on the nightstand, and then ease out of the room. A few moments later they heard the front door open and close.

Ryan wrapped himself in a towel and stepped out into the bedroom of the extended stay hotel on the northwest side of Houston, Texas. His grandfather turned to him and raised an eyebrow.

"She stayed all night, huh? And from what I just heard she didn't charge you extra."

"Yep," Ryan said as he reached into a drawer next to his bed to fish out a pair of boxer shorts.

"You ain't *that* good, you know," Dan assured. "She just wants the repeat business."

"Tell me something I don't know," Ryan returned as he walked over to the door leading to the rest of the apartment, which consisted of one large room that contained both a living area and a kitchen. When he was sure the room was empty, he turned back to his grandfather. "So how was your company?"

"Honey was a great conversationalist," Dan said.

Ryan cocked his head. "All you did was talk? Bullshit. Unless the pipes don't…"

"The pipes work fine, boy. She just wasn't my type…too skinny. Not even a dog wants a bone with no meat on it."

Ryan chuckled. "So why didn't you look for someone else? The club was full of women of all shapes, sizes and colors."

"I saw you checkin' out Synn, and since she and Honey like to work together, I thought I'd help you out. You needed it more than I did. When you get my age you have a few more things to worry about than a little tail…" he glanced at the door with a lewd smile as if Synn was still there. "…Or a *big* one."

"Thanks, gramps," Ryan said sarcastically. "So what did you two talk about?"

"Life, my boy. We talked about life. I explained to her that she has a lot of other options and she didn't have to do what she was doing."

"What are *you* doing?" Ryan chuckled. "Savin' souls now?"

"You know I ain't no angel," Dan assured. "But I saw some promise in that girl. I could see her potential if she made the right choices."

"And I'm sure she just ran right outta here ready to change her life," Ryan teased.

Dan shrugged. "Probably not. I'm sure she looked at the night as easy money without having to break a sweat for a heathen like you. But who knows? If there's a chance that something took root in her mind, it was money well spent."

"Whatever you say," Ryan scoffed as he looked over at his bed. He noticed that Dan had already laid out a pair of slacks and a golf shirt on the bed for him.

"What?" Ryan asked. "You're dressing me now?"

"You always agonize over what to wear like you were a broad or something," Dan answered. "I don't feel like waiting around for you today." Dan whirled his wheelchair around and rolled out of the bedroom.

There was nothing wrong with the clothes his grandfather set out for him, but the mere fact that he did so irked Ryan. Dan was exaggerating, too. Ryan was always dressed and prepared to move before Dan. His grandfather was obviously in a hurry.

As Ryan dressed, Dan called to him from the other room. "You know, boy, it might do *you* some good to try to save some souls every now and then. I know you gave up the whole murder-for-hire thing but there's more to rehabilitation than just giving up killing."

"One sin at a time, gramps," Ryan called back. He thought about the prostitute's nickname and couldn't help but snicker. "No pun intended!"

"Just hurry up so we can go!" Dan snapped. He was visibly anxious about something. So Ryan took his time getting dressed just to tweak the old man a little.

In another ten minutes the two of them were motoring south on I-45 to a storage facility on the city's southeast side. It took them another half-hour to reach their destination. When they pulled into the storage facility's small parking lot, Dan's impatient irritability disappeared. He was almost giddy with anticipation.

"I have something to show you, boy," Dan said slyly.

"What is it this time, Gramps?" Ryan asked suspiciously. He remembered the last time his grandfather "had something to show him." That "something" was Demonsbane, his enchanted battle-axe. Dan had revealed it to Ryan just before Ryan was pulled – or fell – into the Kingdom of Lorr.

Dan opened the passenger side door of his grandson's van and flipped the necessary switches to bring the wheel chair lift to life. The hydraulic system lifted Dan's wheelchair a few inches from the floor of the van and then smoothly extended itself and the chair outward until it was clear of the van door. It was on the ground by the time Ryan exited the driver side door and walked around to the passenger side. He closed the door after the lift contracted back into the vehicle.

Ryan had to walk briskly to keep up as Dan steered his wheelchair to the closed door of the leased storage unit. The Houston winter day was brisk, like mid-Fall in Chicago, and the wind blew almost as fiercely as the Windy City's famed Hawk. Without looking back at his grandson, Dan fished a set of keys out of his pocket and tossed it absently over his shoulder. He threw it wide to the right, or so Ryan thought, but a strong breeze caught the key ring and blew it back to the left.

"Show off," Ryan said as he held out a hand to let the keys drop into his palm.

He went to the door, unlocked the big padlock securing the storage unit, and then lifted the garage-style door, revealing a fifteen by ten foot room filled nearly to the ceiling with unmarked boxes of various sizes.

"I hope you can find whatever it is you want to show me," Ryan said.

"I don't have to," Dan replied. "You can find it."

"What do you mean?" Ryan asked. "I've never been here before. I didn't even know this place existed, let alone what's in here."

"You can't feel that?" Dan inquired, somewhat surprised.

"Feel what?"

"Just shut up and *feel*." Dan advised. "It should be something like the pull you felt in Lorr when you were near the demons. Not as oppressive or intense, but it should be a similar kind of tug."

"That was involuntary," Ryan argued. "I didn't have to reach out for it or anything. The tug found me."

"Exactly," Dan agreed. "So shut up and feel."

Ryan did as he was told. Instead of trying to focus on any particular sensation, he relaxed his mind and body and simply became aware of everything around him.

That was when he felt it. Like his grandfather said, it was a much less intense version of the feeling he experienced when Demonsbane pulled him in the direction of the demons that were released from the Seven Hells. It was a warm tingle that compelled him to move in a particular direction.

Ryan followed the pull through a tight maze of cardboard boxes until he came to two in particular, one nondescript box stacked on top of another, tucked into a dark rear corner of the storage facility. The bottom box was nearly two feet square and one fourth as deep. The other was about two feet long, nine inches wide, and had a depth of only about four inches.

"Bring them out here," Dan called from the entrance.

"This is way too familiar…" Ryan whispered as he lifted the two boxes easily and brought them back to his grandfather. He placed them on the storage shelter floor near the wheels of Dan's chair.

"Well?" Dan said impatiently. "You gonna open them or not?"

Ryan breathed deeply and pulled open the narrow box. The flaps were sealed with thick tape that easily gave way. He reached into the box and pulled out a short, relatively wide sword. The blade was flat, with no ridge or fuller. It looked almost to be made of ivory but Ryan could tell it was some sort of metal. The blade did not shine with the reflective brilliance of Demonsbane but it was a beautiful weapon nonetheless.

There were incredible carvings on the blade that reminded Ryan of the WorldGate and Hell Keys. The carving depicted seven people – three men and three women – following a man. All of them were dressed in ragged clothes. The men wore tattered shirts and britches held up with thin lengths of rope. The women wore torn, loosely fitting dresses and had kerchiefs tied around their heads. The leader stood tall and confident and pointed ahead eagerly to an unseen destination.

The artist, whoever it was, did an amazing job with the impossibly intricate detail on the small surface area of the blade. Ryan could easily make out the wrinkles in the people's clothing, the subtle shadows defining facial features, and the expressions of hope and determination in the tired eyes of the six followers. Even though the images were carved into the nearly white metal, the facial features of the people made it obvious they were of African origin. Ryan quickly realized what he was looking at. It was a group of people held as slaves being led to freedom. An identical carving adorned the opposite side of the blade.

The seven-inch long grip of the short sword was almost as long as the blade and was made of a silvery metal identical to that of his enchanted battle-axe. From the bottom of the handle spread a knob-like pommel, round except for its flat base, about the size of Ryan's fist. Like Demonsbane, this short sword seemed to fit his grasp flawlessly and its balance was perfect.

"That's Questblade," Dan informed.

"This can't be a weapon created by the Gatekeeper," Ryan said, still transfixed by the beautiful carving. "This etching is from the nineteenth century…*our* nineteenth century."

"No, it wasn't made by the Gatekeeper," Dan answered. "My father made it."

"Wow," Ryan said, impressed. "What does it do?"

"Questblade does what the name implies. It helps its owner find things."

"What kind of things?"

"Whatever the owner is looking for," Dan said. "As long as it's a noble search."

"Define 'noble.'" Ryan urged.

"I can't," Dan admitted. "The blade's magic defines what's noble. If it decides the quest is worthy, it will lead in the necessary direction."

"Cool," Ryan decided. "An excellent time saver."

"You've got the wrong idea, boy." Dan chuckled. "It doesn't take you in a straight line to your target the way Demonsbane leads you to demons. It might take you all around the world to find something that may have only been a mile away. Questblade takes you in the direction you *need* to go."

"Whatever that means," Ryan said doubtfully.

"As you can see from the image," Dan continued, "the carvings depict a man leading a group of men and women to freedom. The guide is my father. He worked on the Underground Railroad and created Questblade to assist in leading people held as slaves to freedom. Even though the destinations were known to the freedom fighters, the route was still dangerous, of course. Questblade guided them along the safest paths."

"Where were you during that time?" Ryan asked. "If you're closing in on two hundred, you were alive then."

"My father sent my mother and me to Asia," Dan explained. "He'd lived in Northern China for years, way back before he met my mother in the States. While he lived in China he studied and became friends with a Shaolin monk. The monk agreed to take us in while my father stayed in the States to help in the fight against slavery. I spent the first fifty years of my life in and around China. My mother provided a link to my African and American heritage while I studied martial arts and Buddhism."

"I never knew that…" Ryan breathed. "Why did he have to send you China?"

"It was the early eighteen-hundreds. Slavery was thriving in the south and black folks weren't exactly loved by white America in the north. My father didn't want my mother and me in America. This country was an ugly, shameful place back then and he didn't want my magic to be nurtured in such a hateful atmosphere. He was afraid I'd use my abilities to exact some type of revenge."

"Didn't you want to come here and help your dad?"

"Hell yes," Dan said. "But my father insisted I stay in the Far East. He said the fight against slavery was *his* war, not mine. His gift of foresight was strong and he knew my destiny was to fight in future wars. The lessons I learned in China were a great help to me when I did finally get to America in nineteen hundred."

"How so?" Ryan was genuinely curious. He never imagined his grandfather's life was so interesting.

"You know your history, boy," Dan fussed. "The practice of slavery might have been outlawed but the oppression was worse than anyone living in America nowadays could imagine. China was no paradise back then either. Between the Opium Wars, the Taiping and Boxer Rebellions and the Sino-Japanese War, China was constantly in violent conflict. The Chinese fought against each other and against foreigners all through the late 1800's and into the turn of the century.

"For a while my mother and I were in safe seclusion at one of the Northern Shaolin Temples but it was just a matter of time before the violence reached us. The Temples were under attack again and, since we were clearly *not* Chinese, we had to stay hidden most of the time.

"The lessons I learned from Buddhism helped me find inner peace and avoid getting infected by the hatred and animosity that permeated China and the United States. It was especially hard to be peaceful in this country when I watched people that looked like me get tortured and murdered just *because* they looked like me.

"I was almost glad momma passed away several years before I came back to the States. If old age hadn't claimed her then, despair at how our people were treated in this country almost certainly would have."

"Especially when you had the power to stop it," Ryan added.

"I didn't have that kind of power," Dan corrected. "Not even your great grandfather had that kind of power. To stop an atrocity so deeply rooted in a nation's culture takes the power to change men's hearts. We only had the power to stop hearts from beating. And believe me, I was more than a little tempted to stop a lot hearts back then. The peace and discipline I learned in the Far East are the only things that kept me from doing just that."

A faraway look clouded Dan's eyes. His mouth contorted slightly into a barely perceptible grimace as he recalled memories that were best left forgotten. "Enough about that," he concluded. "Open the other box."

The second box contained a small, round, slightly domed shield with a diameter of about eighteen inches. The front and rear surfaces of the shield seemed to be cast from iron. There were no intricate carvings or other distinguishable marks. There was only the dull gray ore, except for the fine edges that were rimmed with that same silvery-blue metal that adorned the haft of Questblade.

Ryan slid his forearm through the two straps screwed into the inner surface of the shield. Like his enchanted armor and other weapons, this one felt as if it was made specifically for him. One strap fitted comfortably around his wrist and the other fit perfectly around his forearm about an inch away from the crook of his arm. As expected, the weight of the shield was heavy enough to ensure Ryan of its sturdiness but light enough to not be a burden.

"What's so special about this shield?" he asked his grandfather.

"It's called the *Shield of Innocents*." Dan answered, his chest swelling with pride.

"Kinda plain compared to the other stuff, eh?" Ryan asked.

"Thanks, ass," Dan replied dryly.

Ryan's eyes widened. "*You* made this one?"

"Sure did, Sherlock."

"Sorry, gramps," Ryan chuckled. "I didn't mean to offend you. It's just that the other stuff is so elaborately decorated and this one…well…it isn't."

"Look, damn it, I didn't have the time, inclination, or skill to carve pretty pictures."

"Alright, gramps," Ryan held his hands up defensively. "I just didn't know if the carvings had any significance."

"The carvings are just decoration. They have nothing to do with the weapons' power. Your mother, like many of the Children, had that artistic flair. I don't. You don't either, by the way. But it doesn't matter. The magic doesn't come from the art. We don't need to carve runes or symbols into our talismans. The magic in the enchanted weapons we make comes directly from us."

"I can see why the Keys, Demonsbane, and Questblade were created, but why did you make the shield?"

"I was a soldier," Dan explained. "I fought in both World Wars, the future wars my father foresaw. My specialty was POW extraction. I used Questblade during both wars but I found out pretty quickly during WWI that the blade wouldn't be enough."

"Why not?" Ryan asked.

"It led us along the safest and surest paths as it's created to do," Dan said. "But you know what combat is like. During a war of that magnitude 'safe' is a relative term. Not even the best paths are free of danger. I still lost people – too many people – to surprise attacks and cross fire from unexpected fire fights."

"I see what you mean," Ryan said.

Dan went on. "After WWI, it wasn't too hard to see another one coming and I knew I would have to do my part in that one, too. I didn't want a repeat of the first war so I created the *Shield*."

"So what does the *Shield* do? And don't tell me it shields, old man. What's so special about it?"

Dan laughed. "It shields, boy!" He laughed again when Ryan bristled and then he continued. "It shields any kind of physical assault, much like your armor. And it shields an area much greater than the actual surface area of the shield."

"Does it grow or something?" Ryan questioned seriously.

"It doesn't grow, but it emits a semi-invisible field that expands in every direction. It protects not only the person holding the shield, but anyone close enough to him, as well."

"I'll bet that came in handy during WWII," Ryan said.

"It did." Dan confirmed. "I didn't lose very many the second time around, only the ones too stupid to follow orders or stay nearby."

"Damn, gramps," Ryan breathed. "I didn't know you were such a hero. That's pretty cool."

"There's a lot you don't know about me. But don't worry. I'll teach you as much as I can."

"This weapon-making legacy of ours," Ryan began, "Did it ever pass down to mom?"

"Probably, but she never had occasion to use it," Dan answered. "Cynthia was too young for Korea, and she disagreed with the US involvement in 'Nam. Your mom was kinda drawn to the military, though. I guess it's in our blood. But ours is the blood of warriors and she didn't appreciate the subordinate role that women were forced to play in law enforcement and the military back then."

"So mom went into psychology and counseling?" Ryan asked, recalling her vocation. "That's a big jump, eh?"

"She specialized in counseling abused women and children," Dan explained. "A different kind of war but a war just the same."

"I wish I had known her longer," Ryan mused.

"Me, too," Dan agreed. "Me, too."

After a brief, sad pause Ryan said, "Maybe I should make a weapon. You think I could make an enchanted weapon like you did?"

"I'm sure you could," Dan told him. "But it's not something we can do on a whim. There has to be a reason for it, a cause."

"If I'd known, I could've made something while I was in Lorr," Ryan realized.

"When the time comes for you to craft a weapon, you'll know," Dan promised. "And the weapons you make may not necessarily be for you. When Raxe and the Gatekeeper made Demonsbane, it obviously wasn't for them. They didn't need a talisman to destroy demons. It was for their descendants, the less powerful Children of the Old Ones. Questblade wasn't just for my father. It's for anyone on a noble search. The weapon you make may or may not be for you. Your magic will let you know."

"Now that I think about it," Ryan leveled an accusing glare at his grandfather. "*These* weapons might have been useful back in Lorr."

"Nah," Dan said. "You did fine without them. If I thought you would need them I would've given them to you. But honestly, what good would either of these things have done against what you faced?"

Ryan thought about that while Dan continued. "You had old Shandie as a guide during your quest for Raxe's armor and the King of the Dragons, and she did as good a job – if not a better one – than Questblade could have done. The Shield works against projection based attacks: bullets, arrows, even energy streams. Your combat was up close and personal for the most part, and your armor took care of the rest. These weapons would've been just extra gear for you to lug around."

"But you didn't know about the armor," Ryan argued. "Hell, Shandie didn't even know about it. How did you know I wouldn't need the shield?"

"I had a vision, boy," Dan reminded him. "The way I interpreted it, you only had need of Demonsbane. Everything else was provided for or accomplished by you alone."

"That's flimsy, gramps. Real flimsy."

"That's foresight," Dan returned. "I don't expect you to understand and I don't care if you do or not. It's irrelevant now, anyway."

"So you had another vision..." Ryan realized. "Something that told you it was time for you to pass these weapons on to me?"

"Now you're getting it," Dan said sarcastically.

Ryan raised a hand to stall him. "Hold on." He looked around the storage area suspiciously before he continued. "So how many other useful weapons are in here, gramps? There's gotta be something else around here that I can use."

"Not right now, there isn't," Dan countered. "The vision sent me for the *Shield* and Questblade. I won't jinx things by getting ahead of myself."

"So I guess that means the shit is about to hit the fan again, right?"

"Give that boy a cigar!" Dan declared. "Let's get the hell outta here."

3.2

It was late afternoon when they got back to their apartment at the extended stay hotel. Ryan placed the boxes holding the sword and shield on the coffee table in front of the couch before seating himself. Dan wheeled over to the side of the table and eyed Ryan expectantly.

"What?" Ryan asked.

"What do you mean 'what'?" Dan returned. "Use Questblade."

"For what?"

"Whatever you want, boy. What is it that you would most like to find?"

"I want to find a way to keep from going to hell," Ryan said, only half joking.

"Try a person, place, or thing," Dan amended.

"The supervisor," Ryan said. "You know that. I want to find out why the organization is trying to terminate me. Is that noble enough?"

"There's only one way to find out," Dan answered. He pointed his chin at the box containing Questblade.

"So how do I use it?"

"Clear your mind and control your breathing, the same way you were taught to find your *chi*," Dan explained. "Concentrate on what it is you're looking for. If it's something you've seen, visualize it. If it is something you haven't, repeat its name in your mind. Then balance Questblade on the base of the pommel. If your quest is worthy, it will stand on its own for a few seconds before it falls. Whichever direction the tip of the blade points is where you will need to start your search."

"That sounds a little corny, gramps," Ryan started as he took the enchanted blade from the box. "But after what I've seen, who am I to argue?"

"Hold the grip in your right hand and the rest the blade in your left palm."

Ryan did as he was told. He slowed his breathing until it was smooth and rhythmic, inhaling slowly and deeply through his nose and exhaling through slightly parted lips.

When his mind's eye saw nothing but darkness he began to filter out all noise. The constant rumble of traffic outside their hotel faded away, as did all other sound both external and internal until all he could here were six words: *The one who ordered my assassination.*

The words were repeated over and over. They began to echo, to bounce off the walls of his mind. The words resonated at different psychic volumes and different rhythms until they coalesced and morphed from intelligible individual words into a simple awareness.

Questblade grew warm in his hands. The warmth spread through his fingers, then his wrist and arms, working its way up his neck and into the base of his skull. The sound in his darkened mind burst into white light. The light shined for a moment and then shrank in on itself, as if going down an invisible drain in his mind's eye. Blackness crept back in where the light bled away, shrinking into a vision. The vision was of Questblade pointed upright against a screen of total darkness.

Ryan opened his eyes. The awe he felt was hidden poorly as he placed the enchanted sword on the table with the flat base of the pommel down and the blade pointing at the ceiling. It was perfectly balanced and still. Ryan watched the sword expectantly while Dan watched Ryan. A moment later, without any physical catalyst that he could see, the sword fell over onto the flat side of the blade.

The blade tip pointed at the television set across the room and directly in front of the coffee table.

Ryan chuckled. He did not know what to expect, but it was certainly not that. Even though his grandfather explained exactly what would happen, Ryan still half expected the blade to glow or bark out a clap of thunder, perhaps even make some kind of weird noise. All it did was fall. And its tip pointed in the general direction of the television.

"It wants us to watch TV," Ryan teased.

"You think so?" Dan asked seriously.

"Of course not," Ryan said. "It's pointing north. It's telling us to head north."

"Then why did you mention the TV?" Dan challenged.

"Because it's silly," Ryan argued. "I was joking."

"And it was the first thing that came to your mind. Wasn't it?"

"Well, yeah," Ryan concurred with a sigh. "But – "

"But nothing," Dan cut him off. "What do you do, listen in shifts or something? Questblade is not a simple damn compass. It's a guide. The blade is pointing at the TV and that was the first thing that came to your mind. Trust the magic and turn the damn thing on."

"All right already," Ryan said as he snatched up the remote control and turned on the television. "Look, it's the news, OK? It's a national weather report."

"Shhhh!" Dan admonished.

Ryan rolled his eyes and fell silent. He looked at the television set as the national weather report was followed by the local weather, which was replaced two long minutes later by a news story. Dan was watching intently enough to convince Ryan to at least act like he was interested. A Hispanic woman wearing a thick red skullcap and a heavy red parka appeared. Fat snowflakes drifted lazily down around her as she held a microphone with one black-gloved hand. The other gloved hand was held out to the side, calling the camera's attention to the long stretch of snowy highway a few feet to the side of her.

In the background, a barricade of yellow tape surrounded a crime scene. Uniformed state and county police officers milled around a green Honda Civic. Dan listened closely to the reporter.

> *We're here in southern Illinois, just fifty miles south of* Carbondale, *where state troopers found a car in the early morning hours stranded on the side of the highway. Two men were found dead; shot to death apparently almost twenty-four hours earlier in what law enforcement officials believe to have been a drug deal gone bad. The victims were shot execution-style,*

and both men carried high caliber weapons.

Investigators have since confirmed that the Honda Civic was stolen. The identification found on both victims have proven to be false, so State Police have released these photographs in the hopes of discovering the men's true identities.

Dan's mouth dropped open and Ryan's eyes widened when the pictures popped up on the television screen. Ryan caught his grandfather's expression and was intrigued even further.

"Do you know those guys?" Ryan asked.

"I've seen them," Dan confirmed. "What about you?"

"They work for the organization," Ryan shared. "They were on the team that came to kill me at my apartment in Chicago."

"You told me a hell of a lot of men were at that building," Dan said. "How do you remember those two particular faces out of so many?"

Ryan turned to his grandfather. "Just like I remember the face of every man and woman I've ever killed, I remember the face of every man and woman that's tried to kill me…at least the ones that I've actually seen up close." He looked at the screen and studied the pictures again. "Those two were there. They were a part of the group that came through the door just before I went out the window."

Dan grunted. "They came to my room at the center, pretending to be my nephews," he informed. "They're probably the ones who planted the bomb there."

"You never told me how you were able to see them without them seeing you," Ryan recalled. "Where were you hiding?"

"That's irrelevant," Dan eluded. "What is relevant is that the blade worked. You do realize this ain't a coincidence, don't you?"

Ryan looked at the blade and shrugged. Ok, then. The sword was magic. Who was he to argue? "Then that was definitely *not* a drug deal gone bad," he surmised. "It was the organization."

"A botched assassination?" Dan asked.

"Had to be," Ryan returned. "And to take out two agents like that, the target must've been good. Damn good. This is a huge stroke of luck."

Dan scoffed. "Not for them."

"I mean for us," explained Ryan. "I've been dying to take the fight to them for years but I've never had a lead. During our training we never knew where we were. We were always either drugged or blindfolded as we were moved around. Our handlers always wore masks or talked to us over the phone. The only people we trainees saw unmasked were each other. Only a few of us saw each other and I haven't seen any of them since. I've never been able to find any intel that would help me find my supervisor.

"But now… If the organization missed, they'll keep trying until the target is dead. We have to find the target before they do. Once we do, all we'll have to do is trail them and wait for the organization to take another shot. And, knowing the organization the way I do, I'm pretty sure it won't be a long wait."

"OK," allowed Dan. "So how do we find the target?"

3.3

Ethan looked through the porthole of his cabin at the obsidian waves stretching out beyond the horizon. The dark water and the nighttime sky blended in the distance to form a void as infinite as the concerns that crowded Ethan's thoughts.

He wondered what type of spell was being conjured near Tohrfell's Valley, and if the Hounds had managed to stop them in time. He wondered what would become of the Keeper's Hounds now that the last demon had been destroyed. And despite himself, he worried that he might never see his teammates again, Arrowhead in particular, if the Hounds were disbanded.

He turned his head at a soft knock on his door. Curious as to who would be coming to his room at such a late hour, Ethan hurried to the door, pulled it open, and had to stifle a gasp of surprise. Arrowhead stood before him. She was wreathed in the soft, mist-diffused glimmer of the three moons' light. The silver glow illuminated the long, straight, black hair that cascaded down her shoulders and rested gently on the wool cloak that she held closed tightly against the cool night air.

Ethan was taken aback for a moment. He had never seen her wear her hair down. It was always drawn up in a tight bun or hidden beneath a scarf or hood. He was amazed at how such a simple thing as removing a few pins and combs could transform a woman's entire appearance. Framed by those long, straight tresses, her round face looked softer. Her hazel eyes, usually intense, seemed more relaxed. Even her fair skin looked smoother and more delicate than usual. She looked younger. And even prettier.

"Are you going to let me in or just stare at me while I freeze?" She demanded in a whisper.

"It's not that cold out there, Arrowhead," Ethan said softly in a weak attempt to conceal his embarrassment. He stepped out of her way.

"No," she said as she padded quickly into the room. "But that damp, cold deck was giving me a chill all over."

Ethan stepped out of his corner cabin peaked around at the adjacent deck to see if anyone was watching, wondering if this was some kind of joke. When he was satisfied no one was there, he stepped back into his cabin and closed the door. He looked down at her bare feet and slim ankles and realized he had never seen her without boots. Her feet were pale and tiny, and Ethan realized he was staring at them. He looked up to find her looking at him with a half-smile.

"Are you done with all the gawking?" she asked sternly.

"I'm sorry," he said quickly. "It's just that I've never seen you with…or I mean without…well, you know what I mean."

"You do realize that I'm not *always* dressed in hunting gear, don't you?"

"Of course," Ethan scoffed. He was lying, of course. With the exception of a few – well, more than a few – fantasies, he had never seriously thought about her in anything else but her gear. That was all he ever saw her wear. All of the Keeper's Hounds slept in full gear when they were on the hunt, and even though they had sailed to other lands in the past, she had never visited him after everyone had bedded down for the night. He was used to seeing her looking like a fighter; armed, wary and intense. Now she looked like a girl. *No*, he corrected himself. She looked like a woman.

"What are you doing here this late?" Ethan said, forcing distracting thoughts from his mind.

"I wanted to talk to you about what happened last night."

"A lot of things happened last night, Arrowhead," Ethan said, his mood darkening at the memories.

"No doubt," Arrowhead agreed. "But I'm talking about my leaving you alone with that mercenary."

"I was curious about that," Ethan admitted. "I thought maybe One-Shot had suggested that you two leave me. At least I thought that until he dressed down you and Hammer for it just after we boarded this ship."

Arrowhead shrugged and smiled mischievously. "You mean dressed us down *again*. You should have seen him when I first told him. He turned beet-red. I thought his head would explode. But it is like I told him and you: I felt you were ready."

"The commander obviously did not," Ethan said.

"And he never will," Arrowhead assured. "Your age barely matters. The commander is overly protective of you because he and your father were such good friends. Your father was his mentor, you know."

"Tell me, Arrowhead," Ethan said, regarding her thoughtfully. "What made you decide that I was ready?"

"You can call me Nicolette," she shared as she sat down on a small stool placed a few feet away from Ethan's bunk. "We're not in the field now."

"I can see that," Ethan said, his thoughts and eyes beginning to wonder again. Nicolette's woolen cloak and the long shift she wore beneath it raised a few inches when she sat down, just barely revealing the smooth curve of her toned calves.

"In answer to your question," Nicolette said with just enough emphasis to call Ethan's attention back to her eyes. "That's what I came to tell you. On our last few hunts, you've acquitted yourself well. You followed orders without nearly as much whining as in our earlier missions. You stopped taking the foolish chances that made One-Shot even more adamant about leaving you with chaperones. I was impressed, and it made me believe that you could handle yourself responsibly."

Ethan could feel warmth as his face grew flushed. With great effort, he was able to constrain his flattered smile to what he thought was a nonchalant half-smile.

"I hope I did not disappoint you."

"Not at all," Nicolette said. "But One-Shot will not allow himself to share the confidence that I have in you. That's why it is very likely that he will no longer leave you in my company in future missions."

"Future missions?" Ethan questioned. "But that was our last hunt. That was the last demon gazed upon by Sollustre's Eye."

"I know," Nicolette said. "But I have heard whispers that the Hounds will not be disbanded. General Ramos, the Head

Mage and the King are pleased with our work. It is believed by many that they will call upon us for special missions in the future."

"That's great!" Ethan exclaimed. "That means we can continue to work together."

"*We?*" Nicolette teased.

"The Hounds, I mean," Ethan clarified after loudly clearing his throat.

Nicolette's response was an incredulous grin. "You are a horrible liar, you know," she told him.

"Liar?" Ethan asked defensively. "Please understand, Arrowhead – "

"Nicolette," she corrected.

"Nicolette, yes," Ethan said. "If I seem uneasy, it's because I'm not accustomed to seeing you so…so comfortable. You just look so different without your gear."

"What do you mean by *different*?" she asked.

Ethan's complexion, usually as fair as Nicolette's, was growing ruddier by the second as he struggled to find the right words. He had always been attracted to her but he never imagined that she might be attracted to him. She was two years his senior and had never shown the slightest romantic interest. And now here she was in his cabin, with her hair down, teasing him. He did not know what to say.

The thought occurred to him that because of how he felt about her, he might be misinterpreting her words and actions. The last thing he wanted to do was embarrass himself further by saying something to betray his feelings. On the other hand, he considered, this was their last demon hunt. Even if they were called upon in the future, who knew how much time would pass until then? Who knew how long he would have to wait before he saw her again?

He finally decided that if there was the slightest chance she was attracted to him, a little embarrassment was well worth the risk.

"Nicolette," he started awkwardly. "Do you think perhaps we could see one another sometime…when we are not on official business, I mean?"

"I was wondering when you would get around to asking," Nicolette chuckled. "You may be quick with a sword but you're terribly slow when it comes to other matters. Of course we can. What took you so long to ask?"

"What do you mean 'terribly slow'?" Ethan demanded. "I had no idea you had any interest in me. You certainly did a great job of hiding it. I always thought you liked Shadow Blade."

Nicolette scoffed. "Magnus? Why? Because he likes to flirt with me? Because he likes to flex his muscles and show off his scars from our hunts?"

"I thought you ladies liked that kind of thing," Ethan said. "Does it not make him seem more of a man to you?"

"Are you daft?" she asked. "It makes him seem too slow to dodge fangs and claws."

Ethan laughed as Nicolette stood up and started walking toward him.

"You've grown so accustomed to the fawning young strumpets that follow you around back home that subtlety is completely lost on you," she said, stopping just a few inches away. Her hair and skin smelled faintly of lilacs. Her breath smelled sweet.

"I mean, really, Ethan," she continued. "I had to let my hair down and walk in here barefoot just to get you to notice me."

Ethan smiled and shook his head slowly. "No, Nicolette. I noticed you long ago." He leaned toward her. She closed her eyes and waited. She was only inches away but it seemed to Ethan that it took forever to cross that distance to kiss her.

When he was just close enough to taste her breath on his lips, the cabin door came crashing in. Both Nicolette and Ethan jumped. Ethan, whose back was to the door, noticed a look of shocked surprise on Nicolette's face before he turned.

Shadow Blade, or Magnus, stood in the doorway. He was still dressed in full gear but his hood was pulled back. Magnus was usually a strikingly handsome man, but his face was twisted into a frightening mask of rage. His slate gray eyes were maniacally wide and spittle dribbled from the corner of his snarling mouth.

"I *knew* I'd find you here," Magnus said, pointing a trembling finger. "Harlot!"

"You talk as though there's something between us," Nicolette said icily. She once again wore the face of Arrowhead: her eyes intense and her thin lips set in a firm, tight line. "As if there was *ever* anything between us. What is the meaning of this foolishness?"

"And *this* is why there has been nothing between us?" Magnus growled, turning his pointing finger to Ethan. "This boy? This little pup? He's barely off of his mother's tit and you'd spread your thighs for him and not me?"

"Where is your honor, Magnus?" Ethan demanded. "Where is your respect?"

"Quiet, *boy*," Magnus commanded, pulling his dark gray, double-edged long sword from its sheath with a shaky right hand. "Adults are talking." He leveled his mad glare back onto Nicolette. "Are you afraid you cannot handle a man?"

With one powerful yank with his free left hand, he tore away his leather overtunic and the cloth shirt beneath. He had a washboard stomach and a lean, muscular chest. His shoulders were broad and his arms were long and well defined without being bulky.

"By the gods, I have earned *battle scars*!" Magnus swore, gesturing at the jagged and hardened slash marks that crisscrossed his chest and shoulders. "What has he done? Sat trembling with fear on the perimeter of the real action!"

Both Ethan and Nicolette noticed that the long-healed scars had opened and were slightly oozing bright yellow puss, but both were too angered by his insane words to point it out at that moment. Instead, Nicolette took a step toward her raving teammate.

"I know not what type of madness has overtaken you, Magnus," she began, "but you had better leave here. And take your lies with you!"

"I will leave here," Magnus said in a threatening tone. "But I will take your head with me!" He lifted his sword and took two quick steps toward Nicolette.

Nicolette took a step back. There was not much room to maneuver in the small cabin so she braced herself to sidestep the oncoming downward strike, hoping she would be quick enough to avoid a critical injury.

Magnus brought the sword down with a grunt but the blade was snagged and halted in mid-strike by the loop of a lasso that fell and tightened around the wrist of his sword arm. He stopped short and turned to the left to see Ethan holding his lasso in both hands, tugging at the blade.

Ethan pulled as hard as he could in an attempt to snatch Magnus off-balance, but all he managed to do was stop the arcing sword. Magnus sneered and snatched his sword with his left hand. The blade sliced easily through the lasso and Ethan, who was still tugging at it, went stumbling backward into the wall.

The moment Magnus's attention was diverted Nicolette reached into her cloak and pulled out a long hunting dagger. By the time Magnus turned his horrible glare back to her, she had already thrown the knife. He had just enough time to gasp as the long blade sunk deeply into his heart. He looked down at the handle protruding from his chest and then back up at Nicolette. His bulging eyes had yellowed and looked even more insane than before.

"Whore!" he gurgled as he crumpled to the floor.

Ethan ran to Nicolette and put his arms around her. "Are you all right?" he asked.

"No," she answered, voice low. "Are you?"

"No," Ethan answered truthfully. "We just killed a fellow Hound. What in the name of the Lord Ascendant got into him?"

"I don't know," Nicolette said. "But you can't believe that he and I were involved."

"I don't," Ethan assured. He looked at his fallen teammate. "His scars. You see how they are running? Maybe the wounds were somehow infected and the sickness damaged his mind."

"Perhaps," Nicolette said. She knitted her eyebrows thoughtfully. "But some of those scars are over a year old. That would be a very slow-acting infection."

"Those are demon scars," Ethan pointed out. "Who knows what effect they can have? Do you think perhaps that spell that was being cast last night might have caused it?"

Nicolette shrugged. She suddenly looked at the door and then turned to Ethan with a curious stare. "Why has no one come to see about us? Surely they heard the commotion."

It was at that moment that they remembered. "Magnus was not the only one of us with demon scars," Ethan said. "And if it really was Magnus's wounds that caused him to go violently insane..."

He went to retrieve his broadsword from the other side of his bed.

"I'll get my sword from my quarters," Arrowhead called back as she bolted toward the cabin door, leaping over Magnus's still body. "Meet me at my – "

Ethan yelped as Nicolette suddenly fell to the floor. He quickly snatched up his broadsword when Magnus roared and rose from the floor holding Nicolette's right ankle in his left hand and his long sword in his right.

Magnus brought his sword down toward Nicolette's back. Ethan's broadsword cross blocked it at the halfway point of its arc. Even though the broadsword was heavier than the long sword and Ethan's footing was solid, the force of Magnus's blow drove him to his knees. Magnus lifted the sword to hack at Ethan but Ethan turned his broadsword in a quick motion and drove it into Magnus's stomach.

Nicolette snatched her foot away and rose to her feet, turning as she did so to face Magnus and help Ethan if necessary. She turned just as Magnus kicked Ethan in the chest, sending him flying into Nicolette and sending both of them out of the cabin door.

They landed on the deck and rolled across the damp planked flooring, dazed and breathless, until the ship's railing finally stopped them. Magnus snarled at them as he snatched the broadsword from his belly and charged with both his and Ethan's swords held high to attack. Ethan saw him coming and tried to untangle himself from Nicolette, but at the speed Magnus was moving Ethan knew he would not get free in time. Magnus was halfway across the deck before Ethan could roll Nicolette off of him. The berserker Hound was just about to reach them when a big blur rose up in Ethan's leftmost peripheral vision.

Hammer stepped around the corner, his huge shoulder crashing into Magnus and sending the smaller man stumbling up the deck. He fell in a heap but popped quickly to his feet and roared at Hammer with a wide, frothing mouth. The big man frowned in surprise at his teammate's terrible appearance.

"Magnus," Hammer cried. "Stop this now!"

But Magnus only charged Hammer with the point of both blades thrusting toward Hammer's barrel chest.

"NO, MAGNUS!" Hammer yelled as he hoisted his huge war hammer. He swung it like a club, and with his long powerful arms and the weapon's long handle, the flat side of the massive hammer caught Magnus on the shoulder before the blades could make contact. The blow made a sickening crunching sound and catapulted Magnus over the ship's railing and into the great Lake Onyx.

Hammer turned to Ethan and Arrowhead with a look of stunned disbelief on his face.

"What in the Seven Hells is going on here?"

Ethan and Arrowhead were both standing, but they were leaning on the rail trying to catch their breath. They met his gaze and shrugged.

"Magnus went mad," Ethan said. "He accused Arrowhead and I of...having a relationship. And then he attacked us."

Hammer looked even more puzzled. People tended to underestimate his intelligence because of his appearance. They seemed to think that someone with his size and brute strength could not be as intelligent as he was powerful. But now, as he tried to decipher what was going on, Hammer looked every bit the big dumb oaf for which he was often mistaken.

"But you and Magnus weren't...?"

"No, we *were not*," Nicolette said firmly.

"And you and *Ethan* aren't..." he continued.

Both paused before saying in unison: "No."

Hammer studied their expressions and noted the pause.

"At least not yet, eh?"

Their silence and flushed faces answered his question.

"It matters, not," Hammer concluded. "There's no justification for his actions. We have to tell the commander immediately."

"No," Nicolette disagreed. She answered Hammer's questioning glance before he could speak. "We have to find Lance. We fear he may be suffering from the same malady as Magnus."

"I left him almost an hour ago," Hammer informed them. He and several other Hounds were down in the cells playing bones when I left them. It was a spirited game," Hammer's big head tilted to the right. "And come to think of it, Lance was the most spirited of the bunch."

"And he's usually the quiet one," Ethan noted.

The young Sureblade retrieved his broadsword. When he came out to join Hammer he saw Arrowhead disappearing into her cabin. He and Hammer ran to her door just as she emerged with her short sword and crossbow. Her quiver was slung over her shoulder.

"Wait," Ethan said. He dropped to his knees and lightly grasped her ankle.

"Eagle Eye?" Hammer asked.

"Why did you have a hunting knife in your cloak?" Ethan asked as he inspected her slim ankle closely. "Did you think you would need protection from me?"

Arrowhead smiled. "I carry at least one knife with me at *all* times," she told him. "I learned long ago to never be without protection, no matter the circumstances."

"Good lesson," Ethan noted.

"Is the skin broken?" Arrowhead asked nervously.

"No," he answered. He and Arrowhead exhaled heavily.

The three of them dashed toward the bow of the small ship. As they approached the door that led below deck, Hammer had to ask.

"What was that business with Arrowhead's ankle?"

"We're afraid that Magnus's demon-inflicted wounds are what caused his malady," Arrowhead explained.

"Lance," Hammer breathed as he quickly made the connection. And then he quickened his pace.

3.4

They heard the screams the moment Ethan opened the stairway door. The pounding of their footsteps echoed through the narrow stairwell as they descended, all of them fearful of what they would find.

What they found was Cobra and four other Keeper's Hounds standing breathless and shocked in the hall outside the cells below deck. They watched with anger and confusion as Lance raged within the cell just beyond them. He threw himself violently against the bars over and over, sending a shudder through the hall with each strike, roaring obscenities and spitting feral snarls and thick yellow phlegm at the group. The cell bars held, though. Lance rebounded off of them each time and crashed to the floor, only to get up and try again.

A wooden table was smashed into several pieces that were scattered all over the hall. Chairs were smashed to splinters. White, palm-sized pyramids with various patterns of lines and dots etched and painted on each surface littered the floor. The pointed end of a long, dull gray lance, half as broad as the traditional jousting lance, was embedded into the wall a few feet down the corridor. The haft was still vibrating.

"What took you three so long?" Cobra asked, raising her voice above the din of the berserker inside the cell. "Surely you heard us. We could have used your help a little earlier."

"Sound from down here doesn't travel upstairs very well when the stairway door is closed," Hammer reminded them.

"And we were fairly occupied, ourselves," Arrowhead added. "I see you managed to imprison Lance."

"And it wasn't easy," said the Keeper's Hound named Tygra Claw. "We were enjoying a friendly game of bones. When he started losing badly he accused us of cheating and attacked us." Claw was a little shorter than Hammer and a few pounds heavier than Magnus. A trident and a spiked chain were his chosen weapons, but neither was evident. It appeared Lance was the only Hound to bring his weapon to this "friendly" game.

“It took all five of us to herd him into the cell,” said Fang, the Hound to Claw’s immediate left. “He was as strong as a bull, and he’s never been known for his strength.”

Fang was right, Ethan knew. Lance was named for his choice of weapon. He was good with it, but speed and precision were his specialties, not raw strength.

“Were any of you injured?” Ethan asked worriedly. “Any scratches or bites?”

“Of course not,” said Cobra. “When he brought that damned lance of his with that weird look on his face, we were all a bit wary. We could see the attack coming well in advance from the way his strange rage built up. He never laid a finger on us. We used the chairs and table legs to drive him into the cell.”

“Good,” Ethan said.

He was about to continue when Lance suddenly fell silent. They all looked into the cell at Lance sitting on floor, his back propped against the back wall of the cell. The group thought he must have finally knocked himself unconscious but when they looked at him they saw that his eyes were wide open. His gaze was no longer enraged or maniacal. In fact, he wore a completely blank expression. They would have believed him dead but his eyes shifted this way and that as if searching for something that only he could see.

The commander, the two remaining Hounds, and the ship’s captain and first mate came pounding down the stairs and into the hall. One-Shot glanced at the carnage around him, the breathless men and women who looked like they had just survived a battle, and the vacant-looking Hound locked in the cell.

“I wake up to a god-awful racket and search the ship to find Eagle Eye’s cabin door kicked in, his room in a shambles, and a bent and broken railing just outside of the room. We have to almost threaten the good captain’s crew back to their stations and cabins for their own safety. Now I come down here to see *this*. Is anyone going to explain this?”

He looked around at everyone in the small area. “And where is Shadow Blade?”

"I wish we had a chair for you all to pull up," Cobra said, inspecting the remains of furniture scattered all over the floor. "After hearing this story, you may need one.

The Hounds took turns explaining the strange events that had taken place. Ethan and Arrowhead smartly left out the near-kiss and shared their theory about infections from their demon scars and the possible connection to the spell they interrupted the night before. The commander took it all in with a calm, thoughtful expression. The only time his expression changed was when he was informed about Magnus, and how the long sword wielder was not killed from a knife to the heart or a broadsword to the gut. By the time the story was done, his calm expression had returned.

One-shot turned to the captain. "We must make haste, Captain Whelker," he declared. "We must report this to the Head Mage as soon as – "

Everyone turned abruptly when Lance gave a grunt and shot to his feet. His facial expression was still vacant but his movements were purposeful. The Hounds expected him to start throwing himself against the bars again, but Lance turned and launched himself at the wood-planked back wall of the cell. His head crashed all the way through the inner wall and outer hull, revealing the darkness of the night sky and black water.

All of the Hounds gaped in astonishment as Lance began tearing though the wall with his bare hands, shredding the skin and staining the wood with thick dark blood and yellow puss. No one knew what to do. The Hounds did not want to engage him again but they could not let him sink the ship.

"We have to stop him!" the captain ordered.

But with Lance's newfound strength, the hole was already large enough, just barely, but large enough for him to squeeze through. The jagged edges of the hole tore deep, wide gashes of flesh from his body as he pulled himself through yet he never cried out in pain. It was as if he had not felt a thing.

By the time they had the cell door open Lance was dropping out of view and splashing into the great lake.

"Get the crew down here to patch this hole before we start taking on water," the captain said to the first mate.

One-Shot frowned deeply. "If their demon scars and that blasted spell are what caused this madness, we must return to Lorr as swiftly as this tub can carry us!"

Chapter 4: Progeny

4.1

Rionn Lorr was a busy man, much busier than usual. His current, incredibly hectic schedule made him even more appreciative of the rare quiet times he got to spend with his wife and their beautiful daughter at their modest cabin on the Island of Cartha.

Rionn thought about the island's name and smiled. He remembered when several advisors to the king had suggested that the name of the island be changed. The island was part of the Kingdom of Lorr and many people, citizens and government officials alike, did not like the fact that the island shared its name with the kingdom to the south with which the Kingdom of Lorr had several conflicts over the years. Rionn's response was that the island had been named by the Old Ones themselves and that not even one of their Children had the right or authority to change it.

He wondered what his daughter Shandie would do when the island was passed to her. And then he thought of her name, Shandie, and his smile broadened. Catherine insisted on naming the child after the late sorceress, her beloved friend and mentor Shanderah. Even though he had respected her power and knowledge, Rionn had always thought the old conjurer was so eccentric that he often questioned her wisdom and dependability.

But fortunately for him and all of the citizens of the Kingdom of Lorr, Shanderah more than proved her value and dependability during the Cursed Opening. Without her help the land would surely have fallen under the control of the evil wizard Mar-dah. Rionn gained a newfound respect for the old sorceress and wished he had known her better before she gave her life for their struggle. So when Catherine suggested naming their first-born daughter after Shanderah in tribute to her love and sacrifice, Rionn did not argue. It would not have done him any good, anyway. He could count on one hand the number of times he had won an argument with his wife.

On this pleasant evening, Rionn and Catherine lay out in the middle of the meadow looking at the three moons and countless stars in the clear night sky while little Shandie chased fireflies. The Lord Ascendant had indeed blessed them with a beautiful child. Her hair was as blonde as her mother's, her eyes the same pale green. Those eyes, however, did not have the same Elfish tilt as her mother's, who was half elf. Shandie's eyes were round and wide. They were also bright and inquisitive. The top of her ears had the faintest hint of a point, but it was not noticeable without a close inspection. She had Rionn's tanned complexion and by all indications she would have his height, as well. She had long legs and was taller than most children her age.

The magic of the Old Ones was strong within her. Even though she had not yet demonstrated any of the abilities of her divine ancestors, Rionn could nonetheless feel the power burning within her. Whenever it was finally released, Rionn knew it would be awesome.

Not only did she have the magic of the Old Ones, she possessed Elven magic from her mother's side of the family. She had also inherited her mother's gift of foresight. That particular ability had been revealed almost as soon as she learned to talk. He and Catherine believed her divine heritage strengthened her foresight. It was already nearly as active as her mother's.

They both knew that they would have to be diligent with this one. Her intelligence was astonishing for a child of her age, and that intelligence was coupled with a curious nature that had the potential to be troublesome. Catherine and Rionn vowed to do everything they could to preserve her innocence for as long as possible.

When Catherine first told Rionn she was pregnant, his initial reaction was that of joy. That joy, however, was tempered with a bit of anger because she had known that she was pregnant for weeks before finally revealing it to him. Catherine found out only shortly before the beginning of the ordeal with Mar-dah and the demons and was waiting for the perfect time to tell Rionn. Before she could, the attack on the town of Silverleaf took place and things escalated from there with terrible swiftness. Catherine did not want to give him the news during such trying times, knowing that it would have been just one more distraction that would have done more harm than good.

Rionn was upset for another reason when she finally told him. She had worked incredibly hard and had undergone a great deal of stress while working with the other healers to care for wounded soldiers and citizens during the Cursed Opening. She knew full well that he would have forbid her from participating for fear of harming their unborn Child. As a healer and the Head Mage's wife, Catherine felt it was her duty to give as much aid as she could. And it was a good thing she did. She used her gift to save the lives of many people, including Jon the Firemaster, who happened to be one of Rionn's best friends.

After the Child was born and Rionn looked into those big green eyes for the first time, all of his earlier trepidation was quickly swept away. He smiled every time he watched or even thought about his daughter. For a fleeting moment, her image could make him forget about all of his troubles.

But those moments were all too fleeting, indeed, because in the next instant he would once again be distressed by everything that was transpiring.

A second search party was missing. The mage that was sent along to assist the soldiers in their quest had not communicated with the Head Mage for over two weeks. The first search party that was sent out to scour the Demon's Spine Mountains for Mar-dah's stronghold had disappeared in a similar fashion. Twelve of the king's best soldiers and trackers, along with one of Rionn's handpicked wizard agents had simply vanished.

Rionn wanted very much to accompany the second search party, but Catherine, King William, and Queen Mary had convinced him not to. His presence within the boundaries of the Kingdom was too important. No one but the Head Mage himself was trusted to guard the body of Mar-dah. He was not expected to stand over the body at all times the way sentries were required to guard prisoners, but as long as he was in the Kingdom, his magic could transport him to within an arm's reach of the body in a matter of moments. It would take just an instant longer if he was outside the Kingdom, but they were all aware that that mere instant could very well be the difference between safety and catastrophe.

The body was contained within an iron coffin filled with salt and the coffin was stored in the deepest recesses of the palace dungeons. The salt, along with the iron walls of the coffin, could contain Mar-dah's evil essence indefinitely until his soul could be cast into the Seven Hells. Unfortunately, the Hell key was needed to accomplish that task.

Mar-dah did not have the Key to the Seven Hells on his person when he attempted to seize the palace three years earlier. It was assumed by all that the talisman had been left in his hidden base of operations. A search party was charged with the duty of finding the wicked mage's stronghold and all of the magic it contained, especially the Hell Key, before it could be found by anyone else.

Rionn was not initially concerned with anyone else using the Key because only a Child of the Old Ones could invoke the magic. After Mar-dah's death, Rionn and Raxe were the only surviving Children.

That, however, was no longer the case. He was not worried about his daughter ever using the Key, but Rionn knew that she was not the only member of the newest generation of Children. Roughly nine months after the ordeal with Mar-dah and the demons, Rionn began to sense the presence of a Child besides his daughter.

Its presence was distant and faint, so much so that not even he could trace its origins. Rionn was certain that one of his greatest fears had come to pass: Mar-dah had sired an offspring. Rionn would not rest easy until this Child was found, or at the very least, until the Hell Key had been recovered so there would be no threat of that Child ever gaining possession of it. It was not that he expected the Child to be born evil, but he or she would be powerful. Rionn feared that if someone even approaching Mar-dah's malevolence had the ability to control or manipulate the Child, they could use him or her to re-open the gates of the Seven Hells.

Rionn had been using his magic to try to pinpoint the exact whereabouts of the Child for three years, but as of yet he had no success. He could vaguely sense the Child's presence but pinpointing it was like trying to catch a speck of dust floating around a drafty room. Just when he thought he was close to verifying its location, it seemed to flit away to the deep shadows of his awareness.

And those were not his only worries. Shara Dune, Queen of the Forsaken Desert, had been able to evade him as well. Not only had she been able to avoid his magical probes, she had also been able to avoid physical detection from both his and the King's agents. Her sand creatures were used to aid Mar-dah's Legion Midnight and Rionn knew that Shara Dune was the sole mistress of those monsters. Not even Mar-dah could employ them without her compliance. She had to be found and imprisoned for her participation in Mar-dah's failed bid to overthrow the Kingdom of Lorr.

He had no idea how she was able to avoid his detection and that made him uneasy. She was a fairly accomplished sorceress but Rionn was confident that he had an accurate measure of her ability. She should not have been able to hide from him this long. He had always been able to locate her in the past. Shara Dune was well aware of this fact and as a result she had been very diligent about not perpetrating any act that would draw his ire…until, of course, she threw in her lot with Mar-dah. It was then that she disappeared from Rionn's awareness. But Mar-dah was gone now and so was his protection. Yet he still had not found her.

Glynhallah the Weather Witch, another ally of Mar-dah's who assisted him in his assault on the kingdom, had been relatively easy to locate. She was currently jailed in the royal prison along with Lo Garath the Lupine, who had led his wraith wolves on an unsuccessful attack on old Shanderah and the offworlder Raxe on Infinity Isle. The Lupine's efforts were rewarded with capture and imprisonment.

Shara Dune, on the other hand, proved to be far more resourceful and elusive than her fellow conspirators. The Forsaken Desert and Shara Dune's subterranean fortress beneath it had been searched thoroughly. The Queen of the

Forsaken Desert was nowhere to be found. Rionn assumed she had fled to either the Kingdom of Darshay or Cartha because they all shared the continent of Lorr. But he could not rule out the possibility, however remote because of her aversion to water, that she could have crossed one of the bordering oceans to flee to another continent. But he still should have been able to find her.

While Rionn used his magic, both he and the King had dispatched agents to search for her throughout the Known Lands. A group of agents, two of which possessed magic, were left in Southborough, a town in very close proximity to the Forsaken Desert, to keep watch over the vast expanse of desert in case she returned. Still, she managed to elude them.

The worst part of it all was that he was fairly sure the disappearance of the Desert Queen and his inability to pinpoint the location of the Child were not coincidences. Knowing Mar-dah the way he did, and knowing how attractive Shara Dune was, it was very possible that the Child was hers. They had been working together, after all. His evil cousin would not have been able to resist her seductive beauty...whether or not she wanted him in return. If indeed the elusive Child was the progeny of the Desert Queen and Mar-dah, it was all the more critical that the Hell Key be found.

But not all of the occurrences following Mar-dah's defeat had been unfavorable ones. At the Head Mage's request, King William sent an excavation team across the Sea of Spirits to Infinity Isle. Rionn had hoped that there were more ancient magical artifacts in the ruins of the underground palace where Raxe's armor had been found. This was the only time since Mar-dah's death that Rionn actually left the Kingdom of Lorr. The possible presence of ancient, potentially dangerous magic and the monstrous havocs that roamed the isle made it imperative for the Head Mage to accompany the team.

Fortunately, the havocs paid them no mind. They were still on the island but they were herbivores, so the massive primates would not hunt humans for food. Havocs were not aggressive creatures by nature, so without the divine imperative of guarding Raxe's armor, the simian creatures had simply dispersed into the depths of the island to live out their days foraging and procreating. All the excavation team had to do was stay out of the creatures' way.

Under Rionn Lorr and Master Mage Delthar's direction, the team excavated the ruins without incident. To Rionn's delight, many useful artifacts were discovered. Spell books, lost volumes of his world's history, and various tools of magic were found and brought back to the Kingdom of Lorr. Rionn gave Delthar, his trusted friend and mentor, the challenging task of overseeing the identification and cataloguing of the artifacts so that Rionn could concentrate on one recovered talisman in particular:

Sollustre's Eye.

Sollustre's Eye, a blood red orb six inches in diameter, was carved from a stone denser than marble but with a semi-transparent appearance that resembled glass. The surface of the stone was smooth and reflective and shone with a soft inner glow that revealed, to those very few with the right type of vision, a smaller sphere of darkness at the center of the orb that was similar to the pupil of an eye. Rionn could sense the talisman's significance the moment he saw it. In addition to its odd appearance, it fairly thrummed with divine energy, insistent and imploring.

Rionn's subsequent studies revealed that the orb was used as a tool of the First Generation of Children of the Old Ones during Heaven's War. A pinpoint of golden light, even more difficult to see than the dark pupil, illuminated to reveal the presence and location of demons.

The orb was a representation of the entire earth sphere, and the pupil represented the location of the orb. Sollustre's Eye was like a compass, with the location of the demons it exposed always indicated relative to the orb's position; and the pupil's positioning was, without exception, relative to the person holding the talisman. A golden point on the right, left, above, or below the stone's pupil indicated that a demon was to the right, left, in front of, or behind the holder respectively. Distances were often difficult to gauge but the direction was never wrong.

Once he learned how to read the orb, the Head Mage trained a team of his most trusted agents to do the same. He then set up a round-the-clock vigil of the orb to keep track of the location and number of demons that managed to escape death at the Tyne River and other battles against demons during the Cursed Opening. With the help of the Head Mage and the magical talisman, the King commissioned a group of elite trackers and soldiers to find and kill those demons. The group called itself the Gatekeeper's Hounds, fancying themselves as hunting dogs for the divine blacksmith and warrior of the Old Ones, the Gatekeeper himself.

Others simply called them the Demon Hunters. They were very good at what they did. Fortunately, none of the gilded points of light were located in the Unknown Lands. Rionn often wondered if the Eye could even penetrate the barriers that separated the Known and Unknown Lands, but he assumed that something crafted by the Old Ones would have no trouble doing so.

The group that kept a vigil over the Eye allowed Rionn enough free time to devote to studying the histories, memorize newly discovered spells, and to learn how to use the other enchanted tools that were excavated from Infinity Isle. As the Hounds did their dangerous work, the scattered pinpoints of gold that sparkled ominously on the surface of Sollustre's Eye eventually dwindled down to one, and that one had disappeared just a day earlier. Now the glassy surface of the beautiful crimson orb shone undisturbed.

Yes, the excavation of the ruins had gone much better than anticipated, but that was about the only thing that had.

"What troubles you, husband?" came the melodic voice of his wife.

"The usual," Rionn admitted. "Everything. I must trek to the castle in less than two sunrises only to tell the King that most of my investigations are still fruitless."

"You must take at least a little time to enjoy yourself and the wonders of the world around you," she advised. "Else your worries will consume you."

"I know," Rionn agreed. "But whenever I turn my mind away from one crisis it is confronted by another."

"Such is the life of a guardian of the Kingdom of Lorr," Catherine reminded him. As if he needed reminding. She scooted closer to him and rubbed her fair, soft hand down his leathery cheek. "Perhaps I can turn your mind to something pleasurable for a change."

A sly half smile lifted one side of Rionn's mouth. "Perhaps you could," he agreed. He looked up at the position of the moons and stars. "It *is* getting to be Shandie's bedtime, is it not?"

Catherine and Rionn looked out at their daughter, her giggling drifting to them from across the field like music on the soft night breeze. She had caught dozens of fireflies by then, but she did not catch them in her hands the way most children would.

The luminescent insects twirled around her in a succession of artistic patterns, one intricately beautiful design shifting smoothly into another, while the young Child skipped and spun gleefully and moved her hands to conduct the insects' patterns of flight. The bright yellow light of the fireflies cast a glow upon Shandie as she danced to the rhythm of nature. She moved in time with the sounds of chirping insects, the cries of night birds, and the soft whistle of the breeze as it wafted through the boughs of the tall ash trees surrounding the clearing.

"Elven magic," Rionn whispered with wonder.

"Indeed," Catherine added. "She does have an incredibly strong connection to nature." She gave Rionn an alluring look that caused a wave of warmth to flow through him. "Too bad it is time for her to go in for the night."

"Indeed," Rionn said. Husband and wife rose to their feet, clasped hands, and went to usher their daughter back to their cabin.

As they neared little Shandie she was skipping and jumping amid the fireflies, singing to them as they twirled around her small, flailing hands. Both Rionn and Catherine grinned. But then the toddler suddenly stopped cold and the fireflies shot away from her as if a predator had just entered their midst.

After a startled pause, both parents ran to their daughter, who stood frozen with her hands hanging at her sides. Her back was to them so they could not see her face.

Rionn reached Shandie only an instant before Catherine. He ran around in front of her and gently grasped her shoulders. Catherine went to the little girl's side, dropped to her knees, and put a comforting arm around the tiny waist. From the vacant look in her eye, Rionn knew what was happening. Catherine did as well. They looked at one another and mouthed the same word simultaneously:

"Vision."

Shandie's eyes stared into nothingness. No part of her body so much as twitched until her lips began to move. The Head Mage and his wife leaned in closer to the little mouth to hear what she was saying. In pitch and softness, her voice was the same as always, but her tone and words were not at all those of a three year old.

"From the depths of blackness to the heat of flames, from desiccated valley to raging river, from sand to stone… A Child's wrath will span."

4.2

Shara Dune – self-proclaimed Queen of the Forsaken Desert – was accustomed to being pampered. She was just not accustomed to being pampered by humans. If she had been at her home beneath the desert sands it would have been the massive, four-tentacle sand-creatures tending to her. Instead, strapping young men and alluring young women were massaging her with exotic oils and painting the nails on her fingers and toes. Another lithe, scantily clad female attendant brushed her long, fire-red hair where it cascaded down from the small bejeweled golden comb that sat at the crown of Shara's head like a tiara to keep several looping curls out of her eyes.

It was a nice change. Mage Stratham Glund, Second High Adviser to the Kingdom of Cartha's Head Mage, took excellent care of his consorts. Shara Dune was his favorite.

The other women of the House envied her. No one knew who she was or where she came from. They were aware of the existence of the infamous Queen of the Forsaken Desert, of course, but none of them had actually seen her in person. None of them would imagine that such a notorious personage would be working among them.

All they knew was that she came in and immediately replaced the previous mistress of the *E'Strahil Vah* House, the most prestigious pleasure house in the Carthan capital city of Crystalline Bay. And she did so without ever having to work her way up from its famed Gallery. Glund brought her in and immediately placed her in charge of the pleasure house. He even allowed her to have her pick of male attendants from among the brutish, thuggish bodyguards that served her every whim like eager schoolboys, even while they brutalized the other women who worked and lived there.

No one understood how the woman accomplished such a feat. In the past, Glund always appointed the Mistress of the House from among the women who had worked there the longest and demonstrated the proper amount of loyalty, dependability and "motivation."

That had not been the case with Shara Dune and they all resented her for it, though none would dare show their resentment or voice it aloud. Not only were they afraid of losing their lucrative employment at the bustling pleasure house, they were also afraid of losing their very lives. Shara Dune ruled the *E'Strahil Vah* House the same way she ruled the Forsaken Desert: Loyalty and production were generously rewarded. Failure was punished vigorously. Disloyalty was met with death.

Shara looked over at the tiny, thin, red headed toddler that was giving his nanny such a hard time while she tried to feed him. As she looked at her child the desert queen was thankful once again that she did not follow through with her first impulse. When she had discovered she was pregnant with the spawn of Mar-dah, her first instinct was to abort. She was sickened by the mere thought of that twisted wizard's seed within her womb.

But then she considered that what she carried was the progeny of a Child of the Old Ones. This meant the child would very likely be imbued with considerable power. A Child of the Old One's divine magic was passed to only one of his or her offspring, and it was usually the firstborn that received this birthright. She assumed Mar-dah had not already fathered children. The perverted wizard had a steady flow of whores who were blindfolded and brought through his stronghold to work as servants and consorts, but Shara was certain he would be careful not to impregnate such lowly creatures. And even if he had, they apparently had not been gifted, for her son surely was.

The Child would not be as powerful as his father. Everyone knew that each offspring born of a Child and a human had incrementally less power than its supernatural parent. The essence of the human parent diluted the magic. Shara, however, was not without considerable power. The elemental magic that gave her telekinetic control over sand and hypnotic control over species of lesser intelligence was well recognized throughout the Known Lands.

She was confident that her own magic would minimize the depletion of power and make her Child nearly as formidable as his father.

That powerful Child belonged to the Queen of the Forsaken Desert to shape and control as she wished. She named him Tariin, after her gypsy father. And in giving birth to him she would make herself into the mother of a new age in the Known Lands. Her toddler was already showing signs of impressive power. Those signs revealed themselves sporadically in involuntary, reflexive bursts when his feelings were intense. Shara, who was not easily impressed, was very impressed by what she saw in him.

She would first have to solidify her power base among the minor mages and elementals that were enemies of Lorr, both the Kingdom and the man. Then, as Mar-dah had attempted before his death, she would form and lead an alliance that could stand against King William's army and Rionn Lorr's magic. If she was clever enough, as she knew she was, she would accomplish this sooner rather than later. She was growing weary of living her life on the run and constantly shielding herself and her Child from the Kingdom of Lorr's agents and the wizard's magical probes.

While she resided in Mar-dah's mountain during the assault on Lorr, she learned as much as she could from the libraries that Mar-dah allowed her to visit. There were some libraries, she knew, that he would never allow her to enter, so she made the most use of the ones she could. She was surprised that he allowed her to enter *any* of them, but then again, the egotistical man believed himself to be too powerful to be harmed or manipulated by anything she could learn from those tomes. And he was right. While she found many spells that could be useful for different types of endeavors, she never found anything that could be effectively used against the powerful and wily Mar-dah.

Shara had been inspecting her demon-spawn troops of sand creatures in the Forsaken Desert when she found out that Mar-dah had been killed. She gleefully rushed back to his mountain, believing that with his death she could finally access the forbidden areas of his stronghold. What she discovered was that his fortress was warded against intrusion by powerful magic that she had no hope of circumventing. The bastard refused to give up his secrets even in death.

Fortunately for her, she found and taught herself a spell that could hide her from even the most powerful magical probes. Initially she did not think she possessed enough inner magic to power the spell appropriately, but it had been over three years and Rionn Lorr had not located her. Shara was more than pleased with her ingenuity and surprising power.

But Shara was thoroughly *dis*pleased with her current situation. She detested the Kingdom of Cartha and longed to return to her desert home. Unfortunately, the Forsaken Desert bordered the Kingdom of Lorr. Rionn would no doubt have both people and enchantments monitoring her desert and the surrounding region. She and her son had to be kept far away from the Head Mage. He would no doubt act as guardian to her son if she allowed herself to be captured. Shara would not let her son be subverted by Rionn's repugnant righteousness and altruism. Glynhallah was already in his custody and Shara was determined not to share her fate. The desert queen had too many plans for her son and herself.

Tariin was her trump card. Her fellow conjurers...no, the word "fellow" was inappropriate. That word implied the others were her peers. The *other* conjurers would recognize straight away the kind of power she controlled as the mother of a Child of the Old Ones. A few of them would even try to take possession of that power or destroy it outright. She would happily deal with those fools as necessary. Most of them, however, would be wise enough to ally themselves with her for fear of the repercussions should she come to power without their requested aid.

She had another trump card, as well. Of all of the magic workers in the Known Lands, she alone knew the location of Mar-dah's stronghold. With the exception of a very select few, visitors were blindfolded or rendered unconscious in some fashion before they even got within visual distance of his mountain.

Many correctly suspected that his stronghold was somewhere in the Demon's Spine Mountains but the exact location was a secret to all save herself and two of Mar-dah's highest ranking officers of the now disbanded Legion Midnight. One of those officers was killed during the attack on the capital city of Greenglenn. The other was captured during that same failed campaign.

Shara was not concerned about the captive voluntarily or involuntarily divulging the location of the mountain. She knew Mar-dah had taken certain precautions for such an occurrence. If the general had been interrogated, and she knew he had been, as it is the standard procedure for captured high-ranking enemies, any questions about the location of the stronghold would have invoked a deeply implanted spell that would attack his brain and result in his immediate death.

Mar-dah's mountain contained volumes upon volumes of spell books, alchemist's chemicals, and talismans that could be used at her discretion. Before his ill-fated trip to the Lorrian Palace, he had apparently put wards in place to protect his mountain from anyone unfortunate or foolish enough to find it. No one, not she nor Mar-dah's select charges knew how to bypass those defenses to gain entrance to his fortress.

But Shara was determined to find a way. She would use their son to accomplish her goals. Shara was convinced that this was her destiny and she would bring it to fruition. There had been too many sacrifices and far too much suffering over the years, both willingly and unwillingly, for her to be denied the power she was owed.

She had been born to an older couple that resided in the arid and barely-habitable regions just south of the Forsaken Desert. Her mother had been told that she could not bear children, so her birth was considered a blessing and a good omen for her family. They were part of a large group of nomads that formed the Gypsy Nation. The nomadic nation wandered the mountains and desert fringes of the Kingdoms of Lorr, Darshay, and Cartha. They were a superstitious and contradictory people.

Their shamans were warlocks who, while not naturally imbued with their own inner magic, had enough sensitivity to magical energies to learn how tap into them. That sensitivity, along with the proper training, allowed the shamans to wield magic through the use of spells and talismans.

The shamans were revered by their people and acted as spiritual leaders, protectors, and advisors. But, true to their contradictory nature, the shamans accused people actually born with magic of being demonic abominations to be expunged with all haste. The obvious truth was that the shamans considered them threats and potential rivals. They had more than enough influence to convince the superstitious Gypsy Nation that those born with magic were threats to the entire nation. The result was sanctioned infanticide. On the rare occasions when an infant or toddler showed signs of instinctive or spontaneous magic, they were summarily burned as demon-spawn. That meant that any potential wizards or elementals like Shara Dune were killed at almost the moment they were identified as such.

Shara Dune's father was a fierce warrior in his youth and a respected military leader among the tribe when Shara was born. He did not, however, share many of the superstitions of his people. One of the most prominent superstitions he secretly rejected was the belief that those born with magic were inherently evil. So when Shara displayed the ability to seemingly communicate with and control creatures native to the Forsaken Desert and its surrounding region; and when he began to take notice of the small sand and dust devils that seemed to materialize out of nowhere when she was upset, her father took every step imaginable to conceal her abilities.

In the years just prior to her teens, when her father was elevated to the rank of Elder, a rival Elder found out what she was and exposed her. Her father sent her away with strict instructions that she not tell him or her mother where she was going and to never contact them again. If she had, he knew the shamans would use torture and magic to pry the information from them.

She went to the only place she knew she would be safe: the Forsaken Desert. Her abilities made it the logical and obvious choice. Her elemental abilities, coupled with her ability to control the only slightly intelligent sand creatures, allowed her to quickly come to power in their subterranean realm. Contacting her parents was never a concern, for they were swiftly executed for concealing their daughter's magic for so long.

A search party was then sent into the desert to find her. The gypsies were a hearty people and better suited to survive the harsh conditions of the dry and scorching landscape better than anyone in the Known Lands, but not even they could survive that harsh environment indefinitely.

The first search party returned empty-handed after two months, having tolerated the desert for as long as they could. They believed she must have been dead but the shamans knew better. They knew she was a desert elemental and would find a way to not only survive, but also thrive in the Forsaken Desert. Another search party, this one even better prepared than the first, was sent to find her.

Only one of them returned alive. That lone survivor came back broken, driven mad, and barely alive. He told them of the horrors he and his team encountered when they finally found Shara – or better yet – when she found them.

The survivor wore several grizzly necklaces as evidence that she was no longer a fugitive. Shara Dune made it clear that she was no longer the hunted and was, in fact, the huntress. Desiccated eyeballs and ears, fingers and toes and even testicles were strung on cords weaved from strings cut and dried from human intestines. All of this was done to convey one clear message to the shamans:

Anyone who dared to enter her desert without permission would share the fate of that final search party.

That was more than enough to convince the Gypsy Nation to leave her alone. It was not nearly enough, though, for the Queen of the Forsaken Desert.

As the tribe continued to wander the edges of the vast, desolate wastelands that separated the Kingdom of Lorr from Darshay and Cartha, Shara led her hideous sand creatures, oversized scorpions and fatally poisonous desert snakes from the Forsaken Desert on raid after brutal raid until all of the shamans and elders were dead.

But still her vengeance was not sated. She had learned well the painful lesson that kindness was weakness. In her youth, the only reward for weakness had been misuse and death. She learned that those born without magic would always envy and despise those born with it, and that the only way to avoid death at their hands was to kill them first or dominate them.

To that end, she spent years learning as much as she could about her inherent magic as an elemental as well as the manipulation of external magic. She learned to extend her control over desert creatures to other creatures, including – to a lesser extent – weak-willed humans. And then she used her lessons to embark on a ruthless campaign to decimate her own people lest someone else rise up and dare to hunt her. Those who escaped death went into hiding, spreading out among and blending into the populations of the surrounding kingdoms.

When she was done, the Gypsy Nation was no more.

Shara frequently traveled outside her home beneath the great sand dunes of the Forsaken Desert. When she did so, she usually wore some sort of disguise. The legend of the Queen of the Desert, also known as the Desert Witch, grew with each passing year. In different guises, she took lessons from any magic worker that she could threaten, pay, or seduce to teach her.

After years of planning and plotting in secrecy beneath the sands of the Forsaken Desert, the Desert Witch learned that to truly rule, she must have a king and an army. She had built a loose but obedient cult following consisting of powerful allies within the Kingdom of Lorr and other kingdoms as well. Mayors, sheriffs, dukes, counts, and even high-ranking military officials were under her influence in various kingdoms, but none of them commanded the type of political and military might she needed to reach her goals.

So when Mar-dah recruited her for his bid at domination, she allied herself with him immediately. Believing Rionn Lorr to be too compassionate to overcome his ambitious distant cousin, she was sure Mar-dah would win and go on to usurp Lorr, the mightiest kingdom in the Known Lands. Like Mar-dah, she did not expect the interference of Raxe, the off world descendant of the Gatekeeper. Now that Mar-dah was vanquished she had to find a new ally. She had done just that in the Kingdom of Cartha.

The King of Cartha had never been an ally of King William. He, like many of the other kings in the Known Lands, resented and envied the Kingdom of Lorr because of its direct support from the Children descendants of Lorr. The King of Cartha's Head Mage, a powerful wizard named Ghotahn Koufee, had two primary advisors. Mage Stratham Glund, the younger, impetuous, and more powerful of the two, was ruled by his lust. Shara enthralled him and let him believe that he controlled their relationship.

He was so taken by her physical beauty and subtle, enchanted charms that he gifted her with the golden comb bejeweled with small but priceless jade and ruby gems that presently adorned her long fire-red hair. She had hesitated to take the gift but could not deny her attraction to it. The decorative styling comb securely held her thick, full coif in any style she chose, and it perfectly complimented the color of her hair. In addition to that, the long handle was narrow and tapered to a point like a long golden nail, which allowed it to serve as the perfect hidden weapon.

Most importantly, it was a constant reminder to the other women in the pleasure house exactly who was the favorite of Mage Glund. The only time she removed it was when she bathed, and even then, it was always within arm's reach for fear that one of her jealous underlings might gather enough courage and stupidity to swipe it.

Through Glund she manipulated Cartha's Head Mage, who in turn influenced the king himself. So the Queen of the Desert had her army, at least indirectly. But Cartha's military alone would not be enough to overcome the great army of Lorr and the Child of the same name. That would be accomplished with the help of her son and his father's stronghold. Not only was there a treasure of magic of all forms, there was also the Hell Key, the god-forged broadsword that Mar-dah used to open the gates of the Seven Hells and commence the Cursed Opening. Shara Dune had the means to wield that very same power by controlling someone who could.

Her son would be the key. She knew enough to be certain of how the magic of the Children worked. Their magic was always accessible to their progeny, passed on from generation to generation. She would unlock that key, and in the meantime she would take all necessary steps to insure her rise to power. Yes, Queen Shara Dune of the Forsaken Desert would eventually take her place as the pre-eminent magic worker in the Known Lands.

Her musings were interrupted when a female attendant stepped into her chambers.

"Master Glund has arrived, mistress," the young raven-haired girl informed. "He should be here within a few minutes."

Shara nodded her acknowledgement and banished the girl with a wave of her manicured hand. She then shooed her male attendants away with a similar gesture and instructed the females attending to her son to take him and leave. When she was the only one left in the chamber, she removed the towel that covered her otherwise naked body and quickly dressed in a sheer, emerald green, low-cut negligee that she covered with a soft silken robe of the same color. The robe was left open to reveal just enough of her ample bosom to distract. Even though she had the ability to mesmerize, she had long ago found that she did not have to exert quite as much persuasive magic when the man – or woman, in many cases – was already preoccupied with her body.

She could envision the sneers and envious glares of the whores as they watched Glund and his guard walk through the establishment. Glund had never come to see the previous mistress of the house. The women who pleasured him were always delivered to a discreet location of his choosing.

But he came to Shara. Of course he came to Shara. She was the Queen of the Forsaken Desert. It was bad enough she had to suffer the indignity of being surrounded by these inferiors. She would *not* be inconvenienced with a half-day's ride to go to him. They did often not meet in person, however, so she knew he had news for her that he did not trust with a messenger. That meant he was about to ask another favor of her. This was a good thing. It meant that their plans were moving along.

One of her male attendants opened the door to announce the Second High Advisor to the Carthan Head Mage. Master Stratham Glund swept into the room, leaving his personal guards out in the corridor as he closed the door behind him. Stratham Glund was a man of average height and build, but those were the only things about him that were average. His long, shimmering, dark brown hair was pulled back and tied in a neat braid. He was a handsome man with straight, aquiline features and piercing steel-gray eyes. Even with his dun-colored, unornamented riding cloak to conceal his wizard's traveling robes, his station was unmistakable. His bearing alone marked him as a man of considerable power and influence. His cold gray eyes met her light brown eyes in a penetrating gaze that would have unnerved someone of lesser confidence than Queen Shara Dune.

"You are as ravishing as ever, my Queen," Glund said with a deep, polite bow.

Unimpressed, Shara sighed irritably. She was fully aware of the wizard's lustful glance at her full breasts heaving against the laces of her bodice.

"What is it that you require, Glund? I assume it is important if you could not trust it to a messenger."

"Right to business, as always," Glund observed. "Very well, then. Our benefactor is once again in need of your considerable skill."

"I have many skills," Shara reminded with a suspicious side-glance. "Which of them does he require?"

"He would like you to travel to Eastedge to speak to our contact there," Glund explained. "He needs to be convinced to assist us further."

"You mean Tauran?" Shara asked.

A brief look of surprise passed quickly across the Second High Advisor's countenance.

"Has his handler finally lost control of him?" Shara continued. She knew this was privileged information. She purposely divulged that small tidbit to let Glund know that she was not without resources, and to make him wonder how much she really did know about their secretive operation.

"Impressive," Glund complimented. "I would expect no less from the Queen of the Forsaken Desert. And that is why we have no doubt that you can ensure Tauran's continued cooperation."

"Your compliments do not interest me, wizard," Shara said, impatience sharpening her tone. "Do not think for a moment that your gifts and your favor entitle you to waste my time. What would our benefactor ask of me? Surely the two of you don't expect me to whore myself to that barbarian to secure his cooperation?"

"I would not insult you so," Glund assured. "Your varied and considerable powers of persuasion are well known. While I have no doubt that you could seduce him, I would never presume to tell you how to ply your skills."

"That is wise of you," Shara said coolly. "But Eastedge is quite far away. I would require a bit more incentive than your past compensations for such a journey."

"And you shall have it, I promise you. Only name it and it shall be yours."

"First tell me exactly what it is you require from Tauran," Shara demanded. "And then I will decide the price."

"The King and Head Mage of Lorr are growing desperate to retrieve the Hell Key," Glund told her. "We believe they will, at some point in the very near future, recruit otherworldly assistance. We need their next exhibition to meet the same fate as the first two – should they survive that long – and Tauran is critical to that end. But he has grown more squeamish as of late. He seems not to have the stomach to do all that is necessary for us to achieve success."

Shara twitched an eyebrow in concealed surprise. She knew Tauran worked for the Second High Advisor in several capacities aimed at crippling the Kingdom of Lorr, but she had no idea he had actually participated in Rionn Lorr's two ill-fated missions to recover the Hell Key.

She was immediately offended that such a self-absorbed buffoon would be entrusted with the type of power that was used to halt those quests. She should be the wielder of such power. With that in mind, the price for this assignment would be doubled.

Chapter 5: Mr. and Mrs. Harvey

5.1

Joel was winded nearly to the point of collapse but he continued to run. He had to run, for the dark thing that chased him continued to pursue. Despite tight, burning lungs, Joel kept his fatigued legs pumping as the thudding footfalls upon the pavement behind him grew louder and nearer. He pushed on through downtown Montgomery, Alabama, coming upon the intersection of Monroe and North Hull. He turned south on Hull and ran on. The historic Dexter Avenue King Memorial Baptist Church was just around the corner and he knew that there he could find sanctuary from the evil that hunted him so relentlessly.

As he approached the corner of Hull and Dexter Avenue, he expected to see the red brick building that represented his safe haven. But when rounded the corner his surroundings changed abruptly. His momentary disorientation did not slow his flight, though, because any hesitation would mean certain capture by the thing that dogged him. A moment later he recognized where he was: Jeffery Avenue on the South Side of Chicago. A quick glance at the address on a building revealed that he was on 82nd street and heading south toward 83rd. There was another church there, he knew. Another sanctuary.

Then he noticed that he could no longer hear or feel the evil that had been chasing him for so long. He risked a glance over his shoulder and saw that there was nothing there, nothing but the abandoned sidewalk. All he could hear was the rough wheezing of his own heaving chest. He kept running, anyway, just in case the evil had concealed itself. When he turned to look forward again…

The evil was right in front of him. It was just yards away from him and it took the form of a hulking shadow. Its shape was vaguely human. Joel could make out a disproportionately small head set atop a wide stump of a neck, which in turn sat atop a pair of shoulders that were easily five feet across and bulging with muscle. Besides that, all Joel had time enough to notice were blazing golden-red eyes that seemed for all the world like small triangular windows into the depths of hell.

Joel could not stop his momentum in time and crashed into the barrel chest of the evil. One of its pectorals was almost as wide as Joel's torso. The thing was as solid as a brick wall and just as immovable. The smell of musk and sulfur assaulted Joel's nostrils and suffocated him as he bounced off of the monster and crumpled to the ground. The evil was upon him before he could even try to recover.

Long, vice-like fingers clutched his throat and the monster put its full weight behind its knee upon Joel's chest, crushing the very life out of him. Joel's head throbbed and his eyes bulged so violently that he feared his heart had been forced up into his skull. The cavity in his chest, where his heart had been, burned like fire. The evil's vomitus breath joined with its stench of musk and sulfur until breathing was completely impossible.

The evil's hellish lantern eyes lowered until they were only inches away from Joel's own, their brightness casting just enough illumination for Joel to make out some of the evil's features. Its features were horribly distorted and horribly familiar.

They were his own.

With the last ounce of his all-but-faded strength, Joel brought his hands up to the thing's shoulders and surprised even himself by pushing the massive creature off of him. He rolled over and reversed their positions. Now Joel was on top of the evil and had his own hands, which had morphed into long blades of bone, at the throat of his pursuer. Just as he was about to plunge his talons into the evil's jugular vein, the creature called out his name...

In *Lisa's* voice!

The darkest shadows fell away from Joel's intended victim to reveal, to his horror, the terror-stricken face of his wife. Her brown skin was tinted with the stark yellow light of a street lamp outside their hotel window, the pale glow intensifying her terrified expression. They were not on the asphalt streets of Chicago. They were in a bed. His right hand pressed down forcefully against her chest, pinning her helplessly to the bed, but the fingers of his left hand were still inhuman talons pressed against the tip of her throat.

Lisa's bulging eyes watched with morbid revulsion as Joel's talons retracted back into human fingers. Joel thrust himself away with so much force that he flew from the king-sized hotel bed to the floor, tears streaming from his eyes. Lisa lay frozen on the bed. She was holding her breath so her chest did not move. The only parts of her that did were her wide, fearful eyes, which followed Joel to the floor where he sat trembling and panic stricken.

"Oh God," she finally managed to whisper.

Joel wanted to reply, but even if he could find the words, he realized that he still could not breathe. His chest was still burning and his lungs were still impossibly tight. He was wheezing violently and still could not understand what was happening to him.

"Your inhaler!" Lisa said, coming to her senses before her husband.

She rolled quickly over to his side of the bed, snatched his albuterol pump from the nightstand, and then scrambled over to where he huddled on the floor. Joel recovered from his shock just enough to take the inhaler from her. He took two deep pumps and remained still until his wheezing subsided and he could speak once again.

"What's happening to me?" Joel whimpered.

"You didn't take all of your meds today," Lisa said. "That's why you were having such a bad attack. I thought I heard you wheezing so I woke you up to take your albuterol and you...went a little crazy."

"What's happening to me?" he echoed softly, more to himself than to his wife.

"You were having a nightmare," Lisa noted. "But hell, I must've been waking up from one, too. I could've sworn your fingers were, I don't know, claws or something."

You weren't dreaming, Joel wanted to tell her. But he refused to say it aloud, hoping his silence would keep it from being true.

5.2

To Ryan's amazement, Dan had a connection in the Illinois State Troopers office. Dan used that connection to quickly find out the approximate time of death of the agents and also that the car they used was stolen from a small motel in Paducah, Kentucky. With his knowledge of organization agents' standard procedures, Ryan guessed that the agents probably picked up the trail of their target near that hotel. They would have then followed the targets to an isolated stretch of road to kill them and make it look like a robbery or bad drug deal. Taking the time of death and the distance from the Kentucky hotel into account, they estimated that the agents left the hotel trailing their target around six o'clock in the morning.

So Dan and Ryan drove to Paducah. Dan used another connection that Ryan did not know he had to obtain a pair of forged but extraordinarily authentic-looking state investigator identifications. Ryan was surprised, impressed and even a little envious. Most of his resources had been affiliated with the organization and therefore were off limits. He had a few independent connections that he was sure were not on the organization's radar, but none of them were of any use in this particular endeavor. How many other surprises were up his grandfather's sleeve?

At the Paducah motel they interviewed the desk clerk on duty on the morning in question. They were informed that two men and a married couple checked out that morning. One of the men headed south while the other man and the couple went north. As Ryan had assumed, none of them fit the description of the dead agents. The man who was headed north drove a sports car and the couple drove a full sized pick-up truck. The motel paperwork included the license plate numbers of the travelers' cars.

From there, Dan and Ryan canvassed every gas station near the highway between the hotel and the spot where the stolen car and victims were found. It was tedious work but Ryan welcomed it.

In his search for answers to why the organization was trying to "serve him a pink slip," he had spent the better part of the last three years feeling like he was chasing his tail. Finding his ex-employers while simultaneously hiding from them was a more than challenging proposition. After running into dead end after dead end, and after being sidetracked by the occasional misadventure just when he thought he had gotten close, it was a relief to be performing tedious legwork on a legitimate lead.

They checked the surveillance tapes at the gas stations that had working security cameras and noticed a pattern. The green Honda Civic stopped at several of the same gas stations as the pick-up truck described by the motel clerk. Ryan guessed that in the instances where the recordings contained the pick-up but not the Civic, the Civic had simply stopped outside of camera range. One of the cameras got a clear view of the truck's license plate number. It matched the plate number given to them at the hotel.

The entire process took three days. But from there, they were able to track the car back to one of Ryan and Dan's favorite cities.

"Chicago," Ryan said with a smile as he drove north on the two-lane highway. "It's good to be going back. I still wish you could've made Questblade work like a metal detector, where it just beeps or glows at different speeds or intensities to show whether or not we're going in the right direction."

"Listen for a second," Dan commanded. "You might learn something. When making a weapon of magic, you have to determine how best to employ the magic according to the intended use of the weapon. Sometimes you want to make it real specific, like with Demonsbane or the Shield of Innocents. But sometimes a broader scope is needed. Questblade's scope of magic is so broad because often the things you find along the way of search are just as important, if not more so, than the actual object of your search."

"If you say so," Ryan said with a shrug. "I'm just glad to be going back to the Windy City."

"Same here," Dan agreed.

They rode in silence for a while after that. Dan distracted himself from boredom by reminiscing about Chicago and thinking about what restaurants he would visit upon his return. He looked over at his grandson. He, too, was deep in thought, but the firm grip he had on the steering wheel and the near scowl on his face betrayed that his thoughts were not as whimsical as his grandfather's.

Dan tried to peek into Ryan's mind to see the cause of his intense expression. As had happened each of the previous times he tried to read his grandson's mind since Ryan's return from Lorr, Dan encountered only haze. It was as if Ryan was unconsciously blocking him.

Ryan turned to him. "Why don't you just ask, gramps?"

Perhaps it wasn't unconscious. "You knew?" Dan asked.

"Every time you peek, I feel it," Ryan said. "That's a bad little habit you've got there. Have you always eavesdropped on me like that?"

"I don't know if 'eavesdrop' is the word I would –"

"Gramps?"

"Always," Dan confessed. "Ever since you were a kid. It was hard not to. I had to know how you thought, how you made decisions. I had to know what kind of person you really were. Your destiny was too important. I couldn't take a chance on letting you go to Lorr if I didn't think you were ready."

"So all of the things I've done, all the people I've…"

He stopped short of saying the word "killed" but Dan was sure that was where he was going. "I wasn't looking *all* the time," Dan assured. "Not literally every second of every day. I did have my own life to live, you know."

Ryan gave his grandfather a sidelong glance. "What have you seen, old man?"

Dan stared at his son for a moment before he finally relented. "Let's just say I've seen enough."

Ryan had done many things in his life that he had come to be ashamed of after the Kingdom of Lorr changed his perspective on life and death. If having to involuntarily share his shame with the one person whose opinion he valued was part of his penance, then so be it. Instead of re-hashing his dissolute history or allowing himself to be angered by past invasions of privacy, he decided to leave well enough alone.

"You say you couldn't take a chance on *letting* me go, gramps, but Rionn pulled me over there. You didn't send me. How could you have stopped him?"

Dan gave a sly smile that increased the depths of the crow's feet at the corner of his eyes. "You should know by now that I'm a man of many resources."

Ryan could only shrug his agreement as Dan continued. "How did you learn to detect me...and block me?"

"I don't know," Ryan admitted. "But I think it has something to do with what Shanderah did to me."

"You mean when she passed the location of WorldHopper's mountain from her mind to yours?"

"Yeah," Ryan said. "Only I think she might have passed more than that. A *whole* lot more than that."

Dan's age-thinned lips set firmly together and he glanced out of the window as his mind worked. He turned back to Ryan. "Why do you say that?"

"Ever since then, I've known things," Ryan explained. "Things about magic. It's not an instinctive thing, either. Stray thoughts pop in and out of my head at random. They're like recollections of voices I've never heard, of pages I've never read. I see words written in a language I've never seen but I understand them as if they were written in English. I see the faces of people I've never met."

"Like someone else's memories," Dan concluded.

"Shandie's memories," Ryan agreed.

"Makes sense," Dan said. "She's not in our direct blood line, so it took a great effort for her to do that transfer. She was dying, too, so it had to be hard for her to focus.

"She knew her time was short and I'm guessing she didn't have the clarity to zero in on a specific recollection. Hell, she may have even forgotten what she was trying to do. I'll bet she put a huge chunk of her memories into your mind to make sure she got you the information you needed."

"Overkill," Ryan said. "Kind of like blowing up an entire building to kill one person."

"Still thinking like a hit man? That's a bad little habit *you've* got there."

Ryan shrugged again as he stared at the road. "Gramps," he said. "Exactly how does Demonsbane's magic work?"

Dan's eyes narrowed. "Shanderah knew, so you tell me."

"This is what I 'remember,' I guess," Ryan started. "Most of the magic; the enhanced strength, speed, and the higher pain threshold in the presence of demons, that's mine. That's our legacy from the Gatekeeper. Demonsbane does something else. It helps to focus the magic and controls my actions if they don't coincide with what Demonsbane knows is best. And somehow, it sends the demons back to hell."

"That's right," Dan concurred. "When the Old Ones, the parents of the Leaders, created the demons to help their Children battle the Protectors, they did more than splice different creatures together. They breathed a small bit of their own essence into the demons to increase every aspect of their power. The fortification of that energy is incrementally greater with each level of hell. If the lower level demons' bodies receive too much physical damage, they can't retain their damned souls, which are quickly sucked back into the level of hell they came from. But with the upper levels demons, their stronger essence keeps their souls from being pulled back."

"So Demonsbane strips that essence, that magic, away from them. And then they're pulled back," Ryan realized. "And it can cut through anything as long as its user is strong enough to drive it."

"Which you are in the presence of Demons," Dan added. "So you can cut through even the toughest demon hide."

"Interesting..." Ryan mused. His thoughtful expression lingered as he gazed out at the road ahead.

Dan turned to the passenger side window and smiled. He missed the philosophical debates and thought-provoking discussions he used to have with Shanderah across the WorldGate. He had hoped that with Ryan's exposure to a world of magic, his grandson could provide him with the knowledgeable conversation for which he longed. For so many years Ryan simply refused to believe in magic. When he first returned from Lorr, he was too busy trying to process everything that had happened, and too self-determined, to seek his grandfather's counsel. But now it seemed Ryan was willing to talk about it and Dan did not want to miss out on the opportunity.

"Is there anything else?" Dan asked. "You must have a load of questions."

"I guess I do," Ryan admitted.

"Fire away, boy."

"What about the prophecies?" Ryan asked. "I've had dreams where I…or Shanderah, was learning to recite memorized passages from long-lost texts. She must have been a little girl at the time. She was standing in front of a man and a woman. The man was her father, a Child of the Old Ones. The woman was her mother, a priestess of a lost order of nuns or something. The one passage that keeps replaying in my head is the one about the re-emergence of Raxe's progeny." Ryan recited the prophecy as Dan had told it to him:

"And there was a Child; a son of Raxe; grandson to the Gatekeeper. When the evil rained down upon them, that son would be far too young to help them overcome the hordes of evil that would descend upon the house of the Gatekeeper, so the Gatekeeper and Raxe would send that son across the WorldGate, into a land that would provide him safe haven. The progeny of that son would bear Children. One of his progeny would bear the weapon. *That Child would have the power to fell both demon and man, and a day will come when the progeny of that son finds the other to save the Kingdom of Lorr and beyond."*

"So you remember it?" Dan said with more than a little surprise. "I didn't think you were paying attention."

"Thing is," Ryan went on, "Shanderah didn't remember it that way. In the way she was taught the verse, she was told 'The progeny of that son would *be* the weapon,' not *bear* the weapon."

"Semantics?" Dan offered. "And think about it, there's not much difference in pronunciation between the words 'be' and 'bear.' You know stories can alter with each telling or writing, especially when passed down for as long as this one has been."

"True," Ryan conceded. "But tell me this, who do you think 'the other' is?"

"Rionn Lorr," Dan said thoughtfully. "Why? Do you think it could be someone else?"

"Couldn't it be?" Ryan asked.

"But that would mean that somebody in our line had more than one Child with magic," Dan said. "A split blood line." He thought for a moment and then shook his head. "But how could that happen? Raxe's son was a Child of the Old Ones, not an Old One, and a Child can have only one offspring with magic."

"How do you know Raxe's son wasn't an Old One?" Ryan posed.

"Well," Dan conceded. "I don't *know* any of this for a fact. All I know is that's how the story was passed to me. So let's say there were two bloodlines. That would mean there could be another Child around here somewhere." He thought about that for a moment. "But how could another child exist without us knowing? We would be able to feel his or her presence."

"Yeah," Ryan agreed. He considered his heightened sensitivity to magic as a result of the time spent and lessons learned in the Kingdom of Lorr. He thought about his grandfather's advanced sensitivity to magic and his decades of experience with it. If there were another Child in this world, one of them, particularly Dan, would have known.

"I guess I don't have an answer for that one, gramps. Unless he or she is in a different world, neither here nor in the world of Lorr."

"True," Dan said proudly. "You know, kid, I'm glad to see you thinking about this whole magic thing."

Ryan scoffed. "After all I've been through? Hell, it's hard not to."

5.3

Joel and Lisa sat restfully on wooden crates in the living room of their apartment. They had just brought in the clothes, cot, and the few pieces of furniture they were able to pack into the bed of their pickup truck. They had worked up a sweat even in the Chicago winter, so they both shed their coats as they rested.

"Is that all?" Lisa gasped as she cracked open a bottle of soda.

Joel chuckled and coughed a bit. "Yeah," he answered. "This should hold us until we can make arrangements to have the rest of our stuff brought up from 'Skegee."

"What's with the cough, baby?" Lisa asked.

"Just dusty in here, sugar, that's all." Joel opened his beer, took a long swallow, and exhaled heavily with satisfaction. "All better."

"Be careful," Lisa said as she took a sip of her soda. "You've got a nice little beer-belly starting there."

Joel patted his stomach with proud smile. "Just a sign of good living."

He smiled on the outside but he knew it had not been long ago when his stomach was flat, when his back and knees did not hurt from light lifting the way they ached now. His asthma was growing worse as he was growing older and he let it scare him out of exercising the way he once had. That's when the weight started to creep up on him.

"I promise I'll start working out again as soon as we get settled in," Joel vowed.

"Mm-hmm," Lisa said incredulously. "Where have I heard that before?"

Joel laughed, and then coughed again, more roughly than before. When he finished he took a deep breath and Lisa heard a wheeze.

"You sure you're OK?" Lisa said. "Sounds like –"

"Yeah, I'm wheezing a little," Joel admitted. He fished his small white inhaler from the front right pocket of his loose-fitting jeans. "A little hit should fix me right up."

He took his usual double-pump from his inhaler and waited for his breathing to clear. And he waited. He took another pump but his breathing only got worse.

"Baby?" Lisa asked.

Joel took a deep, hissing breath and rubbed his chest. A frustrated and fearful expression descended on him like a shroud. It was that old familiar feeling. When his emergency inhaler did not work, which happened once every few years but far too frequently for him, he always had to fight to keep from panicking.

The congestion in his chest cut his breath shorter with each labored gasp. In a while, perhaps hours, or possibly even minutes, his head would grow light from lack of oxygen.

"Lisa, we need to find an emergency room."

Just over an hour later Joel sat on a gurney in an ER treatment room. A transparent plastic facemask covered his mouth and nose. A small clear vial containing bubbling liquid was attached to the bottom of the mask, transferring air from a buzzing wall spout through a thin plastic tube. White vapor wafted up from the mask as Joel took deep breaths. Lisa sat next to him, rubbing his arm comfortingly, when she saw his thick eyebrows knit into what she easily recognized as frustration.

"Is the medicine helping?" she asked worriedly.

Joel nodded slowly.

"Then what's wrong?"

Joel shrugged. "So how do you like being married to such a high-maintenance man?" he asked, his voice muffled through the mask and the hiss of the vapor.

Lisa flashed a frown. "Shut up and breathe, man."

"I don't think this is gonna work," Joel said.

"I thought the medicine was helping." Lisa's eyes widened with worry once more.

"It is," Joel mumbled. Then he turned and looked at the oxygen spout. "I'm feeling better," he assured. "Turn that thing off for a minute. I'd do it myself but I might turn the wrong knob and mess myself up for real." Lisa gave him a doubtful look. Joel rolled his eyes. "It's almost finished anyway." Lisa did not budge. "Look, I'll finish it up when I finish telling you what I have to tell you. I promise."

Lisa reluctantly did as he asked. "If you're not going to be quiet," she muttered under her breath, "we might as well not waste the medicine." Joel pulled the elastic strap holding the mask to his face and lifted it over his head. "This better be important," Lisa warned. "So what's not going to work?"

"Us," Joel said, not willing to look her in the eye. "I'm not good for you."

Now Lisa was annoyed. "What are you talking about, Joel? You think we should break up because you have asthma? That's silly. If that was a problem for me we would've never gotten together in the first place."

"It's not just that," Joel went on in a somber whisper. "What about what happened on the highway?"

"We were in danger," Lisa reminded him.

"But I lost it!" Joel snapped, straining to whisper. He took a deep, clear breath and composed himself. "What if that ever happened with us?"

"Do you think I could ever threaten you or piss you off enough to make you lose it like *that*?" Lisa asked, her annoyance softening into sadness.

"Of course not. I just don't know what else might set me off," Joel explained. He continued with noticeable reluctance. "The dream you had that night at the hotel…when you saw me with those claws… What if it wasn't just a dream?"

"What else could it have been?" she asked suspiciously. "It couldn't have been real. People's fingers don't grow into claws in real life."

"Maybe it was a warning," Joel offered.

"It was a nightmare," Lisa concluded with finality. She sounded as if she was trying to convince herself as much as she was trying to convince him. "And if you think I'm going anywhere," she put a dainty right hand to her stomach, "If you think *we're* going anywhere, you're crazy." Her left hand caressed his cheek softly. "And if you think I'm letting you go anywhere you've *completely* lost your mind." She put the mask back on his face and turned on the oxygen. "Now shut up and breathe."

They sat together in silence until the doctor stepped into the room a few minutes later. He inspected the medicine connected to his facemask, nodded his head, and turned off the oxygen spout. "Are you feeling better, Mr. Harvey?"

Joel nodded as he removed the facemask. "Much better. So what was it?"

"Looks like an allergic reaction to the dust in the apartment triggered your attack," the doctor explained. "I'm guessing there were mold spores in the dust particles. Moisture can build up when an untended apartment isn't cooled and ventilated properly.

"Your albuterol inhaler doesn't affect your allergies and your allergies aggravated your asthma. Once we got the allergic reaction under control the asthma meds kicked in. There are steroids in your IV for your lungs and we gave you a small shot of diphenhydramine for your allergies. We want you to stick around for a few hours so we can watch you but you should be on your way home later this afternoon."

"So what do we do about the apartment?" Lisa asked.

"Get it vacuumed out," the doctor suggested. "Well. They have services for that. In the meantime, though, you'll need to stay somewhere else. If you have to go into the apartment, Mr. Harvey, you'll want to stay for a short time and wear a garden face mask, one of the ones that filter allergens."

"Will do, doc," Joel said.

5.*4*

The ride home was a quiet one. Lisa was understandably disturbed by Joel's suggestion and Joel felt guilty about making it, but he had to convince her that what she saw that night at the hotel was not a dream. He feared for the safety of his wife and unborn child far more than he feared for his own safety and he would do anything to protect them. If that meant leaving them, no matter how heartbreaking it might be, he would force himself to do it. He left the topic alone for the moment because he could tell from her tone in the treatment room that there was no way she would accept the truth.

The couple arrived at their apartment building and took the elevator to their third floor apartment. When they stepped out into the hall, they saw a stranger standing at their door. He wore an unbuttoned, long leather trench coat over a dark blazer, a white cotton button-down shirt, and dark slacks. His long dreadlocks were tied fast behind his head. His bearing was familiar to Joel. He looked like – hell, he even *stood* like a cop. And if he was not a cop, Joel was almost positive he was a law enforcement officer of some sort.

Ryan recognized the couple stepping out of the elevator from their descriptions and the choppy surveillance videos. He wasted no time in providing his false FBI identification for inspection. When they were satisfied, Ryan continued.

"I hope everything is alright, Mr. and Mrs. Harvey," he said with genuine concern. "Your neighbors said you rushed out of here in a hurry. They heard something about you going to the hospital."

"Asthma attack," Joel said guardedly. "What can we do for you, agent Franklin?"

"I was hoping we could talk inside," Ryan said.

"We're kind of in a hurry," Joel insisted.

"I know about the incident on the state highway," Ryan said softly. "Downstate."

"We don't know what –"

"I'm not here to bust you for it," Ryan promised. "I'm on a completely different case. I'm after the men that sent those assassins after you."

"Assassins?" Lisa breathed. Ryan glanced at her but Joel placed a silencing hand on her shoulder.

"We don't know what you're talking about," Joel lied.

"I found a witness," Ryan lied in return. "There were a couple of kids out there hiding behind snow banks. The ordeal frightened them into silence for a while but I found them and they told me everything." Ryan watched as Joel's feigned confusion faltered into worry. "Like I said," Ryan continued, "I'm not here for that. I want to find out about the men that accosted you. We can go inside now or I can turn this lead over to the detectives who *are* looking for you."

"Why haven't you done that already?" Joel challenged. He knew this stranger was trying to deceive them, but could not tell what was true and was not. Besides, this guy knew way too much. "This doesn't sound like standard procedure to me."

"You're right," Ryan agreed, pulling a nine-millimeter handgun from the inside of his open trench coat. "Let's follow standard procedure, then. I arrest you both and hand-deliver you to the local police. Or we go in and talk."

Joel and Lisa looked at one another for a long moment and then silently went to their door and unlocked it. Ryan followed them in, closing and locking the door behind them. He eyed Joel carefully as the husband reached into a plastic drug store bag and produced a garden facemask. He took it out of the packaging and secured the strap to the back of his head.

"What's with the mask?" Ryan asked, hesitating in his move to holster his pistol.

"Allergies, asthma," Joel reminded.

The couple found crates on which to sit and Ryan followed suit.

"Beer?" Lisa offered.

"Sure," Ryan said as he put his gun away.

"Aren't you on duty?" Joel asked.

"Right at this very the moment?" Ryan asked slyly. "Nope. I could use a beer."

"No beer for the agent," Joel said. Lisa gave the visitor an apologetic shrug and stayed seated. Joel turned his attention back to Ryan. “So what is it you want to know? And why did you say they were assassins?”

“I did a background check on the two of you,” Ryan said, truthfully this time. His grandfather’s connections had come into play once again to get them everything they could find on the couple. “There was nothing in there to explain why two covert agents would be after either of you. Maybe you can fill me in.”

“Agents?” Lisa asked. “Those were thugs, gang bangers.”

“That was their cover,” Ryan said. “So talk to me. How could a veterinarian and a CAD teacher manage to kill two trained assassins? Or are those jobs *your* cover?”

Joel leaned forward. “They were punk-ass, wanna-be bangers. I snapped and they panicked and they got killed. I blacked out, OK? I have no idea how I did it. If you’re gonna arrest me for it, arrest me. Just leave my wife alone.”

Ryan studied him closely, searching his eyes and the rest of his body for any signs of deception. He could find none. If this were a trained agent, Ryan knew, the man would be adept at lying. Ryan wished he could read minds the way WorldHopper could. He almost wished for a moment that the dragon was there. But knowing the ill-tempered, fire-breathing, man-eater the way he did, Ryan quickly banished that thought and went with his instincts.

All three of them started at the chirping of Ryan’s cell phone. He pulled it from his pocket and answered it.

“Watcha got for me?” he asked.

“What we were looking for,” came a voice from the other end, speaking much louder than necessary.

“Good,” Ryan said. “I’m on my way.” He turned to Joel and Lisa. “I believe you,” he said. “But be careful. Mistaken identity doesn’t happen very often with the guys who came after you. But if you *have* been mistaken for marks, you’re still in danger.” He stood up quickly and went for the door.

“You’re leaving? Just like that?” Joel questioned. “Aren’t you supposed to help us?”

Ryan turned after opening the door. “I’m trying to get to them before they get to you.”

“What about protective custody?” Lisa asked.

Ryan shrugged. "Not my department. And, honestly, I'm kind of freelancing on this. The people after you are above the Bureau's pay grade…way above their pay grade. But don't worry. Once we get them, you'll be safe."

Lisa and Joel stared at the closed door after Ryan left. Joel turned to his wife and voiced his suspicion.

"I don't think he was a real agent."

"Why?" Lisa asked.

"I just don't," Joel answered. "He didn't seem right. He didn't, I don't know…he didn't smell right."

"Didn't *smell* right?" Lisa echoed.

"Yeah, well, I don't know…" Joel was trying to explain but he could not find the words. So he found other words. "It's just that I thought he was an agent at first, but now," Joel shook his head. "I mean, I don't give a damn if he was freelancing. A real agent wouldn't just let us go like that, especially after we fessed up. He'd have to arrest us or put us in protective custody or something."

"So you think he was lying about everything?" Lisa asked hopefully. "You don't think those guys were agents?"

"Hell no," Joel assured. "I think the fake agent's maybe ex military or law enforcement or something. I heard guys like that work as private investigators."

Lisa chuckled. "Where'd you hear that? Mystery novels or TV detective shows?"

"Hey, a lot of that stuff is researched and pretty accurate," Joel argued.

They shared a laugh that lasted for several seconds before withering into awkward silence as uncertainty crept back into the room. They looked back at the door and spoke in unison:

"With everything else we've got to worry about—" they started. They looked at each other and chuckled worriedly.

5.5

Ryan ran down the hall and the stairs to the ground floor foyer, where he stopped short just as he reached the front entrance. Through the large glass panel on the front door he saw a tan sedan parked across the empty and silent street. The tinted windows were rolled up and too dark for Ryan to make out anything inside the car. He eased to the side of the door and peeked back out through the glass to where his van was parked a half block behind the sedan. His breath caught in his throat when he saw that his grandfather was no longer in the front passenger seat.

Between the two vehicles he saw a man wearing a long hooded parka about fifteen yards away from the sedan and approaching stealthily. His stealth would not have been obvious to the average observer. Ryan, however, was not the average observer. He could see the feigned casual nature of the other's approach, the pace neither too slow nor too fast to attract attention. And even though the man's head faced straight ahead, Ryan noticed his eyes were locked on the sedan. As he closed the distance between himself and the parked car, his right hand eased into and out of his parka so smoothly that the Glock 17 9mm pistol, equipped with a suppressor, seemed to magically appear in his grasp.

A deep breath allowed Ryan to focus on the rhythm of his heartbeat and the soft echoes deep within his mind. A moment later he felt the secondary, almost subconscious rhythms that he immediately recognized as his grandfather's presence. It took another moment to pinpoint the direction from which the feelings originated to confirm his fear.

Gramps was in the sedan.

Ryan reached into his trench and put his hand on the Smith & Wesson M&P 45 caliber pistol nestled in his shoulder holster. His vow to stop killing came to mind but that was least of his concerns. He was an expert marksman with any type of firearm, more than good enough for a debilitating but nonlethal shot. Unlike the agent across the street, though, Ryan's gun was not fitted with a suppressor.

The small side street, lined with low-rise apartment buildings and brownstones, was still empty except for his grandfather, the agents, and a few parked vehicles. It was midday, after lunch but before the public schools let out, so the street was almost eerily silent. Ryan did not want to risk shattering that silence with gunfire that might bring people to their windows, or spur them to call the police. He reached into is trench again to the smooth, cold, reassuring handle of Demonsbane where it hung from the axe frog at his hip.

He would have a harder time explaining the battle-axe than he would a silencer on his .45, but it would make less noise. Besides, he had a hard time leaving the enchanted weapon too far away from his person for too long. That had not been the case at all when Demonsbane was new to him. In fact, he had dreaded the gothic weapon and would have happily let anyone other than himself handle it. But in the years since, Demonsbane had come to feel like a part of him.

Ryan took another deep breath as the agent across the street lifted his .9mm and inched closer to the sedan. When the gunman was almost directly across the street from him, Ryan exhaled, pushed open the door, and sent Demonsbane spinning through the air with a powerful overhand throw.

The gunman turned at the sudden movement, bringing his Glock around in a two-handed grip to meet the unexpected threat. Before he could squeeze the trigger, or even finish turning, for that matter, one of Demonsbane's twirling crescent blades sheared the pistol in half, missing the gunman's fingers by less than half an inch. The enchanted battle-axe stuck with a thunk into the wall of the building beside him. The agent was stunned for the briefest of moments as he spared a glance over his shoulder at the antique weapon. When he turned to see who threw it he saw Ryan sprinting toward him across the cold, wet street.

"Axe," the agent said with a smile, invoking Ryan's old organization moniker. "What an unexpected surprise!" He turned back to the battle-axe, rushed quickly over to it and extended his hand. "Let me show you how to use this thing."

It was Ryan's turn to smile. He also covered his eyes.

When the agent touched the handle of the battle-axe, the blinding white light still managed to burn Ryan's shielded eyes. A muffled *whump* cuffed his ears. Ryan's vision cleared quickly and he immediately leapt into the air to avoid the agent that had been hurled in his direction by the magic of the battle-axe.

Ryan hit the slippery ground, slid, and fell heavily onto his backside. He bounced back to his feet quickly and ran over to retrieve Demonsbane. The agent, however, did not get up. He did not move at all and he would never move again. Ryan did not bother to check the fallen man's vital signs because he knew the man was already dead. Once Dan bequeathed the enchanted weapon to his grandson, no one but Ryan could so much as touch Demonsbane and survive.

Ryan slipped the battle-axe back into his coat and retrieved his gun as he snatched open the driver's side door. He had to catch an unconscious man before he fell to the concrete. Ryan looked over to see his grandfather sitting in the front passenger seat. The wheelchair rested just outside the open door. Dan was binding the man's hands with long plastic ties. Long-range audio surveillance equipment lay sprawled across the back seat.

"I told you not to move on him, gramps," Ryan complained. "You could've gotten yourself killed. How the hell did you do this?"

Dan smiled slyly. "My legs may not work all that well but my hands still do. Don't forget who taught you and your mom to fight. Besides, people don't expect much from old men in wheelchairs. I played a homeless disabled man begging for spare change. The son of a bitch was rude so I was a little rougher than I had to be. Nice toss, by the way. I just hope that flash didn't call too much attention to us."

Ryan frowned. "The plan was for you to I-D him so *I* could take him down."

"And it was a good plan," Dan said sarcastically. "But it was gonna take too damn long, so I improvised. Now stop griping and tie his legs."

5.6

"What's the problem Johnson?" The director made no attempt to hide the irritation in his voice or his expression. He did not have to hide his irritation. He was a member of the organization's Board of Directors. These were among the most powerful men in the world. The agents that worked for them called the directors the Four Horsemen. This particular director was the head of the Deactivation Branch, and he had been so for the better part of forty years. Deactivation was the organization's synonym for termination, or assassination. Presidents and kings had died at his command.

"His pink slip was served over three years ago," the director continued. "I know he's skilled and surely has independent resources to call upon, so I've tried to give you ample time and latitude to resolve this. But we are the *organization*, Johnson. Axe and his grandfather should have been located and removed by now. What am I supposed to make of this? Of *you*?"

Supervisor Johnson made a show of trying to disguise the shaking in his three hundred dollar Italian loafers. It was rumored that the Horsemen enjoyed intimidating their employees. This director did not even have a visitor's chair in his office. He did not want his visitors comfortable. He wanted them working. The director was seated and Johnson, a taller than average man, towered over him as he stood on the other side of the narrow oak desk. Johnson knew that under normal circumstances he would have been intimidated by the shorter, plumper man's cold gaze and irritated scowl.

But these were not normal circumstances. Johnson was not intimidated in the least, yet he still played the role of the apprehensive underling. He knew his act had to be subtle, though. If a subordinate was overly shaken it could be taken as a sign of weakness. Or worse, it could be construed as mocking if the director was acutely insightful or overly suspicious. Johnson had no fear of the director. Not anymore. But the time was not yet right to play his hand.

"Well, sir," Johnson began. He swallowed against a feigned dry throat. "Axe, as I have said, is our most effective employee."

"I know," the director said. "But explain to me again how this was possible."

"Axe apparently enlisted outside aid, sir. According to reports from the surviving members of the deactivation team, a group of heavily armed operatives surprised and outnumbered them. They were able to overcome the deactivation team and extract Axe."

Johnson was telling an outright lie. The director would never believe the truth, anyway. How could he tell the director that Ryan Franklin, AKA Axe, jumped out of a third floor window and then disappeared into a one-dimensional black hole that appeared and then disappeared in mid-air?

"I'm starting to believe that another branch is aiding him," Johnson added. "That would go a long way toward explaining his ability to escape and elude us for so long."

"That possibility is being looked into," the director assured. "What about the video crew? Have they ever been able to produce anything that would give us a clue as to Axe's extraction team?"

Johnson was ready for that one. "No, sir. His team was obviously well briefed. The video crew was deactivated and their equipment appropriated. Even the hidden micro cams and bugs were removed."

"So the story you've been telling me all this time is still hearsay, with no evidence to support it," the director stated.

"True," Johnson admitted. "But these reports came to me first hand from the deactivation team. I see no reason for them to fabricate this story."

"I do," replied the director. "It very well could be that the team simply failed. Perhaps they would rather liquidate the video crew and dispose of the evidence than admit to their own ineptness."

Or maybe I *had them killed,* Johnson thought. *And everyone outside who saw what happened...except, of course, for the survivors, my hand picked operatives who killed them.*

"True again, sir," Johnson said aloud. "I will continue the internal investigation and report to you immediately if I discover that your supposition is true."

"And what of the Harvey's? I approved their pink slips because your sources revealed them as Axe's civilian assets. I trusted you to deal with them. How have they been able to elude you?"

Johnson lied again. "Apparently, he selects his CA's as well as he does his other assets. The couple is more capable than their dossier's indicated. I'll make sure that the next team to go after them is fully prepared."

"You do that." The director looked at Johnson with an impassive, appraising eye. He then went about the task of inspecting a mound of paperwork on his large oak desk as if Johnson was no longer there. That was Johnson's cue to leave. He turned and walked toward the door.

"Johnson," the director called. Supervisor Johnson froze in his tracks as he opened the door and turned to his superior. The director continued, "Too much time has passed without a resolution to this situation. Fortunately for us he's been quiet, but who knows how long that will last? I can't stress enough how important it is to deactivate this agent. If he is as problematic as you say, he could cause an undue amount of trouble for us." The Director paused for emphasis, and then continued. "Your continued employment with the organization depends on how well you complete this assignment. And your time is running frightfully short."

Johnson swallowed again and made a point to do so louder than he did the first time. They both knew that the only way to leave the organization was in a body bag. The supervisor nodded his head in understanding and hurried from the room.

He had to stifle a chuckle as he walked down the hall, knowing that hidden cameras lined the walls. It was a common practice of most supervisors. Why would the Directors be any different? Johnson kept an expression of subdued nervousness plastered to his face.

In the past, that nervousness would have been genuine because he had no one to blame but himself for his predicament. It was his own greed that drove him to use organization agents to do side jobs to fill his pockets. Unfortunately, his director found out about the last couple of unauthorized assassinations and asked the Director of the Organization Intelligence Branch to conduct an independent investigation.

News of the investigation filtered back to Johnson and he knew it was only a matter of time before the OIB discovered the truth. Johnson covered himself by saying that Axe was the rouge agent. He assured the Directors that Axe would be dealt with.

And being the keen-eyed, opportunistic sort that he was, he quickly found a way to use the situation to fatten his secret bank accounts. The organization had targeted Marco Katsaros, a Greek arms dealer with more than his share of government influence. It was to be Axe's next job. Johnson decided to make a deal with Marco. In exchange for five million dollars and limited, but significant access to the arms dealer's vast global resources, Johnson would arrange for Axe to disappear.

Axe, however, had proven to be an incredibly difficult man to deactivate. Johnson was sure that at that very moment Axe was doing his own investigation to find out why he had been targeted. In the past, that knowledge, as well as his superior's disfavor, would have had Johnson fearing for his life. But things had changed recently, and they had changed decidedly in his favor.

One of Johnson's many advantages was the fact that Axe was a mere field agent. Field agents were lower-level operatives and neither they nor assistant supervisors had direct contact with the Board of Directors. Only upper-level management such as Johnson had personal and direct contact with directors. And even then, they only had contact with the director of their particular branch. There was no way Axe could go over Johnson's head.

Johnson would either find Axe or Axe would find him. Johnson was more than ready for either occurrence.

That thought reminded him that he needed to appoint a new Field Supervisor. Tracker, his previous FS, was “deactivated” by Axe three years earlier in an attempt to serve him his pink slip. The interim FS he appointed failed at the simple task of terminating Axe’s grandfather, who was just a crippled old man in a retirement home. The men sent by the interim FS to dispatch the Harvey’s had failed as well. Johnson responded to the failures by ordering the FS to perform reconnaissance personally on the couple. He had not been heard from since.

There had been far too many mistakes. Some adjustments would have to be made. But once Axe, his grandfather, and the Harvey’s were removed, the way would be clear for the next phase of Johnson’s grand scheme.

5.7

An angry and pained roar erupted from an old abandoned warehouse near the lakefront on Chicago's south side. The old building was just one of several derelict structures in the area. The citywide building rehabilitation project had not reached this particular area, but it would eventually. In the meantime, the seemingly useless building served *some* purposes very well. The building was structurally sound, although its outward appearance hinted otherwise. Old gray paint, faded and peeling from years of hot summers, cold winters, and the famed Chicago hawk lent the building a brittle, frail look that masked its sturdy foundation, beams, studs, and columns.

The windows of the warehouse were boarded, allowing only small rays of sunlight to stab through the cracks and spaces between the boards. This sparse light was not enough to allow good visibility, but it was just enough to cast weird shadows throughout the dim space. The room was dry and musty and the air was stale and thick with dust. There were no partition walls inside the warehouse, only one huge, empty room with a twenty-foot high, unfinished ceiling.

On the inside of the warehouse a man sat handcuffed to a steel chair. He had been trying to work himself free of the handcuffs but every time he tried, the cuffs would bite deeper into his wrists. While he struggled, a man sat on the dusty floor a few feet away from him drinking beer from frosty silver can. Another man, an elderly one in a wheelchair, ate popcorn from a red-striped bag. Every now and then the old man tossed a kernel at the man bound to the chair.

"C'mon, Axe," the frustrated captive said, spitting out an unpopped kernel that landed in his mouth while he talked. He gave the old man an angry look and continued. "There's no way I'm telling you who the supervisor is. You'll just have to kill me."

"First of all, don't call me Axe. That was my organization handle, and since those bastards no longer employ me, I prefer to be called Ryan. Second, I'm gonna get the name from you eventually so I don't have to kill you. Third, I'm not in the killing business anymore."

Clay chuckled. "If you don't kill anymore, *Ryan,* how in the hell are you going to stop them from killing you? Blackmail? It has to be. But if you don't even know who the supervisor is, what could you have on him?"

Ryan took a long swig from his can. "Why does the organization want me dead?"

"You know the deal, Axe. We don't ask questions. We follow orders."

"I know you do your homework on a target just like I do," Ryan accused. "Like I *used* to. No matter who the target is. You know why they want me dead and you are going to tell me."

Clay chuckled, and then gagged a large popped kernel of corn zipped into his mouth and lodged in his throat.

"I'm tellin' you, Clay, it would be best for you if you gave me what I want before my friend shows up. He doesn't have a lot of patience. I won't kill you but he will without a second thought."

Clay hacked and gagged until he worked the soggy kernel of popcorn out of his throat and then spit it back at the old man, who showed surprising reflexes by lifting the bag to block the streaking kernel. "I'm not afraid to die, *Ryan*. You know that. They train us that way."

Clay was deadly serious and Ryan did indeed know he was right. "Believe me," Ryan said, "I know. But there are a lot of ways to die. Sometimes the actual dying is not as bad as the manner of death."

"What the hell are you babbling about?"

"You'll find out if you don't talk to me," Ryan warned.

"Fuck you." Clay spat again, but Ryan leaned to the side to avoid the liquid projectile.

Dan frowned when he saw the cool, indifferent expression on his grandson's face transform into a glower of heated rage. And then he almost jumped when Ryan became a blur of movement. He shifted on the floor and his foot shot out to violently kick the bound agent in the chest.

Clay hit the floor back first with a crash and a grunt. Before he could take another breath, Ryan's knee was in his chest and his right hand was crushing the captive's windpipe.

"Spit at *me,* you son of a bitch? You must be out of your fucking mind."

Ryan growled in a low, fearsome tone. His damaged voice lent a menacing timbre to the sound that Dan imagined could only be matched by Satan himself. From the way Clay's eyes bulged, Dan could tell Ryan was really strangling him. Dan guessed the agent was expecting to die quickly, with a bullet to the head or something of that nature. The slow death of strangulation added an element of fearful surprise to his painful expression.

Dan was surprised as well, although he hid it effectively. This was not part of the plan. Ryan had insisted on not killing the agent if it was at all possible. While Dan did not agree, he respected his grandson's oath and did not want to see him break it because of something as trivial as being spit at.

"Looks like you're having trouble with the whole 'not killing' thing," Dan observed. Ryan ignored him so Dan continued. "This is probably what he wants, you know. Dead men can't give up secrets."

Ryan's expression did not change but his grip shifted so that his fingers clutched the sides of Clay's neck instead of his trachea. With one hand he yanked Clay and the chair up and righted them with seemingly no effort. And then as quickly as it appeared, the angry glower faded.

"He tried to spit on me," Ryan shrugged. "I guess he managed to get under my skin."

It was out of character for Ryan to lose control so quickly. He had always been adept at keeping his emotions in check. Dan concluded that the stress of their predicament was finally taking its toll. He was about to say as much when suddenly there was a sharp crackling of static just outside the front door, followed by a muffled boom that caused the building and everything within it to shudder.

A bright shimmer of light streamed under the door and into the room. The noise and light lasted about three seconds and then all went quiet.

"Last chance, Clay."

Clay smiled, clearly unafraid. "Nice special effects, Ryan, but you can save them for an amateur. Do what you're gonna do and get it over with."

"You probably thought you'd die from a gunshot, or a knife wound, or a car accident or something like that, huh?" Ryan rasped with a sly smile. "I'm sure you thought I was about to strangle you to death just now.

"But did you ever think you'd be eaten by a dragon?"

Clay laughed. Loudly. The laugh, however, was cut short when the door leading to the outside creaked, bowed inward, and then flew violently off of its hinges and into the room. Ryan backed away to the far wall. Dan giggled and rolled his chair backwards to the opposite wall.

A cold silence engulfed the room as an icy breeze and pale sunlight poured through the doorway.

A huge, weird shadow materialized in the pool of daylight cast on the floor. At first the shadow engulfed all of the light but then it began to shrink and take shape as its owner moved closer to the doorway. Clay unconsciously held his breath as he watched the shadow define itself. It soon became clear that the creature casting that shadow was not human.

The captive agent resumed his work at the cuffs but the outcome was the same as it had been since they were placed on his wrists. Warm blood ran slowly down onto his palms, over his fingers and dripped into a small puddle of spreading blood on the floor. Clay ignored the pain and blood and worked harder to free himself as the shadow moved closer and closer to the doorway.

A foot-long lizard crept into the room. Clay looked down at the lizard and then looked up at Ryan and Dan. Ryan looked puzzled while Dan smirked. The bound man looked at the lizard again and laughed.

"This is the *dragon*!?" he guffawed. "You've lost it, Axe! Am I supposed to be afraid of –" His laughter stopped short when the little lizard reared up on its hind legs…

And began to grow.

Within seconds the lizard morphed into a huge, squat serpentine monster with massive shoulders that bulged against the ceiling joists of the warehouse. The leathery wings folded tightly against its back ruffled a bit against the straining structural members, causing the building to quake as if from a deep roll of thunder. Its hind legs were splayed, but its weight still buckled the flooring beneath its wicked claws. Dappled sunlight from the cracks and seams of the boarded windows danced on the creature's dark green, glimmering scales.

The beast swung its head down so that its burning gaze was level with the captive's face. Clay stared with bulging eyes. His mouth dropped open and froze in a silent scream. Dan and Ryan heard the legs of his chair tap rapidly against the floor as Clay's whole body shuddered with fear.

"Last chance, laughing boy," Ryan warned.

The beast blew a puff of rancid steam from its nostrils for emphasis. Clay yelped from the intense heat and could feel blisters popping up on his scorched skin. The steam turned to searing liquid when it touched Clay and his face was instantly dripping with foul moisture that smelled of sulfur and rot.

"His name is Johnson," Clay hissed through ragged breaths. The words poured out with panicked speed. "He gave the order to serve you at your apartment and he put me on the Harvey's after the two agents got taken out downstate he's calling me at six tonight at a pay phone outside a grocery store on 79th street the ring sequence is two-one-four I'm supposed to answer the phone and press one if your pink slip was served and two if it wasn't."

"What happens if it wasn't?" Ryan asked.

"They give me further instructions."

A thought from WorldHopper popped into Ryan's head. *He's lying about pressing one or two.*

Ryan shook his head. "I can't believe it," he said. "I'm impressed, though. Even scared three-quarters to death you can still manage to lie. You do realize that dragon in front of you is no hallucination. Now tell me the truth or your next incarnation will be a pile of dragon shit."

To further emphasize the point, WorldHopper opened its mouth wide to display rows and rows of sharp curved teeth. It looked as if it had a mouth full of dripping elephant tusks. The dragon's forked tongue darted out and touched Clay's forehead three times in quick succession, making the man's skin sizzle from the contact.

Clay hesitated in disgust and fear then spoke: "Press 'y' for yes and 'n' for no. That's the truth! I swear it!"

He speaks true. WorldHopper projected.

"Great," Ryan said. "Now –"

He never got a chance to finish his sentence.

Clay's scream lasted only a second as the dragon's mouth snapped shut around his torso and the back of the chair. WorldHopper lifted his head and proceeded to gobble both the man and the chair down with three large, loud bites and a gulp that echoed throughout the room. Dan gasped with surprise and morbid fascination. Ryan bristled.

Unfortunately, he had seen this before.

"What the hell was that?" Ryan yelled. "He told us what we wanted to know!"

"Exactly," WorldHopper acknowledged. "*And then* I ate him. Was I supposed to do it *before* he told you?"

"You weren't supposed to do it at all!" Ryan argued. "This is the strongest lead we've had in three years. First you pop up out of nowhere, uninvited, insisting on helping us. And then you freaking eat our best chance to find the son of a bitch that's trying to kill me!"

"Uninvited?" WorldHopper asked indignantly. "You called me here, foolish Child."

"No the hell I didn't," Ryan countered.

"An hour or so ago you wished I was here," the dragon revealed with a bored tone. "I heard you."

"What?" Ryan said in disbelief. "You heard me think that back at the Harvey's apartment, from across the WorldGate? But how?"

"I am the King of the Dragons," WorldHopper reminded. "I am the closest thing to a god you humans will ever during you earthly lives. Do you have any idea what that entails?"

"I don't care what that entails," Ryan shot back. "I didn't 'wish' you here. I only thought your mind reading would come in handy. And why would the King of the Dragons be at the beck and call of a lowly human, anyway?"

"I was bored in my cave," WorldHopper answered in a disinterested tone. "Your desire for my assistance amused me."

"Since you know so much, you should know that I didn't wish for you to eat that man. But you did it anyway."

"I told you I would feed here in this world when I ferried you from the Kingdom of Lorr three years agone," WorldHopper said. "There is no Treaty of the Dragon here." The dragon's lantern eyes flared in warning. "And you would do well to lower your voice when you speak to me."

"OK," Ryan replied with considerably less volume. "But promise you won't eat anyone else."

"I will not promise that."

Dan chuckled.

"I have an even better idea, then," Ryan said. "How about you just leave us alone? I don't give a damn if you stay in this world or go back to Lorr or even to Mars. As long as you're not hanging around me."

"Are you *telling* me to leave?" WorldHopper snarled, his eyes flickering evilly.

"I'm asking," Ryan answered, being careful to speak in calmer and more even tones. "With all due respect, I would rather not have your company on this endeavor."

The dragon thought for a moment and then said:

"No."

"No?" Ryan echoed. "You mean you're gonna stay with us even though you're not wanted?"

"That is correct," WorldHopper answered. "As surprised as I am to admit it, I'm vaguely interested in your dilemma. I'm going to stay with you two until my amusement passes or until the stench of this world becomes too much to bear."

"OK. That's it," Ryan said. "I'm not asking you anymore. I'm telling you. Leave us. Now."

WorldHopper lowered its reptilian head until its eyes were level with Ryan's and his lower jaw was nearly resting on the floor. The scaled face was motionless and Ryan heard a deep rumbling sound from somewhere in the dragon's long throat. Ryan knew that sound. WorldHopper was gathering its fire.

Even though they had helped each other in the past, this monster still frightened Ryan. How could it not? He just witnessed the King of the Dragons eat another man.

The rumbling grew louder as it made its way closer to the dragon's maw. Ryan visibly flinched as heat, steam and a thunderous roar exploded from WorldHopper's mouth. The steam smelled of methane, sulfur, and decay. Ryan gagged on the fumes and doubled over, expecting flames to engulf him at any second. He remembered when the dragon showered him with flames during their first meeting, he remembered the pain he felt even through his enchanted armor. This time he was not wearing his armor. There was nothing to protect his flesh from the dragon fire.

This time, however, there were no flames. Instead, he entire warehouse shook in time with short bursts of deafening thunder that erupted from the King of the Dragons.

Ryan knew that sound, as well. The dragon was laughing.

"Your defiance is comical," WorldHopper roared. "You thought you were about to be reduced to an odious pile of ash, did you not?"

Ryan's fear turned quickly back into irritation. "I don't want you traveling with us, WorldHopper. Leave us. I'm serious!"

"That is what makes you so comical!" the dragon chuckled sickeningly. "You know there is absolutely nothing you can do to compel me yet you keep giving commands. Any other human would be fodder by now, boy, but you somehow continue entertain me."

"Are you going to leave us or not?" Ryan insisted.

WorldHopper's laughter stopped abruptly. "Of course not," he answered matter-of-factly. "Not until I choose."

"Then promise not to eat people in my presence, at least," Ryan said, almost pleading.

WorldHopper's answer was a guttural harrumph that shot a plume of smoke out of flared, manhole-sized nostrils.

"C'mon, your highness," Dan bade, "that's a gross spectacle for us humans. Our stomachs are a lot weaker than yours. We get queasy a lot faster than dragons."

"True," WorldHopper agreed. There was a thoughtful pause. "Alright, then. Not in your presence. But you will not decide whom I feed upon."

Ryan sighed in unspoken agreement.

"Now that all of that's settled, what's our next move?" Dan asked.

"We need to get to that payphone and answer it." Ryan said. "But there's one problem. The organization's gonna have someone watching that phone. If Clay isn't the one to answer it, and he obviously won't," Ryan cast a sidelong glance at WorldHopper, "they'll be on to us."

"No, they will not." WorldHopper assured. His gigantic form shimmered, shrank and morphed into an exact physical duplicate of Clay. "I do not know why I continue to help you," he said in Clay's voice.

"I didn't know you could take a human form," Ryan said.

"There is much you do not know." WorldHopper-Clay huffed.

"I'll be damned," Dan said. "You never cease to amaze me."

WorldHopper turned to Dan. "I am WorldHopper. It is only natural that you are awed by my presence and power."

"Gimme a break..." Ryan mumbled.

PART II

FOUND

Chapter 6: The Ranger Elf

6.1

A cloaked, hooded figure climbed easily down the ship's rope ladder and dropped silently into the one-passenger rowboat. There were no moons out but the night sky was clear and the stars provided more than enough light for the sharp eyes beneath the cowl. They could clearly see the island shore more than six miles away.

A pair of strong, calloused hands untied the last towline and gripped the shafts of two abnormally long oars with paddles much larger than standard rowboat oars. The oars were actually spare barge oars purchased from the vessel's surly captain. The barge oars would propel the boat much faster than rowboat oars. The price paid for the oars and the rowboat was way too high, but time was of the essence and there was none of it to waste on wrangling.

Of course, the oars and rowboat could have been quietly stolen or taken by force. Either scenario could have taken place without anyone finding out until the morning. But then there would be a search. People would come looking to retrieve their property as well as for revenge…unless the barge was somehow tragically lost at sea. Surely this mission was important enough to justify such drastic measures. In the end, however, the quickest route was the one that went against his frugal nature. It was easier to simply pay the exorbitant prices and have done with it.

It took three strong men to handle one of the oars in the rowing chamber at the bottom of the barge. The dark figure handled two of them as if their size was inconsequential. The rowboat glided smoothly and swiftly across the calm sea surface toward the shore of a small island.

In less than twenty minutes the rowboat was floating nearly fifteen yards from the island shore. The boat's occupant let it drift to a stop. He knew to go no further without taking the proper precautions.

A strong sensitivity to magic easily detected the invisible aura of power surrounding the island. And even without that sensitivity, the danger of trespass here was well known. The wall of magic protecting the island sent a telepathic warning to man and beast alike that any contact on the shore of that island without its master's invitation would be fatal. In fact, the barrier reached high enough into the sky so that even birds had to fly around the island as opposed to flying over it.

The stranger, however, was not without significant magic of his own.

While he knew his trespass would not go undetected, he also knew it would not be fatal. Long, slender fingers reached into the folds of his heavy cloak and came out with a small, polished, dark green marble of stone. The cloaked figure climbed out into the waist-high seawater and waded to within a few feet of the barrier and then tossed the green stone at it.

There was a white flash of light that faded to reveal an oval-shaped, six-foot tall by three-foot wide panel of glowing red energy, the bottom third of which extended down into the water. Knowing the panel would last for only a second, the stranger rushed quickly through the oval, successfully passing through the protective barrier. The red panel blinked away the moment he was safely on the other side.

He moved soundlessly through the water and gained the sandy shore, but before another step could be taken, a constricting force seized his throat as well as all of the muscles in his arms and legs. The force was enough to send just about anyone else to their knees. But the stranger, who was unlike just about anyone else, remained upright even though he could not move. His keen eyes searched the shadows for the expected host and saw nothing but a forest of towering and densely packed ash trees beyond the sand of the beach. The keen ears, however, detected a nearly inaudible whiff of misplaced of air from behind and to his left.

"It takes great magic and even greater gall to come onto my island uninvited," came a deep, menacing voice.

A tall man with tanned, sun leathered skin stepped around in front of him. A heavy cotton tunic hung loosely from his broad shoulders. The hem of the shirt draped over a thick leather belt holding up loose fitting woolen breaches that were tucked into short leather boots. Average sized hands held firmly onto a weathered, crooked wooden staff that was nearly as long as its owner was tall. The staff looked more like a fallen branch than anything carved by hand.

Dark blonde hair hung to his shoulders and was trimmed neatly above light brown eyebrows that were knitted tightly above intense blue eyes. The dangerous look in those eyes belied the otherwise calm expression on his face. The cloaked stranger's sensitivity to magic allowed him to feel the magic radiating from his host. And well he should have, for this was one of the most powerful magic workers in the all of the Known Lands. This was the Head Mage Rionn Lorr, a Child of the Old Ones.

And he was not happy.

"Who are you, and to what do I owe the dishonor of your trespass?" Rionn Lorr demanded calmly. "And have no doubt that I will know if you lie."

"Allow me to remove my cowl," the stranger managed to say despite the unseen pressure on his lungs and growing pain in his throat. It sounded neither like a request nor a demand.

The Head Mage said nothing, but a moment later the invisible force released the stranger's arms. He reached up slowly and pulled back his cowl to reveal sharply slanted eyes of a greenish-brown so pure and intense that their color was easily discernable even in the starlight. Above those eyes, with the same severe slant, were thin, yellow eyebrows. His were the eyes of a hunter. His glare and his angular features gave him the look of an avian predator. Long, pointed ears protruded from light blonde hair that was parted down the middle and pulled to the sides and back where it was twisted into a thick braid that coiled once around his neck and fell over his left shoulder. Rionn recognized the coif as that of an Elven Ranger.

Even with the pain caused by the paralysis spell, the elf managed to mask his suffering with a casual, almost disinterested expression. His fair skin grew even paler and the lack of oxygen was starting to add a blue tint to it. His cheekbones were high and sharp, but his jaw line was square and strong. The thick, taut muscles in his neck were quivering against the force being exerted against it.

Rionn relaxed the invisible grip on the elf's throat just enough for him to take a gulp of air and speak clearly.

"I am Rell Kallen; Ranger captain of the Elf Land's Thâlstrën Kingdom," the stranger offered.

Rionn's eyes narrowed. He walked closer to the Ranger captain, who stood about four inches shorter than Rionn's six feet and two inches, which was tall for an elf of the Thâlstrën Kingdom. Rionn studied him for several seconds.

"I recognize that name."

The corner of the elf's thin lips curved upward slightly. "I thought you might."

"And did you think that recognition would work to your favor?" Rionn asked.

"I thought that a Child of the Old Ones would be above petty jealousy," Rell Kallen said.

"Why have you come upon my island?"

"My queen sent me on a mission of grave importance."

"She would ignore the proper protocol to contact me?"

Rell Kallen's smile faded. "There was no time for protocol. An emissary is travelling here to request counsel with King William, but it was imperative that you be contacted as soon as possible. The sooner we act the better chance we have of stopping the evil that is loosed."

Rionn Lorr studied the elf for a long moment. He walked a slow circle around Rell Kallen, probing him with his eyes and his magic; observing and cataloging every weapon – exposed and hidden – and every talisman; even the short, thin string tucked under his tunic that hung around his neck and supported a small pouch. The imprint was invisible to the human eye, but not to the magic of the Head Mage.

Rionn was determined to continue his inspection until he was satisfied that there would be no surprises. He even decided to utilize one of the many talents that he loathed.

This would mark the second time he had used this particular talent in the last three years, and only the third time he had ever used it. But this elf, this dangerous Ranger Elf, had violated the Head Mage's island with his presence. He did so by using a formidable magic that a Ranger Elf does not usually command. Any possible threat to his wife and daughter would have to be detected and put down by any means available.

Even the Mind's Eye Whisper.

Rionn Lorr's gaze bore deeply into Rell Kallen's eyes. The Ranger Elf tried to look away but he could not. Once the Child of Old One's cold blue eyes locked upon the dark green eyes of the Ranger Elf, arcane energy locked Rell Kallen in an unbreakable link in both mind and body. He could not even lower his eyelids to blink.

The Head Mage stared *into* him more than at him, as if he could look into Rell's very essence. The elf's entire field of vision focused to the blue orbs of Rionn Lorr's irises. So intense was Rell's attention on that glare that his pointed ears almost missed the soft whisper escaping from Rionn's barely-moving lips.

The Ranger Elf, who could hear a grain of pollen settle upon dewy grass at over ten yards, could not make out the words coming from the mouth of a man less than an arm's length away.

The Child of the Old Ones no longer saw Rell Kallen's sharply angled eyes. He saw the elf's mind. But there was something amiss. He was staring into a canvas of shadow when he should have been seeing the soft swirling colors of the first level of the other's consciousness. He should have been hearing the soft murmur of the other's thoughts, but all he heard was the sound of a rushing stream. It was a peaceful sound, a soothing sound. It was a…distracting sound. The Ranger Elf was trying to block him with a strong will and a well-trained mind.

A lesser practitioner than a Child of the Old Ones would have been stayed by such an impressive effort. Rionn Lorr was not deterred.

However, he did not want to risk damaging his subject's mind with too powerful an assault. Instead of brutally forcing aside the obstacle, he breathed a tentative psychic breath to gently waft the darkness and sound away. But the breath merely caused the shadows to stir and turned the soft trickling flow of water into a brief splash.

The Head Mage was impressed but undaunted. He reached deeper into his being and brought more of his magic to bear, gathering it into a thin stream and channeling it through his appendages and into his right hand. In moments his staff began to vibrate. The movement quickly built up until the vibration became a deep, audible thrum. Using the staff to focus and augment his magic, he blew a measured psychic gale into Rell Kallen's mind.

The trickling sound turned into the crashing of waves. The mental shadows began to tremor in time with the thrumming of the staff. The shadows parted and broke away, revealing a vision of a quaking stream cutting through a meadow blanketed with thick, dark green grass. If it had been still, Rionn knew the vision would have been beautiful. As it was, it appeared to be a meadow caught in an earthquake.

The water began to roil. Large clumps of earth broke away from the banks of the stream and sloshed into the water. Grass and black dirt slid down into the stream and churned it to mud. Roots shrugged out of the soil and the quaking grew ever stronger.

In the next moment, the vision shook so violently that it agitated into a blur of greens, blues, and browns. The thrum of the magic became an extended roll of thunder that built up and built up until it became a deafening explosion that blasted the blur of colors into whiteness. It finally softened into the familiar slow swirl of rainbow hues. Rionn pulled back quickly and quieted the droning staff. When he peered into the Ranger Elf's mind again, the sound of dashing water faded and turned into the expected murmuring of conscious and subconscious thoughts. Rionn Lorr was relieved to find Rell Kallen's mind undamaged.

He was doubly relieved to find it far less disturbing than the last two minds he had entered. The seasoned warrior elf had seen more than his share of violence and death, but Rionn did not feel the sickening excitement that was evident in the mind of the captured High Captain of the Legion Midnight two years ago. Nor did he feel the disturbing erotic satisfaction that he felt in the mind of the mad Wizard Drake when Rionn had performed the Mind's Eye Whisper on him several years earlier in his efforts to curtail the start of a second Dragon War. The Legion Midnight's High Captain and the Wizard Drake stood witness to – and performed – atrocities that not even Rionn Lorr had seen firsthand in his years as Head Mage.

That was one of the many reasons he so hated to use the Mind's Eye Whisper. The spell was not only a spell of telepathy, but also empathy. He experienced the emotions his subjects' memories evoked within them. To make matters worse, he could not go directly to the targeted thoughts or memories. He had to search for them, which meant he had to sift through disturbing thoughts, memories and emotions that would revisit him in his nightmares for years to come.

Another reason he despised the spell was because he was vulnerable, as well. While using the Mind's Eye Whisper, his subject had as much access to his mind as he had to theirs. Often times he had experienced the emotions of awe and sinister curiosity that his surface thoughts and memories stirred within his subjects. Very few people, thankfully, had the knowledge, talent and sheer magical power to conduct any kind of directed search of his mind or to inflict any kind of assault against him.

Fortunately for Rionn, Rell Kallen did not have that kind of ability, either. In addition, the Ranger Elf was as repulsed by his own more violent memories as Rionn. As a result, Rionn did not have to endure the sickening recollections of sadistic pleasure that his other subjects had felt when they committed their heinous acts.

Rionn finally found what he was looking for: the events that led to the Ranger Elf's visit to the Island of Cartha.

Through Rell Kallen's eyes he saw the beautiful Elf Queen, so similar to his wife yet so different. She was nearly two centuries older than Catherine but only the slightest hint of shadow beneath her brilliant emerald eyes belied their age difference. Where Catherine's skin was fair, her grandmother's was almost pure white and flawless, like porcelain. The points of her ears, as well as her pencil-thin eyebrows, stood higher and sharper than those of her half-elf granddaughter.

The memory Rionn came upon was that of the Elf Queen telling Rell Kallen about the distressing news concerning the future of the Known Lands. She spoke to him of the Banners of Omniscience and their Readers' warnings. And then she sent Rell Kallen to find the Head Mage and beseech him for his help.

Satisfied, Rionn Lorr quickly ceased his scanning of Rell Kallen's mind. He could have stayed in longer and learned more, but he did not enjoy using the Mind's Eye Whisper. Whenever he did, he felt like a mental rapist. He realized he was violating the mind of whom he read and it felt like a horrible misuse of his abilities. Of all of his powers, that one frightened him the most. It was potentially the most seductive if he allowed it to be, it was potentially the most corrupting, and it was potentially the most dangerous to him, as well.

Rionn pulled out of the other's mind carefully and then expertly erased all traces of his presence. To Rell, it seemed as if only a second or two had passed, but the new positioning of the stars overhead quickly told the elf that nearly half an hour had gone by. He had no recollection of what had been done to him but he had a fairly good idea. He knew what *he* would have done if he was in the Head Mage's position and in possession of that kind of power.

"I hope you found what you were looking for, mage," Rell growled. "I do not appreciate intrusions into my mind."

"And I do not appreciate intrusions onto my island," Rionn returned.

"Do not think that we are even," Rell warned.

"By no means," Rionn agreed. "You trespass on the private land of the Head Mage of the Kingdom of Lorr, not a mere trickster or petty magic worker. Your transgression was greater by far."

Rionn Lorr turned and stalked away into the shadows, finally releasing the paralysis spell. The Ranger Elf glowered at Rionn's back for a few seconds warily followed him back to his cabin.

"I knew you would immediately detect my intrusion," Rell Kallen called ahead as he gained on Rionn Lorr. "But I did not think you quick enough to be fully dressed and waiting for me the moment I crossed your barrier."

"Did you think I would not be aware of your presence until you stepped foot on my beach?" Rionn asked. "I knew you were approaching the moment your rowboat splashed into the Sea of Spirits. I am a Child of the Old Ones, Ranger Rell Kallen. Do not underestimate me."

"I'll make it a point not to," Rell mumbled under his breath, knowing full well that Rionn Lorr could hear him.

6.2

A brisk ten-minute walk through the forest brought them to the log cabin that was home to the Lorr family. Catherine, dressed in a soft cotton nightgown and long wool robe, was waiting in the small sitting room that faced the front door to the modest dwelling. Her concerned expression deepened into worry when she saw the look on her husband's face as he trudged through the door. When she saw who entered behind him, she understood Rionn's appearance.

Rell Kallen found her eyes the instant he stepped into the room. A wide smile spread across his face.

"Ah," he said, performing an elegant bow, "The lovely Catherine Eleshaë. As impossible as it seems, you are even more beautiful than when you were my betrothed."

"Catherine Eleshaë *Lorr"* Catherine replied coolly. "I was never your betrothed."

"This home is comfortable, surely," Rell went on, "but it is rather lacking in the proper adornments for the granddaughter of a Queen."

Catherine's only answer was a dagger-like stare, so the Ranger Elf continued with a sly half-smile.

"You cannot deny, Catherine Eleshaë, that you were fond of me at one time. How did you come to think so ill of me that you would shame your family, turn your back on your people, and flee to this land of humans?"

"I will correct you on several counts," Catherine returned. "I have as much human blood in my veins as elven. And while your inflated ego may make this difficult for you to believe, know that my departure from Thâlstrën had nothing at all to do with you.

"My love for Rionn Lorr decided me. But because of Thâlstrën's archaic customs of pre-arranged marriages, banishment of any elf that dares to love someone outside of their race, and the murder of any outsider that dares to love an elf within the Elf Lands, I was of a mind to leave even before I met him."

"Execution, Catherine Eleshaë," Rell corrected, "not murder. The difference between the two is vast."

"My name is Catherine Eleshaë *Lorr,*" she repeated in a tone and with a smoldering glare that warned him not to make the same mistake a third time. "The difference lies only within one's perception."

Both Rell and Rionn could see Catherine's fury build as she spoke. Her fair skin flushed and her canted eyes narrowed. "What was done to my parents is unforgivable, and will always be perceived by me as murder."

Catherine's sweet and compassionate demeanor turned to cold anger whenever she recalled how her human father, the son of a wealthy baron on a trading expedition, was sentenced to death for consorting with her mother, an elven princess, and how her mother had chosen to die with her love rather than be banished from the Elf Lands without him. Had her mother not been a princess, Catherine would have been left in her mother's womb to die with her. But the Queen could not bear the thought of losing a granddaughter, even a half-human granddaughter.

Rionn half-believed his normally peaceful wife might strike out at the Ranger Elf, but she maintained her composure when she was done. She turned and walked to the door leading into the short main hallway. Even in her thick robe, her elegant form could be seen in the soft sway of curved hips and the smooth, regal oscillation of her slender shoulders. She paused at the open door and looked over her shoulder at Rionn.

"Make your business quick," she requested. "I do not want this one in my home any longer than necessary." She left the room and closed the door behind her.

Rell Kallen turned his half-smile to Rionn Lorr. "That one has fire. I loved that about her…as I'm sure you do."

Rionn was growing tired of the elf's attempts to rile them yet he kept is irritation from showing on his face. "I agree with my wife about the length of your stay, so have a seat and tell me why Queen Le'Elonda sent you."

The Ranger Elf sat down on a wooden bench set against a wall and looked up at the Head Mage. "As you know," he began, "The Old Ones entrusted the elves, their *first* people, with many of their talismans and tools when they realized that war was on the horizon. They hid the others in different places all over the earth. Some of the other races have uncovered some of these over the years, but no other people besides the elves were *directly* entrusted with any of Their possessions –"

"These are things of which I am already aware," Rionn hastened.

"Among those things entrusted to my predecessors were the Banners of Omniscience. Are you familiar with them?"

"I've read of them," Rionn answered. "They are thousands of small flags, standards less than a foot tall, in a room with no doors or open windows to the outside, where the air is never disturbed by exterior forces. They are placed in a pattern that represents the five continents of the earth, both the Known and Unknown Lands. They detect the dispersal of magical energy anywhere on this sphere and display it by ruffling in the room without moving air. Seven elves are always watching the flags through sealed glass portholes around the walls. They interpret the ruffling standards to know whenever and wherever magic is used anywhere on our earth sphere."

"No matter how miniscule, no matter how great," Rell Kallen concluded. "The Banner Readers have special magic and are trained for over two human lifetimes to learn how to read the Banners. They can determine how great a threat a certain use of magic might pose. They can see patterns forming in the use of magic to accurately predict the end result."

Rionn was genuinely intrigued. "And what have they seen that has your Queen so interested that she would involve herself in human affairs?"

"A magic so subtle that even our best readers almost missed it, and then nearly misread it," Rell Kallen revealed. "It was an old magic, an evil magic. It was magic of a like not seen since Heaven's War."

"Demon magic," Rionn breathed. "But what do you mean 'not seen since Heaven's War?' What about the Cursed Opening? That was demon magic."

"Yes," Rell agreed. "And an ill wind blew through the Banners of Omniscience indeed. But that magic was easy to detect and identify. This more recent demon magic that they discovered was veiled. They discovered it over a year ago and it took them from then until now to trace it back to its origin and make a confident prediction of the potential end."

"The Banners of Omniscience are a magic handed down directly from the Old Ones," Rionn noted. "It would take a being of enormous power and knowledge and cunning to veil its magic so effectively. It would take the magic of demons bred to stand directly against the First Generation of Children, who were only slightly less powerful than the Old Ones Themselves…demons that not even Mar-dah was foolish enough to set free."

The Ranger Elf nodded in affirmation.

Rionn Lorr thought for a moment and then shook his head. "But how could the demon escape the detection of Sollustre's Eye? We monitor it with the same diligence as your Readers monitor the Banners of Omniscience. I have hand picked wizards taking shifts so that the Eye never goes unobserved. Could the demon be *that* powerful?"

"The magic is that of a sixth level demon," Rell Kallen elucidated. "If there is a way to avoid the gaze of Sollustre's Eye, such a demon can find it. But alas, that is not the whole of it."

Rionn frowned. "What is, then?"

"If the loosed demon manages to acquire the Hell Key," Rell warned, "you will not be able to banish Mar-dah's soul to hell. And worse, a sixth level demon would have the might and knowledge to invoke a spell of reincarnation."

Rionn had Mar-dah's body packed in salt and encased in an iron coffin almost one hundred feet underground in the all-but-forgotten bowels of the royal dungeons. The iron and salt, as well as the spells and enchanted runes put in place by the Head Mage, could hold Mar-dah's soul captive for years, but not indefinitely. If the demon could somehow free that soul and successfully reincarnate the evil Child, Mar-dah would be more powerful than he ever was in life and enthralled to the demon that brought him back. He would no longer be bound by the myriad limitations of the flesh.

"He would not be a mere demon," Rionn said aloud, his brow creased with dread. He knew that a demon was a once-earthly creature – or combination of once-earthly creatures – imbued with enough divine essence to fortify it to varying degrees. A demon could also be a once-earthly soul without the additive of a divine essence that was touched by the taint of hell and yet managed to escape.

Mar-dah's divine essence was not something imparted to him that could be stripped away. He was a Child of the Old Ones, so it was an inseparable part of his being. If reincarnated, he would not fall into either category that would mark him a demon.

"So not even Demonsbane would be able to send him to hell," Rionn whispered.

"Yes," Rell Kallen added darkly. "And the Hell Key would be unable banish his soul. It can send an earthly soul to hell or release demons. A reincarnated soul, however, would not be affected by its magic. It would take nothing short of an Old One to banish such a power."

"And that power would be under the command of a sixth level demon," Rionn's voice would have been inaudible to all save one with the sharp hearing of an elf. "As if such a creature is not fierce enough on its own. That would be a fate exceedingly worse than Mar-dah could ever have wrought in his natural life."

"You see the urgency, now, Head Mage?" Rell Kallen asked. "The Banner Readers have seen this potential."

"We must find the demon," Rionn declared. "The demon is a bigger threat than the Hell Key."

Rell nodded. "That is true, but it will not be as difficult to locate the Key as it would be to locate and destroy the demon. If it is indeed scheming to resurrect Mar-dah, at least we can foil that much."

"But what other chaos might the monster bring about in the meantime?" Rionn asked. "How can we not pursue it?"

"You may do as you wish, but the Queen has deemed finding the Key my priority. It has been determined by the

Banner Readers that without my help, the Key cannot be found. But by the same token, I cannot find the Key without your help, not in a timely fashion, at least. And besides, there is one more thing that will make finding the demon nearly impossible."

Rionn's frown deepened. "And what would that be?"

"The Banner Readers were able to uncover signs of another magic that, until the Cursed Opening, had not been seen since the Old Ones lived. They saw that it was employed frequently, even after the offworlder departed."

Rionn already knew. This was a sixth level demon, after all. He sighed a defeated sigh.

"It can cross the WorldGate."

"At will, Head Mage. It can cross the WorldGate at will."

6.3

The wizard Goran opened his eyes to pitch-blackness. He knew he was in the forest because he could smell the pine and the damp grass beneath his feet. However, no moonlight or starlight could penetrate the darkness to reveal which forest surrounded him. He also knew he was near an ocean. The unmistakable scent of seawater permeated the chill humid air and he could taste salt on the breeze. He could hear the soft lapping of waves – which was the only sound he heard because no nocturnal creature, be it animal or insect, dared to come close enough to be heard. This last fact made him certain of what creature was acting as his host.

The darkness and silence unnerved him the first time he came to this place. His initial thought was that his host had struck him deaf and blind before his ears finally adjusted enough to hear the ocean and his eyes enough to see shifting shadows in the darkness. That was when he realized that a concealment spell had been cast upon him in addition to the teleportation spell that brought him to this place. Once that realization set in, all he could do then was what he was doing now: wait.

An undeterminable amount of time passed and the wizard, as always, began to lose patience. His host was watching, the wizard knew. He could not sense the other with any of his physical or magical senses but he knew – in the same way a prey animal knew it was being watched by a predator that it could not see, hear, or smell. He should have been used to this by now but he had far more important things to do than just stand around in the darkness.

His host, the wizard knew, could not possibly care less about his impatience. His host had the patience of eternity and delighted in the discomfort of others. It was for this reason that the wizard tried not to demonstrate his impatience. There would be no fidgeting or sighing or any other outward manifestation of his frustration. He did not want to give his host the satisfaction. Though it was getting more and more difficult to suppress his displeasure.

"Temper, temper, wizard Goran," came the deep, sinister voice.

It was barely a whisper, but the suddenness of it caused the wizard to start – as he always did – even though he knew it would eventually come. He tried without success to pinpoint the direction from whence the voice came. The sound seemed to come from every direction in the darkness. The wizard concluded that this time, like all of the other times, the voice was not coming from any nearby external source. His host was speaking directly into his mind.

"You have brought me here yet again, my master," the wizard said softly. "What is your wish?"

His master was silent for a time. The shifting shadows went still, leaving the wizard in complete blackness. He cringed involuntarily when a soft, but blistering hot gust of air struck his neck just below his ear. Even though the air burned his neck, it sent an almost painful chill through the rest of his body.

"Competence, Goran," his master answered. This time the baritone rumble echoed in his right ear as if it floated there from the bowels of a deep, dark well. "I wish for competence among my charges. Is that too much to ask?"

"If you are alluding to the trouble at the meadow in Darshay," Goran began, "The spell was ultimately cast."

"Just barely," came the menacing voice, its deep tone reverberating on Goran's eardrums. "Had the Keeper's Hounds arrived any earlier, the spell would not have been completed. And the beast was not whole, as is required for the spell to achieve full power. It was damaged by the intruders."

The wizard Goran scoffed. "A couple of arrow nicks on its tough hide would not have had a significant – "

"QUIET!" the host roared with a blast of searing air that drove Goran to his knees. "The beast was NOT WHOLE! Your incompetence has caused a delay in the effects of the spell!"

All was silent again, but Goran knew his host was still there. He could sense the contemplative nature of the silence, this time. Either through the instinct of a cornered victim, or perhaps through an intentional projection of his host's will, Goran was certain that his fate was being decided in that ominous silence.

"We have a very specific *agreement*, Goran," his host finally said. "Break it at your peril."

"I apologize, master," Goran said, staring anxiously up into the darkness. "I will do a better job of fulfilling my part of our arrangement."

"See that you do, *human*," the host warned. "You are all so utterly fallible. It sickens me that I must depend upon your kind in this endeavor."

"What is it you would have me do, master?"

"Retrieve the heart and take it to the Ken," the host commanded. "The bearer and his elder have made themselves known to me. It is very likely that they will be here soon, and possibly with the *Other*."

"The *Other*? So he has survived the test?"

"The first one, yes," the host confirmed. "The next test is forthcoming. If he survives it, he may come or he may not. Either way, the Ken will use the heart to bring low the rest. The *Other* is to be held for me. The rest are to die."

"And what of the red one?" Goran asked.

"He is no longer your concern. Shara Dune will serve as his handler henceforth. You can no longer properly motivate him. He is too stupid to fear you and he believes he is too wealthy now to be swayed by the promise of currency. Shara will be able to appeal to his baser human appetites. She will make a trade with him to ensure his continued assistance."

"I would think he's wealthy enough to purchase women of his own," Goran said.

"Ah, but Shara employs some of the most exotic women in the Known Lands. The red one will want something he has never had, and the sand queen will provide it. But enough of that business. Attend to your own. You have your orders."

Before Goran could say another word, the blackness that surrounded him was violently swept away and the wizard Goran was back in his quarters.

The starlight filtered through the slit in his curtains, but dressed in his black cloak with the large hood pulled up, he was still nearly invisible in the shadows of his bedchamber. Beneath his thick cloak and heavy black robes, the wizard trembled in fear. He knew his host would be upset about the intrusion of the Keeper's Hounds and wondered how close he had actually come to dying.

Great care would have to be taken to complete his remaining tasks flawlessly. That was a necessary part of his own master plan. Besides, it was beyond dangerous to break a pact with a demon.

6.4

Dan and Ryan arrived at a bar on the opposite end of the block from the payphone where agent Clay was supposed to receive his phone call. WorldHopper was supposed to meet them there. Just after the interrogation and feeding at the warehouse, the dragon disappeared to God-knows-where and promised to meet them here at this time.

The plan was to arrive a few hours early and wait, to try to spot the surveillance team that would be watching the false Clay. *If he ever gets here*, Ryan thought as he checked his watch for the fifth time.

"You know what's funny, gramps?" Ryan began, trying to distract himself. "With all of the advanced technology the organization has, it's still old fashioned in one sense: they trust landline phones more than cells."

Dan nodded his understanding. "They can physically control and secure landlines easier than they can signals floating in the air."

"Yeah," Ryan agreed. "They've got access to some of the best signal encryption, but I guess none of that is completely hack-proof. I know a guy who could crack any kind of encryption if he put his mind to it."

"You talking about that Cutter you used to work with?" Dan asked. "That Dr. James guy?"

"How do you know –" He stopped when noticed his grandfather tapping his temple, reminding Ryan yet again of his ability to read his grandson's mind. Ryan shook his head. "I am so glad I can block you now."

"So what are thinking right this moment?" Dan asked. "I notice you *are* blocking me right now."

"I'm wondering if WorldHopper can pull this off."

"Of course he can," Dan assured. "He probably downloaded that guy's entire memory before he…" Dan paused at the unpleasant recollection. "Anyway, I wonder where he is now."

"I don't wanna know," Ryan said. "I just wish he'd hurry up and get here."

It was dark out, but the workday had only just ended and the bar was not yet crowded. Ryan scanned the surrounding people, those inside the heated establishment with him along with those on the outside bundled against the cold and stooped against the strong, icy, Chicago wind.

He wondered what form the dragon would take as he discreetly studied the men and the women. He doubted WorldHopper would mimic a woman, but then again, how could he be sure? The dragon's bearing and his ego were distinctly male, at least by human standards, so Ryan and his grandfather assumed the dragon was male. The truth was neither of them had ever asked.

"Yeah," Dan said out of the blue. "I've wondered about that, too. Should we ask him to lift his leg for us?"

Ryan was taken aback. He had grown so accustomed to blocking his thoughts that he did it almost subconsciously. The fact that his grandfather was in his head again meant that he was so distracted thinking about the dragon that he allowed his shield to weaken.

"Are you always listening?" Ryan demanded. "Always waiting for me to slip? That's really irritating, you know."

"When you're far away I have to make a conscious effort to reach out to you," Dan admitted. "But when we're this close, yes, I'm always listening." His tone was not defiant or flippant but reassuring. "I don't care if you slip or not. Hell, I had even gotten used to the mental silence over the last few years. It's not an intentional thing, though. I listen with my mind the way I listen with my ears."

"I'll keep that in mind," Ryan said as he put his mental shields back up and resumed his monitoring of the patrons in the bar and the passerby outside. "Anyway," the grandson continued, "we might not be able to tell even if WorldHopper did lift his leg for us. For all we know his dragon-thing might be retractable, or her dragon-thing might be hidden by scales. Shit, he could have both."

"Now that's just nasty," Dan scolded with a smirk.

Just then Ryan saw a huge black man walking down the sidewalk. He immediately thought about another teammate from his Cutter days, only that teammate was not as broad and muscle-bound as the man coming toward the tavern. The approaching man wore a tight-fitting black t-shirt with dark, baggy blue jeans and black low-top running shoes; no coat, no jacket, no sweater.

At first Ryan thought the man was a professional football player. That had to be why he looked so familiar. But when he focused more he realized it was not the face that drew his attention. It was the intensity of the eyes. It was the man's confident, arrogant bearing. He stared boldly, almost challengingly, at passing strangers. He was as oblivious to the cold as he was to the irritated and frightened glances he received in return as the passerby gave him a wide berth. It was as if the hulking brute was sizing them up for something sinister, appraising them the way a lion would a young doe.

Ryan tapped his grandfather's shoulder and pointed his chin at the near giant.

"What do think?" Ryan asked.

"Oh, yeah," Dan nodded. "That's him. I can feel his magic from here."

Ryan turned to his grandfather. "How can you feel it? What does it feel like?"

"It's different for different people," Dan told him. "I feel it in waves, like a soft breeze that's usually neither cold nor warm. You probably could, too, if you made a conscious effort and knew what to look for."

Ryan was wondering what he should look for when his attention was drawn to the door of the tavern. Two men were stepping out of the bar when the dark giant filled the doorway. The two men, who were pretty sizable themselves, stepped back quickly and allowed the stranger to enter. He immediately turned in Dan and Ryan's direction.

"We have time to kill," he said in a deep, menacing voice as he passed, never bothering to look at either of them. "I wish to have a drink."

"You could have been a little less conspicuous," Ryan mumbled nearly inaudibly, barely moved his lips, knowing WorldHopper would hear him. He rolled his grandfather in the dragon's wake.

"I like this form, as human forms go," WorldHopper said. "It fits a being of my stature and power."

"And ego," Ryan added.

"Yes," WorldHopper agreed.

He strode to the bar, which had no empty stools, and stood behind a man that looked almost as large as he. The heavy, fair skinned, ruddy-haired patron sipped from a mug of beer and watched the sports news displayed on the ceiling-mounted television at the end of the bar. He saw the weird stranger in the mirror wall behind the bar and out of the corner of his eye but ignored him.

"I wish to sit here," WorldHopper warned.

"I'll be done in a minute," the patron said. He glanced at the half full mug and shrugged. "Maybe two."

"Maybe now," WorldHopper declared. He laid a thick, heavy hand on the patron's shoulder and squeezed. The resulting crunching sound caused the surrounding customers to start with surprise. The unfortunate patron screamed and clutched at WorldHopper's unmoving hand. With a quick flick of his massive forearm, the changeling dragon sent the man sailing into the far corner of the room.

"Here we go," Ryan said, rolling his eyes.

"WorldHopper," Dan said quickly. "Maybe we should –"

"Drink," WorldHopper said, taking his seat. "Barkeep! Two pitchers of ale: one blonde and one stout!"

The bartender, who looked like a shorter, fatter, goateed version of WorldHopper's current form, walked cautiously over to the newcomer.

"I can't serve you, man," he said, making a nearly convincing attempt to hide his nervousness. "I'm gonna have to ask you to leave. I can't have people coming in here assaulting our regular customers."

WorldHopper's big hand shot out and wrapped around the bartender's neck and yanked him halfway over the bar.

"I will not ask again," he growled impatiently before flicking the bartender to the floor behind the bar.

The bartender popped up a moment later holding a sawed-off shotgun. "Neither will I, motherfucker," he growled in return.

WorldHopper popped to his feet so quickly that it startled the bartender, who unintentionally pulled the trigger and blasted WorldHopper several yards across the tavern and to the floor.

"Let's go, gramps," Ryan whispered beneath startled shouts and frightened screams. He maneuvered the wheelchair quickly among the customers fleeing and around those that were frozen with fear or morbid curiosity.

Ryan did not want to look back but did in spite of himself when another round of loud, fearful screams tore through the tavern. He saw the bartender's eyes widen in confused terror as WorldHopper rose to his feet with a gaping bloody hole in his stomach. Ryan saw WorldHopper's face reflected in the mirror behind the bar and gasped.

The wide, blue-black face was split with an evil grin that spread literally – and hideously – from ear to ear, revealing a jagged mess of pointed yellow teeth. His eyes shone with a yellow glow that bounced little pinpoints of searing light off of the mirror.

"Now I'm thirsty *and* hungry," WorldHopper rumbled.

"Damn dragon," Ryan swore as he hurried himself and his grandfather out into the cold.

He rolled Dan down to the middle of the block and turned into the dark shadows between buildings. Screams, thundering shotgun blasts, and pistol fire rang out into the night for what seemed to Ryan like hours. Glass shattered and the sound of snapping wood boomed almost as loud as the gunfire. It felt weird to Ryan, being this close to a fight without being in the middle of it. He did not miss it by any means. It was just strange. When the noise finally and suddenly quieted, he checked his watch and saw that less than five minutes had passed since he checked it last. The critical phone call they came for was only minutes away.

"I'm as close as I've been in three years and he's gonna blow it," Ryan complained. "I can't believe that sadistic son of a bitch."

"You can't believe it?" Dan asked incredulously. "What? Are you just meeting him or something? This is what he does. You shouldn't have wished him here."

Ryan sighed in exasperation and stared out at the street. He and Dan watched panicked men and women sprint past. The night was alive with the sounds of traffic and the fearful exclamations and the countless footfalls crunching against the ice as the last of the bar patrons streamed out into the street. Even that noise seemed eerily quiet compared to the clamor of the riot that had taken place just moments earlier.

"I guess he's finished," Ryan said sarcastically.

"Yes, I am," resonated WorldHopper's baritone voice.

Ryan and Dan turned to see agent Clay standing there wearing a smug, sinister grin.

"The two of you stay here while I go await the call," WorldHopper ordered. "There are men on the rooftops all around watching the telephone. You only just beat them here. They did not notice you among the rush of fleeing patrons and they cannot see you now from their vantage points. They will wait another half hour after I leave. I suggest you wait another ten before you do the same."

Ryan gave WorldHopper a sidelong glance. "So you did all that to create a diversion for us?"

"No," he answered, this time in Clay's voice. He licked a spot of blood away from his lips and strode away.

Chapter 7: What Is Magic?

7.1

Rionn Lorr's brow was set low in an annoyed grimace as he rode Ebony westward along the northern edge of Glennshire Forest. Catherine rode by his side on her stallion Speck, so named because of his mottled coat. The beaches were hours behind them back east. Straight ahead they could see the jagged peaks of the Wyrm Mountains disappearing into a low ceiling of cloud.

They could look to the right and see where, less than a mile to the north, the earth dropped abruptly away. That was the area called the Hallowed Fall, where cliffs over a half-mile high leaned protectively outward over the Sea of Spirits. Further to north they could see the shimmering blue edge of the Sea of Spirits just before it curved over the horizon. Many a time he and his wife had dined beneath the beautiful skies at the Hallowed Fall. The view of the vast sea from those arcing cliffs was one of the most beautiful in the Known Lands. But not even the memory of that breathtaking view could ease his mood.

This distraction was the last thing he needed. While making hasty but careful preparations to deal with the menace revealed to him by the Ranger Elf Rell Kallen, a messenger had come to him with a disturbing message that fishermen off the coast of the Ocean Crystalline had found the remains of a sea creature the likes of which they had never seen. Ordinarily that would not have been a matter of any real significance to the Head Mage. He knew there were all manner of sea creatures that were rarely if ever seen by men. It would not be alarming in the least if one of them washed ashore from time to time. But then the messenger relayed the description of the creature.

He said it was an ovoid creature nearly twice the size of a Royal barge. It resembled a large hill of coral. Its coral-like skin was hard, rough, and craggy and covered sporadically with sprouting growths that appeared to be seaweed.

It was a multi-tentacled creature with vine-like tentacles that varied in size. Some were as thin as a needle and others as broad as tree trunks, and many of them had small openings on their tips that looked like mouths.

From the messenger's description of the creature, Rionn recognized it as a Phillosith. As he understood it, those creatures could live for thousands of years and there were precious few of them in existence. Very few humans had ever laid eyes on one, and as far as he knew, no one had ever seen a dead one. A Phillosith rarely if ever came close enough to land to be washed ashore after death. When they died, they usually settled to the bottom of the ocean, where the corpse would feed a multitude of sea creatures for many months.

As a youngster, Rionn was taught that the death of such a rare and ancient creature could sometimes be a portent of great change in the world. It could sometimes mean that some kind of shift in nature had taken place, such as a change of temperature in the atmosphere or seas, or something else so dramatic that it disturbed the creature's habitat to the point that the creature could not survive. A natural occurrence of that sort was sure to eventually affect humans as well.

Such a death could also be a sign of something much more sinister. Rionn had been taught that the death of such a creature could sometimes be a portent of a great change in the balance of magic. That knowledge, coupled with the dire news delivered by the Ranger Elf the night before, compelled Rionn to make the half-day's journey to the Great Lake Onyx...if for no other reason than to ease his paranoia.

The company of his wife made the trip easier and more awkward at the same time. It was easier because her presence made everything more enjoyable for him. Even the most trying and taxing situations were much more bearable when she was at his side. The trip was made more awkward, however, because of whom he was going to see.

Sabrina, the Mistress of the Sea.

Many years ago, when Catherine was but an intriguing acquaintance to Rionn but not yet his betrothed, Sabrina had made an insistent attempt to seduce him. Her mesmerizing beauty, along with her magic of beguilement, almost won her success. In the end, though, Rionn Lorr resisted her advances. He was not the lustful young rogue that so many of his peers were at the time. Instead, he was a wistful romantic that wanted one devoted woman more than he desired a series of passionate dalliances. He knew that Sabrina, an aloof and mysterious elemental that preferred the company of sea creatures to the company of humans, would never have accepted the kind of relationship that he would insist upon.

Catherine interested him more. He pursued the beautiful half-elf instead of accepting the generous offers made by the stunning Mistress of the Sea. Sabrina, however, made no secret of her desires. Rionn's friends envied him so of course they teased him viciously when they discovered that he had turned down the Mistress of the Sea. Catherine was immensely flattered, and not only because he chose her over the exotic elemental. She was also impressed that the young, newly ascended Head Mage had the strength of will to resist Sabrina's beguiling magic.

And she had mistrusted Sabrina ever since. So much so that when Catherine learned Rionn was planning to visit Lake Onyx, she insisted upon traveling with him. Rionn Lorr was no fool. He never even thought about protesting.

When they finally reached the North Bountiful River they turned their horses south, traveling parallel to the river as it flowed toward Lake Onyx. They had been riding since sunrise and it was near dusk when they reached the North Bountiful. If they rode through the night they would be there by sunrise, but more likely they would bed down for the night in a few hours and resume the trip at sun up.

Rionn wanted to hurry. He wanted to take care of this business and return to the palace as soon as possible to continue overseeing the preparations for the coming crisis. Catherine, however, did not think that they should be in so much of a hurry that they should tax their horses. When he protested, she reminded him that he had left explicit instructions to his master mages and the king's advisors because he trusted them to carry out his wishes.

With their diligent assistance, the time it would take to complete those tasks would take the same amount of time whether he was there or not. And besides, she wanted both of them to be well rested and alert for their audience with the Mistress, not distracted from the weariness of a rushed trip.

As they rode south, when only the crown of the highest sun peeked over the Wyrm Mountains, the two of them caught site of bubbling water out on the river. The spot began to stir more intensely as the seconds passed until it swirled into a small funnel that rose several feet above the surface of the agitated water. Catherine and Rionn reined their horses to a halt when the funnel began to move toward the shore in their direction.

The swirling cone of water came to a stop few feet away from the muddy bank and fell back into the river. In its place, standing atop the gentle waves as if they were solid earth, was a beautiful, long-limbed woman with a bronzed skin tone with just a hint of sea green.

She had aquamarine colored hair that shimmered and undulated in the air. It changed colors subtly as it flowed around her. From foam white to coral brown to azure to pale green, in random patterns, the colors flowed like liquid. So smooth were the transitions, in fact, that it was hard to tell exactly when the change took place, much like the large eyes that beheld the Head Mage and his wife. The effect was soothing, almost mesmerizing for anyone who gazed at her. That, along with her staggering beauty and elegant, voluptuous shape, was enough to bewitch any man and provoke jealous ire in any woman.

"Sabrina," Catherine said as warmly as she could manage.

Rionn Lorr nodded his greeting. "You were expecting us?"

"Yes," answered Sabrina, Mistress of the Sea of Spirits, in a soft and almost musical voice.

Rionn used to wonder why, as the Mistress of the Sea of Spirits, she chose to spend most of her time at Lake Onyx. He had asked her that very question years ago.

She told him that she could travel from the Sea of Spirits north of the kingdom to the Ascendant's Heart Sea to the West, all the way to the Ocean Crystalline to the southeast.

She could travel the Known Lands by the network of rivers that cut through the continents. The harsh climates and treacherous magic that separated the Known and Unknown Lands, however, were too much for even her. As a result, she had not visited the Unknown Lands since the end of Heaven's War. She preferred Lake Onyx because its waters were among the warmest and the calmest.

Humans, she explained, came up with the title of Mistress of the Sea of Spirits. It was not a title she had given to herself. The reason for the title was unknown to her. She was the protector of all of the seas and lakes and waterways of the Known Lands and simply called herself Sabrina.

"How did you know we were coming to see you?" Rionn asked.

"It is common knowledge," she said in a matter-of-fact tone.

"We told only a few that we were leaving, and we told no one of our destination," Catherine said.

"Ah, but the sea gulls spied you on your trek, even heard a little of your conversations," Sabrina revealed. "I heard them speaking of it as they hunted and drank from my waters. I thought I might save you some time."

"The sea gulls know who we are?" Catherine asked with amusement.

"All of Lorr's creatures know of the Head Mage and his half-elf wife," Sabrina said as if it were obvious. "The Head Mage, the descendant of the Old One called Lorr, is connected to all life in this kingdom. As are you, Catherine, through your elven blood, even though your human blood somewhat obscures your bond." She turned her flowing eyes back to Rionn Lorr. "I knew that you were coming, but I know not why."

"These are dangerous times, Sabrina," Rionn explained. "A demon is loose, a powerful one. Another Child of the Old Ones has been born recently, and a dead Phillosith was found on the shores of the Ocean Crystalline. I fear that these incidents may be somehow related."

Sabrina's eyes darkened. "I know of the Phillosith's death," she said, her soft voice hardening a bit. "He had many more years to grace the waters of this world. His life was stolen from him."

"Do you know by what?" Rionn inquired.

"I do not," she admitted. "I fear the demon you speak of may be involved. I am not certain. I do intend to find out."

She studied the Head Mage for a moment in silence. Her captivating gaze seemed to draw Rionn in. Catherine noticed immediately. She stepped in front of her husband to capture Sabrina's attention.

"Is there a reason you study my husband so, Sabrina?" Catherine demanded in a calm, composed voice.

Sabrina smiled. "Yes, but not the reason you suppose. It surprises me, and I must say it impresses me, that Rionn could detect Azhju'lestra.

"Azhju'lestra?" Rionn and Catherine echoed in unison.

"Mine and Raxe's Child," Sabrina elaborated.

7.2

Rionn's eyes widened. "The Child I detected is yours?" he asked in disbelief. "Yours and *Ryan's*?" He was relieved that it was hers and Raxe's Child he had felt and that Mardah had not sired an offspring. But he was as insulted as he was relieved.

"We're allies, Sabrina. We've been friends for as long as I can remember. How could you keep this from me?"

"Because I've known you all of your life," Sabrina replied.

"What is that supposed to mean?" Rionn questioned.

"It means I know you well. I know how would have reacted had I told you."

"Oh?" Rionn asked incredulously. "And how do you think I would have reacted?"

"You would have imposed," she said matter-of-factly.

"Imposed?" Rionn asked, insulted again.

"I mean no offense," Sabrina amended. "Your intentions would be kind, as always, but you would have been an imposition just the same."

"Explain," Rionn demanded.

"Because you and my daughter share a common heritage, you would demand to be a part of her life. You would insist on seeing her regularly, to tutor and teach her about your ways and her lineage."

"And you think that is a bad thing," Rionn said.

"Not bad," Sabrina corrected. "Just unnecessary."

"She *should* know about her heritage," Rionn argued. "Who would be better than an adult Child of the Old Ones to teach a young one about her heritage?"

"Me," Sabrina answered.

"You," Rionn scoffed. "And what makes you think you would be a better teacher than I?"

"I am much older than you," she explained. "Much older than even Shanderah before her death. The only beings in this world older than me are WorldHopper and a handful of his fellow dragons.

"The histories you would teach her would be second and third-hand narratives passed down from generation to generation, subject to slight alterations. And the human side of the Children of the Old Ones can make you all guilty, however unintentionally, of embellishment and other subtle inaccuracies. The histories I have taught and will teach her are first hand experiences and observations, untainted by a faulty human memory or ego."

Catherine raised an eyebrow. "You talk as if you are a creature of faerie," she noted.

Sabrina smiled and nodded.

Rionn raised both eyebrows. "You *are* faerie?"

"A water faerie, yes," Sabrina admitted. "The last of my kind until Azhju'lestra. People believe me to be a mere elemental and I am happy to allow them to. It is actually to my benefit. Humans make too many solicitations of fairies unless they fear us. Many believe all of us can grant wishes. I have no desire to listen to the requests of greedy, self-absorbed or heartsick humans."

"A faerie..." Rionn repeated.

"That is why you attempted to seduce my husband," Catherine realized.

"Ah, but he was not your husband at the time," Sabrina reminded, holding up an elegant and perfect finger. "I would never attempt to persuade a man to break his sacred vow of fidelity."

Rionn turned to his wife. "How did you know that was the reason?"

"It's obvious, Rionn," Catherine said. "A moment ago she said she was the last of her kind. Not even fairies have infinite life spans. She needs an heir, someone to protect the oceans and lakes and rivers once her time has passed. A creature of faerie would not soil her egg with a purely human seed. But I assume a Child of the Old Ones, with his magical lineage, would be a suitable mate. And since it would be better to let her race die out than to bear an offspring of Mar-dah, it makes sense that she would choose you."

Sabrina nodded once in affirmation and then turned to Rionn. "What did you think, old friend? Did you think me promiscuous?" she teased. "Or did you believe yourself to be so irresistible that I simply *had* to have you?"

Rionn blushed and shrugged. "I learned long ago that it is the height of folly even attempt to divine the inner workings of the female mind, whatever her race or species."

Catherine gave him a playful nudge with her elbow. "A good lesson to learn," she assured.

Rionn's embarrassed look turned serious again. "So you persuaded Raxe to mate with you while you helped him heal from the demon attack?"

"I did not 'mate' with him in the human sense," Sabrina explained. "Fairies reproduce in many different ways. While he was in his healing sleep, I took a bit of his essence. Raxe never even knew."

"To have done such a thing without his knowledge was not right," Rionn Lorr chided.

"I do not expect you to understand," Sabrina returned. "Nature Herself, the Ascendant One's *very first* Child, commands these events. Even I must follow her dictates."

"You speak as if you had no choice," Rionn countered. "You did not have to steal Raxe's seed. You chose to."

"Indeed," Sabrina conceded. "But the choice was not a random one. My child had to have a father possessing of powerful magic, for she has an important role to play in the future of our world. Neither you nor Raxe would have willingly provided for me. And as I have said, I would not force or persuade you to break your marital vows."

Rionn's normally warm blue eyes went cold as he leveled an accusing stare. "And Raxe, an unmarried Child of the Old Ones, *conveniently* falls into your lap."

Sabrina's shimmering eyes froze into a shade of pale green that made the ice in Rionn's own glare seem like flames by comparison.

"*Lorrïsh'Estâhn,*" Sabrina chided. Rionn knew that phrase meant 'Spawn of Lorr' in her native tongue. "Do not dare imply that incident was in any way orchestrated by me. He offered his life to bring down the fifth level sea demon sent by Mar-dah, saving not only his companions, but me as well, for I would have been no match against such a creature.

I repaid Raxe by saving his life. It was then that I realized that the time had come for me to play my role in the events set forth in prophecy."

"And how would you know so much of prophecy?" Catherine questioned. "Do you have access to the Lost Books out here in the oceans, lakes, and rivers? Do you have the gift of foresight yourself?"

"No," Sabrina said. Her eyes thawed from frozen green back into rippling waves of shifting aquatic colors. A small smile curved the left corner of her full, perfect lips. "But I am the Mistress of the Sea of Spirits. I am faerie. I have lived a long, long time and have come to learn many things."

Catherine asked the question she knew her husband had as well. "What part does young Azhju'lestra have to play in these prophecies?"

"That, I do not know, at least not exactly," Sabrina admitted apologetically. "I only know that she is meant to play a pivotal role in the survival of the Kingdom of Lorr and beyond, and that somehow, the demon and the death of my long time Phillosith companion are very likely connected. I wish I could be specific, but prophecy is much like foresight. Much of its interpretation is guesswork at best. They are mostly hints that can mean any number of things."

Catherine nodded her understanding. Her own gift of foresight was little more than fleeting shadows of near-forgotten dreams and vague wisps of waking visions. But from the little she knew of prophecy, and from the considerably more that her husband knew from years of study, she knew that acting upon misinterpreted prophecy could lead to surprising and tragic consequences.

Rionn Lorr voiced his wife's concerns. "Let us hope that you have interpreted correctly."

"Why have you chosen to tell us about her now?" Catherine asked.

"Because you have come to me and asked," Sabrina said. "I would never have volunteered the information. My magic should have kept you from feeling her presence, yet somehow you thought to inquire about her existence. That is no coincidence. It is a sign that the wheels of prophecy have been put into motion."

"But I *could* feel her presence," Rionn told her. "We came to ask about the Phillosith, but I was able to feel her presence. I simply could not locate her. I had no idea that the Child I felt was here. Your magic may have hidden her exact location, but I did know she existed."

A small frown creased the smooth, bronze skin around Sabrina's mouth. Her color-shifting eyes turned coral-brown and went still. Both Rionn and Catherine could see that she was in deep thought. Finally, her eyes shimmered once more as the Mistress of the Sea of Spirits slowly shook her head.

"I must disagree, Rionn. You could not have felt her presence. I am being neither vain nor overconfident when I say that I know what my magic can do."

"I felt the Child, Sabrina," Rionn insisted.

Sabrina slowly shook her head again. "When Raxe was being re-fortified at the bottom of Lake Onyx, you thought he was dead, did you not?"

"Well, yes," Rionn confessed.

"Because I shielded him from you. Not even Shanderah could feel his presence. And she was far more sensitive than you. The magic I used to shield my Azhju'lestra was even more powerful."

"These are facts we cannot argue," Catherine added. "But the fact remains that Rionn knew of the Child's existence. He has been searching for her for some time now."

Sabrina cocked her head slightly as she regarded Rionn Lorr. "When did you first detect another Child's presence?"

"Roughly nine months after Raxe returned to his side of the WorldGate," Rionn answered.

"Then you could not have felt the presence of Azhju'lestra," Sabrina confirmed. "Faerie offspring physically mature sooner than normal humans. They have much longer life spans, as well. What makes you think the gestation period would be the same?"

"Enlighten us, please," Rionn requested with a hint of sarcasm. "What is the gestation period for a water faerie?"

"Only five weeks, but it takes fourteen months for the fertilization process to complete within the womb after a successful mating before gestation begins. It would have taken longer than a year after the offworlder's departure for you to feel her presence. And even that is assuming you could feel a Child's aura before birth, which you cannot, because a Child's divine essence is indistinguishable from the mother's essence until birth. The Child you felt was not mine and Raxe's."

The Head Mage was about to argue further but he knew it was pointless. If Sabrina did not want to believe him, he could not force her. But he had to admit to himself the possibility that she was right. In fact, what she said was true about her effectively concealing Raxe's presence. Rionn really believed the offworlder had died. When his aura had returned, Rionn never questioned it. He was so relieved that Raxe was not dead and so preoccupied with the loosed demons that he did not dwell on the mystery of how Raxe's aura disappeared and then reappeared.

The Mistress of the Sea was, he now knew, faerie. The power possessed by a creature of faerie was far greater than that of an elemental. While Rionn's magical abilities were far more diverse, not even he could match her when it came to her specific skills. Who was he to say she was wrong?

The implications of this caused Rionn's head to spin. The relief he felt moments earlier was swept away in a wave of worry and uncertainty. If the Child he detected was not Azhju'lestra, then who in the name of the Ascendant One was it? With a sixth level demon in this world and the Hell Key unprotected – hidden for the time being, but still unprotected – the existence of a mystery Child could be fatally dangerous. If the demon could somehow bring the Child under its control and possessed the Hell Key, it would have power over the very gates of hell.

The near-chime of Sabrina's voice brought him back to more immediate concerns. "What is it you intend to do about this escaped demon, Head Mage?"

"I intend to stop it," Rionn Lorr said, "with the aid of the Gatekeeper's descendants from across the WorldGate."

"I will be journeying to other waters to discover what I can of this new threat," Sabrina revealed. "But before I go, I request that you send Raxe to me when you bring him back to Lorr. It is imperative that I speak to him before he begins his quest."

"Will you introduce him to his Child?" Rionn asked with an accusing tone.

"You have much work to do," Sabrina said, "As do I." The waters began to roil around her bare, perfect feet as they carried her back out toward the middle of the river. Her musical voice faded as the distance between them grew.

"It is very important, Rionn, that you do as I ask."

She reached the river's midpoint and gently raised her arms. The waters swirling around her legs rose until they completely engulfed her. When the water settled, the Mistress of the Sea of Spirits was gone.

7.3

"What is magic?" Master Mage Delthar asked the gangly teen with sandy brown hair that sat before him across a small and sparsely appointed desk. The green student's robe he wore enveloped him completely, except for where the bottom of his long legs stretched from beneath the hem.

"It is energy," Quick answered without hesitation. This was one of his first lessons at the *Chronicai Tul Myst*, a lesson that many of his peers seemed to take for granted and dismiss in the early days of training. Quick, however, always felt like it was one the most important lessons. In fact, he took all of his lessons more seriously than most of his peers.

The changeling would never have dreamt that he would one day walk the same halls walked by the Master Mage Delthar and Rionn Lorr when they were young apprentices. As honored as he felt to receive periodic personal training from Rionn on the Island of Cartha, there was something almost regal about being officially enrolled at the *Chronicai Tul Myst*. And the fact that the Head Mage himself had recommended him to the fabled magic academy was not to be taken lightly.

He continued, noting from the annoyed and expectant look on Master Delthar's face that the three word answer was far from sufficient. "Like any other energy," he continued, "It can be used for good or evil, depending on the wielder."

"Elaborate," Mage Delthar commanded.

Quick thought for a moment and then continued. "Fire can be used by a mother to cook food for hungry children. It also brings warmth during cold weather. But raiders can use it to raze the fields and homes of a victimized village.

"No land mammal can survive without water, but any of them can drown in too much of it. The force of a flowing river provides power for mills, but if a damn is destroyed, that very same river can level entire towns. Unlike most other energies, though, magic can be used for almost any purpose. Its uses are limited only by the wielder's imagination, knowledge, dexterity, and aptitude."

There was a look on Master Delthar's face that Quick could not read. The changeling apprentice saw just the hint of a twitch of the elder's thick whiskers, but not enough to reveal whether the twitch was caused by a smile or a frown.

"Worry not about my assessments until we have finished our lesson," Master Mage Delthar advised.

As sensitive to magic as Quick was, as was his nature as a creature of magic himself, he could not tell if the old wizard's accurate estimation of his thoughts were from magic or simply a keen ability to read the faces and eyes of others.

Master Mage Delthar was one of the most learned mages in all of the known lands. In addition to being First Advisor to the Head Mage, he had been teaching at the *Chronicai Tul Myst* – known in less formal circles as the Mage Academy and even less formally as the wizard school – for almost three times as long as Quick had been alive. Before then, he had served as First Advisor to the previous Head Mage, Rionn Lorr's father. Prior to that he had distinguished himself as an Echelon One mage while serving on the Conjurer's Alliance in the Southborough region.

That was after he graduated from the *Chronicai Tul Myst* with high honors and apprenticed under none other than the previous Head Mage, as Quick was doing now. In short, Delthar was one of the most powerful and accomplished wizards in the Known Lands and quite adept at shielding his use of magic to all but the very few who were more adept than himself. Quick was a long way from that.

Delthar raised an appraising eyebrow as Quick studied the deep wrinkles at the corner of the old man's dark gray eyes. There was a question in the wizard's stare, a question other than the one he asked next:

"From where does magic come?"

Quick was ready for this one. The answer came quickly. "It comes from the same source as all energy. No matter its intended use or how many times its form is altered, all energy comes originally from Nature."

He thought back to some of the discussions he overheard between Raxe, Shanderah and Meldrick on their travels during their adventures opposing the evil Mar-dah and his loosed demons.

"Oil, the raw material from which so much energy is derived on Raxe's Earth, is believed to have come in large part from the remains of massive, mighty creatures that dominated the world's prehistory. Fire and nuclear energy are derived from a certain manipulation of materials originally found in Nature."

Delthar's appraising gaze turned stern and his whiskers moved in a way that Quick immediately recognized this time as a scowl. "I know nothing of 'nuclear' energy, or of this 'Raxe's world' of which you speak so frequently. Please refrain from such references during the lesson, for I have no way of confirming or refuting the accuracy of such references." The fact that Quick possessed knowledge that Delthar lacked clearly irritated the wizard. After a short pause, the Master Mage asked his next question. "So, from what natural source does magic flow?"

A flood of words rushed into the changeling's mind. It took him a moment to organize them before he continued. It was not enough to simply recite the words that were given to him in earlier sessions. He had to describe it in his own words, in such a way as to prove he truly understood.

"Magic is the exhaled breath of the Lord Ascendant," Quick commenced. "Magic is the kinetic energy generated by the rotation and orbit of the planets, suns, moons and stars. A miniscule portion of the energy released when liquids, solids, and gasses change from one phase to another is magic. Magic is the by-product of sadness as it transforms to happiness or love turning into hate. When life is extinguished and the soul is released from a physical host, the residual energy of that transition is magic. When a father's seed fertilizes a mother's egg, again, there is magic. When the seasons change, magical energy is a by-product of the transformation."

"Continue," Delthar bade, his gaze never leaving his student's brown eyes.

"Magic is everywhere." Quick went on. "There are no known man-made instruments capable of measuring magical energy, but there are individuals – both man and beast – that can manipulate it. Some can manipulate it more than others. Some have a greater sensitivity to it than others. But if they have no knowledge of it, or do not believe in its existence, or reject out of fear borne from misunderstanding, as is the case for many in the Far Regions on the edges of the Known Lands, they never have cause nor desire to tap into it."

Quick remembered Mage Delthar's command to not speak of the world across the WorldGate and ceased to speak at that point. But his thoughts continued. He recalled something Shanderah had told Raxe while they rode in a sky sleigh to Infinity Isle. The offworlder made a show of not listening to her but Quick drank the words in like water.

When the Lord Ascendant created your world, Raxe, he made both man and beast much less sensitive to magic than those in the world of Lorr. That lack of sensitivity makes the intentional use of magic so infrequent there that most deny its existence. But the magic is still there. And every so often, some imperceptible anomaly makes a being of your world more attuned to the magic than most.

Many exhibitions of superhuman ability, be they physical or extrasensory, are often the result of magic. The scientists and self-styled intellectuals theorize and suppose and conjure up explanations without ever being able to prove their theories correct. How can they? There is no scientific way they know of to reproduce fantastic incidents because they know and believe nothing of magic. If their explanations sound logical enough, though, others will concur and it will be accepted as "fact."

His musings were cut short by the Master Mage's next question. "How many different kinds of magic are there?"

Quick broke from his reverie and responded. "Despite all of their subcategories and uses, there are essentially two types of magic. First, there is physical magic. This is the residual energy that comes from the elemental and other physical forces that radiate from and act upon a planet.

"The forces mentioned earlier: the rotation of the planets; the phase transitions; the change of seasons; and other forces too numerous to list all produce physical magic. This type of magic has physical effects. It can be used to manipulate weather or to rearrange, disassemble and reassemble matter. It can be used to move matter as well as to produce and control physical energy. This is the most commonly used form of magic. It is the easiest form to master.

"And then there is metaphysical magic," Quick continued. "The residue of emotions, of the lighting and extinguishing of all forms of life, these are the energies that comprise metaphysical magic. This magic is more abundant but much more ephemeral than physical magic. It is more difficult to control but potentially more destructive."

That last sentence was not something that had ever been told to him. It was something he had surmised on his own. This caused one of Delthar's bushy eyebrows to twitch.

"Why is it more destructive?" the Master Mage asked. This time Quick was certain there was a tone of genuine curiosity in his instructor's voice. The teen-aged changeling was happy to continue.

"Physical magic controls *things*," Quick said. "But metaphysical magic controls *beings*. Some of the very sources of metaphysical magic – things like thought and emotion – can actually be manipulated by the residual magical energy they produce. Man, beast, and insect all can be manipulated by metaphysical magic. While the forces of the earth can be manipulated do great physical harm to mankind and all of his works, they can never be made by magic to destroy their own source.

"Man, however, with his intelligence and ability to interfere with the balance of nature, has the power to destroy himself, both physically and spiritually, as well as the earth. That makes him potentially more dangerous than the forces of the earth, no matter how awesome those forces can be."

"And what makes the metaphysical magic so ephemeral?" Master Delthar asked. He leaned forward a bit to emphasize what followed. "And stay within your lesson this time, young apprentice. I want none of your own conclusions or suppositions."

Quick cleared his throat. "Metaphysical magic is in constant motion. It appears in this world and disappears into the nether realms with a quickness that would make the single beat of a hummingbird's wings seem slow. The denser magical energy from the earth's forces quickly pushes it out of this physical plane. For this reason, it takes an extremely powerful command of magic to even capture, let alone employ metaphysical magic before it escapes to the nether realm. Once in the nether realm, only a being of great magic can pierce the dimensional veil to retrieve it."

Delthar sat back in his chair, seemingly satisfied with the answer. His next question, he decided, would go beyond the scope of the lesson. It would break the rules of instruction. But it was his right as a Master Mage to use his discretion to occasionally step outside the boundaries of the established system of training. He would finally catch this young one by surprise.

"We both know why metaphysical magic is so quickly snatched into the nether realm," Delthar started, dismissing that topic with the wave of a bony hand. "So I want you to tell me what you know, or what you *think* you know, of what metaphysical magic fortifies...and why."

Quick very nearly jumped from surprise. While he had an answer, it was not something that was discussed at this early stage of training. Not only that, the Master Mage was instructing him to contradict his earlier directive about not mentioning Raxe's side of the WorldGate. There was no way he could think to answer without referring to Raxe's world. The teen thought it must be some trick, some wizard's game to trip him up. But then he thought of a lesson he had been taught during the first few weeks of his apprenticeship: *Never question a superior Mage's query. Only respond honestly.* Quick did just that.

"Metaphysical magic enters the nether realms for the purpose of fortifying the WorldGate to keep the worlds separate," Quick said confidently. "The WorldGate was not meant to be a portal, but a boundary. The Lord Ascendant never intended for the infinite worlds to intermingle, but in His divine generosity, he gave the Old Ones free will and great power, which included the gift to traverse the WorldGate to view His many works first hand. They in turn created the means for their half-human progeny to cross the

WorldGate. But they overestimated human nature. The Children would eventually abuse the WorldGate."

"You have not told me why the WorldGate is important," Delthar challenged.

Quick gave a nod and sighed. If he was being tricked, then so be it. He *wanted* to talk about this. Rionn Lorr was a busy man and had very little time for long philosophical discussion. Quick's peers had not seen what he had seen so they had no point of reference. But Delthar's knowledge was vast indeed. Quick could learn much from any exchange they might share. Besides, it was his charge to respond honestly.

"To a person from the world of Lorr, the technology of Raxe's world would be as fantastic and alien as magic was to Raxe. We have some forms of technology, but because of magic, we have not needed to learn how to manipulate the physical energy of our earth the way mankind has learned to in the more technical worlds.

"This would sound odd to someone from across the WorldGate, where the term '*super*natural' is used to describe that which their technical knowledge cannot explain. But even though those in Raxe's world make more use of the earth's forces than we, the prevalence of magic in our world has resulted in us being much more in balance with Nature."

"Explain, young one," Delthar urged.

Quick was happy to go on. "According to Raxe, in the technology-dominated world people exploit nature to the point that they are damaging their own world to an almost irreparable extent. They have the power to obliterate massive chunks of their planet's surface. They have the means to ruin great expanses of oceans if they so chose, and to poison the air for thousands of miles.

"This destruction can be wrought with their technology alone. How much more destructive could they be if they could also command magic the way we do? And these are but two worlds out of an infinite number of them, all separated by the WorldGate, including the Seven Hells."

Delthar absently fingered his mustaches as he regarded the youngster. He knew that Quick had learned much during his travels, but this one had far too much insight for a boy his age. Then again, Delthar had to remind himself, Quick was not a normal boy. Stars! He was not a boy at all! He was male, but a male changeling. He held his human form so frequently that many thought of him as such, including the Master Mage, to his embarrassment. In truth, he knew of no one who knew what a changeling's true form actually was. But the old, learned wizard knew their history.

In the early times just after Heaven's War, changelings existed all over the Known Lands and beyond. They were solitary creatures, left to fend for themselves immediately after their birth. They tended to take the form of and assimilate with the creatures that were most prevalent around them at the time of their birth, but no one knew what they looked like prior to taking their first form.

Unfortunately, most creatures could sense that they were different. Changelings were often outcasts and loners among the creatures they mimicked. Additionally, they could not hold any one form indefinitely, and so would eventually have to change into some other creature. That caused even more problems among whatever group of which they were a part.

Their unique magic and solitary nature led both man and beast to fear and mistrust them. And man, as is his nature, sought to purge that which was misunderstood and feared. Dogs were trained to identify changelings by scent so that men could drive them away or kill them. Foolish mages provided various other means of identifying changelings for profit. Changeling hunting became a sport. People bet on who could bag the most. Alchemists ground their bones and burned their flesh to ash to use their essential salts and minerals for potions.

The unfortunate creatures were driven to near extinction. Delthar knew of a few when he was a small boy, but that had been decades ago, for Delthar was coming upon his eighty-third winter. Since then the existence of changelings had all but faded to legend. Since they usually posed no danger to humans they were not vilified by history. At most, they became a whimsical faerie tale to children. No one had seen or heard anything about a changeling since Delthar was in his mid teens, at least not until Rionn Lorr found Quick as an orphaned toddler while traveling in the southern lands of Lorr nearly fifteen years ago.

Quick was believed to be the last of his kind. More likely, the Master Mage believed, he was the last of his kind willing to ally himself with humans. Rionn Lorr was aware of the history of changelings and felt pity for Quick, so he brought him to his home on the Island of Cartha to care for him for a time and learn as much as he could about their fascinating race. Old Shanderah met the boy on a visit to the Head Mage's wife. The moment she laid eyes on him, her foresight told her that he would play a significant role in the course of the Kingdom of Lorr's future. For this reason, Rionn Lorr took a special interest in the boy's well being.

And now Delthar was interested. Quick was a creature of magic, not a young boy. As a creature of magic, he was much more naturally aware of magic and had an inherent understanding of how it worked. Delthar was prideful but he was not blinded by his pride. By helping this young changeling he could learn much. A wizard, after all, was first and foremost a scholar. Delthar used all of his talent, as well as a small bit of magic, to mask his emotions. And yet he was still unconvinced that Quick could not see through his façade.

"What is the most important thing one can remember about magic?" Delthar asked with a tone of finality that indicated this would conclude the lesson.

Quick did not want the session to end, but he knew it must. He had sword training after his lesson with the Master Mage, which he enjoyed almost as much. "Like any other energy," Quick concluded, "magic is not infinite. As vast as the oceans are, and as unlikely as it may seem, they can be depleted. And even more unlikely, but possible nonetheless, so can magic. A wise conjurer is conservative with its use."

The Master Mage sat back in his big chair with an expectant look in his eyes. Quick wondered what he was waiting for. The only thing he could think of was that the mage might have been upset because Quick mentioned Raxe's world after he had been instructed not to.

"Master Delthar," Quick began. "I apologize for referring once again to the place beyond the WorldGate, but that was the only way I could think of to answer your question completely."

At that, the left corner of Delthar's mustaches tilted up in a sad smile as the old man sighed and lowered his head. That was not a good sign. Quick sat quietly and waited for the old wizard to speak. Delthar finally raised his head to return Quick's questioning gaze. Just as the silence was becoming unbearable for Quick, Master Delthar spoke.

"You answered each question correctly and thoroughly, young apprentice. You used relevant examples to support your answers. You added insight gained from your own life experiences – which far exceeds most apprentices of your age – to enhance the knowledge you shared. I am pleased."

"Master Delthar, I must say that our exchange seemed more like a test than a lesson."

"Young one, every experience in life is both a test and a lesson. You either play the role of student or the role of teacher; and sometimes both at once. Remember that."

"Yes, Master Delthar," Quick acknowledged. "So…did I pass?"

"I am afraid, young apprentice, that even though you performed well, you have failed this particular test."

Quick's eyes widened in surprise. "But I answered every question correctly, as you have said only a moment ago."

"But then you made apology for again mentioning Raxe's world. I understand your trepidation at having to disobey a direct instruction, but as you said, it was necessary to adequately answer the question posed to you. A wizard never makes apology for speaking what he knows to be truth, or for doing what must be done, no matter how distasteful it may be. You apologize only for being wrong."

Quick started to protest but Delthar raised a hand to quiet him before continuing. "You did well to remember many of your earliest lessons while responding to my inquiries, but your uncertainty caused you to overlook one: To ask forgiveness for doing the right thing is a direct contradiction. It is a false admission of guilt that in some ways can undo the right that has been done."

The young changeling lowered his head in indignation. Of course the old mage was correct. He raised his head when Delthar concluded. "That, apprentice, was also part of the test. And as you know, tests of wizardry are not graded on percentages. One mistake out of one thousand questions is one too many."

Quick took a deep breath to settle himself. The lesson had been concluded and that was that. There would be other lessons, he knew, and he would be ready. Delthar could read the determination in the other's eyes and smiled to himself as the youngster stood and gave a dignified bow. Delthar acknowledged the bow with a nod that also served to dismiss the apprentice. Quick left the small room, bound for his fencing lesson.

7.4

As Quick slowly and somberly walked the broad halls of the academy, he managed to bow to the mages and nod to other apprentices as they passed. He descended two flights of stairs, crossed the main alcove and then went to the cavernous wardrobe to hang his robe in the appropriate slot. From there, he moped through the foyer before stepping out into the courtyard. Once outside, he became eager to leave the school and his recent failure behind him as soon as possible. The plain tunic and brown pants were a welcome change from the confining green *Chronicai* apprentice robes. He walked so fast he was nearly jogging southward to the main gate. The pair of guards there betrayed their stoic façade and waved at the familiar youngster.

"Give us a quick one," one of the guards called. Both armored men laughed at the play on words.

Quick responded by taking two running strides and jumping into the air. While airborne, he went into a summersault and came out of it as a large bullfrog, landing atop the helmeted head of the guard that made the request. When the laughing guard reached up to grab him, Quick sprung from his head to the shoulder of the other guard. The man shouted a lighthearted "Whoa" at the unexpected move and he also tried to grab the big frog. He was as unsuccessful as his partner. Quick bolted from his shoulder and when he landed, he was in his human form once more. The young changeling gave an exaggerated bow as the guards laughed and applauded.

"Good form, Quick! Good form indeed!" lauded the guard from whose shoulder Quick had just leapt.

"Next time," Quick winked, "I'll perform that feat as a wallowgrump!"

"That would be something to see!" laughed the other guard as the changeling trotted off down the thoroughfare.

The guards lifted Quick's sullen spirits. He felt relieved and pleasantly surprised every time a soldier, or a civilian for that matter, was friendly to him.

Most of his years had been spent hiding the fact that he was a changeling. During his short life he had blended in with several species and races: animals, dwarves, elves, and humans. He could live among them for a while but eventually they would notice he was different. That inevitably led to him being driven away.

And then Rionn Lorr found him. Once the Head Mage accepted him it did not take long for others to follow his example. Quick slowly gained the trust of the crown and the military by acting as an unofficial spy. And then, during the Cursed Opening, he proved himself time and time again. He eventually saved the entire kingdom by killing Mar-dah just as the evil wizard was about to murder the king, queen, Raxe, Rionn Lorr and others. After that he was lauded as a hero and accepted by all of the citizens of Lorr. And now he was a student of the *Chronicai Tul Myst* and the Royal Academy.

Within minutes Quick had passed through the gates of the palace grounds and took the main road southward that led to the city of Greenglenn. He wanted to morph into a form that could travel much faster but there was still too much traffic. In general, he did not like the attention his transformations brought. For those that knew him well and considered him a friend, like the guards back at the *Chronicai Tul Myst*, his morphing was appreciated and a source of good-natured amusement. For those unfamiliar with him, however, his transformations might startle and alarm.

For that reason, he waited until he reached a short stretch of road that was clear of any citizens before changing into a hummingbird and taking to the skies. He landed in a densely wooded area several yards off of the road just outside the city gates and morphed back into his human form.

It would have been faster to fly all the way to the Academy near the southern border of Greenglenn, but he appreciated cities the most as one of its citizens. He was not in so much of a hurry that he would pass up the opportunity to experience the sights, sounds, smells, and camaraderie of the city streets.

He enjoyed swordplay almost as much as he enjoyed magic. The physical release was often an effective way to relax from the mental strain of academic as well as conjuring lessons. Even though Ethan – his favorite sparring partner at the Royal Academy – was off demon hunting with the Keeper's Hounds, Quick would still enjoy his session. His fighting lessons made him feel even closer to the humans who had accepted him as one of their own. Of course there were those who still feared and mistrusted him, and as long as human nature was what it was, there always would be.

But those that really mattered to him accepted him and depended on him, and that was enough for Quick. Ethan Sureblade had become his best friend over the last few years as they both advanced through the Royal Academy. Several other students had befriended him as well. Rionn Lorr had all but adopted him. He took the youngster under his wing and looked after him, giving him guidance and discipline, while respecting Quick's fiercely independent nature.

The Head Mage trusted him and had given him a tremendous amount of responsibility over the years. In doing so, he saved the changeling from a life of pointless drifting between places and species. For that was the curse of a changeling: never being accepted, only tolerated for a finite amount of time until being forced to find somewhere else to live. That lonely, nomadic existence was all Quick had ever known before Rionn Lorr found him.

The changeling remembered their meeting fondly. In the guise of a squirrel, the changeling had been attempting to steal a bit of food from Rionn Lorr while the Head Mage and his wife were camping in the forested foothills just beyond the southern regions of the Runestone Mountains. He would have been successful if Catherine had been fully human. However, being half elf, she shared that magical link with Nature that all elves possess. She thought the squirrel was cute, and when she examined him more closely she realized that he was not a real squirrel and alerted her husband that a thief or a spy was in their midst.

Instead of punishing him for his insolence, the Head Mage saw something in the young creature and took a liking to him. Shanderah did as well, and with the endorsement of two respected and feared Children of the Old Ones, Quick was embraced by the royal family.

In response and gratitude, Quick pledged himself to Rionn and Catherine and the Kingdom of Lorr. As long as he lived, he would do everything in his power to protect and serve the Kingdom, its leaders, and its citizens.

Quick's weapons training at the Royal Academy played an important part of his chosen destiny as one of the protectors of the Kingdom of Lorr, so he was disappointed when he reached the gates of the Academy and was handed a letter by one of the guards. The letter informed him that his lessons had been cancelled. His heartbeat quickened with excitement, though, when he read further and saw the reason. Rionn Lorr left instructions for Quick to travel to Port Lorrian where the Head Mage would join him within the week with further instructions.

A nervous smile crept slowly across the young changeling's lips. It sounded to Quick as if a mission was in the offing!

7.5

The Head Mage strode into the royal conference room nearly fifteen minutes late. He wished he could be later. The spacious conference hall, with its arched ceiling and soaring columns and ornate tapestries covering the walls was wonderfully aesthetic, but Rionn Lorr felt he had spent too much time within these walls as of late. He was never entirely comfortable in this room, though he could not deny the allure of the space. It was regal in every way and befitting of the sovereign of the most envied kingdom in the Known Lands. The gleaming polished mahogany wood of the walls, railings, and framing was dazzling, especially when the sun shone through the high arching windows at midday.

Its splendor, however, was in direct contrast to the man for whom the hall was constructed. King William would have been far more comfortable in the smaller, more utilitarian war room that he used when he served as the High General of the Royal Infantry. Even in times of peace he would use the war room to host meetings despite the fact that as High General he had access to this conference hall. The other generals would use it from time to time, but never William. Now, however, he was king. It would not do for a king to use anything less than the royal conference hall. In his early years as king, Rionn and the high generals would needle William about his clear discomfort in his new surroundings.

During King William's reign, Rionn thought sadly, the days that his land was involved in some sort of armed conflict were starting to outnumber the days of peace. It was not long before the king disliked the room for a reason other than his aversion to its striking adornments. The great hall had become a symbol of crisis for King William and his advisors, the Head Mage included. This day was no different.

Minister Geoffrey, High General of the Home Guard Artemis, and High Admiral Tyus all sat to the left of the king on the long side of the oval mahogany conference table that was large enough to accommodate thirty people. They sat near the door and looked up as Rionn walked to the King's right. He nodded to the King's personal bodyguards. The two tall, heavily muscled and heavily armed men returned the nod before Rionn Lorr took his seat.

"Forgive my tardiness, my king," Rionn Lorr requested.

"Busier than usual these days?" asked William sincerely.

"Only in the last few days."

"I can imagine," the king said. He turned to his left. "Gentlemen, please summarize your reports for the Head Mage and we will see if there is anything he can add. Tyus?"

"The patrol barges report no more curious disturbances in our waters," the naval high admiral informed. "No more rare species of aquatic animals have been found and nothing else out of the ordinary has been spotted since the Phillosith was discovered."

"What of the Phillosith itself?" Rionn Lorr asked.

"We do not know much of the creature's physical make-up, so only a limited examination has taken place," Tyus explained. "But there does seem to be some tearing, or breaking of the coral-like skin. According to the naval examiners, the creature may have experienced some sort of external trauma. Whether or not that was the cause of its death has not been determined."

Geoffrey, as Minister of War, was also in command of the spies that worked in Darshay and Cartha, the other two kingdoms that shared the continent of Lorr. He gave the Head Mage a moment to process Tyus's information before giving his summary.

"My agents report from the surrounding kingdoms the usual griping of jealous lords and politicians about our kingdom's place at the Seat of Power of the Sovereign Council. They have noticed that the anti-Lorr sentiment seems to be growing, not at an alarming rate, but a noticeable one. The churches in Darshay have sent out volunteer emissaries to travel to the border counties of Darshay and Cartha to spread ill will toward the Children of the Old Ones and their position of power here in Lorr."

Rionn Lorr raised an eyebrow. "That is new. So what was once mere envy has taken root and grown into a movement."

King William shook his head in disgust, causing his mane of dark mahogany-red curls to sway. "How can they worship the Lord Ascendant and all of His Old Ones while rejecting the Old Ones' direct descendants?"

"Simple," Rionn scoffed. "They choose to publicly voice doubt that we *are* direct descendants of the Old Ones even though they know it is true. They paint us merely as powerful conjurers masquerading as Children of the Old Ones. That is the only way to preserve their own power and influence."

"I wonder what's worse," Geoffrey mused. "The hypocrisy of their clergy or the fools that believe their lies."

"Perhaps, my Head Mage," the king said, "if you would participate more in the activities of this Kingdom's Church of Lorr and the Lord Ascendant, it would be more difficult for the other kingdoms to perpetuate their lies."

The Head Mage sighed. He and the king had been having this debate for years. Rionn Lorr answered the way he always did. "My king, I am an agent and protector of this kingdom, not a politician or cleric. I believe in our church and what it represents, but I must often make decisions for the greater good that do not run quite parallel with some of the tenets of the church."

The king, as always, shrugged his massive shoulders. He usually let the matter drop at that, but not this time. "At, the very least, Rionn, you could show your face a little more often at Church services. A few words could go a long way toward encouraging the congregation and countering the ill will being fostered by those foreign emissaries."

William's tone indicated that it was more than a suggestion. Rionn Lorr nodded. "Of course, my king. I'll make arrangements with the Church."

"Excellent," the king said. He turned his attention to his war minister. "Geoffrey, has evidence been found that these emissaries are sponsored in any way by their respective crowns?"

"Not as of yet," Geoffrey answered. "Only the church. But in addition to this interesting news, it has also come to our attention that the Carthan Kingdom is preparing to receive a contingent of ships approaching their southern shores. I'm sure they have arrived by now. I should have a report within the coming days."

"Do they think it is an invading force?" Rionn Lorr asked quickly. The Kingdom of Cartha, like Darshay, shared the continent of Lorr with the kingdom that bore his name. This fact made any threat to those kingdoms a potential threat to the Kingdom of Lorr. Those kingdoms unfortunately did not share that sentiment, as evidenced by their refusal to assist the Kingdom of Lorr during the Cursed Opening.

"Their numbers were too small for an armada," Tyus said. "And the origin of the ships have not been determined."

"My agents," Artemis began, "And I mean key agents from every other kingdom with the exception of Darshay, reported that their sovereigns were all out of contact for a time during the last month."

"Kings and queens frequently travel," Rionn Lorr said. "What was so strange about these occurrences?"

"Not strange," Artemis replied. "But curious. They all left and returned at various times bound for various locations for various reasons. This fact, in and of itself, is not out of the ordinary at all. However, there was an overlapping period of two days when all of them were away at the same time. It may not seem like a great deal of time, but I can honestly say that in all my years as high general, it has never happened…"

"Except for one occasion," Rionn Lorr realized. "And on that occasion, all *ten* of the sovereigns are away." He looked at the nods from the other four men at the table. "You think they held an unscheduled council meeting without the Kingdom of Lorr?"

"We have not confirmed that," Artemis cautioned. "And we probably never will. But I think we all would agree that this is the most likely assumption."

"Strangers approaching the southern shores of the continent," King William uttered tiredly. "An anti-Lorr campaign launched in the bordering kingdoms, and in all likelihood an unofficial Sovereign Council meeting that excluded the Kingdom currently holding the Seat of Power."

The king paused as he considered the last two reports. And then he prepared himself to receive the final and likely most troublesome one. "Now, my Head Mage, I fear I must ask what news you bring to this meeting."

"I take it you have met with the emissary from the Elf Lands by now," Rionn began.

"Which only serves to add to my enjoyment," the king deadpanned.

The Head Mage chuckled briefly at the sarcasm and then turned serious once more. Before he could reply, however, the ever-talkative Artemis interjected.

"Surely the elf is not speaking truth," the high general insisted. "Sollustre's Eye would have revealed the presence of the demon."

"We think this may be a ploy to gain possession of the WorldGate Key and the Hell Key," the king added. "Her belief that the elven nation is better suited to protect the recovered divine weapons is well known. What say you, Rionn?"

"The Ranger Elf speaks true," Rionn Lorr admitted. "At least, he believes his words to be true."

"Do you imply that perhaps the elf has been misled by his superiors?" Geoffrey asked hopefully.

"He received his orders directly from the queen," Rionn said. "And while she may be clever, one could even say devious, fabricating a story about a loosed demon is a level of treachery to which she would not stoop. There may be some things she knowingly kept from Rell Kallen to keep those things from me, but I believe the essence of the information is true."

"This is a serious charge," King William declared. "It is a charge that would require a great deal of attention during a time when we are still rebuilding our armies and our kingdom from the aftermath of the Cursed Opening. I am more than willing to devote whatever force is necessary to combat such a threat…but only if the threat is real."

Rionn Lorr heard the unasked question and answered it. "I was able to confirm the information, in a manner. And I feel that there is enough evidence to pursue the matter."

"You said 'in a manner,' Rionn," the king noted. "What does that mean?"

"It means that there are far too many things transpiring at the same time for me discount the word of the Ranger Elf," the Head Mage said bluntly. "The dead Phillosith, in fact, could very well be a victim of the loosed demon. I am in the process of putting together an exhibition to address these matters. I will not ask you to spare any military resources until I have uncovered the truth of things."

"You will ask for whatever you need, Head Mage," the king commanded. "At any time. And it will be at your disposal, as always."

Rionn Lorr knew it was true, but he also knew that the king had to be careful how he used his men. Without concrete evidence that a threat was genuine, or a thorough understanding of what they were facing, his soldiers would be at a grave disadvantage.

Between the enchanted armor of the Legion Midnight and the demons loosed by Mar-dah, Lorr's military lost more men than one would expect in a conflict that lasted a relatively short time. They Lorrian military was comprised of seasoned warriors who could defeat any human threat in the Known Lands. But magic and demons were things that they had never faced. The Head Mage always felt he should have been better prepared for that conflict and he would not make the same mistake here.

He would not hesitate to appropriate military force if it proved necessary, but he would do all he could to assure that he and his charges were prepared for their enemy before he did so.

And he knew exactly what preparations to make.

"In that case, my king," Rionn began, "I ask for only one unit to be placed in my employ."

Chapter 8: Power Unchained

8.1

Dan watched the familiar South Side streets rush past. They were different than the last time he was here, but the same. More buildings were abandoned. Some had been storefronts that were now completely boarded up. There was a building that resembled a popular fast food burger chain in every way except for the sign, which at the moment displayed a pagoda and the title of a Chinese Food restaurant. It seemed that every time Dan came through this part of the city, that same building had a different incarnation.

The people were different, but the same. The faces always changed, but like the fast food restaurant building, they were different incarnations of the same spirits. This time it might be a drug dealer. Another time it might be panhandler or a hooker. And then there were the wary citizens trying to navigate safely through those streets. Young mothers pushing strollers, grandmothers and grandfathers on canes and walkers, thirty-somethings trying to get home safely to husbands or wives or children.

These were the people of his city. There were people like this in cities all over the country and the world. This was just a small sample of the people he was charged to protect. He was a Child of the Old Ones, and as such, he had a duty to protect all of mankind in any way he could. There was something on the horizon that threatened these people. It was Dan's responsibility to make sure that he and his grandson protected them. Sometimes that responsibility weighed on Dan like a physical, tangible thing. He had not felt anxiety like this since World War II.

"So what do you think about the Harveys?" Dan asked to distract himself. "Seeing as how you wouldn't let me talk to them."

"We didn't have time, gramps, I explained that."

"Yeah, yeah, yeah," Dan huffed.

Ryan was driving them to a location several miles south of the rendezvous point discovered by WorldHopper in the guise of the organization agent Clay. To Ryan's relief, the dragon finally decided to part ways with them after the slaughter at the tavern. Ryan shuddered at the memory and shook it from his mind.

"I don't know what to think," Ryan admitted. "They weren't agents, that's for damn sure. You and I both vetted them. I'd usually assume they were CA's…but that doesn't seem right this time."

"CA's?" Dan asked.

"CA stands for civilian asset," Ryan explained. "Assets not affiliated to any intelligence or law enforcement agency; just regular people. I've never used them, but a lot of agents do for different reasons. Some of them act as informants. Others may help to provide a backstory for an agent that has to use a false identity. Most of them don't even know they're being used."

Dan's thin, wispy eyebrows knitted. "Why would the organization kill them?"

Ryan shrugged. "Sometimes they find out things they shouldn't. If the agent's good enough, the CA's stay completely in the dark and off the radar. They stay safe and can be used over and over. But if the agent's sloppy, their CA's can become loose ends without even realizing it."

Dan nodded in understanding and paused before asking, "But how many of these *civilian* assets manage to kill two trained agents?"

"Just a freak accident?" Ryan offered feebly.

Dan gave him a sidelong glance and scoffed.

"Exactly," Ryan said. "That's why this doesn't seem right."

Ryan pulled the van to a stop at the curb. He set the emergency break, climbed out of the driver's seat and climbed into the back of the van. Dan remained seated, lifting the miniature, high-powered binoculars that hung from a nylon strap around his neck.

The paved parking lot they pulled into, five miles south down the lakeshore from the rendezvous point, was separated by ten yards of ice-hardened brown grass from the ice-speckled sand of the beach. The beach stretched out another forty yards before the frothy edges of Lake Michigan rhythmically lapped at the shore, darkening the sand and turning it into a cold brown slush.

As Ryan rummaged and shuffled around in the back of the van, Dan looked through the windshield at the churning Lake Michigan. Its surface had been frozen less than a week ago. Since then the temperature had risen enough to thaw the lake, even though it was still frigid. Despite the cold, dark twilight, he found the Chicago skyline as striking as ever. The low hanging clouds obscuring the giant antennas atop the John Hancock Tower and most of the top third of Sears Tower emphasized the imposing height of the monoliths.

Dan brought his binoculars and swept the darkening horizon from right to left, scanning from the southern curve of the Great Lake to the downtown skyline. When he was done, he lowered the binoculars to his chest and turned to the rear of the van where he watched his grandson pull the hood of his wetsuit over his head and slip his night vision goggles over his eyes.

"Is that suit gonna keep you warm enough?" Dan asked. "That's some cold-ass water out there."

"It better, or somebody's getting their ass kicked," Ryan said as he strapped on his oxygen pack. "I paid a lot of money for this suit. It's thicker than standard wet suits and it's supposed to lock in body heat better. I'm already starting to sweat back here."

The eye, mouth and nostril holes were small enough that the facemask and goggles, both rimmed with rubber that formed an airtight fit on the surface of the wetsuit, kept the cold and the wet from touching his skin. Ryan made a few minor adjustments and double-checked the oxygen feed in his facemask before scanning the lake in a wide arc that ended at the Ferris wheel on Navy Pier. He looked back to his grandfather.

"So how's the view?"

"About what you said," Dan conveyed. "Two fake fishermen about a half-mile out on the lake from the rendezvous point, two watchers in a parked car roughly a half-mile up shore, and two fake joggers on the path just up the rise, about a hundred yards."

“You sure?” Ryan asked skeptically.

“What?” Dan challenged, “You don’t trust me to spot spooks? I’ve been doing this for years.”

“You haven’t done this *in* years,” Ryan corrected.

“Let’s look at the score card,” Dan chuckled. He lifted a finger to check off each incident. “They got to you in your fortified, surveillance-camera-ridden building. They missed me in a next-to-no security rest home. They almost blew you to hell in that same rest home while I was waiting for you in *your* car. And I haven’t done this in years.”

“Alright,” Ryan surrendered. “Mike check, please?”

Dan hooked the tiny microphone-tipped earpiece onto his right ear. Ryan’s small headset, which consisted of a dime-sized earpiece and wire-thin microphone, was already fitted under the hood of his wetsuit. They clicked to each other and nodded that their equipment was functional. Ryan then lifted and inspected the dive propulsion vehicle and opened the van’s back doors. The DPV was a lightweight, submersible, handheld scooter that looked like a miniature torpedo with small wings and handlebars.

“That thing runs silent, right?” Dan asked. Ryan nodded in the affirmative. “They’ll be watching real close. They may have scramblers, you know.”

“Don’t worry, gramps,” Ryan said. “I’ll stay deep enough so they won’t see me. They picked the beach because it’s wide open and easier to watch, so they’ll be scrambling for higher-level, long distance surveillance equipment. This wet suit and the cold water will mask my heat signature when they use night vision after dusk. Besides, they won’t expect anyone to be close as I’ll be. My low-level audio receiver should pick them up fine.”

“Stay low, anyway.” Dan advised.

“I’ve done this before, gramps,” Ryan assured as he opened the back of the van. “I’ll be fine.”

Dan used his binoculars to check their surroundings while Ryan jogged across the grass and then across the beach before easing into the dark gray, icy water.

Ryan went out into the lake until the water was up to his chin. Once there, he ducked low, aimed the DPV north and powered it up. As the DPV towed him along he felt the water flowing over him but the wetsuit effectively kept the cold at bay. He felt a bit of a chill through the diving mask but it was not enough to cause him discomfort. He and his grandfather successfully exchanged two more clicks to make sure their communications were working.

Ryan did not do much work underwater, and on the few occasions he did he had never had a problem with it. But this time was different. The feeling was more comfortable than it had ever been. It was pleasurable, in fact, like he belonged underwater almost as much as the fish. Hc fclt likc he could move through the water just as easily and quickly without the DPV.

And then he realized that this was the first time he had been completely submerged in a natural body of water since his visit to Lorr. He had almost died while killing a sea demon, and if not for Sabrina, the Mistress of the Sea, he would have died. Instinctively he knew that whatever Sabrina did to save him had caused this new connection he felt with the water. Ryan marveled at how, even three years after his return home, the Kingdom of Lorr was still teaching him new things about himself.

8.2

When Dan was satisfied that everything was fine, he used his arms to swing himself over to the driver's seat, buckled up, and pulled out of the parking lot. He may not have walked, but his legs worked well enough to drive an automatic.

It would not do to sit in one place for too long with all of the weapons and equipment they had in the back of the van. The last thing he wanted to do was be conspicuous. The police patrolled the area periodically and there was a slight chance that one of those patrols might be a disguised organization agent. He would drive a few miles up Lake Shore Drive and back a few times and then meet Ryan in the parking lot in two hours, or sooner, if either of them gave the word. Ryan told him that meetings like the one about to take place were usually guarded within a two to three mile radius, but Dan was not taking any chances.

Dan did not particularly miss the covert work he did back before his daughter was born, but he was a warrior by blood. The near-sedentary life he led after Cynthia came along had been almost maddening. If not for his foresight over sixty years earlier warning him about eventual trouble with the WorldGate and the Kingdom of Lorr, he was sure he would have gone stir crazy. But as a result of that vision, as well as the fact that he had no idea of exactly when it would come to pass, he was able to occupy himself by preparing Cynthia and then Ryan for the crisis to come.

Now that he was at it again, even if not in an official capacity, that sense of excitement had returned. Dan's body was nowhere near as strong as it had once been but his mind was still sharp and his resources were still plentiful. He thought about the things he had seen, the places he had been, and the things he had done over the course of his long life. From the training he received from a Shao Lin monk as a child and young adult to both World Wars, from his covert work for the government, to his retirement, Dan had committed acts of heroism as well as acts that he was not at all proud of.

Overall, though, he believed he had done far more good than bad and that he would be welcomed into Heaven for the balance of his deeds. His only real regret was his inability to save his daughter.

Dan knew it was an irrational guilt. He was nowhere around when Cynthia died in that car accident. It was not his fault that his occasional foresight did not warn him of her impending death. But he felt guilty just the same for not being there. That guilt had been with him every day of his life since the moment he identified her body. That was why he committed himself to doing whatever it took to prepare Ryan. He felt he owed it to his daughter for his failure to protect her when she needed him most.

There was a time when he was afraid that Ryan would either not be ready for or worthy of the challenges ahead of him. It was only because of Cynthia that Dan continued to teach and train Ryan despite his strong doubts about his grandson's character. Not that he had much of a choice. With Cynthia gone, Dan and Ryan would be the only people capable of wielding Demonsbane, and Dan knew he had grown too old to do the heavy lifting. It was "Ryan or dyin," he liked to say to himself. His grandson's success in the Kingdom of Lorr made Dan proud.

Unfortunately, it seemed their trials were only beginning.

Dan checked his clock and saw that his reverie had made the two hours fly by. Night had settled in fully but Dan had barely noticed. He found himself turning the van back into the parking lot just in time to catch his grandson emerging from the water. In the darkness, Ryan's black diving suit made him nearly invisible. Dan switched his binoculars night-vision mode and scanned the area to make sure it was clear before turning his attention back to Ryan.

He immediately noticed Ryan's hurried movements. Instead of jogging back to the van the way Dan would have expected, Ryan sprinted as well as he could manage with the rubber flippers covering his feet and the DPV in his arms. He moved as if he were being chased.

"What's wrong?" Dan asked as Ryan made his way around the back of the van. The older man turned to his right when Ryan climbed into the sliding side door.

"I'll tell you while we roll, gramps," Ryan promised, shrugging out of his wetsuit.

Dan drove for five minutes, working his way west, before his curiosity got the better of him.

"So, what happened, boy? They see you?"

"No," Ryan said. "Everything went smoothly."

"So why do you look so spooked? What did you hear?"

"I didn't learn too much," Ryan said. "Johnson showed. I think he was with a director."

Dan's wispy eyebrows rose. "Really? You sure?"

"I know Johnson's voice," Ryan assured. "He uses a voice scrambler but there are little things, like inflection and accent and even word choice that a scrambler can't completely conceal. And he was showing a lot of respect for someone he was with, very deferential. The only people that supervisors defer to are directors."

"A director in a face-to-face with an underling? From what you've told me that's not SOP," Dan observed.

"Not at all," Ryan agreed. "That means this is serious business, gramps. They bitched about Clay not showing up and promised to terminate him if he didn't have a damn good excuse. They talked a little bit about you, me, the Harvey's – who they think are my CA's – and they talked about how we all need to be dealt with. But they didn't go into a lot of detail. They mainly complained about Clay."

"So are you going to tell me why you came running out of the water like your ass was on fire?" Dan asked.

"It wasn't what I heard," Ryan said. "It was something I felt. But it couldn't have been real."

As anxious as Dan was for his grandson to get to the point, he decided to let Ryan go at his own pace. Whatever it was clearly had the younger man shaken. Dan waited as Ryan climbed into the empty wheelchair where it was secured in place of a passenger side front seat.

"I got cold," Ryan started. "Real cold, and not from the water. It was an inner chill." Ryan shuddered momentarily as he recalled the sensation. "Then it felt like every hair on my body was standing on end, even under the wetsuit. And then I saw a reflection of a soft, silver light on my goggles."

"Someone with a flashlight searching the water?" Dan asked hopefully.

Ryan shook his head firmly in the negative. "The light was coming from *inside* the goggles."

"Uh oh," Dan said softly.

"Yeah," Ryan concurred. "Thing is, the silver-glowing eyes thing never happened to me without Demonsbane. The only time it *did* happen…"

"One of those guys was a demon," Dan concluded.

"But how could I have felt it without Demonsbane?" Ryan wondered aloud.

"Demons invoke the magic in *you*." Dan reminded. "Demonsbane's magic just works with yours." He thought for a moment. "So the feeling definitely came from one of the men on the beach?"

"Definitely," Ryan confirmed. "There were five of them. Two were with the director and one was with Johnson. The feeling washed over me from their direction. I was too far away to zero in on specifically which one it was. It took all of my will power not to rush the beach and kill all of them. If I had Demonsbane, I probably would have."

Dan's curious frown tightened into one of fear. "There *are* no human-looking demons, Ryan. The one you felt was either possessing one of those men, or it was a changeling."

"There are changeling demons?" Ryan asked.

"Unfortunately," Dan confirmed. "Apparently this demon can cross the WorldGate."

"Then it's Johnson," Ryan realized.

"Why him?" Dan asked.

"For starters, he's the one trying to kill me."

"But wasn't he was already trying to kill you?" Dan questioned. "Before the Hell Gates were ever opened?"

"This thing can cross the WorldGate," Ryan countered. "It can either possess people or shape change, too. Maybe it's smart enough to take the place of someone with the resources to get to me. It could be impersonating Johnson the way

WorldHopper impersonated Clay. Hell, Johnson was already after me so why not take his identity? It doesn't get any more convenient than that."

The two men drove back to their motel in thoughtful silence.

8.3

A couple of hours passed. In that time, Ryan and Dan went to their rented room so Ryan could shower and dress. They went to a cheap diner to wolf down greasy but delicious burgers and fries. There were too many people around to talk about their plans so they just ate and made small talk. When they returned to their motel Ryan had settled heavily onto the couch facing the front door and adjacent to the television. Dan wheeled himself to within a few feet of the couch. Both remained silent for long minutes as they watched cable news and considered their situation.

"I'll use Demonsbane to track the demon," Ryan finally decided.

"I don't like it," Dan said. "A demon that can imitate a human has to be pretty powerful. I'm talking sixth level at least and possibly seventh. Demons from those levels don't act like intelligent animals. They operate with human cunning. And when they decide to use brute force, nothing short of a God or a first-generation Child can match them."

"Then what am I supposed to do?" Ryan asked.

Dan started to respond and then paused. "You hear that?" he whispered.

"Of course I did," Ryan answered quietly. "I ain't deaf."

Dan's whisper turned harsh. "Then why are you sitting there like a damned stump?"

Ryan's right hand had been resting behind the cushion next to the armrest of the couch. He eased out a Walther P99 and used his left hand to chamber a round.

"Patience, old dude."

They waited for another few moments and then heard the soft sound of a key card being inserted into the lock on the outside of the door. Dan watched intently while Ryan shifted the gun behind the cushion. The doorknob turned slowly. Surmising that Ryan would be the target, Dan wheeled backward and away from his grandson and put himself in flanking position to whoever came through the door. His left hand went into a pouch hanging by the big left wheel of his chair and wrapped tightly around his own pistol.

Ryan was calm because his sixth danger sense never tweaked. He believed that whoever was on the other side of the door meant them no harm. He still held onto his gun. Just in case. The door opened slowly and two men – or better yet a man and a boy – stood in the doorway.

Ryan immediately recognized the six-foot tall man wearing a parka, khakis, and brown snow boots.

"Jorgé Barboza," Ryan said.

It was indeed Jorgé Barboza, ex-army colonel and commander of the Cutters. Almost ten years had years had passed since he last saw Barboza, and Ryan could count every one of them in the deep creases in Barboza's light brown face. Barboza was fifteen years older than Ryan, putting him near fifty, but he looked considerably older. His dark brown eyes, however, were just as sharp and intense as Ryan remembered.

The boy seemed to be in his late teens. He stood about an inch or so shorter than Ryan, who was five feet ten. He was a light-complexioned black teen and wore long corn rolls in his hair, much tighter and neater than Ryan's dreadlocks. The teen wore a three-quarter-length trench coat that covered everything but the bottom few inches of his pants legs and his Timberland-booted feet.

Ryan stood up and eyed Barboza warily. He kept the gun in his right hand, making sure it was clearly visible but letting it hang at his side with the nose pointing to the floor. They were not really friends back when they worked together. They were more like associates. There was never any animosity between them and there was no reason for Ryan to consider him a threat, but he was not in a trusting mood these days. The organization had a very long reach and Ryan could not rule out the possibility of them using an old ally to bring him down.

Barboza held out his right hand when he was in arm's reach of Ryan. Ryan switched his gun to his left hand to shake the offered hand firmly and curtly.

"Long time no see," Ryan said.

"Yes," Barboza agreed, his Hispanic accent faint but noticeable. "It's good to see you, Ryan."

"Why is that?" Ryan challenged.

"No pleasantries, then?" Barboza observed.

"How did you find me?" Ryan asked.

"And why?" Dan added.

"The 'how' is standing right here," Barboza answered, indicating the youngster next to him. "We call him Merge. The 'why' is a little more complicated. Mind if we have a seat?"

"Before you start," Dan urged, "Stop being rude and fill me in on who the hell you are."

"Jorgé was a colonel in the army," Ryan explained. "I worked with him...or rather for him, for a little while. He started the Cutters." He turned back to Jorgé. "What are you doing with yourself these days?"

"I'm a Branch Director now."

Ryan lifted an eyebrow and became that much more aware the Walther held comfortably in his left hand. He was ambidextrous with weapons of all types.

"No shit?" Dan asked. "You supervise supervisors and regional directors? That's a pretty heavy gig."

"I see your grandson has told you all about us."

"I don't have to keep secrets," Ryan said. "I'm not affiliated anymore. But you already knew that."

"Of course I did."

"Can I sit down?" Merge interrupted. "My ass starts to hurt if I stand up for too long."

"Hey," Dan chastised, "Quiet while grown folks are talking."

"I'll be in the car, George," Merge said as he cast a sharp eye at Dan and walked out of the hotel room.

"It's Jorgé," Barboza called as Merge shut the door.

"You're a Director," Ryan noted. "You let him talk to you like that?"

"You know I never gave a damn about formalities. He gets the job done. Well. That's all I require."

"How'd he find us, anyway?" Dan asked. "He's barely old enough to find his own ass. He can't be that skilled."

"That's part of the 'why' you want me to answer," Barboza said. "This really is an involved story...and my ass is starting to hurt, too."

Ryan waved his gun at the empty love seat across the room. Barboza nodded a thank you and sat down. Ryan re-seated himself as well and leaned forward.

"What does one of the four horsemen want with a lowly foot-soldier like me? This visit goes completely against organization chain of command and policy."

"Horseman?" Dan asked.

"I don't particularly care for the term," Barboza admitted. "It's a nickname the field agents came up with. There is a director for each of the four branches of the organization: Deactivation, Intelligence, Global Defense, and Omni-Research. We each wield a considerable amount of power, thus the nickname. I'm the Global Defense Director."

"Global *Organizational* Defense, to be exact," Ryan informed.

"Wait a minute," Dan said. "I get it. Four Horsemen? GOD Branch? I can't believe the egos on you sons of bitches. No wonder my grandson fit in so well with the organization."

"Hey, I didn't make up the name," Barboza replied with his hands raised open-palmed. "But it's fitting when you consider what the branch does."

"Global defense," Dan shook his head. "So you guys protect the 'world,' eh? From what, aliens?"

"If necessary," Barboza said, deadly serious. Dan chuckled nervously as Barboza continued. "But most of time we protect the globe from internal threats."

"I'll ask again," Ryan began. "Why would one of the horsemen break policy to communicate directly with a foot-soldier?"

"*Ex* foot-soldier," Barboza reminded. "You said yourself that you were no longer affiliated. How can I be breaking policy? I'm here in a recruiting capacity."

"Branch Directors don't recruit," Ryan said skeptically.

"We do on occasion," Barboza told him. "We recruit supervisors and regional directors...among other things."

"You want this boy for a director?" Dan scoffed.

"I doubt it," Ryan answered. "I must be one of the 'other things.' "

"One of the duties of Global Defense is to investigate unexplained occurrences of an extra-terrestrial, superhuman, or supernatural nature."

"X-Files type of stuff," Dan said.

"That was the FBI," Barboza corrected. "This is much, much more. We investigate these occurrences and determine whether their source would be of potential use to us or a threat to us and then respond accordingly. We also run sort of a checks and balances on the other three branches. They in turn do the same thing."

"I'm waiting for the part where you get to me," Ryan said.

"During one of our checks of the Deactivation Branch we uncovered evidence that suggested a number of unauthorized deactivations were being carried out by organization field agents. Now we have to engage in the balances part."

"Deactivations?" Dan asked. "Call it what it is: murder, hits, assassinations."

"Habit," Barboza admitted with a shrug. "Anyway, we suspected the hits were being authorized by a supervisor by the name of –"

"Johnson," Ryan finished.

"Coming together, is it?" Barboza asked.

"Why not go to the Deactivation Branch director with this?" Dan asked.

"It doesn't quite work that way Mr. Franklin," Barboza answered. "We all know the checks and balances thing is happening but we don't let each other know when we're doing it. That kind of defeats the purpose. When necessary, we have ways of leaking bits and pieces of information through indirect channels."

"So much bullshit…" Dan started.

"Gramps," Ryan snapped. "Let the man talk."

"Alright already!" Dan snapped back. Then he mumbled something about his grandson needing to learn respect.

Barboza cleared his throat and paused before continuing, allowing Dan to trail off into silence. "We believe Johnson caught wind of the investigation and decided to use one of his agents as a goat."

"Why me?" Ryan asked.

"Simple," Barboza answered. "You're the only one good enough to pull something like that off for so long a time and we all know it. Any other agent would have made his director suspicious."

"But I wouldn't get caught," Ryan said. "Ever."

"Maybe not," Barboza allowed before going on. "But Johnson did a great job of making it look like you were moonlighting." Now Barboza leaned forward and cocked an eyebrow. "We had people in place to observe their attempt to serve your pink slip at your building on the south side."

Ryan sat back in his chair, took a long sigh, and smiled. "So they must've seen my escape."

"I have video of you jumping through a third story window and being swallowed up by a two dimensional black hole. That was the last anyone saw of you for three years. And then, yesterday, we got a call about a man in a near north side tavern transforming into some kind of monster. He left several mutilated…well, mutilated isn't quite right. He left several *partially eaten* corpses in his wake."

"Damn dragon..." Ryan mumbled.

Barboza's eyes widened. "Dragon?" Ryan did not answer. Instead, he beckoned for Barboza to continue. The director did so reluctantly. "Imagine our surprise when we saw you and your grandfather chumming it up with the man-turned-monster just moments before his transformation. He even looked at the security camera and smiled. It was the scariest damn smile I've ever seen. And then he stepped out of camera range. No one knows what happened to him after that. He seemingly just disappeared."

"Chumming it up?" Dan asked. "He said a couple of words in passing and didn't even look at us. He barely moved his lips."

"We have some pretty extensive resources," Barboza reminded. "We noticed the exchange, brief as it was. You followed him to the bar but never got a chance to sit down, and we all know why. With your disappearing act three years ago and now your man-monster friend, you can understand how you'd make a rather large blip on my branch's radar."

"So what do you want from me?" Ryan demanded.

"First of all, I'd like to know what the hell is going on. I want to know what you meant by *dragon*. If the answers are satisfactory I'll offer you a job."

"What kind of job?" Ryan asked incredulously.

"I'm forming a new team and I want you to lead it."

The director reached into an inside breast pocket in his coat and produced a brown envelope. He held it out for Ryan's inspection.

Ryan laughed bitterly. "You think I'd leave one branch of the organization to join another? C'mon, man. You know me better than that. Besides, I don't do teams anymore. I'm strictly solo." He looked over at his grandfather, who was giving him the evil eye.

"And the only reason the old dude hangs with me is because I can't seem to shake him without killing him...and I've sworn off killing. Guess that's another reason I'd be no good for you."

"This job isn't like any other organization job," Barboza assured. "This isn't a glorified hit squad like the Cutters were, either. If you can figure out a way to achieve your objectives without casualties, that'd be fine with me. I'd actually prefer it."

"Completion of global scale defense without casualties?" Dan said in disbelief. "How is that even possible?"

"You'd have to see the group I've assembled," Barboza said. "Like I said earlier, we investigate cases of an extra-terrestrial, supernatural, and superhuman nature. In my time as director I've seen some amazing things. I've met some people who can *do* some amazing things."

Barboza leaned forward to move the envelope closer to Ryan. "I've recruited several of these people in the hopes of putting together an elite force to act as a global defense and enforcement team. I'd like you to be the field leader. The team members' summarized bios are in this envelope."

Ryan reached out and took the envelope. "This is just curiosity, Barboza."

Barboza nodded.

"Kendrick Scott," Ryan read aloud, looking at the color photo of a bespectacled black man with a wide, square jaw, light-brown complexion and full lips. Ryan could see the thick neck bulging from behind his ears. The neck curved down into broad shoulders that expanded out of frame. "Handle: Pillar," Ryan nodded his agreement. If the neck and shoulders were any indication, this guy was huge. "Specialty:" Ryan continued, "Demolition." He handed the sheet to his grandfather.

"Damn," Dan said, appraising the man's picture. "Demolition, eh? He probably uses his bare hands."

Barboza grinned but did not reply. Dan handed the sheet back to his grandson. Ryan set it aside and pulled another sheet from the envelope.

"Peter O'Kelly." The photo was of a Caucasian man with a fair complexion, close-cropped, carrot-red hair, a strong, straight nose and cleft chin. O'Kelly wore an eye patch over his left eye. The right one was pale blue. "Handle: Ace; specialties: sharp shooting and hand-to-hand combat." He frowned and passed the sheet to Dan.

"A one-eyed sharp shooter?" Dan chuckled. He examined the sheet a second longer and handed it back to his grandson.

"Whoa…" Ryan gasped with a wide smile as he looked at the third sheet.

"What?" Dan asked. "Let me see!"

"Hold on," Ryan said, swatting at his grandfather's reaching hands. "Let me read it… It says, wait, I can't pronounce that…"

"Vilamdehsrriath," Barboza offered. "It's pronounced: 'vill-am-DESH-ree-ath.' That's it. No surname."

"What nationality is that name?" Ryan asked, studying the photo of a stunning woman with smooth, almond-brown skin and thick, wavy blue-black hair that fell past a pair of slim but toned shoulders. She had high cheekbones and a softly curving jaw that narrowed down into a smart chin. The firm, no-nonsense set of her wide mouth and full lips was as alluring as it was intimidating.

As elegant as those features were, it was her wide eyes that dominated the image, and not just because of their brightness. Ryan thought it might be some kind of flaw with the photo because her irises were not quite round. They seemed more oval than circular, and the color was a light, pale shade of magenta. The only woman he had ever seen who could match her exotic, unearthly beauty was on the other side of the WorldGate: Sabrina the Mistress of the Sea of Spirits.

"Where is she from?" Ryan asked.

"She's not from *here*," Barboza said cryptically. "I'll leave it at that for now."

"Her handle is 'Light Rider,'" Ryan observed. "It says her specialty is explosives. You already have Pillar as your demolition expert. A little redundant, don't you think?"

Barboza smiled. "Not at all. Let's just say those descriptions are very general. And *very* understated."

Dan put that statement in the context of everything else the stranger had said and then clapped his hands in amusement. "A super team? That's what you're telling us. What is this, a freaking comic book?"

Ryan shook his head. "Whatever you think you know about me, I gotta tell you: I ain't no superman." He handed the envelope back to his old associate.

"I never thought you were superhuman," Barboza said. "Your monster friend from the tavern, definitely, but not you. I'm leaning the other way on you. And I don't mean extra-terrestrial."

"You believe in the supernatural, Jorgé? In magic?" Ryan teased. "I would've never guessed."

"I never believed in magic," Barboza admitted. "Not until almost a decade ago. But running the GOD Branch has made a believer of me."

"I'm not interested," Ryan said seriously. "Like said, I don't do teams anymore. I damn sure won't lead one."

"You showed excellent leadership skills as second in command and field leader of the Cutters," Barboza argued.

"It obviously wasn't good enough to keep the team together," Ryan countered.

"That wasn't about you," Barboza pressed. "That was about Doc Stewart. His pre-charter psych-eval was...well, it was flawed. He should've never been on the team."

"Doc Stewart?" Dan asked.

"Doctor James Stewart," Ryan answered. His eyes looked forward but Dan could tell he was looking to the past. "Yeah, the hacker we talked about. Problem was he didn't have the right temperament for the Cutters. I used all of my 'excellent leadership skills' to convince him to stay but he left anyway and convinced another member to leave, too. The Pentagon got impatient and scrapped the whole program before we could find suitable replacements for them."

"What you didn't know," Barboza added, "What I didn't know until after the fact was that the guys that put the Cutters together wanted Doc so badly they authorized his recruiters to misrepresent the Cutters. That was the only way to get him to join. They falsified his psych-eval to get final approval from the Pentagon. They thought he'd grow into the job but he never did. There was nothing you or anyone else could have done to keep him on the team."

"Those mother – " Ryan breathed.

"That's what I thought," Barboza said. "That was one of the final straws that pushed me out of traditional government service. Understand something, my branch doesn't engage in that type of bullshit. We don't follow standard intra-branch protocol. I hand pick my people myself because I want to know them. I want to look into their eyes. I want to know that I can trust them. And I trust you. As leader of my team you'd have complete autonomy to run it any way you choose. All I ask is all I've ever asked for: honesty and results."

Ryan rubbed his chin as if he was actually considering the offer. Barboza moved in for the kill. "You wanted to know how Merge found you and followed you without being detected? You want to know how a kid could do something that seasoned agents couldn't? You'd never guess how and you wouldn't believe me if I told you, at least not yet. Not until you see for yourself what he and the team can do."

"You'd be surprised at what I'd believe," Ryan intimated. "I've seen some pretty amazing things myself."

"And he's done some pretty amazing things, too," Dan boasted.

"I believe you both," Barboza said earnestly. "That's another reason I want you to lead this team."

"What's in it for me?" Ryan finally asked.

"You mean besides the satisfaction of serving mankind?" Barboza returned. He waited for Ryan to finish scoffing before he continued. "For starters, we'll help get your supervisor off your ass. Finances would never be a concern for you. You and the rest of the team will be among the wealthiest people in the world. You just wouldn't be able to let anyone know about it."

"What good is being filthy rich if no one can see the dirt?" Dan wondered aloud.

"You'll be able to quit at any time," Barboza concluded. "Whenever you think you've had enough, walk away and no one will bother you."

Ryan gave him an openly disbelieving look. "Bullshit."

"Not at all," Barboza countered. "I told you, I don't run my branch like the others. Don't get me wrong; we do have security measures in place. You can retire or resign without penalty, but if you ever told anyone about the organization, you and every individual you told would be terminated without hesitation. Until that time, and hopefully that time will never come, I guarantee you would not be harassed."

"I appreciate your honesty," Ryan answered dryly. "As tempting as this offer sounds, I'm kind of in the middle of something right now. Let me get through this and maybe I'll give your offer some thought."

"Fair enough," Barboza said. "Maybe we can expedite this whole process by helping you find that couple you're looking for."

"We've already – " Ryan's eyes widened. "How the hell did you...?"

"I have resources, my friend," Barboza repeated slyly.

Ryan jumped and suddenly turned to Dan, one eyebrow raised as he stared quizzically at his grandfather. Dan had an even stranger look on his face. A veil of fear and confusion shaded the older man's features as he stared into empty air.

“Gramps?” Ryan asked.

He recognized the look on his grandfather’s face. He had not seen it before but he had seen it on the face of old Shanderah when they were sailing aboard the *Blue Lady* in the Kingdom of Lorr, when the old sorceress came to the dreadful realization that an incredibly evil and demonic presence was near.

“I don’t think we’ll be needing any help,” Ryan said.

8.4

"What the hell is happening to us?" Lisa asked, lying on her back on the motel bed and staring at the ceiling, her brows knitted in frustration. By this time of night she had usually showered and changed into her nightclothes, but there was too much gong on for her to even think about sleeping. "What if he really was with the FBI? We could be in danger."

Joel was silent as he stood at the dresser and placed three different pills in his mouth: one for his asthma, another for his allergies, and a third, a steroid to strengthen his lungs and bronchial tubes. Lisa noticed that his hand was shaking as he lifted the glass of water to his lips. Without looking at her, he placed the glass unsteadily on the dresser and then walked over to the motel door.

He snatched open the southward facing door of their room, which was situated on the southwest corner of the second floor, and looked out into the night, inspecting the parking lot, the street beyond, and even the dark, starless night sky. With a grunt that Lisa recognized as wary satisfaction, he closed and locked door, making sure to secure the lock on the knob as well as the dead bolt and chain. The window on the opposite corner did not open, so when Joel walked briskly over to it, he peered out intently before snatching the drapes closed.

When he finally turned to face her, there was a strange, distant look in his eyes.

"We *are* in danger," he said gravely.

"What are you –" Lisa started. She stopped abruptly when Joel doubled over in apparent agony. "Joel! What's wrong?" Lisa jumped up from the bed and ran over to her husband. *First the nightmares and now this*, she thought. Her nerves were frayed to point of breaking.

She grabbed his shoulders in an attempt to help him to the bed. Joel flicked his left arm and swatted her away with so much force that she was hurled into the wall adjacent to the room next door. The wind was knocked from her lungs and she crumpled to the floor.

As she struggled to catch her breath, she looked over at her husband with wide, fearful eyes. She tried to call out to him but she did not have the strength and the sound came out only as a gasp. All she could do was stare.

Joel dropped to his knees, trembling. He bent forward so sharply that his nose almost touched the floor. Tears streamed down his face. His chin was buried in his chest and his face was contorted into a mask of agony. His arms folded across his midsection, his hands and wrists hidden from Lisa's view. She heard muffled popping sounds like someone cracking their knuckles, only this sound was much louder. She heard a soft tearing sound that she could not identify.

Joel slowly lifted his head and turned it to glare at his wife with eyes turned milky white. Lisa initially thought his eyes were rolled up into his head but she could just barely see his irises behind the weird film that covered them.

The grimace of pain melted away into a blank expression. He opened his mouth as if to speak, the action seeming to move at half speed. When the sound finally came his voice was hollow with an almost metallic resonance.

"Lock yourself in the bathroom," he thrummed.

Lisa could not move. She simply stared at her husband.

"Now!"

That last word was like the slow tolling of a bell that echoed in his wife's ears. Lisa's heart began to race. Her instincts told her to rush to obey. Unfortunately, concern for her husband overcame her good sense. She struggled to her feet as Joel's clouded eyes followed her expectantly. She wanted to go to him again and hesitated when she thought about how effortlessly he had just tossed her aside.

She caught a glimpse of her reflection in the wall-mounted mirror across the room and a strange movement made her turn to view it clearly. Her reflection twisted in front of her eyes until it was distorted as extremely as a fun house mirror. The mirror started to vibrate and Lisa cocked her head, puzzled. She wanted to help her husband but the weird mirror mesmerized her and she could not take her eyes off of it…until it exploded.

Lisa threw herself to the floor as razor sharp shards of glass blew across the hotel room, shredding the lamp shades and shattering the light bulbs beneath them and casting the room into near-darkness. Cold blades of glass sliced through her sweater and the surface of her skin on her arms and back. She could have sworn she saw a bolt of darkness streak through room along with the glass, but with the dim illumination filtering weakly through the closed drapes being the only light in the room, she could not be sure. An instant later she was face down on the floor, her head buried in her folded arms, too afraid to look up again.

An inhuman roar sounded from Joel's direction and Lisa could hear heavy, hurried footfalls, followed by the sudden groan of the hotel bedsprings as something fell heavily upon them. Warm waves of fear rushed up from her shoulders and crashed painfully against the base of her skull. She felt herself trembling as violently as her husband had been only a moment before...

Her husband!

She looked up to find Joel. He was no longer doubled over in pain on the floor in front of her. Now he was flailing wildly on the bed. Lisa shuffled backward on her hands and knees, the terror seizing her trembling legs not allowing her to stand. Joel's hands, forearms and legs were concealed within the folds of writhing sheets of shadow. Lisa saw his face, twisted with maniacal rage as he struggled and got tangled up in something that resembled a mess of dark, opaque rags.

Another shadow streaked out of the broken mirror and threw itself onto Joel, then another, and another still. In a matter of seconds Joel was completely covered with sharp-edged shadows that darted out of the broken mirror every other second. Lisa could hear the sounds of tearing cloth as the battle ripped the bed sheets to shreds. Feathers exploded into the air from decimated pillows.

Lisa tried to back further away from the bed but fear rooted her in place. She was too stunned to scream as she watched yet another shadow burst forth from the ruined mirror, but instead of joining its companions in their struggle with Joel, it stopped short and wavered for a moment, hovering in mid-air, turning opaque then transparent then opaque yet again. Its swaying movements were reminiscent of a charmed serpent, but that was where any similarity between it and anything of the natural world ended.

The deadly shadow-thing seemed undecided as to whether or not it wanted to join the attack. The uppermost edge of the thing reshaped itself into a flat diamond shape, what Lisa assumed was its head. And then it turned in her direction.

Her paralyzing fear eased its hold just enough for Lisa to spring to her feet and rush to the bathroom door. She tried to turn the doorknob but it would not budge. She banged the door with a clenched fist and screamed in fear and frustration. The sound caused the hovering and wavering shadow to coil in on itself and become rigid. Then it launched at Lisa like a deadly spring. She turned just in time to see the thing coming at her. She inhaled sharply and held up her hands in a useless attempt at defense.

A blur of movement hurled itself after the shadow and yanked it violently aside just before its sharp leading edge could pierce Lisa between the eyes. It took a moment for it to register with her that the blur of movement that saved her life was her husband.

Joel pinned the shadow to the wall beside her with one hand while the other hand swiped away one of the shadow-things that had coiled around his upper thigh. A large tear was now visible in his pant leg and it exposed a long, blood red, razor-thin line in his thigh where the shadow-thing had attached to him. Tiny rivulets of blood escaped to trickle down his leg.

Lisa stumbled away and cowered on the far side of the room, looking fearfully at Joel. That was when she noticed that what he was using to ward away their attackers were not hands at all. In the place of human hands, his wrists sprouted long, flat, double-edged lancets of bone that were roughly the same length as his forearms. The bases of the bone spikes were coated in coagulated blood. Ragged tatters of moist skin hung from the end of his wrists.

And then she caught a glimpse of Joel's eyes. Now they were a pure, depthless white that seemed to see everything and nothing. His lips were pulled back and his teeth were bared in a grimace of rage. Inhuman grunts and growls escaped his gnashing teeth while he sheared the shadow-wraiths to pieces.

He was a more frightening sight than the creatures he was fighting.

Lisa watched as Joel wielded his altered, deadly appendages deftly at the shadow things flying at him from the bed and mirror, taking great care to remain between them and his wife. Lisa could not hope to follow the path of his flailing arms but she could see the shadow-things bursting into tiny black specks that disintegrated into nothingness when Joel sliced through them.

But the shadow-things kept coming. Somehow she knew that Joel was the target and that the shadow-things hoped to break him by bringing her down. The evil intentions of the creatures seemed to seethe from their sharp edges.

Lisa also noticed that Joel was slowing down, tiring, and she knew it was only a matter of time before at least one of the nightmarish things got past him and then both she and eventually Joel would be done for.

Joel was starting to falter when the hotel room door came crashing in. A man partially adorned in gleaming silver armor burst into the room waving what looked to Lisa like a torch of blazing silver-white fire. His lean muscular arms, covered only by armbands just below his elbows connected to fingerless gauntlets by thin silver rods, looked as dense as steel. The thin sheen of sweat coating his mostly bare arms reflected the gleaming silver light almost as much as the metal of his armbands, making his arms look more like chiseled bronze than flesh. A silver visor-like helmet covered his face from his forehead down to a pointed tip that covered his nose, leaving his mouth and strong jaw line exposed.

His mouth was set in what looked for all the world to Lisa like a mirthless smile. It was a grim smile of battle-lust.

The medieval armor sharply contrasted his black t-shirt, tan khakis, and suede, ankle high Timberland shoes and the long, thick dreadlocks sprouting from above and below his helmet. Bright silver light poured out of the helmet's eyeholes. Whatever energy ignited his eyes and torch also caused his dark brown locks to gyrate and waver in their own individual pattern as if each were a living entity.

The newcomer threw himself into the battle with no hesitation. Many of the shadow-things that swarmed the room instantly turned and attacked him as ferociously as they had her husband.

The strange torch-bearing knight waded through an endless stream of sharp-edged cutting shadows, leaving streamers of silver light and exploding darklings in his wake, until the two men stood back to back. When the stranger came closer Lisa could see that the weapon he bore was not a torch at all. It was a blazing doubled-bladed battle-axe with a short handle. Together the two men formed an impenetrable wall of protection for Lisa, who could only stare in terrified amazement.

But the shadow-things kept coming. Many of the newest killing shadows that came through the broken mirror did not throw themselves carelessly at the formidable defenders. Instead, they flattened themselves against the walls and defied gravity, creeping slowly up to the ceiling. Once there, they changed direction and oozed over the warriors' heads. Lisa could not take her eyes off of the slow creepers. Breathtaking fear held her voice hostage to keep her from calling in warning to her protectors.

Lisa expected them to fall onto the men from above, but instead, they eased past the deadly duo. Too late she realized that it was not the men they wanted. Dozens of them grouped together almost directly above her head.

A strong hand gripped her shoulder, finally freeing her scream as the shadow-things rained down from the ceiling. She closed her eyes and shielded her head with her hands and forearms, the unfamiliar hand on her shoulder completely ignored. Lisa did not who the hand belonged to because the owner was just behind her and beyond her peripheral vision, but that was irrelevant. Whoever it was would be ripped to pieces right along with her.

Several seconds passed. The sounds of battle still raged in her ears and the smell of sweat and sulfur befouled the air around her. Yet she did not feel the cutting edges of the shadow-things on her flesh as she expected. She became more aware of the hand on her shoulder. It was not only strong, but it radiated a heat so intense that it should have seared through the fabric of her sweater and charred her flesh. But the heat did not burn.

Lisa risked opening her eyes and looked at the hand. It was dark brown and gaunt and heavily wrinkled, the hand of an old black man. But its strength defied its apparent age and frailty. Her eyes followed the right hand to the wrist, to a plaid sleeved arm and shoulder, then to the face. It was indeed an old black man, in a wheelchair, no less. His eyes shone, though not quite as intensely as the other stranger, with that same pale silver glow. She had been so captivated by the shadowy creepers that she did not notice him wheel into the room a few seconds behind the young knight.

In his left hand the old man held up a ridiculously small shield to ward away the attacking shadow-things. He was leaning over at a perilous angle in order to keep himself under the shield while holding it over her head. The shield amazingly held the creatures at bay. When they fell toward the old man and young woman, even outside the circumference of the little shield, they stopped abruptly in mid air just a few inches above them and bounced away as if they had struck an invisible barrier. Several of the things sped across the floor at them from every direction. They too were rebuffed after coming within several inches of Lisa and the stranger. The creatures attacked again and again but made no progress against their intended victims.

They did, however, have success against the outer edges of the big rear wheels of the old man's wheelchair, which apparently extended just beyond the invisible protective barrier. The brakes were engaged so the chair did not roll, but it did jerk and buck savagely as the shadow-things bent the wheel spokes and dented the rims. Soon the wheels were ruined and the chair collapsed, sending the old man crumpling to the floor beside Lisa. He was visibly shaken by the fall but still held the shield aloft and never loosened his grip on the young woman's shoulder.

And still the shadow-things flowed into the room through the broken mirror.

8.5

After they left Barboza and the kid at the hotel and rushed to the van, Ryan saw in his grandfather's eyes the burgeoning glow of power that was ignited by the presence of demons or demon magic. Ryan was taken aback by the sight and suddenly knew how others felt when they saw him under the influence of the same divine energy. As Ryan sped through the city streets, thankful for the first time that this part of the south side was as devoid of a police presence as usual, he saw the glow in Dan's eyes steadily intensify. He could tell from the way Dan looked at him that he was just as fascinated by the growing illumination in Ryan's eyes.

"I know this is nothing new for you," Dan said wistfully. "But I've never felt like this before. I mean, I knew about it, of course, but I never thought I'd feel it for myself. The power is amazing. I feel like I could lift this van."

"Yeah," Ryan agreed. "Almost *god*like, right? It's too bad we only feel this way when demon magic is around."

Dan went on in a tone that Ryan could only describe as giddy: "A demon. I finally get to fight one. Is it bad that I'm kinda excited about it?"

Ryan grinned. "Bad? No. Crazy? Definitely. That's what the magic does. It makes you eager to fight something that a sane person would run from like a bat outta…well, no pun intended. But I have to burst your bubble, gramps…whatever this is, it ain't quite a demon."

"Not *quite* a demon? Ryan, what are you talking about?"

"The feeling is different," Ryan tried to explain. "There's a demonic taint, no doubt, but it's not as intense, not as…I don't know, not as overwhelming as it would be if we were sensing a real demon."

"Then what?" Dan asked. "Is it some kind of demon-spawn creature, like those sand creatures you told me about?"

Ryan thought for a moment and shook his head. "Not really. It's hard to describe the difference. This isn't as substantial."

“No matter,” Dan said excitedly. “It may not be full-fledged demon, but it’s damn sure something that needs killing!”

When the van careened into the motel parking lot, screeching and skidding to a stop, Ryan intended to put on his armored visor and gauntlets and then pull Dan – wheelchair and all – from the van. But by the time Ryan reached behind his seat to quickly grab and put on his gear, Dan threw open the passenger side door and released the clamps that held the wheelchair wheels securely to the floor of the van. He then put one of his bony hands on each rear wheel, turned the chair with a deft twist, and launched himself from the van with one powerful thrust. The chair hit the ground rolling and picked up speed as Dan continued to spin the wheels. With his enhanced strength he could roll the chair much faster manually than he could with the electric motor.

Ryan had to sprint with his own magically increased speed to catch up with Dan. They both came to a stop at the foot of the outside stairway, feeling the evil magic clearly on the second floor. Dan might have been stronger and faster, but he would not be able to make the wheel chair ascend the stairway. Ryan slipped Demonsbane into his belt, stepped behind Dan, grabbed the chair’s armrests with either hand and easily lifted the wheelchair and his grandfather.

He cleared the flight of stairs in two bounding strides and let his grandfather take the chair the rest of the way while he dashed ahead and crashed through the hotel room door. He immediately saw Joel fighting and Lisa a few feet away, cowering on her knees and staring in horror at the shadow wraiths slithering toward her.

His first instinct was to go to the woman, who clearly needed more help than her husband, but his grandfather sent him a mental command to help Joel and assured Ryan that he would protect Lisa with the shield. And sure enough, that’s exactly what he was doing up until the chair collapsed.

Ryan fought back panic and frustration when out of the corner of his eye he saw his grandfather crash to floor. He wanted to rush over to him but there was no way he could. The magic surging through him magnified his strength, speed, and stamina to superhuman proportions but it did not make him physically invulnerable. It was all he could do to keep the countless razor-edged shadow things away from his flesh. If his and Dan's hotel had been a little further away he would have let his grandfather drive so he could to don his full suit of armor, which was stored safely in the back of the van, and he would not have to expend so much energy protecting his chest, shoulders, and thighs.

Then again, if they had been further away Lisa would undoubtedly be dead. Joel might have been a different story. With those weird bone blades bursting from his bloody wrists where his hands should have been, he seemed to be more than holding his own. But he did seem to be faltering just as Ryan and Dan entered the fray.

In order to keep from becoming too distracted, Ryan reminded himself that his grandfather's strength, speed and stamina were also magnified. That fact was evident by the way Dan held the Shield of Innocents firmly despite the pummeling it was taking from the powerful shadow wraiths. Even though the small sheets of blackness looked insubstantial, each one struck with the force of a baseball bat swinging for the fences.

8.6

Lisa was nearly blinded when she looked in the direction of the dazzling light from the axe-wielding stranger. The animalistic sounds continuing to issue forth from her husband could be heard loud and clearly. Razor-edged shadow creatures bounded across the room from every angle, many of them coming to within a finger's length of Lisa and the old man before bouncing away and attacking yet again. The scent of sulfur became nearly suffocating.

Lisa's world became madness and it took several long seconds before she could hear herself screaming uncontrollably. She was convinced that she had somehow fallen into hell and things could not get any worse...and then the window on the west-facing wall exploded into the room.

A tall figure ducked through the ruined frame. Lisa wondered how that could be since there was no balcony or walkway on that side of the outer wall. A flowing, woolen, hooded cloak covered the newcomer from head to toe, revealing no physical characteristics aside from its height. The hood hung low to conceal the wearer's face completely in shadow. The wide sleeves fluttered from his left wrist as his large left hand clutched the upper left side of the window frame. The right hand was tucked deep into the folds of the cloak.

By the time the stranger was completely in the room, the right hand was revealed just slightly as it pulled a long, crooked, wooden staff from the folds of the cloak. The staff was worn smooth from age and use but looked solid nonetheless. It was so long that when its tapered tip contacted the floor, the wider upper end reached up to within an inch or so of its bearer's shoulder. With its length and apparent density, Lisa thought the staff looked quite heavy even though the stranger wielded it as if it weighed only ounces.

Several of the shadow-things immediately attacked him, bolting across the room to engage the newest visitor. Before the dark, deadly edges of the jagged shadows could touch the cloaked figure, he raised the staff high and then slammed the tapered lower tip against the floor. Blinding white light mushroomed out of the top of the staff and exploded into millions of sparks that plumed outward in every direction. Brilliant sparks showered the room, pulverizing each and every shadow creature it touched while bouncing harmlessly off everyone and everything else.

The hidden left hand emerged from the billowing sleeves and flicked small black pellets at the broken mirror. The tiny spheres struck the glass and wood with a startling flash. When Lisa's eyes readjusted, the mirror was whole. There was not a crack or blemish or any other evidence that it had ever been shattered.

The room fell silent. The only sound Lisa could hear was the ragged breathing of the old man beside her. She watched as Joel wavered, slumped to his knees and fell face forward to the floor. The younger stranger was watching the cloaked figure questioningly as he lifted both hands to pull back the hood, revealing a sun bronzed, hard-lined but handsome face wreathed with dark blonde hair and intense blue eyes.

Her vision started to swim. She realized she was shaking violently and struggling to catch her breath. She could feel the pounding of her heart reverberating all the way up to her skull like a lingering bass drum. Then she swooned and fainted into the waiting arms of the old man.

Chapter 9: The Walkers

9.1

Master Mage Delthar was not at all pleased about being summoned to the military graveyard just outside of Fort Bastion. This was a task for the Head Mage. Rionn Lorr, however, had left on important business and his wife was compelled to stay near the castle to watch over the salt-packed, iron coffin-encased body of Mar-dah. So it had fallen upon the Master Mage Delthar, Headmaster of the *Chronicai Tul Myst*, to investigate the strange occurrence reported to him earlier that day.

He would have preferred not to. Fort Bastion was a quarter of a day's ride away and the Master Mage felt that his time would have been much better spent in more intellectual pursuits. But he was the Second Successor to the Head Mage, which meant he became the Head Mage if something happened to both Rionn and Catherine Lorr, and part of that responsibility meant that he had to serve in their place on investigative matters when they were unavailable.

It was a surprise to Delthar that Rionn Lorr would even have an interest in such a case. The Head Mage is notified of cases involving desecration of gravesites as a matter of procedure. However, the task of investigating the issue is usually handed down, bypassing the Master Mage tier altogether, to an Echelon One mage. What would make the Head Mage deem this case important enough for personal attention – or, in his absence, the attention of his immediate successors?

He frowned at the thought of himself as the Second Successor to the office of Head Mage. A Head Mage's wife being in line as successor had never happened prior to Rionn Lorr's tenure. The Headmaster of the *Chronicai Tul Myst* had always been the First Successor. Such a thing as this would never have been considered when Rionn's father, Tavin Lorr, was Head Mage.

Succession of power was only one of several revered traditions that Rionn Lorr had seen fit to break, all to the displeasure of the elder Master Mages. It did not matter that

Catherine's elven heritage invested her with a considerable amount of magic, nor that her years of informal training with the old sorceress Shanderah made her adroit at its use. What mattered was that she was a woman, and a woman holding such a high post was heretofore unheard of.

There had been one exception, of course, but only one. And she was an early-generation Child of the Old Ones, nearly as powerful as the Old Ones themselves. She was Rionn Lorr's ancestor, in fact. Such was not the case with Catherine Lorr. Not only was she a female not of divine lineage, she was half-elf. Her grandmother was the queen of the most powerful elven nation in the Known Lands, for Lorr's sake. There were no hostilities between The Kingdoms of Lorr and Thâlstrën, nor had there ever been in recorded history, but Thâlstrën was a foreign power nonetheless. If there ever happened to be any conflict between the two nations, who could say for certain where Catherine's loyalty would lie?

"Bah," he mumbled under his breath dismissively. This argument was raised years ago and settled by King William himself. He knew there was no point to allowing himself to be annoyed by something he had no authority to change.

Instead, he turned his attention to the mission at hand. Even then, he could not help but bristle. During the Cursed Opening he was not deemed fit to defend the capital city alongside the younger mages of the Conjurer's Alliance at the Tyne. Yet he was the perfect candidate to handle a silly grave-robbing incident while Rionn Lorr was on a mission – with Quick – no less.

Much the same as the decision to appoint his wife First Successor, Delthar could not help but question the Head Mage's wisdom in placing so much responsibility on the shoulders of such a young, brash and under-trained being as Quick, regardless of his untapped potential.

He sighed in resignation, glancing up at the heavens for guidance he knew could not be found there. The sky was overcast and the cool air was so humid that it was sticky, all of which only served to further dampen Mage Delthar's already dour mood. His horse plodded along the soggy trail, following it between old oaks with low-hanging branches that crisscrossed over the path. The branches were slick and leaves drooped from the heavy moisture saturating the air.

Delthar, as well as Minister Geoffrey riding beside him and the five other soldiers behind them, had to duck beneath crooked branches on several occasions before they finally came to the end of the trail. The groundskeeper, a shorter and wider man, rode high in his saddle with no difficulty. The top of his wide-brimmed hat missed even the lowest-hanging branches by inches.

The path ended at a large clearing. Beyond it was a well-manicured expanse of lush green grass that would have been brilliant on a sunny day. The clearing consisted of four plots. Each plot was two hundred yards wide by one hundred yards long. They were horizontally oriented in two rows and two columns and separated by ten-yard wide cobblestone paths. The clearing was called a yard, which was enclosed on all four sides by tall oaks and high walls of smartly trimmed brush.

Each plot contained smooth, polished marble and granite headstones arranged in a neat pattern of fifteen rows and thirty columns. Masterfully carved sculptures and statues adorned the yard as well, ranging from waist high to nearly ten feet tall. Some of the sculptures were of weapons. Broadswords, shields, war hammers and battleaxes, all carved to larger-than-life scale, seemed to thrust upward from beneath the earth as if the occupants of the soil beneath held them high in salute to the Old Ones. Other sculptures were intricately chiseled busts of the people buried beneath them, their brow and chin set in proud defiance.

There were thirty-seven yards such as this in the Warriors' Rest. Each roughly the same size, cleared and filled in response to military actions over The Kingdom of Lorr's history. Usually, the Warriors' Rest Memorial Park was milling with grievers and respect-payers. But due to circumstances that the Master Mage was now investigating, the cemetery had been temporarily closed to visitors. Delthar had seen this place at times when misty skies and ominous clouds did not veil the suns as they did this morning. On bright days the suns' rays danced across the polished stone and bathed the multi-colored flowers in brilliance.

On this gray day, however, there was nothing bright about the place. It was just a place of the dead. Other than that, there was nothing out of the ordinary.

"Nothing seems amiss," Delthar said to Minister Geoffrey.

"The area in question is on another part of the grounds," the groundskeeper explained. He turned, and both the Master Mage and the Minister of War saw the frightened and fascinated look on the shorter man's wizened face. "It is in the newer area we cleared for those who died during the Cursed Opening."

The groundskeeper led them along a wide, worn path that ran through the middle of the yard. Grave markers spread out to the left and right of the riders as they made their way to the far end, where another dense stand of trees closed in on either side. While dense, the stand was not very deep. After fewer than five yards the cluster of trees and brush opened to yet another clearing that appeared almost identical to the first. They went through two more such yards before reaching their destination.

For the most part, this yard was very similar to the ones through which they had just ridden. There were, however, a few notable differences. The gravestones were only three years old, so they were not as weatherworn as the markers in the other yards. And even though the same amount of area had been cleared, there were only three large plots. As terrible as the Cursed Opening was, the number of casualties was small when compared to campaigns on the scale of the Carthan Defense or the Dragon War. But Delthar's eyes grew wide when he noticed the most terrible difference.

On the rear right plot, over a third of the graves had been dug up.

"All of this happened overnight?" Delthar asked.

The groundskeeper nodded. "But not last night. It happened three nights ago."

"And you are just telling us?" the Master Mage asked with more than a hint of irritation.

"We initially assumed grave robbers," the groundskeeper said, withering somewhat under the harsh glare of the wizard.

Delthar spurred his mount to a trot and stopped it at the tenth row. All but eight of the graves on that row, as well as the entire eighth and ninth rows, had been severely disturbed. The wizard dismounted and approached one of the unearthed graves.

"Grave robbers?" Delthar inquired of the groundskeeper as he inspected the scattered clumps of soil. "It would have taken an army of them to accomplish this much overnight."

"That was our first thought," the groundskeeper answered. "We've had grave robbers here before, and the Echelon One mages that investigated always caught out the offenders. We've caught the sodders ourselves in the act many times and had local law enforcement take custody of them so there was no need to contact the castle."

The old man pulled his hat from his balding head and wrung it in his wrinkled hands. "But grave robbery is an offense that doesn't usually require a speedy response, so there's never been an urgent rush to notify the castle. The process has sometimes taken as long as a week. We'd filled in several of the graves over the first couple of days before one of the diggers slipped and fell into one of them. He noticed that, other than the number of disturbed sites, this case was very different."

"What was different about it?" Delthar asked. He was not familiar with grave robbers or their methods.

Minister Geoffrey and his men rode up with a metallic jingling of weapons. "No tracks," he revealed. He dismounted and peered warily at the grave. "At least not grave robber tracks."

Delthar raised a bushy eyebrow. "What do you mean 'at least,' Minister?"

Geoffrey was leaning over the hole as he beckoned Delthar closer. The old wizard came to his side at the edge of the open grave and looked down. There were clear tracks, but not like any Delthar had ever seen. He did not have to be a tracker to recognize a boot print or a bare footprint. Human feet did not make the prints leading from this disturbed grave, at least not human feet covered in flesh. The prints looked…skeletal.

"See that?" Geoffrey pointed down the hole, dread beginning to shroud his features. "Grave robbers usually steal jewelry or sometimes even clothes. Not entire bodies. There's nothing there but a moldy old pair of boots. And look at the coffin. Grave robbers pry coffins open or break off the hinges and lift the lid. This one has been busted open. See how splintered and ragged the hole is. The pieces are scattered around the outside of the coffin…as if…as if it was torn open from the *inside*."

Delthar frowned. "I suppose all of the disturbed graves have similar tracks: only one set leading away from the site?"

The groundskeeper nodded. "And the dirt. The way it is spread, it does not look as if it was dug up with a shovel. It looks like it has been pushed out from below."

The Master Mage's frown deepened. A shiver went through his bones despite the warmth of his heavy cloak. Geoffrey could see in the wizard's eyes that the old man feared to say what they all were thinking, as if not speaking the words aloud would make them untrue.

"It cannot be," a soldier whispered to the soldier next to him.

Geoffrey shot him a sharp glare to quiet any further comment. Even so, his eyes mirrored the fear shared by all of them. Delthar stared in silence, his mind working. After a time, he asked:

"Have you seen the death records of the men who were buried in these graves?"

"Yes," the groundskeeper answered, looking even more disturbed.

Delthar's mustache twitched. "From the look on your face, my good man, it is clear that you discovered something that worries you."

"Well, yes, Master Delthar," the groundskeeper admitted. "All of them died in a similar manner."

"And what manner is that?" Delthar asked

"Yes…well, as you well know," the groundskeeper stammered, "All of the men in this particular yard died during the Cursed Opening. Most fell during the battles at Southborough, Silverleaf, and the other cities that fell to the Legion Midnight. But most of the soldiers in these last three rows fell...in a different manner."

"And what manner is that?" Geoffrey echoed with more than a hint of impatience.

"Against demons," Delthar realized.

The groundskeeper wrung his hat even harder and nodded in confirmation. "They fell at the Tyne in defense of the capital city and also at Bluethorn. Each occupant of the unearthed graves died at the fang or claw of a demon."

Geoffrey's heavy brow bunched up in anger and worry. "They were not supposed to be buried here," he rumbled in low tones. "Strict orders were given that their bodies were to be burned."

"Surely if they would have known – " the groundskeeper began, but he was cut short by the fuming minister.

"Of course no one knew *this* would happen," Geoffrey snarled. "Our concern was that the demons' taint on the dead bodies might poison the soil over time. That would have been bad enough! But *this*..." the minister looked at the grave again and shook his head dejectedly.

The Master Mage immediately began considering the implications of what he was hearing and seeing. "All of these men died at the Tyne and Bluethorn? No exceptions?"

"Not according to their death records," the groundskeeper said softly.

"We must follow those tracks," Geoffrey advised. "But I fear our group is too small for the number of graves that have been unearthed. We'll have to send for more troops and then follow at a distance while the tracks are fresh. It would not be wise to confront...whatever this is...until our numbers are greater. Far greater."

Delthar turned to Geoffrey. "Who keeps the military medical records?"

"Most of the records are kept in the offices of the Royal Infirmary at Fort Bastion," the minister informed. "But these men's death records are here."

"It is not these men I am wondering about," Delthar explained. "It is fairly obvious what appears to have happened here. At present, I fear for those who were wounded by demons but not killed."

Fearful realization widened Minister Geoffrey's eyes. His head snapped to one of his men. "Lieutenant, take two men and ride hard to Fort Bastion. Have them search through their records to find and locate everyone wounded or killed by those monsters during the Cursed Opening. Find where they live or where they're buried." The lieutenant saluted in acknowledgement but then hesitated. Geoffrey raised his eyebrows. "What is it, soldier?"

"I fought at the Tyne," the soldier said. "I wasn't wounded by a demon but I know of one who was. Witnessed it with my own eyes, I did. It was Captain Johnican."

Delthar turned to Geoffrey. "Minister, we should take a few men and go to his home. Perhaps we can ease our fears by finding Captain Johnican well."

9.2

Gwendolyn Johnican reluctantly let the wizard Delthar and Minister Geoffrey into the two story wood and stone house. The stench of sickness greeted them the instant they crossed the threshold. The captain's wife had obviously tried to hide it behind the scent of strategically placed flowers and fragrant candles but the unpleasant odor lurked beneath.

Geoffrey immediately noticed the fresh scars and bruises on Gwendolyn's face and gave Delthar a sidelong glance. Delthar gave a slight nod to acknowledge that he, too, noticed the marks. They followed the woman through the foyer into a parlor that led to the main hallway. Her stiff posture and short, hurried steps betrayed her nervousness.

"Please have a seat, sirs," Gwendolyn offered. "I will fetch my husband for you."

The two men seated themselves on a plush and large but stained couch. Their hostess exited the room at a near jog, leaving the Master Mage and the Minister of War alone. Geoffrey turned to Delthar.

"Already I dislike this," Geoffrey murmured. "Something is wrong here."

"Her bruises," Delthar said, "and the smell of this place..."

"The woman is clearly afraid," Geoffrey observed. "I can understand surprise at such high-ranking officials paying an unannounced visit, but she looked genuinely frightened. Why would she fear us so?"

Delthar considered the question. "You saw her bruises. Perhaps it is not us that frighten her."

A short, malnourished man walked unsteadily into the parlor. His cheekbones threatened to poke through the ashen skin hanging from his face. His tunic draped from his skeletal shoulders, the fabric failing to hide his starkly protruding collarbones. He wore nothing to cover his long, bony feet. His toenails, like his fingernails, were long and unkempt, almost claw like, and colored a dull brown. A look of perpetual exhaustion clouded his filmy blue eyes.

The Minister of War and Master Mage stood to greet him. Geoffrey was struck at his height – or lack thereof. He was stooped to at least two inches shorter than when Geoffrey last saw him. As weak as he looked, Geoffrey was surprised the sickly man could carry the long sword sheathed at his bony hip without tipping over.

"Captain Johnican?" Geoffrey asked. He stopped himself from frowning but could not keep the shock from cracking his voice. When last he saw Johnican, the tunic that hung from him like a sheet would have fit him snugly. His eyes had been bright and alert, his skin tanned and taut. "What has happened to you, man? You are ill."

Delthar wore an impassive mask as he watched Johnican. The Master Mage's long, thick whiskers hid any facial signs of emotion, but he watched Johnican with an intense, scrutinizing gaze as the sickly man settled himself uneasily on a smaller couch facing the one occupied by his visitors. After the visitors had seated themselves, Johnican tried to speak but was seized by a fit of coughing that lasted for almost thirty seconds. When the fit abated, he took two deep, ragged breaths and composed himself as much as he could.

"A bit of the flu," he said. The phlegm in his lungs rattled as he spoke. "Nothing that rest and proper care can't fix."

Delthar and Geoffrey exchanged incredulous glances but decided to go on with the purpose of their visit. Geoffrey leaned forward in his chair. "We paid a visit to the Warriors' Rest and were disappointed to find the graves of hundreds of soldiers that were not supposed to be there."

"Yes," Johnican rumbled. "I suppose you would have."

"Why?" Geoffrey demanded. "You were given direct orders to have those bodies burned."

Johnican's yellow eyes darkened as he barked out a wet cough and spit a glob of thick, greenish brown fluid onto his own floor. Gwendolyn frowned and looked away disgustedly. Johnican leveled a maniacal glare at his superior.

"What was ordered was blasphemy," the sick man argued. "Those warriors fought and died valiantly in the service of the Kingdom of Lorr. They deserved better."

"By order of the Head Mage and King William, himself, you were commanded to burn those bodies," Geoffrey admonished.

Johnican's limp posture straightened. Delthar felt something at that same instant. It was reminiscent of a swift breeze carrying the scent of carrion with it as it rushes past, there one second and then gone the next. The difference in this case was that Delthar did not smell something foul. He felt something foul, a fetid pulse in the incorporeal lines of magic that pass through every living thing. The sensation was fleeting and only the most sensitive of wizards would have been able to catch it.

The Master Mage Delthar was one of those wizards. He leveled a suspicious glare at Captain Johnican.

"I fought alongside those men against accursed demons and watched them fall with my own eyes," Johnican spat. "You would have me dishonor their families and desecrate their memories by burning them like diseased dogs?"

The man was clearly sick, and Geoffrey could understand if his mood was as foul as his appearance, but he was still the Minister of War, and he could not abide the disrespect being shown to him.

"Did you think the order was given gleefully?" Geoffrey questioned, the volume of his voice rising with frustration. "If you did, then you were a fool. The order was given to protect the living. It was not your place to disobey."

The dark look in Johnican's eyes was quickly turning to madness. "Minister or not," Johnican growled, "I will *not* be insulted in my home."

It was Delthar's turn to speak. He looked over at Gwendolyn. "My good lady," he began in a soothing voice, "I think it would be best for you to leave us now. This discussion seems to be taking an unpleasant turn."

"Thank you Master Mage, but I will be staying by my husband's side," Gwendolyn graciously declined.

Delthar looked at the bruises on her face and wondered why she was even still in this home. He shook his head with sadness and turned his attention to the simmering captain.

The wizard inspected Johnican with his eyes and with his magic when he spoke.

"When you fought against the demons, captain, did you sustain any injuries?"

"No!" Johnican barked quickly. Too quickly.

Delthar caught Gwendolyn's quick glance at her husband's left ribcage. The woman's brow knitted for a fraction of a second before she regained control of her emotions and expression.

Delthar's gaze darkened with suspicion. "It is not wise to bc untruthful to a Master Mage, Captain Johnican."

Johnican jumped to his feet. "This one calls me a fool and you call me a liar!" he roared as thick mucus frothed from his mouth. "In my own home! I'll not have it!"

His long sword was unsheathed in a flash and he leapt at Delthar with a quickness that utterly contradicted his near-death appearance.

The wizard had long since conjured a shield to protect the three of them from just such an instance, but Geoffrey did not know that. The Minister of War was nearing his sixty-third winter, yet he moved quickly enough to draw his broadsword and rush to meet the crazed captain.

Johnican's strength was as deceptive as his speed. Geoffrey outweighed the captain by at least seventy pounds, yet the overhand blow drove the minister to one knee. But while Johnican's strength and speed were greater than they had ever been, he was in a frenzied state and Geoffrey was far more skilled. When Johnican raised his sword to strike again, Geoffrey shifted his sword to thrust upward and outward. Using his legs to power his thrust, he pushed his broadsword through Johnican's abdomen all the way to the hilt. He kept going forward until his thick shoulder struck Johnican's chest and lifted the lighter man from his feet.

Gwendolyn screamed.

Minister Geoffrey barreled across the parlor with her husband impaled on his broadsword until the two of them crashed into the far wall. Delthar waved his hand in Gwendolyn's direction and mouthed a silent spell, causing the frantic woman to fall to the couch unconscious. He turned back to where Geoffrey stood breathless several feet away from Johnican, who was pinned firmly to the wall and unmoving. Geoffrey looked over to Gwendolyn lying asleep on the couch and gave Delthar a small smile of gratitude. The look in his eyes, however, betrayed his guilt for what he had just done.

"Perhaps I went a bit too far, eh, wizard?"

"Perhaps not, minister," Delthar answered.

"Perhaps not," Geoffrey echoed. "I've known Johnican for years. Even when he was healthy his strength was no match for mine. How could such a puny and clearly sick man be so formidable? What form of sorcery was that?"

"It was more than just magic, of that much I am sure," Delthar said. "I probed him thoroughly. There was an initial pulse of magical energy before he went berserk. After that there was nothing, at least nothing magical."

Geoffrey approached the still form pinned to the wall and reached for his broadsword. "So what do we—?"

Johnican's eyes bulged open and his arms snapped out. Pale, emaciated fingers reached for the minister's neck. Geoffrey yelped and backpedaled while knocking the grasping arms away. He stopped at what he thought was a safe distance and watched in morbid fascination as Johnican struggled wildly against the cross guard of the broadsword that held him fast to the wall.

Geoffrey's morbid fascination turned into fear when Johnican began to inch forward. The cross guard held fast, gouging through his flesh and tearing into his abdomen with a soft, squishing sound until it was completely hidden within him. Johnican kept going. He slid along the two-hand length of the broadsword grip, growling like a feral beast, his grimace displaying blue gums and brown teeth. A moment later the sword's pommel was disappearing into captain Johnican's gaping wound.

Johnican's arms stretched closer as Geoffrey unfastened the loop on the handle of the combat hatchet that hung at his hip. There was a wet cracking sound that the two men watching could only assume was the cross guard breaking through Johnican's spine. Geoffrey raised the hatchet and looked over to Delthar.

"Even a small bit of assistance would be appreciated, Mage!"

The minister had been so entranced by the spectacle of Johnican that he did not notice Delthar's hands moving the entire time. The wizard thrust his hands forward, palms out, and sent a ball of golden light streaking across the room. The ball unraveled into thin strings of light that extended as they neared Johnican. By the time the rabid captain pulled himself free, the illuminated strings of energy resolved into a gilded web of light that netted Johnican from his neck to his feet, threw him back onto the broadsword and slammed him against the wall. The light web pinned Johnican as securely as the broadsword had, causing Johnican to struggle even more hysterically than before.

"I would not do that, Johnican," Delthar cautioned. "Your flesh will yield. The light web will not."

Johnican was not listening. He shuddered and snarled and slobbered as he pushed against the webbing, his yellow-eyed gaze burning into the eyes of the Minister of War. As Delthar warned, the light web cut deeply into the captain's pale flesh, yet the determined madman did not stop. He growled as he moved forward, ignoring the strands of light cutting like razors all the way to his bones.

Geoffrey's fear soured to terror when he saw Johnican gather himself for one last push. The captain braced the sole of his right foot against the wall, leaned his upper body forward, shoved with all of his surprising might and went right through the webbing. Or more accurately, the webbing went right through him. Nearly his entire body, from just below his neck to just below his knees, toppled into a pile of diced and bloody pieces of flesh and bone.

The right foot and shin that he braced against the wall thumped wetly to the floor. The shin and foot of his left leg slumped forward but was held upright, suspended by the netting. Other than that, only his head was whole; it tumbled down the pile and rolled near Geoffrey's feet. The terror Geoffrey felt increased tenfold when the severed head rolled around, stopped and snarled soundlessly at him. The brown teeth gnashed and the eyes burned as evilly as they had before.

"By the Gods," Geoffrey swore. "And you say this is *not* magic?"

"None that I can detect," Delthar admitted, "at least not now. There was a faint trace and then there was that instant when I felt something pulse, but that was all. After that, all traces of magic disappeared."

This time, not even Delthar's flowing whiskers or years of controlling and subduing his emotions could conceal the astonishment on his face. "The way his blood had thickened and darkened," he continued, "he was virtually a walking corpse. It should have taken much more magic than I felt to animate him to such a degree."

He flicked a finger at the webbing of light still clinging to the wall and made it blink out of sight, causing the suspended remains of the left leg to topple to the floor.

"If you do not mind, Geoffrey, could you have one of your men locate a heavy blanket or sack that can be used to tote the head?"

"Of course, Delthar," Geoffrey said, anxious to be away from the harrying site before him. "I will have another carry the lady to the infirmary at Greenglenn. If this is the result of some sort of...of infection, then that would be the best place for her."

"Indeed," Delthar agreed. "I want her examined and interviewed as soon as she is able to speak. We need to find out how long Johnican was sick." He frowned down at the pile of diced flesh and bone. "You may want to retrieve your weapon now. I am going to burn the rest of him."

Geoffrey slipped on his leather riding gloves, not wanting to touch his bloodied weapon with his bare hands, and stepped carefully around the severed head at his feet. The maniacal eyes followed him and the mouth snapped angrily, causing the minister to hasten his pace.

When he reached the broadsword, he looked down at the gross pile in spite of himself. "Strange," Geoffrey observed as he gripped the broadsword and yanked it free. "I would have expected much more blood."

"There *should* be much more," Delthar agreed. He squinted at some slight movement within the mess and saw a grimy severed finger wriggling amid the gore, worming its way slowly, but relentlessly, toward them. "Step away, Geoffrey, so that I may expunge this abomination."

Geoffrey wiped the thick dark fluid from his broadsword onto the arm of the couch and sheathed it before removing his ruined gloves and tossing them on top of the captain's remains. He then gathered Gwendolyn's prone form in his arms and carried her out. Delthar stoked his beard thoughtfully as he studied the gruesome pile as well as the severed head, which was still scowling and snapping at them.

The Master Mage whispered a spell and reached into the folds of his robe near his ribs. He pulled a wand from his robe, a straight, brown wooden rod about the diameter of his finger and almost as long as his forearm. A very close inspection revealed runes in the form of tiny letters of an ancient alphabet.

Delthar did not usually use a wand. He did not usually need to. He was probably the most experienced and accomplished human wizard alive and he had excellent control of his magic. But the spell he was about to employ was potentially very dangerous, and it was one of the few spells for which he needed the extra focus and control provided by a wand or wizard's staff.

The small runes had already begun to glow with a pale green luminescence, and with a flick of the wrist, Delthar sent a small white spark arcing from the tip of the wand to top of the gruesome pile. The instant the spark came into contact with the wriggling flesh it exploded into whitefyre, a blinding wash of white flames that quickly consumed the pile. Delthar watched the flames and concentrated, willing his magic through his wand to keep the whitefyre on task. One lapse of concentration and the magical flames could easily and quickly ravage the entire home.

But the Master Mage would not lose concentration, not even for a moment. The pile of diced flesh was reduced to ashes in less than fifteen seconds. The whitefyre, its work completed, quickly dissipated, leaving no evidence of its existence save for the white ashes that had once been Captain Johnican's flesh and bones.

When Delthar joined Geoffrey outside of the home, they received a report that two other soldiers in Fort Bastion had just experienced the same terrible transformation as Johnican. One of them went berserk while on guard duty outside of the armory at the center of the town. His comrades immediately struck him down. Tragically, the other victim was home with his family when the change came upon him. He struck down his wife, son, and daughter before leaving his house and heading east. The soldier had traveled nearly half a mile before the bodies were found. Before he could get another half mile further, he was chased down and cut down by pursuing soldiers.

As much as he hated to, Geoffrey knew he would have to give the order to securely bind the bodies and bring them along. After the disturbing sight at the cemetery, he knew they could not risk the possibility of the corpses becoming animated.

"There is one thing more, sirs," the messenger concluded. "The Duke of Emerald Plains has sent a battalion to stop the grave-robbing renegades that desecrated the Warriors' Rest."

Master Mage Delthar's eyes opened so wide that his crow's feet almost disappeared. "No!" he snapped. "He sent them without first seeking royal counsel?"

"Master Delthar," the messenger said, "There was no time. His troops are among the best in the kingdom. Only the royal military is more formidable. Surely they can – "

"Silence!" Delthar commanded. "How long ago was the battalion dispatched?"

"In the early afternoon," the messenger reported.

"The Duke has no idea what he has sent his men to confront," Geoffrey rumbled. "Send word to Duke Hollingfield that he is NOT to send any more troops. Go!"

"Yes sir!" the messenger returned with a firm salute.

As he mounted his steed, the messenger could not help but think that no other troops would be needed, anyway. The battalion of seasoned veterans would be more than a match for a group of grave robbers. The already-circulating rumors had them pegged as a loose remnant of the Legion Midnight seeking to unnerve the military town of Fort Bastion in a weak attempt at retribution for their defeat during the Cursed Opening.

Delthar looked at Geoffrey as the messenger rode away. "We have to get word to that battalion. If Johnican is any indication, those soldiers could be in great danger."

"Let us ride, then, wizard," Geoffrey declared.

They hurried back to the capitol in thoughtful and worried silence. With every mile they traveled the old Master Mage's worry grew.

9.3

Colonel Rheingold Strong thought he had seen it all. From the mysterious sand creatures at Southborough to the loosed demons at the Tyne River, he had led royal soldiers against what had to be some of the fiercest opponents that any human army had faced since Heaven's War. So when this latest threat came within view of his mounted battalion he felt relief that these were not misshapen monsters.

That would be the only relief he felt.

Unlike the land nearly two hundred miles to the northwest that was darkened by overcast skies, the visibility on this cool autumn day was extensive. Despite the chill, the suns shone brightly and the sky was clear. From across the flat, grassy plains of the lands southeast of Fort Bastion, he could see a column of people trudging steadily across the prairie. Glints of the suns' light flickered from time to time along the column, reflected by the metal of armor and weaponry. The colonel did not look forward to testing that metal.

For a group that large traveling on foot, they had covered a great distance since leaving Fort Bastion less than four days earlier. The foothills of the eastern region of the kingdom were already in view. Their targets had set a grueling, nonstop pace while wearing armor and carrying weapons, without pack animals or mounts. They had even been delayed by a brief skirmish and still covered over twice as much ground as a group of that size travelling on foot should have. The battalion had to ride fast and hard to get ahead of the enemy. Now there was nothing for them to do but wait.

Before circling in front, he was able to discern from their tracks that they had never stopped to rest or eat during their trek. The signs of battle they encountered a few miles back, however, made it clear that they had stopped to fight. The evidence of battle confirmed the report that Colonel Strong received about the baron of Briar County and his fifty-man squad of well-trained soldiers confronting the column a day earlier. While the signs of battle were obvious, no bodies were found. Large patches of land were soaked with blood and severed body parts. Spilled organs were scattered throughout the grisly scene. Yet no bodies were found and there were no signs of any graves having been dug.

Their speed had surprised the colonel for the briefest of moments, until he reminded himself that what they pursued needed no rest, food nor drink. He shuddered when he considered the details of their marching orders.

The colonel turned to see one of his scouts approaching from the northwest, giving the approaching enemy a very wide berth, just as the wind shifted and blew in from the same direction. The cold rush of air carried with it an overpowering stench of rot and death. Coughing and retching began to rage through the battalion. Colonel Strong even gagged for a moment before quickly regaining control. He hoped his men would adjust to the smell by the time they confronted their target. For that matter, he hoped that *he* would have adjusted to it by then. But he knew the stench would only get worse as they drew nearer.

When the scout was close enough for Colonel Strong to see his face, the officer's apprehension intensified. The scout's countenance was a mask of fear and confusion. Strong knew the cause of his soldier's unease so he did not bother to speak to it. Instead, he focused on the business at hand.

"What is their number?" the colonel asked. The scout did not answer right away. He simply stared in the colonel's general direction without actually making eye contact. Colonel Strong allowed the man a brief moment before asking more insistently. "Private!" he barked, shocking the scout out of his stupor. "I asked you of their number."

"Thirty score, and then some, from what I could see," the scout answered, attempting to sound stoic but failing miserably.

"Thirty score?" the colonel asked incredulously. "There was barely three hundred at the last count. How could their numbers have doubled so quickly?"

"The last count did not include the others that have joined them throughout the night," the scout said nervously. "Nor Duke Hollingfield's force."

"Duke Hollingfield's forces have *joined* them?" Colonel Strong asked. He thought again about the Briar County battle site and his unease grew even more. "Blades! How are they subverting so many? You say others have joined them? What others?"

"We've received reports that retired soldiers as well as active soldiers on leave, all injured in the Cursed Opening, have been making their way to the enemy force from the southern regions of the kingdom," the scout told him, an uneasy frown etched into his face as he recalled the scene. "They bring others with them, all in a physically injured state, to join the column that began back at Fort Bastion. Many of them were farmers and peasants."

"How do you know they were farmers and peasants?" the colonel asked.

"Our contacts brought the news from family members of some of the newcomers," the scout explained. "And we saw them. Many of them carried rakes, pitchforks, scythes, spades, all manner of farming tools."

"There were enough of them to double their numbers?" the colonel asked doubtfully.

"There is much farmland and pastureland in the enemy's path," the scout reminded. "Almost every ranch, farm and settlement in their path looked as if some of the citizens tried to fight them, to turn them away. The battle sites resembled smaller versions of the aftermath of the Briar County baron's attempt to stop them."

"And now we are to face them," Colonel Strong said, looking to the west at the approaching enemy. He dismissed the scout with a nod and turned to his second in command. The colonel could guess what the younger man would say. Lieutenant Colonel Caleb Godson was an able warrior who had distinguished himself in the Cursed Opening. He was known for charging into battle eagerly and without hesitation. "Have you any suggestions, Caleb?"

"I would suggest retreat, Colonel."

Colonel Strong almost jumped with surprise. "*You* suggest retreat?"

"We are five hundred strong," Caleb said. "They outnumber us now and apparently they do not die. Even the demons we battled at Bluethorn and the Tyne fell to the sword, at least the lower-level ones."

"We cannot allow them unchecked passage," the colonel said grimly. "We are all that stands between them and thousands of other citizens."

The lieutenant colonel shook his head as he gazed steadily to the west. The enemy was growing closer by the moment, keeping a brisk, steady pace. "I love a good battle more than any man I know, colonel, but I fear all we can do is add to their number."

Caleb leaned forward and conspiratorially beckoned his superior officer closer. The colonel spurred his mount nearer, gazing suspiciously at his lieutenant colonel.

"What is it?"

"Permission to speak freely, sir?"

"Granted, lieutenant colonel."

"May I speak as a friend? Man to man, not colonel to lieutenant colonel?"

Colonel Strong cocked his head slightly. "Please do, Caleb."

"They sent us out with less than a day's notice on such a critical mission and did not even send a mage with us," Caleb said softly, not wanting anyone else to hear. "And surely this is dark magic at work. Our superiors have to know this."

The colonel's suspicion started to ease slowly but surely into anger. He did not appreciate or tolerate insubordination, yet he trusted Caleb's instincts and he would hear him out. "What are you trying to say, Caleb? Be honest, but be mindful of your choice of words."

Caleb's serious brown eyes held the colonel's warning gaze. "I will do both, but you may not like what have to I say. I fully expect you, as colonel, to make the decision you think is best. And if that means a reprimand or the dungeons for me, then that is what it means. But I will speak true. I fear we are being wasted, that we are but pawns in a power struggle between the Children of the Old Ones."

"There is no struggle between the Children anymore," Colonel Strong corrected. "Mar-dah is dead. The only Children left are the Head Mage, his daughter, and the offworlder Raxe. They all fight on the same side."

"But this new enemy is a result of that struggle," Caleb countered. "We all know this started with the fallen and living soldiers who fought in the Cursed Opening. I only thank the Gods that we are not already like those…those things. But the Head Mage and the crown would have us throw ourselves at a foe we cannot hope to best. Are we nothing but fodder for their war machine?"

"Of course we are," Colonel Strong said simply. "Did you think we were anything but? By our oath, we have put our faith in the crown and the Head Mage. We fight for them in defense of the Kingdom of Lorr. And do not forget that if not for the Head Mage and Raxe, Mar-dah's demons would have overrun us three years ago."

"Mar-dah's only interest was in bringing down the Head Mage," Caleb returned. "The Head Mage himself was the only reason the demons were set upon us."

"What is the point of this?" Colonel Strong asked. "We are here, now, in this place, by our oath to defend this land and its people. How does this griping move us toward meeting that end?" His eyes narrowed. "Would you defy the crown's orders because you don't agree with them? Would you defy *my* orders?"

"I will fight for land, crown, and fellow soldiers to the death at your command and the crown's command," Caleb promised. "I only ask that if there is a way we can defend our kingdom without needlessly throwing ourselves headfirst into death, perhaps we should seek to find it."

"It would have been wiser for you to say that at the first," the colonel offered. "I will take your words as a confidence from a friend and not your formal position as a soldier. This time."

Lieutenant Colonel Godson nodded in understanding. "Thank you, colonel, sir. That is all that I ask."

Strong pondered his lieutenant colonel's words, still staring at the ever-closing enemy. Their stench had grown much stronger on the wind. The clinking and clanging of their weapons grew ever louder in the distance. He turned to Caleb.

"At their pace and distance, my guess is they will reach us within a quarter of an hour," the colonel said. "We *will* fulfill our charge and stop the enemy from advancing. If it is true that they do not die, then we will cut them into such small pieces that they will not be able to fight. Give the signal."

Caleb nodded. "As you wish, sir." The lieutenant colonel rode into the middle of the battalion and cupped his hands to his mouth. "Form up!" he yelled. "Here is where we make our stand! Form up!"

The men of the battalion, who had been milling about, talking among themselves as they watched the approaching enemy, sprang to life. As they scrambled, the colonel rode among them barking orders and shouting encouragement. In a fast-moving yet organized burst of movement, they quickly formed a wedge. From overhead, their formation was a double-lined, open-ended triangle with its vertex pointing east. The open end was wide enough to encompass the width of the approaching column. Colonel Strong sat on his warhorse at the vertex and glared at the enemy.

If the would-be invaders noticed them, they gave no indication of it. There was no hesitation in their movements. Their pace did not hasten or slow. They trudged on silently and steadily along their path as if the defenders were not even there.

To Colonel Strong, the enemy's approach seemed to take forever. Waiting was almost always the worst part of battle for him. The only thing worse was counting the dead in the aftermath. He wondered if the men at the far corners of the wedge felt as impatient as he. To them, Strong imagined, the approach likely seemed all too fast.

He did not feel the same excited, pulse quickening near-terror he felt when he faced demons during the Cursed Opening. What he felt here was only dread. As frightened as he had been three years earlier, he had still been anxious to fight. He had been eager to engage the enemy and wipe them from the face of the earth. This enemy, however, was not a horde of hideous monsters to be slain without remorse or hesitation. These were brothers of the sword, citizens of the Kingdom of Lorr, civilian men, women and, worst of all, children. It was difficult for him to separate what they once were from what they had become. He wished to the Lord Ascendant that there could be another way.

But there was not. The colonel had his orders, no matter how terrible they were. He scanned the faces of the men close enough to see clearly and could see they felt the same anxiety. They sat straight and tall in their saddles with weapons poised. Their body language exuded fearlessness and confidence. But their eyes belied their true feelings. And with each passing second, the colonel knew their trepidation would – like his – only grow. He decided not to give their anxiety the opportunity to fester.

He raised his hand, a signal to his second in command. Caleb shouted out the order of readiness. The order was passed down the line on both sides, causing the soldiers to shift in their saddles in preparation to attack. All eyes were on the colonel in anticipation of his hand dropping so that they could engage.

And then a shrill whistle sounded from behind Colonel Strong. He snatched his hand back, behind his head, to signal a delay in the order to attack. He turned in his saddle to see nothing but swaying grass covering softly rolling hills. If Caleb had not turned with the same surprised suddenness, the colonel would have thought wishful thinking had made him imagine the whistle.

A moment later the sound of hoof beats floated to them and another scout came charging over one of the eastern foothills on his steed, his horse charging at a breakneck pace. As they came closer, Colonel Strong saw that the scout's expression was just as severe as his near-panicked steed's. The rider struggled to make his mount come to a skidding, reluctant halt at Colonel Strong's side.

"Colonel," he said breathlessly. "More of the enemy is closing on Trader's Parish! A force not unlike this one from

Fort Bastion is approaching the town from Riverside County to the north."

"Merciful gods," the colonel swore. "Many men from Riverside County fought and died at the Tyne. Some of them were buried at the Warriors' Rest but far more were buried in family plots just outside the county."

"Yes," the scout confirmed. "Because of Riverside's nearness to the Tyne, the men from Riverside Company were among the first to form up with the Royal infantry."

"If they are attacking Trader's Parish," the colonel reasoned, "Then they, too are heading in the direction of Ridgeland and the northern ranges of the Runes."

"The men of Trader's Parish are a fierce lot of trappers and hunters," Caleb added. They will surely try to stand against the invaders.

The scout nodded. "They were rushing to do just that when I came this way, sirs."

"They don't stand a chance," Colonel Strong said. "And there is no way we can dispatch the enemy here and reach Trader's Parish in time." He looked to the northwest again and saw the walking dead coming ever closer. He estimated less than a quarter mile of grassland between them and his battalion.

"There's something else," the scout informed. "As strange as it sounds, it is possible that the enemy will *not* attack Trader's Parish."

The colonel turned to him, his eyebrows knitted in an incredulous glare. "What makes you think that, soldier? Have you seen the carnage these things have left in their wake? We have. The chances of them passing through Trader's Parish peacefully are slim to none."

"But they passed through Riverside without incident," the scout informed. "There weren't enough deputies there to organize a decent defense, so instead of fighting, everyone hid. They went into their homes, climbed trees, some merely hid in the brush, anything to stay out of their way. Those that could not get away in time simply hid around corners or ducked behind water troughs and hitching posts. The enemy stalked in, through, and then right out of the other side of the county without even so much as glancing in the civilians' direction. It was as if the citizens were not there at all."

Colonel Strong was mulling over this new information when he noticed multiple dark figures emerge from the cloud-darkened western skies. He called to one of his soldiers to bring him a spyglass and within seconds he was looking through it to see a squad of Gryphon Ryders wearing the colors of the Lorrian Royal military.

"What is it, sir?" asked Caleb.

"Gryphon Ryders," the colonel said. "But only one squad, not nearly enough to stand against the numbers we face."

"Colonel," Caleb said. "The enemy is nearly upon us. What are your orders?"

"Let us test this new piece of information, the colonel declared, turning to Caleb. "Order the men to stand down but ready. We will open the wedge and let them pass."

And they did. By the time the vertex had opened wide enough to turn the wedge into parallel lines, the head of the enemy column was among them. The defenders opened the lines wide enough to allow for twenty yards or so between themselves and the enemy at the far edges of their column. The battalion watched in horrific amazement as the ragtag group passed. All of them looked straight ahead, without so much as a glance at the soldiers to the right and left. Their pace was moderate but constant. They made no sound other than heavy footfalls, uneven shuffling, and the ghostly jingle and clang of metal weapons and tools of varying size. The silence was unsettling. The entire scene was something out of a nightmare.

The head of the column was the most surreal. One glance immediately revealed them as the resurrected soldiers from the Warriors' Rest at Fort Bastion.

They were terrible parodies of human beings. Their eye sockets were empty, shadowy holes. Much of their gray flesh had long since sloughed away, revealing various parts of yellowed skeletons where tattered burial clothing, assaulted by moisture and time, had disintegrated during the years they were underground. Fingers and toes had wasted away to claw-like, skeletal digits. In almost every case, at least a portion of their skulls and facial bones were exposed.

But what was even more amazing to Colonel Strong was that they had any flesh on their bones at all. After three years of death, he thought there would have been more decomposition than what he was seeing. He then reminded himself that he was looking at the product of evil magic. He could only assume that there was something about their deaths at the hands of the demons that somehow preserved the bodies longer than if the victims had died a natural death.

Some of them shuffled along relatively upright with uneven gaits. Even the ones with a missing foot managed to stagger on the bottom edges of their shinbones at a surprisingly fast pace. Others, with one or both legs missing, dragged themselves along the ground with ruined hands.

The stench was overwhelming. That, along with the revolting sight, was too much for many of the colonel's men to take. The eerie silence of the stalkers was soon interrupted by the sounds of the soldiers' retching and gagging. The colonel himself had to stifle a wretch as he watched the grisly march. Only moments earlier he was determined to attack in order to overcome the growing apprehension that was spreading among his men. Now, he was all too happy to let the enemy pass.

The infected, as well as the more recently deceased, made up the rest of the hellish processional. Their appearance varied greatly depending on their station in life and their wounds. In many cases it was difficult to determine who was merely infected and who had been killed and resurrected. In other cases it was all too obvious. In the end, Colonel Strong surmised that it did not really matter who had been infected and who had been killed. The awful result was the same either way. Only their appearance differed.

The recently deceased were marked by gaping chest or abdomen wounds as well as missing limbs that clearly went untreated and would have caused the victim to bleed to death. Others were marked by jagged slits to the throat oozing thick dark liquid that had once been blood. Some were riddled with so many flesh gouges, bite marks, cuts, and stab wounds that there was no way they could have survived. Many of the walkers bore scars that on the surface did not appear to be fatal, but they trudged right along with the rest of the processional. And even though their eyes were still in their heads, they were as devoid of life as the empty sockets of the long-dead walkers.

The worst of them, by a great margin, were the children. Colonel Strong took some solace in the fact that there were very few of them, but even one child was far too many for such a terrible fate. Their tiny bodies stood out in stark contrast to their measured, sinister gait and the gaunt, worn expression on their small round faces.

The colonel could not begin to imagine the kind of evil that would unleash such abominations. He turned his attention back to the head of the column, forcing himself to look elsewhere before a tear escaped. And then the most heart-wrenching cry of anguish he had ever heard tore through his ranks.

"BEN! MY *SON*! NO! *NNNNOOOO*!!"

Colonel Strong looked down the line to see one of his men sprinting frantically toward the walkers. His eyes were wide with shock and his face was twisted into a mask of dread. A handful of other soldiers raced after him and called him back, but panic drove the stricken father to easily outpace them.

"Stop that man!" the colonel called needlessly.

"Bernard!" several of the pursuers called. "Come back!"

The nearest pursuer made a desperate dive in a failed attempt to tackle Bernard. In the next instant, the panicked father was darting through the walkers' crowd, dodging several of them before finally reaching his son. Amazingly, they ignored him even as he passed just inches away. The father snatched up the child, who could not have been older than four.

"Ben!?" he cried, tears streaming down his face.

The child turned wide, dead eyes to his father and answered with an ear-piercing combination of a hiss and scream. The expressionless face twisted into a hellish grimace and the child dug his fingers into the flesh of his father's face. The man's scream of pain and despair was cut short in the next instant when the trailing walkers stumbled into him and his son. Their blank expressions instantly morphed into enraged snarls and they swarmed him like famished hyenas. The rest of the walkers simply continued their march, walking past on either side as if they did not notice the attack.

Several of the soldiers that pursued the anguished father resumed their charge to save their fallen comrade.

"Fall back!" Colonel Strong ordered uselessly.

Four of the soldiers dashed into the midst of the walkers. The small number of men right behind them were stopped abruptly and repelled backwards. It was like they had hit an unyielding, invisible wall.

The four soldiers among the nightmarish procession made it only a few yards before they bumped into a densely clustered group of walkers that they could not avoid. The walkers burst into a crazed frenzy the moment they made physical contact with the soldiers. The soldiers fought savagely but their blows had no effect and they were hopelessly outnumbered. Cries of pain and anger rang out across the flatlands to the west and foothills to the east.

"Fall back, damn it all!" the colonel repeated.

To the colonel's dismay, a third of the battalion ignored him and tried to rush into the ranks of the walkers to help their fellow soldiers. The invisible wall repelled all of them. Strong looked to the squad of Gryphon Ryders who were touching down a few yards to the north of the battalion's northern line.

He immediately caught sight of the lead Ryder, who wore flowing brown robes instead of a Ryder's uniform and carried a long, straight walking staff instead of a bladed weapon. His staff was held high in one hand and his attention was locked on the column of walkers.

"He's conjured the invisible wall," Caleb said anxiously over the colonel's shoulder.

"Thank the gods," the colonel said. "Send a unit over to get those men to stand down," he ordered as he spurred his mount in the direction of the newcomers.

"It is good to see you, wizard," the colonel called. "This situation was about to get much worse."

"Colonel Strong, I am Echelon One Mage Jonathan Markus," the robed man said. "We have come to relay orders from Minister Geoffrey and General Ramos. They command us not to engage the enemy. More information, critical information, has come to light since you received your original orders." He looked over at the soldiers as they relented in their attempts to get into the walkers' ranks. "It looks like you've already come to that conclusion, even if some of your men did not comply."

"Corporal Bernard Nathan saw his son among those creatures," the colonel said defensively. "And his comrades witnessed him being massacred. That is a difficult situation to control."

The mage sighed and softened his tone. "Understood. But *they* must understand that this may only be the beginning."

Caleb rode up behind his colonel and frowned. "That is understood, wizard, I assure you. And all too well."

"So, colonel, have you any suggestions?" Mage Markus asked.

"I think we can better serve the kingdom by riding further ahead of the enemy," Colonel Strong said. "Their path is fairly direct. We can warn away as many citizens as we can reach, instruct them to clear a path and let the enemy pass without confrontation. And then we will send word to the duke that we are now outnumbered and in need of reinforcements and a new strategy. Perhaps he can petition General Ramos to dispatch a larger force."

"Trader's Parish lies directly in our path and theirs," Caleb added. "Perhaps we can ride to the town and save as many as we can."

"Yes," the colonel agreed. "And then it's on to Ridgeland. If the gods will it, reinforcements will be waiting and we can make a stand there."

By the time they looked again, the procession had completely passed the battalion, leaving a trail of crimson-slicked, trampled grass and churned earth in their wake along with the bloody, broken, and torn corpses of the five soldiers that intruded upon their march. The surrounding battalion looked on. A few from both lines attempted to approach the bodies, but the magic wall was still in place. One of them turned toward the colonel, his second command, and the newcomers.

"The enemy has passed, as you can see," called the soldier. "Please ask the wizard to let us through, sir, so that we can at least give them a proper burial."

"That cannot be allowed," Mage Markus said to Colonel Strong. "The bodies must be burned."

"Burned?" Caleb challenged. "You would desecrate the fallen defenders in such a fashion?"

"Would you rather your men end up like *them*?" Mage Markus returned, pointing toward the departing march.

"But surely there must be another way," Caleb argued.

Before the Echelon One Mage could reply, blood-chilling roars pulled all of their attention to the newly worn path.

What they saw shocked them even though it should not have. The fallen soldiers had already risen, snatched up their discarded weapons, and charged the soldiers to either side of the path. The battalion backed away from the path and raised their weapons. The invisible barrier repelled all of the resurrected attackers, sending them staggering back clumsily, but that did not stop them from charging again and again. They hacked at the barrier with their weapons. They stubbornly threw their wrecked and impossibly animated bodies at the invisible wall. The sound of heavy thuds and breaking bones could be heard clearly through the barrier as they continued their ineffective assault, screaming and roaring savagely all the while.

This went on for long minutes before the resurrected soldiers finally and abruptly ceased. Their twisted faces relaxed into the blank expressions shared by the other walking dead before they were provoked. Without another look at the battalion, the five men turned to the southeast and followed the rest of the column.

The colonel looked over at the walking dead and felt his heart drop. "Mage Markus, how can we fight them? Even if they did fall to our swords, how can we fight them? These are our citizens, our comrades… our *children* for God's sake."

Mage Markus shrugged and shook his head. "The Head Mage will find a way."

"If there is a way to be found," Caleb mumbled.

"We'll fly ahead," Mage Markus said. He gave a hand signal and whipped his reins. His gryphon went airborne and flew southeast with the entire Ryder squad following suit.

"Let us ride," Colonel Strong commanded. "I want to put as much distance between our enemy and us as we can." He turned to his second in command. "And Caleb?"

"Yes, sir?"

"They sent a mage after all, and an Echelon One mage at that. Does that allay your concerns about the Children of the Old Ones?"

"A bit," Caleb answered with a frown. "But *only* a bit."

Chapter 10: Decisions

10.1

When she regained consciousness, Lisa saw that she was lying comfortably in the queen size bed of another rented room. The small slit in the closed curtains revealed that it was still nighttime and the clock on the wall displayed eleven o'clock pm. The cold fear that she felt before fainting rushed back to her and kept her frozen on her back. Without rising, she slowly moved her head and eyes around to see that this room was much larger than the one she and Joel occupied earlier that evening. She saw Joel, his back to her and sitting upright at the foot of the bed. Her fear eased substantially.

She sat up and looked at him. His elbows rested on his knees as he watched and listened to a conversation between the old man and the robed, longhaired blonde man. They were seated across from each other at a small, round, polished wood table, on the top of which rested the long, crooked staff that the blonde had used to banish the shadow-wraiths. The younger man, with a bored look shrouding his features, was seated on a recliner on the opposite side of the room. She had not recognized him when he charged into the room wearing an armored visor with bright silver fire pouring from him, but now with his helmet gone and the light show ended, she recognized him as the FBI agent that had questioned them. Lisa scooted down the bed until she was next to her husband. She folded her legs beneath her thighs and leaned against his left shoulder.

"Where are we?" she whispered into his ear.

"The Drake," he whispered back.

Lisa looked at the clock with a puzzled frown. "We're downtown? I've only been out a few minutes. We came from South Chicago to downtown and checked into a hotel room in less than fifteen minutes?"

Joel shrugged. "I woke up about five minutes before you did," he informed. "We were already here."

"But – "

Joel held up a hand to cut her off. "Hold up, baby," he bade gently. "You have to hear this."

"...glad you were able to bring the van," the old man was saying. "We have a lot of gear in there. So what did you use to fix the mirror, Rionn? Was it some kind of living glass?"

Rionn chuckled. "No, nothing like that, Dan," the Head Mage said without taking his eyes from the television. "They were rocks. I always carry rocks with me. The spell to transform their physical makeup is a simple one that allows me to use them for many different purposes. The energy required to power the spell is minimal. I changed a few rocks to brittle glass that shattered when they hit the broken mirror. Then I fused the shards to the gaps."

"So that part wasn't a spell," Dan realized. "Just some sort of telekinesis."

"Not quite," Rionn corrected as he pressed the button on the TV remote again and again, watching in awe as the picture changed with each click. "I used my own internal magic, just an exercise of will, really, which manipulated the matter far more precisely than telekinetic energy. But you have the gist of it."

Dan sat back and grinned as Rionn Lorr paused on one station for about two seconds longer than the others, for a grand total of three seconds, before he was channel surfing again with a look of awe on his face.

"I guess TV is pretty fascinating to you, eh?" Dan asked.

"As fascinating as magic is to you, my friend," Rionn answered.

Joel looked over at his wife and saw that she still wore that little perplexed frown that he found so adorable. It almost made him forget their weird and worrisome situation.

Almost.

"What language are they speaking?" Lisa asked.

"What language are they speaking?" Joel mimicked. "What do you mean? They're speaking English. You can't understand them?"

"*You* can?" she asked incredulously. "Cause that's damn sure *not* English they're speaking."

"Hold up," Joel said, his thick eyebrows bunching up in confusion. He turned toward the blonde named Rionn and the old man he called Dan. "What language are we speaking?"

"English, man," Dan said with a raised eyebrow. "What kind of question is that?"

"We're actually speaking Lorrian," Rionn revealed.

Joel was shaking his head when he felt Lisa squeezing his arm. "How do *you* know their language?" she demanded.

"What are you talking about?" he asked Lisa. He looked at Dan and the man he knew as agent Ryan – both of whom looked as confused as he felt – before turning his eyes to the blonde stranger. "And what are *you* talking about, man?" he felt Lisa's hand tighten once more.

"You're doing it again," she said. "Every time you talk to the blonde guy you switch languages. The least you can do is translate for me."

"Wait a minute," Ryan interjected, directing his attention to Lisa. "When we talk to Rionn Lorr, you can't understand us. When we talk to you or each other, it's perfect English?"

"Not *perfect*," Lisa answered dryly, "but it's English."

"That's fascinating," Dan said before turning to the Head Mage. "What do you know about this, Rionn?"

"I can understand you, Joel, and Raxe whenever you speak, whether to me or to each other or to the young woman," Rionn explained. "When she speaks, however, her language is foreign to me. It is fascinating, Dan, and it is obviously because of our shared heritage as Children of the Old Ones."

"What are they saying?" Lisa asked impatiently. "All I could understand was your name. What is a Raxe?"

"Rionn Lorr, the blonde, said the four of us are children," Joel translated. " 'Children of the old ones,' whatever the hell that means. And Raxe is what the blonde calls the fake FBI agent."

"How can that be?" Ryan asked the Head Mage. "Neither gramps or I can feel his aura. Can you?"

"No, I cannot," Rionn admitted. "But I have no doubt that he is a Child. In fact, based on the power he displayed at the other inn and the fact that I understand him as well as you, I'm sure he is a descendant of Raxe just as you and Dan are."

"But how do you *know*?" Ryan challenged, "If you can't feel his aura?"

Lisa listened intently, as if she could understand what was being said. She finally tapped her husband on the shoulder for a quick translation.

Joel turned his head a bit but kept his eyes on the three strangers. "Sounds like some *Jedi* stuff, baby. They're saying we're all descendants of people that had some kind of powers or something. They're wondering why they can't 'feel' my aura. It's crazy."

Dan turned to Lisa. "We're the descendants of *Old Ones*, sweetheart." He was talking directly to Lisa, so she understood the words even though she had no idea what he was talking about. "They were god-*like* beings, but not like *God*. In Rionn's world, they call God the Lord Ascendant. The Old Ones were similar to angels, but unlike angels, the Old Ones had free will like humans and more interaction with humans.

"The Gatekeeper and Raxe were Old Ones who lived a few thousand years ago in another world," Dan continued.

Lisa and Joel shared amused looks, but Dan, accustomed to the expression because he had seen it on his grandson's face so many times in the past, patiently ignored them and went on.

"Children of the Old Ones are their human descendants and we can feel one another's auras. Rionn Lorr is telling us that Joel is a Child but none of us can feel him." The old man turned a questioning gaze to the Head Mage. "So we're wondering how that can be."

"No doubt your grandson told you about how he acquired his armor," Rionn began.

"Yes," Dan confirmed, "He found it in a sanctuary that had been buried on Infinity Isle."

"We excavated the underground temple and uncovered many priceless and powerful artifacts and texts. We were able to translate the ancient writings and found some very interesting histories and prophecies. One prophecy in particular reveals the fact that Raxe's son had two Children. It caught my attention because Shanderah had once told part of it to Catherine, and she in turn told me. From the telling, it seemed Raxe's son had only one child after he was sent here, just before the Leaders and their demons overwhelmed him and his father, but that was only the half of it."

Ryan's eyes went wide as he jumped to the edge of his seat. "Gramps and I were talking about that not too long ago. I know Shanderah's version, but the one Gramps was taught was a little different."

"Almost identical," Rionn said knowingly. "But with a few subtle differences. They were not slightly changed versions of the same story. They were consecutive passages that were broken apart over time. It seems the Old Ones purposely told different parts to different Children so that when they hid the texts during Heaven's War, the histories would not be lost completely. But no one individual would possess all of the knowledge."

"One would *bear* the weapon," Dan said wistfully, "The other would *be* the weapon."

Ryan nodded his understanding. "Gramps and I suspected that somewhere along the line a Child had two gifted offspring, which confused us because that's not supposed to be possible. And it's not. A Child can only have one gifted offspring, but the Old Ones themselves could have as many gifted Children as they wanted. And Raxe, an Old One, had *two* Children."

"Exactly," Rionn confirmed. "Raxe, you are the bearer of The Weapon, of Demonsbane. From what I saw of Joel, the way his hands were transformed and the way he battled, he most definitely *is* a weapon. *The* weapon."

Joel turned quickly to his wife with an expression of alarm. "He says my hands were transformed?"

Lisa nodded slowly, remembering that Joel could not recall anything about his episodes. "They turned into blades," she told him as if she still could not believe it. "They looked like bone, though, not metal." She looked down at his hands, which were normal now, and grasped them tightly. "The skin tore away and everything…"

"I get the picture, baby," Joel interrupted. He spoke softly but pulled his hands away self-consciously.

"I hate to sound like a broken record, mage," Ryan said. "But how can we be sure he's a Child if we can't feel his aura? Sure, he has some weird stuff going on with his hands but that doesn't make him a Child of the Old Ones. He could just be some kind of mutant or something."

Joel frowned. Lisa gave him an expectant look, waiting for him to translate. He did not want to translate the "mutant" part, so he only said: "They're just debating whether or not I'm one of them."

"I may not know why we cannot feel him, but I do know it is no coincidence that he is here right now," Rionn shared. "He can understand us, and we him. And those…things you were battling at the other inn, those were hell spawned creatures, born of demon magic and sent here after Joel. That is why I've come. We fear a sixth level demon has escaped. It has the ability to traverse the WorldGate."

Recalling the fearsome fourth and fifth level demons at the Tyne River, especially the one that almost killed him at Lake Onyx, Ryan's curious expression changed to fear at the mention of the sixth level.

"So it *is* a sixth level demon," he said worriedly.

"You've seen it?" Lorr asked.

"I felt it," Ryan answered. "We figured it could shape-shift or possess people because it appeared to be human. It was posing as a high-ranking agent in the organization."

Rionn Lorr nodded. "My guess is that it knows about the Children Raxe sent through the WorldGate, and that Joel is one of the descendants. It's trying to kill him to keep the prophecy from coming true."

Joel translated for his wife, who exhaled heavily with a look of dread shrouding her features. Her grip on Joel's shoulder would have been painful if the shock of what he was hearing was not so all consuming.

"What prophecy?" Lisa asked in a near whisper.

Dan spoke directly to Lisa so that she would understand him. "I'll give you the short version, sweetie:

> *The progeny of that Son would bear Children. One of his progeny would bear* the weapon. *That Child would have the power to fell both demon and man, and a day will come when the progeny of that son finds the other to save the Kingdom of Lorr and beyond."*

Ryan elaborated. "That 'Son' is the son of the Raxe, who was a warrior Old One from ancient times. I'm the progeny that would bear the weapon. Rionn Lorr here thinks your husband is the 'other,' and apparently so does this escaped demon. It wants to take Joel and me out of the picture so that we can't join up to stop it."

Rionn Lorr turned a grave stare to Joel, his intense blue eyes radiating with a conviction that sent a chill up the other's spine. "The demon will set events in motion in this world and mine to ensure that none of us can threaten it. Once it has done that, it will go on to poison both worlds with its insipid evil. If it is a shape shifter or possessor with the ability to cross the WorldGate, there is no telling what other powers it may possess."

"For that matter," Dan contributed, "there's no telling how much damage it's done already."

"Exactly," Rionn Lorr agreed. "Our only chance is to seek out and destroy the demon and its works. For that we will have to go across the WorldGate. We have a better chance of defeating the demon there than here."

"We?" Joel scoffed. "Go to your world? You must be out of your mind."

Rionn leaned forward. "You are a part of this, Joel, whether you want to be or not. Yours and Lisa's lives now depend on how you deal with this reality."

Joel chuckled nervously at the lunacy of the suggestion. When he translated, Lisa found nothing amusing about it.

"This is too much," she gasped, rubbing her forehead. The thought of them having to go to another world seemed like a sick joke.

In spite of all that had happened: from the failed attempt on their lives on that southern Illinois highway to the shadow things that attacked her and Joel to the awesome displays of power that vanquished them, logic would not let her accept the possibility of another world. Her head spun as she struggled to process it all without hyperventilating.

"This is not happening," she murmured, to herself more than to anyone else, rubbing her forehead faster. "This can't be happening."

Joel saw his wife wavering. Fear for her and their unborn child seized him. He hugged Lisa firmly against his chest. "It's *not* happening, baby," he assured. "Damn prophecy. To hell with what these freaks are babbling about. I'm not joining anyone. I'm not going anywhere."

Rionn Lorr's gaze softened. He felt badly for the couple but the truth could not be ignored. "I understand your reluctance," he said in the most comforting tone he could manage. "But your unwillingness to accept the things that have happened won't undo them. And it won't stop what's to come."

Lisa did not want a translation this time. She could tell from his tone and from the look in his eyes that the blonde stranger was trying to explain to Joel why they had to do as he asked. As far as she was concerned, there was nothing any of them could say that would make her believe the nonsense she was hearing.

Joel heard Ryan rise from the recliner and felt him sit on the bed behind him. He held Lisa closer and refused to turn, as if refusing to acknowledge the others' presence would make them all go away. When Ryan placed a consoling hand on his right shoulder, Joel knocked it away.

"I understand what you're going through," Ryan shared. "I once felt the way you feel now. I didn't believe it. I couldn't believe. But it's real, man, and so is the danger. You don't have to believe in demons. It doesn't matter if you believe what we say about the WorldGate. The one thing you can't deny is that someone tried to kill you a few days ago and some*thing* tried to kill you tonight. Both of you."

"And your Child," Dan added.

Joel and Lisa, as well as Ryan, looked at him in surprise. "How in the hell did you – " the couple started in unison.

"The wizard and I are very sensitive to magic," Dan explained. "Ryan will be too, eventually. He's just a little slow right now. We can't yet feel the Child's aura because it's still intermingled with the mother. And we probably wouldn't sense it anyway, seeing as how we can't feel Joel's aura. But life in and of itself is the most powerful magical energy there is. Pregnancy radiates it like nothing else."

"You have organization agents after you," Ryan added. "They're trying to snuff that magic out. You can't hide from them for long and they won't stop until you're dead."

"How do you know so much about this organization?" Lisa challenged.

Ryan met her gaze. "I'm not a fed, as you've probably guessed by now. I used to be in the organization. I know how they work."

"Are they after you, too?" Joel asked.

"Yeah," Ryan confirmed. "And believe me, the only way to stop them is to face them head on. To do that, we have to destroy this demon that's manipulating them, and for that we have go to Rionn Lorr's world. You've got to come with us."

"We don't have to do a damn thing," Joel said stubbornly. "Why should we have to go there? Why can't you stop it here?"

"A demon is a creature of magic," Rionn Lorr explained. "And as such, it will take magic to defeat it. This world, while not bereft of magical energies, is sorely lacking. Much more magic can be brought to bear against the demon and its forces in my world."

Joel shook his head in refusal. "What if it just stays on this side of the gate you keep talking about? What's the use of going there if it's here?"

"We can flush it out, lure it back by attacking its machinations on my side of the WorldGate," the Head Mage answered. "I already have a plan to do just that. From what I understand after talking to Dan and Ryan, it will be more difficult to do so here. I'm not at all familiar enough with this world's technology. Dan and Ryan do not have the sheer manpower to fight it *and* the organization here."

"Look, Joel," Dan said. "There are times when you have to look behind you to see the path that lies ahead of you."

When Joel gave him a questioning look, Dan explained.

"Think about what you've been through. You can't believe that you'll solve your problems by running from them. They'll find you again. If you somehow luck up and escape once or twice they'll keep finding you again and again until they finish you. You'll have more of a chance if you go across the WorldGate."

"But we –" Joel protested.

"Not *we*," Rionn Lorr interrupted. "You. I'm sorry, but Lisa cannot come with us. It would be too dangerous for her and too distracting for us."

Joel turned slowly to his wife. "He says you can't come."

"So what?" Lisa huffed. "I wasn't planning to go. And neither are you, right?"

"Of course not," Joel started. "But –"

"But what?" Lisa demanded. "You can't possibly be considering this. How can you believe this craziness? How could you even think of leaving me? Especially now?"

Joel looked down at the floor. All eyes were on him, waiting for his response. He deliberated for what seemed to him like forever before he finally met his wife's gaze.

"There might be something to what they're saying. I knew those shadow things were coming. I could…I could *sense* them before they got here, before I blacked out."

He wanted to tell her that he could sense the three men in a similar fashion. It was not a feeling he could accurately describe. It was an awareness lurking in the corners of his consciousness. The best way he could explain it was a vague recollection of a long-forgotten scent. But even if he could accurately describe it to Lisa, he would not do so in the presence of these strangers. For some reason they could not feel his essence at all, and a preternatural instinct warned Joel that there was a reason for this.

The sound of Lisa's voice drew his attention back. "And?" she questioned. "You're saying that's enough to convince you to leave with them?"

Joel paused again. He could not argue with Lisa on that point. That by itself would not have been enough to make him consider leaving. Unfortunately, though, there was more. As much as he loathed bringing it up, there was no other choice. He had to make her understand.

"Remember when I had the nightmare and asthma attack the other night?" he started. Lisa nodded in the affirmative. "You said you thought you saw something weird. You just figured it was a fading dream."

Dread crept into Lisa's eyes. She vividly remembered what she dismissed as the remnants of nightmare. She could still smell his sweat as his weight pressed down on her. She could still see the claw like fingers at her neck. She thought again about how his hands had transformed earlier that very evening and knew what was coming next.

"It wasn't a dream," Joel said finally. "If I hadn't woken up when I did…" he could not finish his thought.

Lisa only stared without reply. She took several deep breaths to calm herself and pressed the heels of both palms to her forehead.

Joel sighed. "It's not just the agents that I'm afraid of," he concluded.

"But what will I do without you?" Lisa's tone was pleading. "What if they keep coming after me once all of you are gone?"

Joel had not thought about that. He assumed the danger would follow him but it made sense that as close as she was to him, with as much as she had seen, her life would still be in danger. He shook his head and was about to verbally refuse again, but Dan chimed in before Joel could speak:

"I'll stay."

All heads turned to the old man. The lack of enthusiasm in his voice was telling. Ryan knew how hard it was for Dan to volunteer to stay. All the old man had ever talked about was the Kingdom of Lorr, how badly he wished he could go there. As a child, Ryan remembered the look of wonder and longing that came over Dan whenever he told his stories. He knew it was not easy for his grandfather to turn down an opportunity to cross the WorldGate. The fact that he did was enough to convince Ryan of the level of danger Dan believed was facing the young woman.

Joel gave the old man a harsh look. "How the hell are you going to protect her? How old are you anyway, seventy, eighty-something?"

"Add one hundred to that and you'll be just about right," Dan answered with a straight face. "But don't think for a second that I can't take care of myself or her." He turned to Lisa. "I saved you tonight, didn't I?"

"No offense, *gramps*," Joel mocked, "Huddling on the floor in a corner is one thing. On the street, how are you going to protect her from a wheelchair?"

Dan sighed. His wrinkled eyes studied the floor for long moments before he looked up at his grandson. He pursed his lips and gave Ryan a guilty shrug just before he gripped the armrests of his wheelchair.

Ryan raised an eyebrow. "What's wrong gramps? You having a spasm or some –" he stopped short when Dan began to rise slowly from his wheelchair.

Ryan's mouth dropped open as he watched, seemingly in slow motion, his grandfather go from sitting in the wheelchair to standing with no support. It was something he had not seen since he was eight years old, and something he never expected to see again.

"No. Freaking. Way," Ryan breathed.

10.2

"Ryan," Dan started, taking two easy steps forward.

"No freaking way!" Ryan barked as he shot to his feet.

Ryan stepped away from his duplicitous grandfather. The respect he felt for the man's voluntary sacrifice only moments ago crumbled beneath the weight of betrayal.

"All these years of pushing you and lifting you and even carrying your ass… And you can walk!"

"It was part of my cover," Dan explained. "In our world, when you live as long as we do, people eventually start asking questions. Nobody expects someone that looks as old as I do to be spry. You can't stay in one place for too long. You have to move around, change your identity. You have to periodically reinvent yourself."

"You don't have to reinvent yourself to *me*," Ryan argued. A thought suddenly occurred to him. "Did mom know?"

"Yes."

"I'll be damned." A hot rush of anger darkened Ryan's face. "I don't believe this. I would never have thought the two of you would lie to me for so long."

Dan bristled at the accusation. It was his turn to be angry. "Boy, don't you ever say something like that about your mother again. We didn't do it to trick you. We didn't do it because I wanted someone to chauffer me around. Your mother understood what we were. I tried to explain it to you for years but you never took me seriously. She understood what it meant and accepted the choices we have to make."

"What does that have to do with anything?" Ryan snapped. "That's no excuse for lying to me all these years."

"Technically, I didn't lie," Dan countered. "I never said I couldn't walk. I just got used to the chair whenever I was around people. I didn't think you'd understand when you were a kid. When you were older, I was older, too…" Dan lowered his head again. Ryan thought he saw an embarrassed frown flash across his grandfather's face. "It's just that when you get this old, you have to start thinking about…"

Dan stopped suddenly, put his bony fists on his hips, and turned a defiant glare to his grandson. "Wait a minute," he said. "I don't have to justify a damn thing to you. I'm damn-near two hundred years old. I fought in both World Wars. I helped raise your ungrateful ass. I prepared you to save the Kingdom of Lorr. Hell, I *deserve* to be pushed and lifted and carried! You should be thankful for the privilege!"

Ryan did not back down, but his tense expression relaxed a bit. He thought about what Dan had said just before his angry outburst. "What do you have to start thinking about when you get as old as you, gramps?"

"Don't worry about it," Dan said with a disinterested wave of his hand. "Just know that I can take care of myself. I'm more resourceful than you can imagine."

"No shit," Ryan huffed. He would not excuse his grandfather, and would probably never forgive him, but if what he suspected was true he could at least begin to understand. He had a pretty good idea what Dan had been about to say, and that was the only thing that kept him from pressing the issue.

"So you can walk," Joel sneered. "How is that going to help if more of those shadow things show up? Or if more agents come after you?"

"He has the shield, for starters," Ryan said.

Dan held up his hand. "No. You're gonna need the shield, Ryan. I gave it and Questblade to you for a reason. There's no telling what you'll face over there this time."

"Tell me gramps," Ryan countered. "When you had the vision that led you to pull the two weapons from storage, did it tell you they were specifically for me or did it just tell you they were needed?"

Dan's eyes narrowed suspiciously. "What are you getting' at, boy?"

"He's saying that if the vision did not communicate that the weapons were specifically meant for him," Rionn Lorr offered, "Perhaps the shield was meant for you."

"Listen, youngsters," Dan said, eyeing each one of them in turn. "Don't try to tell me how to interpret prophecy and especially my own visions. I've been at it a lot longer than even you, Head Mage."

"You never answered my question, gramps," Ryan pointed out.

Dan folded his arms. "I know what's best."

Rionn Lorr walked over to Dan and placed a strong hand on the old man's bony shoulder. "Sir," he began, giving the older Child the respect he was due. "I have no doubt that you are resourceful. Even a Child of the Old Ones would not get to be your age in these treacherous times without a great deal of resourcefulness. But please, do not allow pride or worry for your grandson to goad you into making a poor decision," Rionn held an open hand in Lisa's direction. "If not for yourself, then for the young lady."

Both Dan and Rionn looked at Lisa. Dan gave the Head Mage a sly look.

"How old are *you,* anyway, Rionn Lorr?"

"A little older than I look," was Rionn's response. "But – and I mean no offense – you have seen far more summers than I."

Lisa caught the mention of the shield before the magician joined the conversation and caused the language to shift again. From the mention of the shield, however, and the gestures and looks the men gave when they spoke, she knew they were having a debate about the use of the weapon. She decided to add her own two cents.

"The shield is nice and all, but it would take more than that to protect us if something like tonight happens again."

Dan leveled a serious gaze on the young woman. There was no pride, bravado, or humor in his visage, only truth.

"I've *got* a lot more than the shield," he assured. "This walking thing is nothing compared to some of my other surprises. I promise both of you," Dan's serious brown eyes met Joel's. "I can and I will keep her safe while you're gone. And I'll use the shield, okay?"

Joel and Lisa looked at one another in silence. There was something convincing about the old man, and both of them knew it. Each knew what the other was thinking. They were both considering everything they had heard, weighing their wishes against reality. Even though logic defied everything they had seen recently, they had seen it nonetheless.

"I don't want to go, baby," Joel whispered.

"But you *have* to," Lisa finished for him. Her big brown eyes looked deeply into his. A tear rolled halfway down her cheek before she could wipe it away. "Don't you?"

"This could be the only way to find out how to control whatever it is that's wrong with me," Joel admitted. "If I can't, I might hurt you," he looked at her still-flat belly. "And the baby."

Lisa turned to Rionn Lorr. "Can he do that?" she questioned. "Can he find a way to control it?"

Rionn gave her a questioning look that went away once Dan translated. The Head Mage smiled and nodded. He said something that Joel translated. "He says if there is a way, we will find it in his world."

Lisa wanted to question the "if" part of Rionn Lorr's response. Instead, she decided that she preferred "if" to the making of a promise that could not be kept. Instead of replying, she wrapped her arms tightly around Joel's shoulders and buried her face in his chest. She took a few deep breaths to hold back sobs that fought to escape.

Joel straightened. "We don't know you guys from Adam. What if this is a trick to separate the two of us?"

"Search your heart," Rionn Lorr advised. "Each of you. I know this is a great deal with which to come to terms in a very short time. The truth, however, is before you."

"Sometimes all you have is faith," Dan told them.

"Yeah," Ryan added, giving his grandfather a knowing look. "A wise old man once told me that sometimes you have to go where the current takes you."

Lisa pulled her face from Joel's chest and looked at him once again. "I don't want you to go, but you're right. We can't live like this. If there's any chance you can control it, you have to take it. And if going with them is the only way to keep us from having to run from assassins for the rest of our lives, you *have* to go."

"Then I'll go," Joel said quietly. He pressed his cheek against the top of Lisa's head and held her slim waist firmly in his arms. He squeezed his eyes shut to force back his own tears before finally looking up at Dan. His eyes were red and filled with dark menace and unspoken warning.

"You'll keep her safe, Dan." It was not a question.

"I will," Dan said. "You have my word as a Child of the Old Ones."

Rionn Lorr exhaled with relief. Ryan Franklin relaxed in the recliner. Dan settled himself back into his wheelchair.

"When do we leave?" Ryan asked.

"Mid morning," Rionn Lorr said tiredly. "I would like to return tonight, but opening the WorldGate and travelling here took quite a bit out of me. I must rest."

"How far did you have to travel to get to the hotel, anyway?" Dan asked.

Rionn rubbed his neck. "I emerged in a land thousands of miles to the west, where just about all of the people I saw had dark hair, almost black. Their eyes resembled those of the elves of Hendragorn, not canted as sharply as the elves' but much narrower than ours. I had to cross a vast ocean and over half of this continent to get here."

"Eastern Asia," Ryan realized. "You came over in the Orient and flew across the Pacific. That means the last of your bloodline crossed the WorldGate either into or out of the Far East."

"The Orient…" Dan said, recalling his father's acquaintances at the Shao Lin temple and wondering whether or not it was a coincidence that Rionn Lorr crossed over into the same part of the world. "How long did it take you to get here?" he asked.

"A little over two hours," Rionn answered in a tone betraying that he was none too proud of the fact. "It was a treacherous flight, as well. I lost count of the number of flying metal crafts I saw, and I narrowly avoided smashing into several of them. I believe you mentioned them, Ryan, as 'airplanes' on your first visit to Lorr. The complexity of those machines is fascinating. A few of the smaller, faster ones pursued me and even shot metal projectiles at me before I left them behind."

Ryan gave a wry half-smile and turned to his grandfather. "The military. He must have really freaked them out. I'd love to have seen their faces."

"Two hours?" Dan gasped. "It only took two hours for to get here from the Far East? That's incredibly fast."

"Over mach-four speed," Ryan confirmed.

"How fast is that?" Lisa asked.

"Four times the speed of sound," Ryan answered.

Joel and Lisa's mouths dropped open.

Rionn Lorr huffed his displeasure. "Very nearly not fast enough, my friend, and the effort has drained me mightily. I barely had the strength to destroy the shadow wraiths."

Ryan noticed that the Head Mage did not specifically mention the sacrifice he had to make just to open the WorldGate. That had to have drained him at least as much as the trip from Asia and the dispatching of the shadow wraiths combined. Rionn's sun-tanned face bore a pallor that spoke to that sacrifice. As he wondered how the Head Mage was even standing, Joel's voice broke Ryan out of his reverie.

"You could feel Dan and Ryan's presence from that far away?" Joel was asking.

"Not at first," Rionn admitted. "The distance was too great. I had to cast a searching spell, and even then, they were so far away I had only a vague sense of the direction from whence their auras emanated. I followed the trail as fast as I dared in your perilously crowded skies. Eventually I had to fly at such a height that it was difficult to even breathe."

"Breathe?" Joel suddenly remembered. "I can't go."

"What do you mean?" Ryan asked. "I thought everything was settled."

Lisa responded before Joel could. "His asthma," she said. "He could run out of, hell, he could lose his meds!"

"That's a helluva long way to go just to suffocate to death before I can even help you."

"It may not be a problem in Lorr," Ryan offered. "They don't have the pollution that we have here. You wouldn't believe how fresh the air is."

Rionn Lorr nodded his agreement almost emphatically. “Yes,” he said. “I’m surprised any of you can breathe at all in the polluted air over your cities.”

“My condition is chronic,” Joel argued. “I’ve had it all my life. It’s not just air pollution. My allergies can trigger attacks, and I’m allergic to damn near everything: pollen, grass, dust, animal dander, you name it. And sometimes attacks are triggered by things that not even my doctors can identify.”

There was silence for a time. Ryan never had asthma so he was in no position to argue. He’d known of people who had died from attacks and understood Joel and Lisa’s fears. Rionn Lorr watched curiously before he broke the silence.

“Suffocate?” he asked. “This ‘asthma’ you speak of is a breathing disorder, then. We call that ‘constriction’ in Lorr. My wife, Catherine, is a healer, and she has had great success in dealing with it.”

“And I can vouch for Catherine’s skill as a healer,” Ryan contributed. “If anyone can get you fixed up, she can.”

“My medicine is the only thing that I know for sure will help me. You’re asking me to trust my life to some strangers telling me that a healer in another world can treat a potentially fatal breathing condition. Do you have *any* idea how that sounds?”

“Then tell me how this sounds:” Ryan countered, “Facing shadow-government assassins and demon attacks without me, gramps, or Rionn Lorr here to help. Believe me, your chances are better with an asthma attack in Lorr. At least over there you’ll have a fighting chance.”

“What about this?” Rionn Lorr offered, “Gather as much of your medicine as you can carry. If you run out or lose it, I promise that I will send you back to acquire more if we have not found another way to relieve your asthma. Then the choice to return to help us will be entirely yours.”

The answer was so obvious, Joel knew. This was ludicrous. How could he concede to something as impossible as leaving his pregnant wife to go with strangers who claimed they were going to take him to another world? But at the same time, he could not ignore what they had seen or what he had done.

Joel felt as if he were in a vacuum. His breath came in rapid pants that had nothing to do with his asthma. Fear started to form a cold and biting feeling in the pit of his stomach. He turned to Lisa with an imploring countenance. The lost and hopeless look with which she answered mirrored what he was feeling. His heart fluttered and his ears suddenly clogged, as if invisible hands covered them. Only a dull hum reverberated inside of his ears. Hot tears almost stung his cheeks as they escaped every few seconds.

Lisa's usually bright brown eyes were dulled from fear and red from crying. But even her sadness was beautiful to him. It was a somber, tragic beauty, but beauty nonetheless. She was his world, his life. How could he leave her like this?

He thought of the danger she had been in earlier that night. The danger she had been in on the southern Illinois highway.

And then he thought about his fingers, extended into nine-inch long razor-sharp talons, at his wife's jugular vein while she slept. Joel's breath caught in his throat as he felt his heart breaking. Lisa could see it happening and it immediately betrayed his answer. Instead of the stream of tears he expected, which in all probability would have made him change his mind again, a look of sad but firm resolve masked her features.

"Do what you have to do, sugar," she told him as she wiped the tears from his face. "And bring your ass back here to me."

Joel allowed a half smile to lift the left side of his mouth. He turned to Dan, Ryan, and finally, Rionn Lorr, and nodded gravely. The Head Mage returned a nod of gratitude and then slumped in his chair for the briefest instant, as if his exhaustion had momentarily broken him down. And then he quickly stiffened, assuming a posture of determination.

"The more I consider the threat we face," Rionn said, "The more convinced I am that we should leave tonight."

"What about your rest?" Dan asked.

"I can rest when we get back to Lorr," Rionn said stubbornly. "Time is far too precious." The Head Mage turned to Joel. "Gather your medicines."

The abruptness took Joel by surprise. "Now?"

Lisa's chin dropped and her eyes grew wide. Her voice was barely a whisper.

"Now?" she asked.

"We don't know how long it will take for who hunts us to find us again," the wizard explained seeing the question in her eyes. "And we don't know what form the next attack will take. A sixth-level demon has, in all likelihood, command of many types of magic. If its next assault is not one of demonic magic, Raxe's power will not aid us. I have enough energy left to get us across the WorldGate but I may not have enough to counter the assault if it is one of formidable magic. The sooner we are on our way, the safer we will be."

Even without understanding the words, Lisa knew exactly what the wizard was explaining. Her resolve began to crumble. She had been hoping they would have at least a few more hours together. Everything was happening so much faster than she could handle. But then again, she feared she would never really be able to handle this insane situation regardless of its pace.

"What about our things?" she almost pled. "Our apartment? Our car? What are we supposed to do about all of that stuff?"

Even as she spoke, she knew how silly and petty those concerns were compared to the unbelievable and catastrophic dangers they had been discussing. But Lisa was in a near panic. She desperately sought a way to keep her husband with her for as long as possible. Ryan and Dan shared a sadly amused look that Lisa would have found condescending had they been looking at her instead of each other. When they did turn to her, they were considerate enough not to sound or appear patronizing.

"All of us will be doing quite a bit of moving around, Lisa," Dan explained patiently. "We'll have to travel light. We brought the bags you had at the hotel so you'll have a few changes of clothes. That's about the most you should carry. Do you have any meds yourself that you have to bring along?"

Lisa shook her head slowly.

Joel simply sat and stared, grinding his teeth with worry and frustration. Lisa knew that even though his expression was blank, his mind was working frantically. Like her, he was more than likely looking for a reason to justify yet another refusal, as if the implausible circumstances in which they found themselves were not reason enough. He sniffed once, then a second time. It was almost like he had caught a strange scent but Lisa assumed he was only sniffling from an allergic reaction. Suddenly his expression hardened into icy determination.

"Rionn Lorr is right," he said to Lisa without meeting her eyes. "It's time for *all of us* to leave."

10.3

After Joel had hurriedly gathered his meds and placed them into a duffle bag, Rionn Lorr rose from his chair, aimed the remote control, and, with a bit of reluctance, turned off the television. He grasped the round wooden table and easily slid it against the closed curtains covering the window that dominated the wall facing the street. He looked to Dan, who had been sitting on the opposite side of the table.

"I'll have to ask you to move from this area, sir," the Head Mage instructed respectfully.

Dan wheeled quickly over to the foot of the bed next to where his grandson was now standing. The old man watched with rapt attention, as did everyone else in the room, as Rionn Lorr rolled up the left sleeve of his cloak.

Ryan knew how the WorldGate Key worked. He had never seen its magic invoked, though, so his interest was just as keen as the others. And since he knew what to expect, he was probably even more anxious. He wondered what part of Rionn's body bore the scar that marked his departure from his home world.

Rionn reached into the deep folds of his cloak with his right hand and produced the most beautiful sword Dan had ever seen. He had seen the sword in visions but that was nothing like seeing it in real life. Dan had been a collector years ago, before having to leave his collection behind when he had to change identities and locations for the first time. He still read and researched swords as much he could and attended exhibits at every opportunity. From far eastern Samurai and katana swords to mid eastern scimitars; from French rapiers to Scottish Claymores, dirks to medieval broadswords, Dan had seen and studied some of the most finely crafted blades in existence. But the craftsmanship of the broadsword before him was breathtaking. Even Joel and Lisa, who knew nothing about swords, gasped at its beauty.

The cross guard was pure silver, and from its underside protruded a two-handed grip of the same silver bound with strand upon strand of gilded thread woven in intricate, braided patterns. The round, flat pommel resembled a three and a half inch silver coin. The double-edged tapered blade, a slightly lighter shade of silver than the cross guard, was three and a half feet long and nearly five inches wide at the hilt. But even more awesome than the sheer size and beauty of the shimmering blade was the image engraved in it just short of its midpoint.

The carving was so detailed that it almost looked like a gray scale – or silver scale – photograph of a bare-chested, heavily muscled man. He held a key almost as long as he was tall. He stood before a high, closed and locked gate composed of thick metal bars. By his bearing, there was no doubt in Dan's mind that this was a god in human guise.

Every curly hair on his thick mane and every strand on his closely trimmed beard were carved with incredible precision. Dan noticed that the Old One's strong, sharp chin appeared very similar to his and his grandson's. His face was set in a scowl of grim defiance. Intense eyes, that to Dan resembled Joel's eyes, dared anyone and everyone to approach the gate behind him. Somehow, the artist even managed display a gleam of light in those eyes.

"The Gatekeeper," Dan said in reverence.

"It's beautiful," Lisa breathed. Joel nodded wordlessly.

Soft strokes expertly detailed reflected light on the bars of the gate and the surface of the giant key. Impossibly delicate cuts illustrated shadows of differing intensity to define realistic looking muscles in the Gatekeeper's torso and arms. Even the wrinkles in his fitted breeches were crafted in a way that made them look like real cloth.

Rionn Lorr held the grip in his right hand and let the heavy blade rest in his left palm. He held it for a time, staring at it in what to Lisa appeared to be dread. She wondered how he could be anything but captivated by the beauty of the treasure in his hands.

The Head Mage stared down at the engraved image. Even with the Gatekeeper being upside-down from Rionn's perspective, the Old One's fearsome eyes still seemed to stare knowingly at him, daring him to invoke the magic. It occurred to him that the way he was holding it might have been making it seem like he was displaying the broadsword to the others, giving them a few moments to revel in its splendor. In truth, he was taking time to build up his own courage, to steel himself against the pain.

All magic had a price. All energy had to have a source. The price and source of this blade's magic – like its sinister twin that opened the gates of the Seven Hells – was blood.

Rionn Lorr took a deep, agitated breath and placed the razor sharp edge of the broadsword against his left forearm. With a slight wince, he slid the edge only a couple of inches along his flesh. Lisa felt a wince distort her own features and she saw the same look on her husband's face. The wince quickly turned into wide-eyed shock when she watched the wizard pull the blade away. The blood from the cut, instead of obeying the laws of gravity to run down his arm and drip to the floor, continued to flow into the blade as if it was being pulled through a transparent catheter.

Lisa stood up in alarm, mouth agape, when the Head Mage allowed the tip of the wide blade to fall to the carpeted floor with a loud thunk. He continued to hold the two-handed broadsword grip with one hand as the rope of blood continued to snake through the air from the cut in his arm to the downturned blade. The blood did not run off of the sword as a liquid was supposed to. The blood disappeared into the polished pale silver as if it was a sponge instead of metal. Rionn Lorr, meanwhile, was looking up at the ceiling in an attempt to ignore the spectacle as the others stared with morbid fascination.

As a veterinarian, Lisa's healer instincts urged her to rush over and help. She may have worked exclusively on animals, but a bandage was a bandage. Common sense, however, kept her from interfering. She simply stood and watched, unable to tear her eyes away from the weird scene.

The wizard's tanned face grew more ashen before their eyes and his left arm started to tremble. Lisa estimated more than two pints of blood were absorbed into the ravenous broadsword before the flow finally ceased, and not a drop had touched the carpeted floor.

The Head Mage fell heavily to one knee. The broadsword, including the hilt and pommel, was only a few inches shy of five feet long, and if Rionn had not been using it as a crutch he would have fallen on his face. Head hung low, he took several deep breaths and placed his left hand flat on the floor to steady himself. Everyone watched in silent awe and waited for something else to happen.

Lisa looked back at her husband. "Wow," was all she could manage.

Joel stood up next to her, never taking his eyes off of the blade. His mouth was moving, as if he were whispering too low to be heard. Lisa placed a questioning hand on his shoulder.

"The magic is in the blood," he mumbled.

"What?" Lisa asked.

"The magic is in the blood," he said as if he had just figured it out.

"It sure is," Dan confirmed in a soft voice. Both he and his grandson continued to stare expectantly.

Just when the true wonder of what had just taken place started to settle in on Joel and Lisa, the huge broadsword began to shimmer. The light was so bright they almost had to shield their eyes. The illumination seemed to rejuvenate Rionn Lorr. He wrapped his left hand around the pommel while squeezing his right hand tighter on the grip and used the sword for balance and leverage as he rose to his feet. He continued to hold the sword with its blade tip on the floor and allowed the light to wash over him.

Lisa had to quickly stifle a cry of surprise when she saw something on the blade that she could not believe.

The brilliantly engraved image began to move.

Lisa told herself that it was only a trick of the fluttering light. It had to be the shimmering, near-blinding rays that made the Gatekeeper appear to hold the giant key high in the sky and swing it around in a big, slow circle. Dancing shadows had to be the culprit for making the corded muscle and sinew in the Old One's barrel chest and massive arms seem to flex from the effort of wielding the key, as well as making the tall gates behind him swing slowly open.

But when Rionn Lorr hoisted the broadsword with two hands and mimicked the Gatekeeper's motions with the key,

Lisa realized that she must have indeed witnessed what she thought she had. As the tip of the blade traveled in its slow circle, a thin, lingering arc of silver flame trailed behind it. When Rionn completed the large circle, the ring of silver flame hovered perpendicularly above the floor. The lower part of the ring hung roughly three inches over the carpet. Within the ring, the view of the far wall began to waver and then spin as if liquefied and caught in a slow drain. As the twirling image shrank, broke apart and finally drained away, complete blackness crept in behind it.

Lisa swooned and feared she might faint for the second time that evening, but Joel put his arm around her and held her close. His comforting embrace helped to clear her head and she continued to watch the shimmering rim of silver fire that outlined a void as dark and infinite as space, absent the illumination of stars.

Dan wheeled a few feet to his right and positioned himself at the necessary angle to peer behind the void. To his further amazement, he saw that the hole was two-dimensional, flat and thinner than even a sheet of notebook paper. Only the silver glimmer made it visible from the side. He shook his head in disbelief.

The Head Mage turned to the others. His tall, brown-robed form looked strangely intimidating framed in the silver-rimmed disc of blackness. His blue eyes were dim from exhaustion but his voice carried a strong, commanding resonance.

"It is time." He declared.

Ryan, lifting over his shoulder a heavy duffle bag that obviously contained his armor because it clanked as it was moved, bent down and gave his grandfather a long, firm hug.

"You be careful, boy," Dan commanded.

"Always, gramps," Ryan said. He stepped to Rionn's Lorr's side right after the Head Mage retrieved his staff from the table and returned the broadsword to his cloak, where it amazingly disappeared within the folds of fabric. Joel remained next to Lisa as the two younger Children spoke.

"Where will we come out on the other side?" Ryan asked.

"If we link arms and I lead the way," Lorr explained, "We will emerge at the place where I last crossed the WorldGate: Port Lorrian."

"The city at the southern shores of Lake Onyx," Ryan recalled. "It's southwest of Lakeside."

Rionn Lorr was impressed. "You remember?"

"I remember a lot about Lorr," Ryan admitted. "But just holding hands will ensure that we all end up in the right place? What if one of us loses contact?"

"Then you will emerge in the last place you, or the last of your bloodline crossed the WorldGate using this Key."

"The Badlands," Ryan said. "That's damn near a thousand miles from Port Lorrian."

"Then the two of you had best hold tight," the Head Mage warned with a weak smile.

Lisa clutched Joel's shoulder with both hands. "You can't go into that thing."

It appeared Joel was about to agree, but he suddenly turned and grasped his wife's shoulders. His brown eyes gazed longingly into hers for a long moment before he kissed her. He kept his eyes opened as they kissed, wanting to see her for as long as possible. Time lost its hold over him and he began to feel weightless in her kiss. His entire existence became the firm press of her soft lips to his, the sweet smell of her warm breath as she exhaled through her nose and he inhaled through his. He felt the urgency of her kiss, as if she intended to convey all of her love and faith in him through their physical connection in that all too brief moment.

When he pulled away they both had to gasp for air. Joel took a deep breath and squeezed her shoulders. The thin streaks of dried tears on his face softened his resolute scowl, but the determination in his eyes was almost frightening.

"I have to go, but I'm coming back," he promised. "I don't care what it takes. I'm coming back to you, baby."

Any doubts and fears Lisa felt earlier were swept away with the kiss and his passionate glare. She nodded and managed a melancholy smile and said: "You'd better."

Joel turned to Ryan, who had already clasped arms with Rionn Lorr. He stopped suddenly and genuflected, dipping one knee to the floor and making the sign of the cross.

He was not baptized as a Catholic but he was raised in the Catholic Church, and he figured he needed as much divine assistance as possible. He said a brief and silent prayer, asking God to watch over his wife and to guide him safely back to her.

A tear rolled down Lisa's face as she watched her husband. He stood and checked his pockets to ensure that he had all of his meds, especially his emergency inhaler. It was the same thing he always did in the past while standing at the front door before going to work in the morning. He called it his "pocket check." A smirk came to his face after he checked his back pocket and pulled out his wallet.

"I guess I won't need this," he said, holding the wallet out to his wife.

Lisa stepped forward and took it from him, all the while fighting the urge to grab him and pull him away from the madness. She stepped back to the foot of the bed. Far too much had happened for her to continue to doubt her eyes. The fact that she was still standing was almost as amazing to her as some of the other things she had seen that night.

She tried to smile but her lips would not cooperate. She gripped the wallet so tightly that the sound of crunching leather reverberated in the otherwise quiet room.

Joel and Ryan locked arms. Rionn Lorr turned to Joel and Ryan to give one last warning.

"Again, gentleman," the Head Mage said, "Hold tight."

The blonde man stepped into the circular void. First his left foot and ankle were swallowed by the darkness. The rest of his body followed until only his right arm, which Ryan clasped with his left, was visible. Soon that, too, was engulfed in the darkness. Ryan's dreadlocks fluttered as he disappeared into the darkness next.

Joel looked back at his wife as he trailed the other two into infinity. The fear in Joel's eyes, fear for himself as well as her, broke Lisa down. She collapsed to a sitting position on the bed, head spinning, but managed to stay conscious.

"I'm coming back to you," he promised again. The conviction of his tone was at odds with the fear in his eyes. "I love you."

"I love you, too," she said as her husband vanished into the void.

The darkness swallowed him like a pool of inky black water. But there were no ripples to signal his passing. A moment later the silver ring of flame winked closed. The concussion of the closing ring sent a stunted breeze through room and caused Lisa and Dan's ears to pop. A moment later it was gone as if it had never been there.

"God be with the three of you," Dan prayed.

Lisa stood and stared at the empty space. She could not see the dresser set against the wall on the far side of the room or the rust-colored carpet on the floor. All she could see was the empty space that her husband had occupied only seconds earlier. Tears started to stream from her eyes just before she dropped the wallet, covered her face with both hands and tried unsuccessfully to muffle her sobs.

"This isn't real," she mumbled again and again, trying to will it to be true through the force of her anguish.

Dan wanted to put a comforting arm around her but he opted not to. He did not know her well enough to assume she would accept his comfort. Instead, he sat silently and allowed her to vent for a time. With each minute that passed, her sobs grew louder instead of subsiding. Dan checked his watch and after the third minute he decided that was as long as they dared wait.

"We have to go, Lisa," he said softly. "They may be able to track Rionn Lorr's magic to this place."

Lisa controlled her sobs long enough to answer. "What difference does it make? This is all a dream, anyway. Let them come. Maybe I'll wake up faster."

"And maybe you'll die in your sleep," Dan countered. "Then you'll never see Joel again. You want to take that chance?"

The thought of those cutting shadows returning motivated her. Lisa took a deep calming breath. She stopped the sobs but the tears could not be held back.

"Where are we headed?" she sniffled as she scooped up Joel's wallet.

"As far away from here as we can get," Dan assured.

PART III

THE RETURN

Chapter 11: Back to Lorr

11.1

Joel felt the sensation of riding with his eyes closed on the tilt-a-whirl ride at the state fair. But instead of spinning and twirling around only a vertical axis, he would suddenly and violently shift to spinning and looping around a horizontal one, and then a diagonal one. That sickening feeling was aggravated by the impossible speed of the forces being exerted upon him. It was as though he was in some kind of cosmic centrifuge that threatened to separate the mass of his body at an atomic level. He could no longer feel Ryan's powerful grip on his arm and he had no idea if he had lost contact with him or not. Waves of panic battered him when he thought that he might be hurtling lost through nothingness for eternity.

And then the centrifuge turned into a blender, and then a microwave, and then a trash compactor. There were flashes of pain that dwarfed anything he had ever felt interspersed with patterns of color that were alternately more beautiful and then more terrible than anything he could ever imagine. An invisible wind screamed agonizingly in his mind the entire time. There were times when his own identity seemed to creep away from him, scaring him to the brink of hysteria. But then he would recall his wife's dark brown eyes and radiant smile and everything else would come back to him.

All of the movement and sound snapped to a stop so violently that the physical shock of it made Joel's ears pop. The colors all at once sharpened into two horizontal stripes, the top one azure and the bottom one green. The green suddenly rushed upwards, as if the horizontal hold of a television screen had been scrolled up, until it filled his vision. He thought the color would actually touch him but the green froze just inches in front of his nose.

The scent of grass suddenly filled his nostrils and almost made him sneeze. That sensation caused the rest of his senses to finally focus. He could feel earth under his knees and strong hands gripping both of his shoulders, keeping his face out of the bright green grass just below him. The hands lifted Joel to his feet and helped to steady him.

Joel looked around at a lush green field and a bright, beautiful blue sky dotted here and there with startlingly white clouds. He was reminded of a big Texas sky on a sunny day, only on an unbelievably larger scale.

He looked down and saw his shadow stretching out on in front of him on the grass and found that his vision was not quite as clear as he thought. He had to be seeing double. It was as if there were two shadows, yet they were so close together that he almost missed it. But then he realized that everything else he saw had no twin, only his shadow and the shadows of the men to either side of him. He turned to look up at the sun and had to catch his breath when he saw two beaming yellow orbs side by side high above the peaks of a mountain range.

The spectacle was as terrifying as it was stunning. He stood there staring at the suns, mouth agape, so dumbfounded by what he was seeing that he paid no mind to the painful suns' light lancing his eyes. The suns burned into him the realization that, in no uncertain terms, he was no longer in Chicago or the United States or anywhere else on Earth. The dread of this revelation caused his already uneasy stomach to lurch as if it had just arrived from the WorldGate to catch up with the rest of his body. His knees turned to jelly as he dropped to all fours and vomited in the lush green grass.

Ryan and the Head Mage waited patiently for Joel to finish coughing, hacking, and heaving. Once he was breathing evenly again, still on his hands and knees staring blankly at the mess in the grass, the other two helped him to his feet once more. Ryan saw Joel's embarrassed expression and gave him a reassuring pat on the shoulder.

"Same thing happened to me on my first trip across the WorldGate, man," Ryan confided. "Hell, it almost happened to me just now."

"Where are we?" Joel asked after regaining just enough of his breath to speak.

"You are in my home world," Rionn Lorr said in a proud but weak voice. "You are in the Kingdom of Lorr, in Onyx County, just west of the city of Port Lorrian."

The Head Mage waved a trembling hand toward the north. Joel's eyes followed his hand. There was an open plain to the left of a jumble of cottages and squat buildings that revealed a large body of water just north of the city. It reminded Joel of Lake Michigan. The surface of the water was dominated by all manner of sailing vessels. Wide sails stood out against the broad blue skies in a colorful mosaic of constantly shifting patterns as boats of all sizes came into and out of port.

Joel followed the shoreline west and in the distance he could see the rise and fall of the land as foothills evolved into a breathtaking mountain range. The peaks were not quite high enough to conceal themselves in the clouds, but the highest peaks were just tickling the underside of some the lower hanging mists. The range swept from north to south, subtly curving inward as it spanned the western horizon for as far as the eye could see.

"It's like a wall," Joel said wistfully, struck by the beautiful panorama.

"Indeed it is," Rionn Lorr confirmed, following Joel's western gaze. "That range forms a natural barrier between the Kingdoms of Lorr and Darshay. As does the Wyrm Mountain range on the north shores of the Great Lake Onyx."

Joel peered hard to the north and could just see several peaks in the distant mists. The beauty of the landscape and the invigorating freshness of the air lent a welcoming atmosphere to this place that Lisa would love if only she had been able to come with him. And then he chastised himself for almost forgetting the severity of his predicament.

Ryan looked north toward Lake Onyx as he took another deep breath of the incredibly fresh air. There was something about it that was different than he remembered, and different in a good way. Even though the invigorating air was the first thing he noticed on his first visit to the Kingdom of Lorr, this time there was something more.

There was an added familiarity about it. It was a comforting feeling, like the smell of his mother's home on Thanksgiving. There were none of the savory smells of cooked and cooking food, but what was the same was the familiar warmth that spread through him and over him, that made him feel safe and strong.

An altogether familiar and strange brightness shimmered off of the lake. Ryan knew that he had never consciously noticed it before, but somehow he knew that it had always been there. That same shimmer rose softly from the grass around him and the peaks of the mountains to the west. It rose in barely perceptible waves from the people in the distance and was even brighter around the Head Mage.

But not around Joel.

At first Ryan attributed the visual sensation to the two suns. Somehow, though, he knew that was not the cause. When he tried to narrow his focus to the shimmer around any particular individual, it vanished like an airborne dust mote that reflects a ray light for a moment before abruptly disappearing along its journey. So instead of concentrating on the strange phenomena directly Ryan simply allowed himself to be aware of its presence. Almost immediately he realized that the shimmer was not only a visible entity. It lent vitality to the air he breathed and a faint tingle to his skin when soft breezes wafted by.

Instinctively he knew why he had not noticed this on his first visit. At that time he had no sensitivity to it. His sensitivity had grown so gradually during his first visit that he became aware of it only at a subconscious level without ever truly recognizing it. But now, returning to the Kingdom of Lorr after living for over three years in a world where it was in much less abundance, Ryan appreciated the phenomena for what it was.

Magic.

"We're earlier than I'd planned," Rionn Lorr said. "That is good. We can greet Ethan and the Keeper's Hounds as they come into port. We can begin our preparations earlier. They will accompany you on your quest."

"That's great!" came a voice from behind them.

Both Ryan and Joel were startled but Rionn Lorr only turned and smiled. Ryan looked closely at the newcomer. Despite the deeper voice, the several inches he had grown and the neatly trimmed, jaw line-length hairstyle he now sported, Ryan immediately knew who the young man was. The sandy brown hair, the wiry frame beneath a loose fitting cotton shirt, and the long legs under woolen breaches, and most of all, the narrow face with the straight nose, easy smile and sincere gray eyes would always give him away.

"Quick!" Ryan called with a grin.

When a few more long strides brought Quick within reach, he and Ryan clasped their right forearms firmly and gave each other a warm hug. Ryan grasped the younger man's shoulders and held him at arm's length.

"Got a few more inches on you, I see," Ryan grinned. "Still skinny as a rail, though."

"And you look the same, Raxe," Quick returned. "Almost exactly."

"It's only been three years," Ryan said. "Adults don't change that much in three years."

Quick took in the slight streak of gray spiraling through a few of the long locks above Ryan's right temple, lingering evidence that he had once fought against the magic of Demonsbane. And then he looked at Ryan's straight brow and dark brown eyes. The young changeling's acute vision, hypersensitive sense of smell, as well as a subtle scan with a tendril of magic brought Quick to a confident conclusion.

"You've barely aged a moment," Quick declared. "The longevity of the Old Ones has begun to bloom within you."

"You notice it, too?" Rionn Lorr asked with something resembling surprise. "Impressive, young one."

The Head Mage was not merely impressed. He was *very* impressed. Quick had an uncanny intuitive connection with his gift. Rionn presumed it had something to do with his inherent changeling magic but that was only a guess. This was the only changeling he had ever known so he had no source for comparison.

Rionn resisted the urge to tell Quick – or anyone else, for that matter – just how exceptional the young changeling really was. He also made it a point to order the instructors at the *Chronicai Tul Myst* to do the same.

They moved Quick through the training sequences at the same pace as all of the other top-level students. The mere fact that he was a changeling set him apart as it was. Rionn did not want to encourage the changeling's alienation by showing him preferential treatment, no matter how much he deserved it. Nor did he want the other students to feel any more intimidation or envy than necessary. A powerful person with an inferiority *or* superiority complex could be dangerous. When that power took the form of magic the results could be catastrophic. Mar-dah had proven that.

"Apparently," Rionn observed, "The longevity trait awakened in Raxe sometime shortly after he departed our world three years ago."

"Anyway," Ryan began, somewhat embarrassed by the scrutiny. "Enough about me." He turned to Joel. "This is Joel Harvey, another offworlder and Child of the Old Ones."

Quick's bright eyes widened. "How can that be? The histories only speak of one Child crossing the WorldGate, and the Children can only produce one gifted offspring."

"It's a long story," Rionn Lorr said. "We can discuss it in detail at another time."

"Of course," Quick agreed. He turned to Joel and smiled. "It is an honor to meet another Child." The changeling smiled and extended his right hand. "And a pleasure."

Joel grasped Quick's wrist the way Ryan had moments earlier. "I wish I could say it was a pleasure for me," Joel said with a dour expression. "I'd much rather be back home."

Quick's smile faltered for a moment. But then he considered the circumstances of the visit and decided not to take Joel's impoliteness personally. "I understand," Quick said as the two broke contact.

There was a moment of awkward silence as Ryan and the Head Mage were also taken aback by Joel's curtness. Rionn Lorr broke the silence by reminding them of their current destination.

"Let us make our way to the docks," Rionn said, turning away from the group and striding south, leaning on his tall, crooked staff as he walked. "We have Hounds to greet!"

Joel had been so distracted by his disorienting trip through the WorldGate and the dazzling landscape that he did not notice the rider-less horse trotting towards them from the south. The beautiful jet-black horse resembled a Clydesdale in height and bearing, but it was not quite as bulky. The horse cantered a few yards ahead of the two lead horses of a four-horse drawn carriage. The carriage was steered by a man in a wool cloak and wide-brimmed straw hat, but to Joel's surprise, it appeared as if the rider-less horse was actually leading the carriage.

"Ryan, is that wagon following the horse?" Joel asked.

"Yeah," Ryan confirmed as the horse stepped right up to Rionn Lorr and stopped. The Head Mage produced a handful of grain from his cloak and held it out in his right palm. The horse immediately began to nibble from his hand. "That's Rionn Lorr's horse, Ebony," Ryan went on. "She and Rionn have some kind of telepathic connection."

The driver steered the carriage past the wizard and his steed and brought it to where Ryan, Joel, and Quick waited. The two younger men climbed aboard the carriage while Rionn Lorr struggled to swing himself onto the saddle on Ebony's back.

Ryan walked over to Rionn Lorr. "Can I ask you something, cuz?"

The Head Mage gave a half smile to the familiar reference. "Yes."

"Ethan's what, fifteen, sixteen years old by now? That seems kind of young for what we're about to do."

"He is sixteen," Rionn confirmed. "And Quick is a year his junior, yet you don't question his inclusion."

"Quick's a changeling," Ryan needlessly reminded. "And I know he can handle himself. I've seen it. Besides, we couldn't stop him from tagging along if we wanted to."

Rionn grinned. "I'll admit Ethan's a bit young. Other than serving as a groom, porter or stable hand, seventeen is the normal age for a young man to join any of our ground forces, and twenty is the minimum age for our elite forces, the navy, and Gryphon Ryders. Ethan is a special exception. Not only is he a gifted fighter, but he is also more mature than his age would indicate."

"Mature or not," Ryan argued, "Except for Quick, I'm not comfortable taking a kid that young on a mission."

"Ethan has been with the Keeper's Hounds since their creation over a year ago," Rionn returned. "I was reluctant, as you are, in the beginning. But his impressive attributes gave all of his mentors in the Royal Military academy – and me – confidence that he was ready. And it was a good thing. His tracking skills and his ability to read the shard of Sollustre's Eye have made him a key member of the Keeper's Hounds."

"Why not get someone else to read it?" Ryan pressed. "There has to be an adult soldier that can read the Eye."

"No, there is not," Rionn assured.

Ryan's incredulous expression caused the wizard to cast a wary glance around them to make sure no one was too close before continuing. He spoke in low, conspiratorial tones.

"Raxe, do not think for a moment that this was a decision made lightly. There are, in fact, only a few that can read the Eye. It takes a special kind of vision, an ability to see things in a different way than others, to see things that others cannot. It is called the Gifted Sight and is only found in the most powerful wizards and, in extremely rare cases, those without internal magic. Ethan is one of those extremely rare cases. That is why he is invaluable to the Keeper's Hounds. And the Hounds will be invaluable to you on this mission."

"Does Ethan know about this Gifted Sight?" Ryan asked.

"No," Rionn confided. "He knows he has abnormally sharp vision but he has no idea it is something as profound as the Gifted Sight. I'd like to keep it that way for a while yet."

"Why?" Ryan asked. "Don't you think he should know?"

"Only a select few know of the existence of this gift because, like any other power, it can be used in the wrong way. Ethan has a good heart but at his age the temptation to misuse such a gift could easily overcome him. I will tell him when he is an adult unless it becomes imperative for him to know sooner. I tell you now because you must have a complete understanding of how important he is to this undertaking. I know you will keep the secret."

"I'll keep it quiet," Ryan promised with a disapproving sigh. "Damn. You wizards keep a lot of secrets."

"All conjurers do," Rionn Lorr agreed with a grim frown. "We do indeed."

"Can you at least tell me why I would need the Keeper's Hounds?" Ryan questioned. "I've got the demon hunting part covered." He patted the demon-killing battle-axe hanging at his hip.

"We have no idea what's in store for us," Rionn countered. "This demon has found a way to conceal itself from Sollustre's Eye. How do we know it has not concealed others? The Hounds have hunted and killed all of the demons located by the Eye and I believe this experienced will be of great assistance. We need as many accomplished demon hunters as we can find."

"Can't argue with you there," Ryan admitted reluctantly. He had experience fighting demons but he had never hunted them. If a demon was too far away for his magic to detect, he would have no idea how to track the beast. He shook his head and turned toward the wagon. After taking two steps he turned and looked over his shoulder at the Head Mage. "OK. I'll take the kid. I still don't like it, though."

The offworlder climbed aboard the wagon. Joel stared out of the window but listened as Ryan and Quick immediately started up an engaging conversation. Each one summarized what they had done during the three years since they had last seen each other. Ryan was impressed by Quick's rapid advancement through the wizard's academy. Quick was fascinated by Ryan's, or – as Quick and Rionn Lorr insisted on calling him, *Raxe's* – summaries of his encounters with the organization as they hunted him and he hunted them.

Raxe admitted his lack of success for three years and talked about a few interesting adventures his grandfather and he had stumbled upon during their travels. Joel noticed that the youngster was particularly fascinated by any references to electronic and mechanical technology, and he would continuously ask Raxe to elaborate any time those things were mentioned.

As much as Raxe enjoyed his give and take with Quick, he would have enjoyed it more if Joel had joined in. He knew from his and Dan's thorough background check of the Harvey's that Joel knew a lot about computers in general and computer-aided drafting in particular. Quick would have loved to hear about those subjects, but Joel only stared blankly out of the side window of the carriage.

Raxe was tempted to invite Joel into the conversation, mainly because he wanted to climb outside to talk more with the Head Mage. He had been having a strange feeling since they crossed the WorldGate. It was hard to identify, like a muddled whisper that fell silent when he tried to focus on it. He thought Rionn Lorr might help him to identify it but he did not want to leave the inquisitive Quick without someone to talk to. He realized that his fellow offworlder's current mood might not be conducive to pleasant conversation.

At that moment, Joel actually turned to him.

"Ryan," Joel asked. "Or, is it Raxe, now? I was wondering. Why did you let your grandfather off the hook when you found out how long he'd been lying to you?"

"Lying to you?" Quick asked. "Dan?"

"Yeah," Raxe said with a sigh. "The old man can walk."

"Blades…" Quick swore in disbelief. On Raxe's previous visit, he and old Shanderah had talked about Raxe's grandfather so much that Quick felt as if he knew him.

Raxe turned back to Joel. "Kinda felt sorry for him," he admitted. "Sure, he can walk, but he's two hundred years old. He can probably only take a few steps at a time. His pride would never let him admit it, though. I think he was just trying to make a point."

A frustrated frown shrouded Joel's face. "If that's the case, how can he protect Lisa?"

"Wheelchair or not," Raxe insisted, "Gramps *is* as resourceful as he claims to be. There's no one in our world that can protect her better than that old man. He's the only one there that knows what's really going on. He has a better understanding of magic than I do. He knows how covert organizations work. Hell, I think he even used to be in one."

"You *think?*" Joel accused. "That's not good enough!"

"I couldn't protect her any better," Raxe said seriously. "You couldn't protect her anywhere near as well. Believe me, she's in the best hands she could be in."

"Let's just hope they don't have to literally *run* from anybody," Joel sneered.

Joel resumed his blank staring while Quick and Raxe returned to their conversation. A short ride took them around the outskirts of the town to the ship docks on the shore of the great lake.

A long line of piers extended out into the lake and almost every one of them was crowded. People were loading and unloading cargo from docked vessels. Some people were dressed in fashionable clothing that marked them passengers on pleasure cruises. The ships they boarded displayed colorful designs on sails and outer hulls. Most of the people, however, were the more modestly dressed – and in some cases, shabbily dressed – passengers of the larger utilitarian transport ships out at the far end of the public docks.

As people noticed the Head Mage, who was conspicuous only because he was atop the majestic Ebony, the men bowed deeply with a fist to their hearts while the women curtsied with an open palm to theirs. Joel noted how the Head Mage nodded or waved continuously, almost mechanically, and figured this was an everyday thing for him. He wondered if Rionn Lorr's smile, assuming he was smiling down at the people humbling themselves before him, was genuine. Joel could not tell because Rionn was riding ahead of them and only his back was visible. He wished he could see the wizard's face.

Joel had a knack for accurately assessing a personality from someone's smile. He could tell if a smile was genuine or not. From a smile, he could tell if a person was duplicitous or honest, confident or insecure. He had not yet, however, gotten a good read on the Head Mage or Ryan Franklin. Their smiles were genuine when they saw Quick, but that just meant they were genuinely happy to see the youngster. He needed to see more to be sure.

Joel had to admit that he got a positive vibe from the Head Mage. The man was powerful and obviously a celebrity but Joel could not detect even the slightest hint of arrogance or vanity. Had he been riding a less noticeable horse he would not have even been recognized. The cloak he wore was not at all distinguishable from the cloaks worn by many of the other people here. His long blonde hair was not uncommon, either. The horse and the long, crooked staff were the only things that set Rionn Lorr apart from the everyday citizens.

Raxe's vibe was a little more difficult to read. The ragged, gravelly voice and nasty knot on his throat seemed like evidence of a bout with throat cancer but his lean, muscular build was more indicative of a health and fitness enthusiast that would loathe cigarette smoke – or any other kind of smoke for that matter. Joel guessed he and Raxe probably weighed about the same, but he knew his burgeoning beer belly and years of on-again-off-again fitness regimens made him appear a little heavier. Raxe's body language and overall demeanor was relaxed but there was a dark edge just beneath the surface.

Joel imagined that edge was a direct result of Raxe's experiences within the mysterious "organization." It was an almost imperceptible tension, like a coiled spring that could pop at any moment, and Joel was sure he did not want to be around when that spring finally did pop.

11.2

The carriage stopped at the end of a pier that was far less crowded than the others. A group of a dozen women, barely women, actually, stood among each other talking and giggling. Their ages ranged from late teens to early twenties. They wore low-cut, cleavage-exposing, frilly blouses that were cinched tightly at the waist and tucked neatly into skirts that hugged their hips before flaring out gaudily. The flowing portion of their skirts drifted down to the top of high-heeled, polished laced boots.

Their huddled conversation continued until they noticed the Head Mage, at which point they blushed and curtsied with an open hand to their left breasts.

Raxe turned to Joel as the two stepped out of the carriage. "Groupies," he observed.

"Groupies?" Quick asked as he followed them out of the carriage.

"Admirers," Raxe explained. "Women who will go to great lengths to show their admiration."

"Groupies indeed, then," Quick confirmed with a knowing smirk.

A few yards further up the pier stood another woman, who was most definitely a *woman*, probably in her early to mid thirties. She had smooth, almond-brown skin and full, shapely lips. A pre-teen girl and boy, both with lighter brown hair than their mother and a shade lighter in complexion, flanked her. Raxe quickly recognized the woman's curly dark brown hair and full figure.

She wore a loose-fitting, off-white blouse with thin leather laces keeping the collar closed snugly. Her long woolen skirt hung down to the ankles of her scuffed, thick, animal hide riding boots. Her modest clothing, while in sharp contrast to the younger women, still failed to completely conceal her appealing curves and generous dimensions.

"Annastace Sureblade?" Raxe asked as he approached. The last time he saw her was at the funeral of her husband Meldrick. He thought she was attractive then, but because of the sadness of the occasion, he failed to take full notice of how attractive she really was.

"Master Raxe," she said with a slight blush and curtsey of her own. "I am flattered that you remember me."

"Beauty is hard to forget," Raxe said as he gently shook her hand.

The compliment earned him a beaming smile. It had been many years since a smile jolted him the way Annastace's had. The women he dealt with socially during most of his adult life usually wore well rehearsed, alluring smiles that promised as much satisfaction as the target of that smile could afford. But Annastace's smile was sincere and heartfelt, and as a result was more captivating than those others could ever be. And, if his ego was not playing tricks on him, he could have sworn he saw a bit more than friendliness in that smile and in her hazel eyes.

He decided to stop his wandering thoughts by reminding himself that she was the widow of the honorable Meldrick Sureblade.

"It's good to see you again," Raxe said. "And please, no 'master.' It's hard enough just getting used to being called Raxe again."

"But you are the descendant of the Gatekeeper Himself," Annastace argued. "You are the slayer of demons, the dragon rider…"

"That dragon part isn't quite right," Raxe corrected her quickly, wary that the worrisome and seemingly omniscient WorldHopper might be listening. "I'm not really a 'dragon rider.' WorldHopper just decided to help me out that one time. So please, just call me Raxe."

"As you wish…Raxe." She said his name in a way that sent a second jolt through him. Raxe had to tear his mind away from distracting thoughts yet again. "Arielle, August," He greeted the children. Both grinned, flattered that Raxe had remembered their names.

"Quick has told us so much about you, Raxe!" Arielle chirped suddenly. "Tell us about the demons! The Legion Midnight!"

"Yes!" August chimed in. "What about WorldHopper! And the WorldGate!"

"Arielle! August!" Annastace chided, "Leave him be! Surely he has more important things to do than regale children with tales of his adventures."

"It's alright," Raxe said. "We're waiting for Ethan, just like you. I can tell them a couple of stories while we wait."

Annastace's smile faltered at the mention of her oldest son. "Why are *you* waiting for Ethan?" she asked suspiciously. "He is just returning from hunting demons. You would call him out on another mission?"

"Not me," Raxe assured. "You'll have to take that up with the Head Mage and King William."

Annastace relented and her smile returned. "I'm sorry, Mast—, I mean Raxe. I suppose I'm an overprotective mother. After –" she trailed off, stopping herself before mentioning anything about losing her husband on the last of his many missions for the King and the Head Mage. Then again, she did not have to. Raxe could see it in her eyes.

Thankfully, Arielle's tug on Raxe's shirtsleeve reminded him that he had just promised her a story. "Oh yeah," Raxe began. He mentally ran through many of the events that had taken place on his first visit. Most of them were too violent for an eleven-year-old girl's ears.

Annastace placed a soft, but firm hand on Raxe's shoulder and leaned in to speak in a confidential tone. "My daughter wants to hear tales of battle," she said as if reading his mind. "She fancies herself a soldier, and between you and me, she has a greater affinity to the life than even her brother Ethan. But I implore you, try to find a tale that does not involve blood. She is still a young girl, after all."

Raxe thought about telling them of his experience with Sabrina, the Mistress of the Sea. That was an interesting, non-violent occurrence. He sighed deeply at the thought of the hauntingly beautiful and mysterious creature and looked out at the vast Lake Onyx. Their encounter had changed him. She had saved his life, and in the process, had somehow enhanced him in almost every way possible.

He felt a greater connection to nature, to this world, and even to his sensitivity to magic. Raxe felt cleansed as a result of her and her Phillosith's efforts to save his life. They had given a little of their essences to him and, according to Sabrina, taken a bit of him in return. He still did not know what that meant, but whatever they did definitely made him better somehow.

Even now, the great lake called to him. The whisper he felt after crossing the WorldGate was even stronger now that he was on the shores of Lake Onyx.

"Have you heard of the Mistress of the Sea?" Raxe asked.

Arielle's bright eyes widened with wonder. "The Lady Sabrina? Of course! Do you know her?"

"Do I?" Raxe said. For Annastace, he left out the battle with the sea demon that led to him meeting the Mistress of the Sea of Spirits and instead began the story by saying "A ship wreck on the Bountiful River left me almost drowned…"

He went on to tell them the story. Several times during the telling, he glanced up at Annastace. She was as interested as the children, and Raxe thought the warm smile gracing her soft features was as captivating as the smile imparted to him by the Mistress of the Sea.

Rionn Lorr and Quick stood shoulder to shoulder and observed the scene. Both of them wore mildly surprised looks on their faces. Quick turned to the Head Mage.

"I never pictured Raxe telling stories to children," the changeling said with a grin.

"This world has brought about a favorable change in the offworlder," Rionn Lorr observed. "Let us hope it has the same affect on the other one."

Both of them looked over to where Joel stood staring out over the great lake with an impatient expression. Shortly after Raxe started the tale, the ship they awaited appeared on the horizon. To Joel, it seemed to take forever.

All three of the Sureblades were thoroughly entertained by the time the ship came to dock. Raxe surprised himself with the way he had become as engrossed in the telling of the story as Annastace and her children were in listening to it. He began to understand why his grandfather and Shanderah enjoyed telling the histories of Lorr so much. He finished the story as the Keeper's Hounds de-boarded the small ship.

Raxe spotted Ethan the second he stepped onto the gangplank. He had his father's straight, prominent nose, steel blue eyes and pale blonde hair, but his mother's thick eyebrows and full lips. Ethan was obviously in the midst of a serious growth spurt. He was now almost the same height as Raxe. He would grow to be easily at least as tall as his father and – even at sixteen years of age – he was already broader across the shoulders than Meldrick Sureblade.

Ethan saw his family immediately. His eyes grew wide and a smile spread across his face when he noticed Raxe. Ethan pushed his way past the other Hounds and weaved his way through the throngs of fawning young women to get to his family and the offworlder. He gave his mother and little sister heartfelt hugs and grasped forearms with his brother firmly enough to make the younger Sureblade male wince and then chuckle. He followed the clasp with a playful ruffle of August's curly brown hair and August quickly responded by reaching up and ruffling Ethan's straight blonde hair. Ethan's smile turned to a serious expression when he turned to the Head Mage and Raxe. He straightened and proudly gave the royal salute.

"Greetings Head Mage and Raxe of Chicago, Sons of the Old Ones."

Rionn Lorr returned the salute. Raxe extended a hand. Ethan clasped Raxe's forearm and gave it a powerful squeeze. Raxe was impressed with the youngster's strength, impressed enough to give Ethan a reminder of which one of the two was a grown man. He matched and then surpassed the pressure being exerted by the teen, causing Ethan to have to stifle a wince of his own. They released one another and Ethan granted Raxe a nod of acknowledgement and smiled broadly.

"It's an honor to see you again," Ethan said. "Though I fear your presence is a harbinger of troubled times."

Raxe shrugged. "I guess that goes without saying. Are you taking good care of your dad's weapons?"

"Of that you can be sure," Ethan promised. "I would have all of them with me now if the Hounds allowed it."

"Good," Raxe said. "He turned to Joel. "This is Joel Harvey. He is another Child of the Old Ones."

"It is an honor," Ethan said, extending his forearm.

"Try not to break my arm, kid," Joel said in a gruff tone. "You've got nothing to prove to me."

Ethan shot a puzzled look at Raxe and Rionn Lorr as the two shook and released. Raxe shrugged again. "I was kinda like that on my first visit, too."

"Worse!" Quick offered as he and Ethan clasped arms and lightly punched each other on the arm with their free hands.

Rionn Lorr put a hand on Ethan's shoulder. "I'm afraid you were right about the portent of the offworlders' presence. We have much to discuss, but that is scheduled for the morn. You should spend this evening with your family."

"Thank you, Master Lorr," Ethan returned. He had to make an effort to keep from frowning as images of the incidents on the ship flashed through his mind. "And there is much that the Keeper's Hounds need to discuss with you, Master Lorr. You may want to talk to my commander as soon as possible."

"You are welcome to join us," Annastace said with a smile to Raxe. She looked around quickly as if just remembering the rest of them were there. "All of you," she amended. "The lodging I've rented has a kitchen and enough room to seat you all for a good meal. It would be an honor."

Raxe looked expectantly at Rionn Lorr. The invitation sounded good to him, but apparently not to Rionn, who was shaking his head slowly.

"Thank you for the invitation," the Head Mage replied. "But we will have to decline. I have to talk to Ethan's commander and then Raxe and I have an engagement."

"We do?" Raxe asked.

"We do," Rionn confirmed with a serious nod.

"I'll not hear of it," Annastace insisted. "By the bags under your eyes, Rionn, you could surely use at least a little rest. You do not have to stay overly long. Just stay long enough to finish a good, hot meal and I promise to release you to your engagement."

Raxe thought back to the delicious feasts that were served at Lorr Palace and gave Rionn a hopeful glance. "Is she as good a cook as the royal chefs at Lorr Palace?"

"I've had the pleasure of sampling her cooking," Rionn said. "Catherine and I have dined at the Sureblade's on several occasions. She is even better than the royal chefs."

"I'm in!" Raxe said excitedly. "I'm sure our engagement can be pushed back an hour or so… Right?"

Rionn exhaled tiredly. "I suppose it can. But my meeting with One-shot cannot. I will meet you there."

Annastace smiled again, causing Raxe's heartbeat to quicken. He could only hope he was successful at concealing it. She then turned that radiant smile to the other offworlder.

"You and Quick are more than welcome to join us, Master Harvey," she offered.

"I appreciate the offer, ma'am," Joel told her. "But I think I need to go somewhere I can get myself a nice, stiff drink."

"A word of advice," Raxe interjected. "Not to brag or nothing, but back on our side of the WorldGate I'm known as a man who can hold his liquor, so believe me when I tell you to respect the drink over here. If you don't, it *will* put you on your ass." He shuddered at the memory of the wicked hangover he earned from the relatively small amount of alcohol he consumed in a tavern on his last visit.

"So noted," Joel said. He turned to Quick. "You know of a place, kid?"

"I can give you the directions to a couple," Ethan offered.

Annastace shot him a suspicious glare. "And how would *you* know of such places?"

"I've heard the other Hounds speak of them," Ethan said quickly. But he could not to stop the flush on his cheeks.

11.3

Raxe sat back in his chair and sighed, rubbing his full belly with a contented smile. He was glad he decided to take off his armor. With all of its magical properties, Raxe doubted the metal would stretch to accommodate the size of his blissfully swollen stomach.

Annastace had cooked up the best meal he had eaten in years. In fact, the last time he had eaten so well was the last time he had visited Lorr. Back then a big delicious feast had been cooked in honor of his arrival. Raxe had very few pleasant dreams, but more than half of the few nice dreams he did enjoy in the last three years included that feast. He thought he would never be fortunate enough to again experience a meal as good that one. This meal, while nowhere near as expansive, was even better than the feast at Lorr Palace. It was more rustic, which was more to Raxe's liking. It was also more flavorful. The difference was similar to that of a five star restaurant and mom's thanksgiving dinner. One was elaborate where the other was familiar and comfortable. The unique personal touches from the chef of the smaller, rustic meal gave it a warmth and soul that were often missing in more formal spreads.

"I take it you gentlemen enjoyed your food," Annastace said with a chuckle.

Raxe looked up and across the table to see the three Sureblade children looking at him and Rionn Lorr. Ethan was stifling a chuckle while the children were openly giggling. He turned to his right and saw that the Head Mage had assumed the same contented posture and expression. Like Raxe, Rionn was rubbing his full stomach.

"I enjoyed my meal, indeed," Rionn assured. A look of worry flashed across his face, but he quickly whisked it away. He looked to the head of the table where Annastace sat. "Your culinary skills are as sharp as ever."

"Wow," was all Raxe could say.

Annastace looked at Raxe with a curious smile. She clearly did not know what "wow" meant but she guessed it was a compliment. Her smile lingered on Raxe for a moment, as his did on her, before she turned to her children.

"Ethan, take your brother and sister to the parlor and assist them with their studies," she instructed.

"Yes, mother," Ethan said dutifully. What he did not say aloud was made apparent by the frown on his face. Ethan wanted to stay and be a part of the conversation that they were obviously about to have. He wanted to tell his mother that he was no longer a child, that he had fought battles against men and demons. But he could tell from his mother's tone that her directive was not up for debate.

"Tell us of your hunts!" August asked as Ethan led the twins out of the dining area.

"Yes!" Arielle chimed in. "How big was the last one?"

"After your lesson, maybe," they heard Ethan say from beyond the threshold.

Annastace called after them. "Mind the details when you tell them of your journeys. Do not cause them to have nightmares as you did the last time!"

"Yes, mother," Ethan's voice floated back. The eldest Sureblade son wondered if the others heard the tremor in his voice from the thought of the inevitable nightmares *he* would have from the horror of the Keeper's Hounds' last mission.

When they were satisfactorily out of earshot, Annastace returned her attention to the two Children of the Old Ones. Her dazzling smile had been replaced by a look of worry.

"Does Ethan *really* have to go with you?" She asked Rionn. "Surely you can do without one Keeper's Hound."

"Annastace," Rionn answered, "I'm sorry, but Ethan is the one Keeper's Hound we cannot do without. His abilities could prove to be essential to us."

"But he is barely more than a child," Annastace argued. "He should be studying at the Royal Academy, not out fighting for his life against demons."

"If I thought we could be successful in this endeavor without him, I would gladly leave him," the Head Mage promised. "I need him for the same reason the Keeper's Hounds needed him. His tracking skills are unrivaled. He is the only person I trust, other than myself, with the ability to read the shard of Sollustre's Eye. That ability is critical to this mission. I would take his place if I could, but that is just not a possibility at this time."

"For what it's worth, Annastace," Raxe said, "I agree with you. But to be honest, I don't think we could keep him away from this mission if we tried."

"I *know* you could not," Annastace told them. "I am aware that his service has always been voluntary. I've had those arguments with him many times, just as I had them with his father. I never win. That is why I've come to you instead of trying to convince Ethan not to go."

Raxe shrugged. "He and Quick just seem to have this weird trait of always wanting to be in the middle of the action, no matter how dangerous it is."

"I can't speak for Quick, but Ethan gets that unfortunate trait directly from his father," Annastace admitted.

"I understand what you're feeling," Rionn Lorr said. "I used to feel that way about Quick. When the time comes I know I'll feel the same way about my daughter. Please understand what we do is for the wellbeing of not just the Kingdom of Lorr, but for all the Known Lands and beyond."

"Yes," Annastace said with a defeated sigh. She was silent for a moment before turning her gaze slowly to the offworlder.

"I have no right to ask you this," she began carefully, searching for the right words. "It's not a realistic thing to ask. But I am Ethan's mother so I will ask it, anyway. Will you promise to see my son back safely from this mission?"

Raxe looked into her big hazel eyes and was captivated by the emotion he saw there. Her eyes conveyed all of the fear and concern and love she felt for her first born. In that instant he would have promised her anything, but all three people sitting at the table knew that would be an impossible promise to keep. He would not make a false promise to this woman. She deserved better than that.

"I will do anything and everything in my power to ensure that Ethan comes home safely," Raxe said sincerely. "That's the most I can promise you, Annastace."

They looked at each other for a long while. Annastace could see the earnestness in Raxe's eyes. She saw the determination in the firm set of his strong jaw.

"Coming from a Child of the Old Ones," she finally said, "that is a most significant promise. I thank you for not trying to placate me with a false pledge."

"Never," Raxe assured her.

"It is us who thank you, Annastace, for this wonderful meal," Rionn Lorr said. "I truly wish we could stay longer, but we must be on our way."

"I wish we could stay longer, too," Raxe agreed.

Annastace stood up and the men followed suit. She smiled softly, but she could not conceal her lingering worry.

"I will cook an even better meal when you return," she guaranteed. "If you think this was good, wait until I have use of my own kitchen at our home in Fort Bastion."

The two men were a step behind her as she walked them to the door. "I'll send Ethan back to your inn after he has visited with us for a while longer," she said, holding open the door to the lodging as the men exited. "I'd prefer that he stay the night, but I know the boy. He'll want to spend the night with you all to make sure you don't leave without him."

Raxe's gaze lingered on Annastace as he studied her lovely figure and the graceful sway of her hips. The meal was incentive enough for him to return both himself and Ethan safely, but he was just as anxious to grace his eyes with her beauty again as he was to treat his stomach to her cooking. Annastace looked over her shoulder as she led them out and caught Raxe staring. He thought he saw her blush as she half-smiled and quickly turned away.

11.4

The whisper that had been calling to Raxe had grown to something more, finally supplanting his thoughts of Annastace Sureblade as he and Rionn Lorr rode westward along the shores of Lake Onyx. They were almost among the foothills of the northern ranges of Hell's Mountains. The southernmost sun had already dipped beneath the mountaintops and only half of the northernmost sun glanced above the jagged peaks, leaving long shadows trailing behind the riders.

The further west they rode, Raxe noticed, the more intense the sensation became. It had blossomed to the point where he was finally able to identify it, and that raised all kinds of questions. He turned to Rionn Lorr.

"There's another Child here besides your daughter," Raxe told him. "Maybe even two. Can't you feel it?"

The Head Mage's head snapped up almost as if he had been suddenly roused from a deep sleep. "I can feel *one* other besides little Shandie," he said. "Not two."

"But you don't look very surprised," Raxe noted. "Is that because you're too worn down?"

"I've been aware of the second Child's presence, but not through the detection of the Child's aura."

"So who is it?" Raxe asked.

"Can *you* tell *me*?" Rionn returned.

Raxe started to get irritated. The nervous anticipation that was building up inside of him shortened his patience.

"I don't have time for this, Rionn. Who is it?"

Rionn looked up at the stars before returning his gaze to the offworlder.

"We have a little under an hour before we reach our destination," Rionn said. "I'd say that was time enough for a lesson. So I ask again: Can you tell me who the child is?"

"Screw you, Head Mage," Raxe said, his patience at an end. He spurred his mount several yards ahead of Rionn and Ebony and rode on in silence.

Raxe knew what Rionn was doing. His grandfather did it all the time and Shanderah had done it as well. Rionn Lorr was trying to teach him something specific. The problem was Raxe did not have the tolerance for it. Not tonight. There was something strangely familiar about the presence he was feeling and he wanted to know why. It reminded him of his grandfather yet was distinctively different. He should have known who it was but he had no idea and his nerves were frayed because of it. A lesson was not what he needed. What he needed was an answer.

By the time the suns had set less than an hour later they had nearly reached their destination. The situation had grown almost unbearable. Raxe was sorely tempted to grab Rionn by the neck and shake the answers out of him. The only thing that stopped him was the fact that he was not wearing his armor and the probability that the powerful wizard would blast him across the lake if Raxe assaulted him. Instead, he reined his mount to a stop and waited for the Head Mage to catch up. When he did, the Head Mage turned left and headed south along the curve of the lake.

Raxe refused to follow. He stubbornly kept his horse still and gazed out over the great lake. Rionn rode for a couple of dozen yards before he realized that Raxe really was not going to continue. He pulled Ebony to a halt and turned her around to cast a questioning look at the stubborn offworlder.

Raxe continued to look out at the vast lake as he spoke. "I'm not going another inch until you give me some answers."

A sultry, musical, and familiar voice spoke from somewhere to the north:

"You do not have to."

"Sabrina," Raxe breathed as he turned.

To his surprise she was already ashore, standing less than ten yards away. The light from the one full and two crescent moons shimmered about her, casting her in a soft warm glow. As always, her multi-hued hair undulated slowly and hypnotically around her beautiful face and her wide oval eyes flowed from one color to another.

There was not enough light to tell the exact colors but Raxe remembered well that the color of her eyes shifted between several aquatic colors; from aqua blue to coral brown to sea green. Her full lips, the same bronze color of her skin but with a hint of sea green, were spread in a glistening smile that almost made Raxe smile despite the frustration, confusion, and surprise he was feeling.

Even though he knew who was there before he turned, and even though he had seen and touched her as closely and intimately as one could without actually having sex with her, his heart still thudded within in his chest when he laid his eyes upon the Mistress of the Sea of Spirits. Her beauty was just that striking.

The near transparent lengths of silk-like cloth waved tantalizingly in the night air, barely covering her full breasts and womanhood while at the same time providing a clear view of every seductive curve of her body. Aside from her flowing locks, long curving eyelashes, and softly arching eyebrows, there was no other hair visible on her smooth bronze skin.

It was somewhat unsettling to see her so far from the water. Somehow he knew there was something significant about that. He also instinctively knew that she was somehow linked to the Child whose presence he felt so strongly.

"As wonderful as it is to see you, Sabrina," Raxe said in a voice barely above a whisper, "I have to ask why you're here. And what do you have to do with this Child I'm feeling?"

Sabrina took several long, smooth steps toward him. He saw her legs moving yet her body still seemed to float across the long grass. She came to within a couple of yards of him before she stopped.

"It is nice to see you, Child of Raxe," Sabrina returned. "I only wish it could be under better circumstances. But I digress. I assume you mean this child," Sabrina raised her left arm and a thin, long-limbed little girl stepped from behind her. She was clothed in the same flowing ribbons as The Mistress of the Sea, but they concealed her small frame far more thoroughly than did her mother's scant coverings.

Just as Raxe knew immediately who Sabrina was from the sound of her voice, he instantly knew the identity of the pretty little girl.

"Our daughter," Raxe breathed.

The familiarity of the aura now made sense. It pulsed in him stronger than ever, easily overshadowing Rionn Lorr's presence in Raxe's consciousness.

He would have known she was their daughter even if could not feel her essence. Her skin was a slightly lighter shade of bronze than Sabrina's. Her long hair did not liquidly change color the way her mother's did, but the moonlight revealed a captivating mixture of marine hues. There was not quite enough light for Raxe to tell what color here eyes were, but he could see that they did not shift colors, either. She did have the same wide oval eyes and long curving eyelashes as her mother.

But that was where the similarities to the Mistress of the Sea of Spirits ended. Everything else he saw in the little girl's face brought to the fore of his mind an image that stole his breath and almost made him stagger. Everything else he saw in her face belonged to his mother.

Raxe vividly remembered his mother's face even from his childhood, and also from a few pictures that his grandfather carried. The little girl had the same oval face and tiny chin, the same thick eyebrows with the exact same arch, which Raxe also shared. Her lips were not quite as full as Raxe's or Sabrina's, but were exactly like his mother's. When the little girl smiled shyly at him, he saw his mother's smile and had to fight back an insistent tear.

He stared for a very long time before he was finally able to speak.

"What's your name, beautiful?" he asked.

The little girl's smile widened at the compliment but she did not answer. Instead, she moved closer to her mother.

"Her name is Azhju'lestra," Sabrina answered. "Please excuse her silence. I've taught her to be wary of strangers. While she knows you are her father, you are still a stranger to her."

Raxe's wonder slowly turned into confusion as he studied the girl more closely. There were two things that really bothered him about what he was seeing and feeling.

"How could she be our daughter?" Raxe questioned. "I was here a little over three years ago, and she looks like a six year old, at least. And I never...*we* never..."

"Copulated?" Sabrina finished for him.

"That's a good way to put it," Raxe said.

"I am faerie," The Mistress of the Sea explained. "Therefore, Azhju'lestra is half faerie. Fairies do not age the way humans do. If she were a full-blooded faerie she would have already physically matured to what humans would consider adulthood. As for your question of our copulation, I must reiterate that I am faerie. We reproduce in many ways and sex is but one. You were unconscious and I knew time was of the essence, so I chose a different way with you."

Raxe paused for a few moments as he took it all in. If her mere kiss enhanced him, made him something more than he was before, what would have happened to him if they made love? The thought of what sex would have been like with such a ravishing creature of faerie flashed through his mind, followed quickly by regret for the lost opportunity. But any lingering feelings of lust were quickly swept away by a wave of irritation as another question came to mind.

"Why?" he asked with a hint of anger. "Why would you steal my seed? Why would you use me to conceive a child without telling me? And why are you telling me now?"

Sabrina turned to their daughter and spoke to her softly. Raxe could hear her voice but he could not understand the words, if they even *were* words. It was more like a sigh with a barely audible undertone of a musical hum.

Azhju'lestra nodded. Raxe caught a glimpse of a small row of slits pulsing on the girl's neck – gills, he realized – just before she moved. She took a few long, graceful strides from the grass to the sandy shoreline and then leapt, soaring over the short strand of beach in a smooth arc that took her over a dozen yards out into the lake. Her slender body broke the water without making so much as a ripple on its surface.

The shifting colors of Sabrina's eyes turned a clear, icy blue and stilled. Her smile withered away as she leveled an intense glare at Raxe.

"I did not *steal* your seed," she corrected. "I gave you a part of myself. I shared with you the magical essence of my world in order to save your life. In return, I took a bit of your essence to conceive an heir."

"How'd you do it?" Raxe demanded. "How do get my seed without my knowing?"

"The Phillosith has tentacles of varying sizes," Sabrina began. "Some, as you know, were small enough to fit down your gullet and nasal passages without ever touching your flesh. There are others, however, even smaller than a strand of hair, that can easily fit – "

"I don't need to hear the rest!" Raxe blurted. He cast a quick, involuntary glance down at the crotch of his woolen riding pants and looked up again. The thought of one of those tentacles going up his urethra, even one as narrow as Sabrina described, made him shudder.

"Again," he went on, "why didn't you tell me?"

"There was no need for you to know. Your human notions of possessiveness and parentage do not apply to faerie. Azhju'lestra is to assume my station as caretaker of this world's waters when my time is past. Her place was here with me. Yours is across the WorldGate."

"You say there '*was*' no need for me to know," Raxe noted. "That her place '*was*' with you. Why are you using past tense?"

"While Azhju'lestra and I traveled the tributaries to the seas and lakes throughout the Known Lands in a quest to discover what killed her mate, I found my sister Phillosith's body in the Sea of Spirits."

Raxe winced involuntarily. The Phillosith Sabrina was speaking of was the same one that helped to save his life. Along with Sabrina, the giant sea creature changed him somehow, and changed him for the better. Their magic heightened his senses and enhanced his strength, speed, and stamina. They made him more attuned to his own magic and magic in general. The Phillosith helped Sabrina to make him more attuned to nature. Hearing of the Phillosith's death struck him harder than he thought it should. It felt as if a part of him had died.

"It was the demon, wasn't it?" Raxe asked.

"It was," answered Sabrina. Her eyes began to flow again, alternating colors hypnotically. "Nothing in the natural world could kill the great Phillosith. She was the last of her kind. The demon slaughtered her mate, as well."

She fell silent for a time, and cast a worried gaze out over Lake Onyx. Raxe followed her gaze and felt his daughter's presence pierce him like a bolt to the heart.

"I'm afraid the demon will target me next," Sabrina went on. "I do not want my daughter to be with me if it does."

"You want Raxe to protect her," Rionn Lorr concluded.

"Yes."

"You think she'll be safer with me?" Raxe asked incredulously. "I'm on a collision course with the demon. I'm trying to find the Hell Key and it's gonna try to stop me."

"But it is afraid of you," Sabrina told him. "It will not confront you directly as long as you have Demonsbane. It may send minions in its name but none of them will be quite as dangerous as it would be. If it comes for me it may very well come personally. I would not stand a chance. Its presence would invoke the magic of the Old Ones within my daughter, but she is too young to survive such an encounter."

Raxe shook his head. "She'd be safer with Rionn. The demon won't confront him directly, either, or it would've done so by now. And he won't be out hunting the demon. He'll be at the palace where it'll be much safer for her."

"She will not stay with anyone else," Sabrina said. "She will only stay with you because of your blood connection to her. If I try to send her with anyone besides you she will leave them and find her way back to me."

"You're her mother," Raxe argued. "Order her to stay at Lorr Palace."

Sabrina chuckled. It was a beautifully sound at once melodic and sad.

"If only it were that simple, offworlder," she said. "I advise you once more: do not apply human notions of parentage to my kind. Fairies are fiercely independent. She does not obey me out of love or fear of punishment as human children obey their parents. She concedes to my wishes only because she trusts that I have her wellbeing in mind. It is purely a survival instinct.

"Although, there may also be a bit of loyalty involved from the part of her that is human," Sabrina allowed. "But understand that she is more faerie than she is Child of the Ones or even human. As such, she will be ruled by instinct more than by what you would consider reason or passion, especially in her current immature state. She will do what she must to survive. As of now, her instincts tell her that she will be best served by staying with her parents."

"There's no telling how rough our travels will be," Raxe countered. "Who knows what enemies we'll have to fight? I can't have a skinny little girl tagging along. She'd be a distraction, a burden that we can't afford."

"Don't let her appearance deceive you," Sabrina said. "She may appear frail to your eyes but she is both Child of the Old Ones and faerie. That is a powerful combination. She may even prove useful on your journey."

Raxe thought about her effortless leap from the lakeshore into Lake Onyx. That was at least a foot-foot bound. There was definitely more to the girl than met the eye.

Rionn Lorr stepped forward. A frown creased his weatherworn face. "As powerful a combination as that may be," he warned, "her human blood makes it a volatile and potentially dangerous one, as well."

Raxe looked from Sabrina to Rionn and back to Sabrina. "Is that true?" he asked.

"Indeed," the Mistress confirmed.

Raxe shook his head. "You ain't doing a good job of selling this."

"I am not trying to sell this," Sabrina declared. "I want you to understand what I am asking of you. You should know the reason, the advantages, and the dangers involved."

"Speaking of dangers, we'll be away from water for long stretches at a time," Raxe pointed out. "Won't that be dangerous for her?"

"She can exist both in and out of water indefinitely, unlike me," Sabrina revealed. "In fact, I am already starting to weaken and will have to return to the water very shortly. I came this far from the water to have this discussion with you to underscore the importance of my request."

Raxe did not respond right away. He again looked out over the waters to where he felt Azhju'lestra's aura. To his surprise he was actually considering Sabrina's request. Normally he would not even have entertained a conversation involving any kid, let alone his daughter. Ethan tagging along was bad enough. He wondered why he was considering Sabrina's request and then turned to the Mistress of the Sea of Spirits with a sharp, accusing glare.

"Are you enthralling me?" he demanded.

"No," Sabrina said sincerely. "You have grown too powerful and our connection is too strong. You would know if I was trying to influence you that way. You would not have to ask. You are considering my request only because you recognize its significance."

She was right, Raxe knew, but he had to ask if for no other reason than to hear the words. He looked over at Rionn Lorr, the look in his eyes asking the Head Mage for his opinion. Rionn could only shrug.

"It is your choice to make, Raxe," Rionn said. "My thoughts on the matter are immaterial."

"Before you make your decision," Sabrina added, "there is one thing more I must say."

Raxe sighed. "Let's hear it."

"If you decide to take her, you must not return her to me until this ordeal is over and the demon has been slain. Under no circumstance should she return to Lake Onyx before this ordeal has been settled. Can you promise me that?"

Logic dictated that Raxe turn her down flat. Reason told him that bringing a little girl with him, even if she was as potentially powerful as Sabrina intimated, was a terrible idea.

And then his heart told him that she was his daughter. A protective instinct unlike anything he had ever felt welled up inside of him. Her essence, the extra little sensation that pulsed in almost perfect synchronicity with his heartbeat, that extra whisper in the corner of his consciousness, all of it had already become a part of him. He began to understand how his grandfather and his mother felt about him.

Even though he had never seen Azhju'lestra before this night, their bond of blood and divine magic made him want to keep her safe. As dangerous and ill advised as he knew it was, he had reluctantly made his decision.

"I'll do as you ask," Raxe told her. "And I promise not to bring her back until the demon has been destroyed."

Sabrina smiled that captivating smile of hers, drawing him in almost as completely as Annastace's smile had earlier that evening. "Our daughter will be there when you begin your journey. I thank you, offworlder, with all of my heart."

Raxe turned to Rionn Lorr. "This is the second stupid promise I've made tonight."

"I suppose you have a weakness for beautiful women," the Head Mage said with a shrug and a half smile.

They turned back just in time to see Sabrina flowing silently and gracefully beneath the dark, glassy surface of the Great Lake Onyx.

Chapter 12: Enter the Ken

12.1

The next day, while the two suns hung suspended at their highest point, Joel stood between Rionn Lorr and Raxe and looked out at the sky sleigh, *Cloud Chaser,* on the sprawling airfield. Rionn Lorr looked on with satisfaction at the men and women scurrying this way and that, carrying tools, supplies, messages, mechanical drawings and the like. The sounds of hammering and sawing and scraping floated across the field as the huge wedge of wooden planks and metal slats and hinges that comprised the sky sleigh were repaired, upgraded, and inspected. All of these sounds, as loud as they were, were sporadically and momentarily drowned out by the occasional booming cry of the avicaws, the colossal birds that transported the sleigh.

Raxe thought back to his first ride on a sky sleigh during his first visit to Lorr. He noticed immediately that the sleigh design had been improved. Overall, the sleigh was clearly larger than the one he rode in three years earlier, and it was more streamlined. There were fewer straight edges and more aerodynamic curves. The pilot box was topped with a half-egg shaped shell of glass with curved wooden framing instead of a box of wood with portal holes cut into it.

Raxe remembered how surprised he was at how smooth the ride was in the original sky sleigh. With the improvements made on the sleigh design he knew the ride would be even smoother now. He also remembered how afraid he had been of riding in the sky sleigh beforehand. He looked to his right and saw that same fear magnified tenfold in Joel's expression. Joel's light brown skin was slightly ashen and beads of sweat rolled down his face even in the cool autumn morning breeze blowing off of Lake Onyx.

"You look a little clammy, there, dude," Raxe teased. "Is it a hangover or is it *Cloud Chaser* over there?"

"My guess is it's both," Rionn Lorr chimed in. His own complexion was back to normal and the bags under his eyes were gone. The Head Mage was clearly well rested.

The same could not be said for Joel, who had risen from bed only an hour or so ago after spending the morning vomiting into buckets provided by various inn attendants; or sprinting to one of the many outhouses that lined the rear of the inn to relieve himself in other ways. The staff thoughtfully provided a bitter drink that managed to rid him of his violent headache, but there was nothing to be done about his nausea. He simply had to expel the liquor from his weakened system.

Joel continued to stare out at the sleigh field with wide, unbelieving eyes. He popped three pills into his mouth, one for asthma and two for allergies, and drank deeply from a water skin, never taking eyes away from the sky sleighs. He had not had to use his emergency inhaler since crossing the WorldGate, but at the moment that was the farthest thing from his mind.

"No way," he finally swore in a low, tired voice. His throat was so raw from throwing up that his voice was almost as raspy as Raxe's. "I have a well-earned hangover, but my head's clear enough to know I'm not getting on *that.*"

"Don't worry, Joel," Raxe said. "I promise it's not as bad as it looks."

Joel shook his head vigorously. "You shouldn't have even brought me out here, man. Ain't no way I'm flying on something like that!"

Raxe had to stifle a chuckle. "C'mon man, it's cool. I thought it looked like something off of the Flintstones, myself. I was scared as hell, too, the first time I – "

"I don't give a damn what you were," Joel snapped. "You and I are two different people. Ain't gonna be no first time for me 'cause I ain't riding on that. No way."

Rionn Lorr placed a strong, comforting hand on Joel's shoulder. "Joel, I assure you all will be well."

Joel promptly swatted the Head Mage's hand away. "You can assure 'til your blonde hair turns gray, Mr. Wizard. Y'all crazy as hell if you think I'm getting on that." Joel turned sharply and began to stride quickly back toward the inn.

Raxe's amusement quickly soured to annoyance as he hurried after his fellow offworlder. "I brought you out here because I didn't want to shock you with it right before it was time to take off. I wanted to give you a little time to digest it and get ready for it."

"Then you screwed up, home boy," Joel returned. "All you did was make up my mind ahead of time. You need to find another means of transportation or you'll be making the trip without me."

"Are you gonna be like this about everything we do here?" Raxe demanded. "If you are, this trip is gonna be a whole lot worse than it has to be."

"Like it's a damned vacation, now," Joel muttered as he quickened his pace.

Raxe put a not-so-comforting hand on Joel's shoulder to halt his retreat. Joel tried to knock the hand away as he did Rionn's, but Raxe's grasp did not budge.

Joel took Raxe's wrist in both hands in an attempt to pry himself free, but Raxe's grip was like iron. Raxe could see that Joel was getting angry. He would not have been surprised if Joel took a swing at him.

"Let me go, mother – "

"Remember why you're here, Joel," Raxe advised, his sandpaper voice going low and cold and sinister. The change of tone had the desired effect. Joel stopped struggling against Raxe's grasp.

"You're right, this *ain't* a damned vacation," Raxe continued. "And it's not about your comfort. It's about protecting this world and ours. Don't forget that no one made you come here. You *chose* to come here in order to protect your wife and baby from demons and assassins."

Joel said nothing. He only stared. Raxe could see Joel's nervousness and worry begin to overcome his anger.

"While you're here, you're gonna be faced with doing a lot of things that you'd rather not do. If you want to get home safely you're gonna have to do them. Bitching and crying won't make it any better. I can help you through this. I've worked with green soldiers and agents on their first missions and I've been to this world before. I can see things from your perspective. If you just listen to me you'll be surprised at how helpful I can be."

Joel shook his head in denial. "We may be from the same world, hell, we're both from Chicago, but we don't share the same perspective. You were new to this world three years ago but you weren't new to fighting. You weren't new to 'missions.' It's different for me. I'm not soldier."

"Yes, you are," Raxe argued. "Like it or not, you're a soldier now. Just look at it like you've been drafted. And since you're here you might as well make the best of it by helping us to help you. Keep thinking about Lisa. Resign yourself to doing whatever the hell you have to do to get safely back to her."

"That's part of the problem," Joel admitted. "I can't *stop* thinking about her."

"I know this is easier said than done," Raxe said, his grip on Joel's shoulder finally easing. "But try not to let the thought of her distract you. Use it to motivate you. Use it to make you more determined than you would be otherwise."

The anger was completely gone from Joel's eyes and replaced by concern. "I'll try," he conceded. "But I can't help but worry about what she's going through back there."

12.2

The mayor's conference room in the Port Lorrian City Hall was more than large enough to host the gathering of men and women and one elf, those who would be going on this latest quest. The fading suns' light necessitated the lighting of the oil lamps that lined all four walls of the space, but most of the group was so engrossed in their individual discussions that no one bothered to light them or send for an attendant to light them. Rionn Lorr was ready to begin, so with a wave of his hand and a thought, he lit all of the oil lamps. The sudden and unexplained brightening of the room startled everyone into silence.

"This is what we face, ladies and gentlemen," Rionn Lorr began in a business like tone that brought all eyes to him. His strong voice carried to everyone in the large conference room. "A demon is on the loose."

"How can that be?" One-shot, commander of the Keeper's Hounds, asked among a sudden drone of excited and worried murmuring. "Sollustre's Eye would have revealed its presence and we would have hunted it down and killed it." Other Hounds nodded and voiced their agreement.

"This is not an indictment of the Keeper's Hounds or the magic of the Eye," Rionn assured. "The loosed demon is a sixth level one."

He paused to give them all time to absorb the significance of that statement. Worried glances and furrowed brows replaced the confidently defiant posture of the Hounds. They had faced mostly first through third level demons. The fourth and fifth level demons released by Mar-dah had been destroyed by Rionn Lorr, Raxe and the dragons three years earlier. The third level demons they faced had been almost too much for the Hounds to handle, so the thought that they would be part of the hunt for a sixth level demon was unimaginable.

"Yes," Rionn reiterated. "We hunt a sixth level demon that has the power to cross the WorldGate at will. Sollustre's Eye cannot detect demons across such a barrier. And since it would have to come to this side at least a few times to plant its seeds of treachery in this world, it had to have found a way elude the Eye. That is why I've brought Raxe back to this world. That is why the Ranger Elf Rell Kallen joins us in this hunt. You all have expertise that we will need to stop this creature before it can do what it has set out to do."

"And what is that?" One-shot asked, this time with a hint of uncertainty in his voice.

"What all demons were created to do," Rionn answered. "They were created to destroy the Children who fought on the side of the Protectors and to bring all mankind to heel."

"I know that a sixth level demon is one of the most powerful," the Hounds' commander said. "But it is still only one being. Surely it could not accomplish such a task alone."

"That is a good point," the Head Mage granted. "And I had the same thought. I researched as many old texts as I could find concerning Heaven's War and found a reference to only one demon that could cross the WorldGate without assistance. It was called the Dierglyorr. It was hybrid of a man, a changeling, and a great beast that has since gone extinct. The beast was something that, according to the texts, could challenge even a dragon.

"The man was a politician from a lost kingdom that, before it disappeared during an epic battle that turned the War in the Protectors' favor, was the most powerful on this earth. I was not able to find specific details but the texts say that the politician was also an accomplished conjurer, a warlock, in fact. He had been instrumental in the kingdom's ascension. He was intelligent, devious, relentless and merciless in his efforts. He believed the Leaders would win the war so he cast his lot with Them. He was a leader of men, and even before the gods took him to make the Dierglyorr, he had convinced many humans to support the Leaders.

"The Leaders made use of his cold cunning," the Head Mage continued. "The Dierglyorr did not only use brute force to accomplish its objectives. In fact, it rarely used brute force even though it had the capacity for much destruction with its bare claws.

"Its cunning was its most dangerous weapon. The Leaders gave it the ability to cross the WorldGate to recruit assistance from other worlds. The Dierglyorr assembled and led a force made up of demons, Leader Children, other hybrid beasts of magic created by the Leader gods, and even creatures from other worlds into the battle that resulted in the destruction of the Gatekeeper and Raxe."

"That is *all* we face?" Cobra whispered sarcastically in Ethan's ear. "All we face is the sixth level demon that killed two Old Ones?"

Ethan shushed her silently but it was too late. The Head Mage was already looking at the woman sitting next to the young Sureblade.

"I understand your concern, Cobra," Rionn Lorr said directly to her. His tone was even but his gaze was stern, a silent admonishment that was clear to all in the room. Cobra shrank before that steely gaze as Rionn Lorr continued. "But we *can* defeat it if we act quickly. It does not have the army that it had then, at least not yet. We have a chance to stop it before it can build one."

Raxe knew the demon was well on its way to creating such an army. With the resources at its command while posing as a high-ranking operative of the organization, its potential for destruction in both worlds was staggering. Neither world would be prepared to do battle against the combination of magical and technological warfare the demon would pit against them.

"We have Raxe," the Head Mage went on, raising his hand in Raxe's direction. The offworlder nodded. "And we have yet another Child," Rionn indicated Joel, who merely stared down at the floor. "The Dierglyorr is as vulnerable to their powers as any other demon." Rionn turned an eye to the commander. "We also have the Ranger Elf Rell Kallen to assist us."

Rionn moved his hand in the direction of Rell Kallen. The motion was not necessary, as everyone had already noticed the quiet yet conspicuous elf standing alone in the corner, his arms crossed and a wary eye on the entire room.

The Head Mage continued, looking at One-shot as he spoke. "And we have your Keeper's Hounds, accomplished demon slayers all."

The vote of confidence put the Hounds in slightly better spirits. Rionn noticed the straightening of slumped shoulders and the prideful rising of chests.

"So how do we bring this demon down?" One-shot asked confidently.

"We find the Hell Key," Rionn Lorr said.

He noticed the curious looks of those who did not get the connection between the Hell Key and the Dierglyorr. They all knew that the Hell Key was created to open the gates of the hells to either release demons or banish to hell the souls of those possessed of divine magic. They also knew that a demon had no soul, and therefore the Hell Key could not be used to banish the Dierglyorr.

"The Dierglyorr will be searching for the Hell Key, as well," the Head Mage explained. "If for no other reason than to make sure no Child can possess it."

What he did not mention was the possibility of the demon manipulating a Child to release and control another host of demons the way Mar-dah had three years earlier.

"If we find the Hell Key we will almost certainly find the Dierglyorr," Rionn said. "The mere search is likely to eventually flush the demon out. And then these offworlder descendants of the Gatekeeper will send it back to the sixth level of hell." When Rionn was satisfied by the look of understanding in everyone's countenance, he went on.

"The first expedition sent to recover the Hell Key was lost somewhere over Hell's Mountains. The second expedition was lost as well, but a survivor managed to send word from as far as the Demons Spine Mountains, Hargathall's Cleft to be exact, before we lost contact with him. So that is where you will start your search. Two royal sky sleighs, *Cloud Chaser* and *Sundance*, have been selected for the trip. We know Mar-dah's lair is somewhere in that mountain range. The survivor had to be very close."

"What is Hargathall's Cleft?" Raxe asked.

"It is a canyon in the northern regions of the Demon's Spine," Rionn Lorr informed. "According to legend, the Old One Hargathall, who fought on the side of the Leaders, cut that great scar into the earth during a battle against Lorr

Himself. Lorr and Hargathall destroyed one another in that confrontation."

"That place is said to be cursed," The Hound Hammer said to no one in particular.

"I have heard that rumor," Rionn Lorr said. "And I have investigated the area on more than one occasion over the years. I will admit the area is barren and has a sinister air about it, but I have yet to find evidence of any curse. But just the same, I would advise you to stay there only long enough to find evidence that will lead you closer to Mar-dah's lair. If you cannot find it within a day's time, you should leave the area and search deeper within the Demon's Spine. I may not have found any evidence of a curse, but the tale had to have come from somewhere.

"As I said earlier," Rionn Lorr concluded. His voice grew louder, projecting strength and certainty. He used a bit of magic to amplify his words in the listeners' minds as well as their ears. "Each of you brings something special to this expedition. Trust that I would not have assembled you if I did not have complete faith that you will be successful. Together we will crush this demon and its schemes and ensure that peace reigns in the Kingdom of Lorr!"

Several of the Hounds, including Ethan, excitedly pounded their fists on the table in response to the Head Mage's inspiring words. Rionn Lorr took his seat and allowed the occupants of the large conference hall to break up into smaller groups to discuss the specifics of their mission. The Keeper's Hounds grouped together in conversation on one side of the room while the Children and the changeling gathered on the other. Rell Kallen stayed for only a moment before leaving to attend to his own affairs. The others did not appreciate his departure but they did not attempt to persuade him to stay.

Each group would periodically send an emissary to the other to relay information back and forth. Finally, the two groups came back together to combine their strategies and conclude their session for the evening. The entire process lasted just over two hours.

12.3

As the occupants filed out of the room, Rionn Lorr came up behind Raxe and placed a hand on his shoulder.

Raxe turned. "What's up, cuz?"

"Be wary of the elf," Rionn Lorr advised. "The Elven Queen Eleshaë believes, as did her predecessors, that the elves should possess the Keys, that the Keys would be safer with them because they cannot invoke their magic so they would not be tempted to use them at all, let alone toward a destructive purpose. They do not understand or agree with the decision to hide the WorldGate and Hell Keys."

Raxe nodded. "Rell Kallen will double cross us."

"At his first opportunity," Rionn confirmed.

"I'll keep that in mind," Raxe promised. "Let me ask you something. If the Keys had been hidden so well for so long, how do you think the Finder located them?"

"I've pondered that myself," Rionn admitted. "The Finder was a legend in his time. Tales abound lost of treasures and charms he recovered over the course of more than four decades. Some say he possessed more talismans than just his dwarf-forged armor and the broadsword Dragon-fang.

"He was one of the wizard Drake's main suppliers of dragon blood years ago. We apprehended Drake, a seasoned and powerful wizard, yet the Finder has always eluded his pursuers. He spilled the blood of both man and monster during his lifetime. Powerful conjurers and the greatest warriors fell to his sword. He murdered the wicked and the innocent alike to fulfill his many contracts over the years. Whatever it took to achieve his goal is what he did."

"You don't have to remind me," Raxe said, the images of the black-armored giant's carnage still fresh in his mind after only three years.

"The Finder was ruthless and effective," Rionn said. "His successes will have to be investigated, lest someone else finds his resources and tries to follow in his footsteps. But we have more immediate troubles to address. How much information did Shanderah impart to you?"

"I'm not sure," Raxe admitted. "When I try to recall any of it I draw a blank. I don't know what triggers bring the memories to me. They seem to come at random. Why?"

"I received some troubling news earlier today," Rionn shared. "I was hoping some of the old sorceresses' knowledge might be helpful."

"What's going on?" Raxe asked.

"I did not mention this to the group because it is not relevant to this mission and would only serve as an unnecessary distraction," Rionn confided. "But it seems the Dierglyorr has already commenced the building of its army. A terrible sickness has befallen many of the royal veterans that fought against demons when you were here last."

Raxe's face went ashen. *He* had fought against demons. He had fought against countless demons. He held his breath and waited for the Head Mage to continue.

"According to Master Mage Delthar, one of the elders of the Conjurer's Alliance and a most trusted advisor, the soldiers who were injured by demons are…transforming into what he describes as 'walking cadavers.' Those who were killed by demons are rising from the grave."

"Shit," Raxe exhaled. His eyes went wide. "I was wounded by a demon right after you brought me through the WorldGate the first time…" his heartbeat began to race as he glanced at the pockmarks on his arms, "not to mention the sea demon that chewed me up and swallowed me."

"I considered that," Rionn replied. "But I believe the blood of the Old Ones that runs through your veins makes you immune to what has befallen the others. And it is very likely that the magic of Demonsbane protects you. It is also possible that Sabrina and the healing properties of the Phillosith cleansed you. These are only suppositions, mind you, but you obviously have not succumbed to the illness that is affecting the others."

Raxe was not comforted. "But what if those things have only delayed the effects?"

"Then the cure that I find will rid you of them," the Head Mage assured. "There is a small army of these walking cadavers moving southeast from Fort Bastion. They have encountered armed resistance along the way but apparently the things cannot be slowed unless they are hacked to pieces. They cannot be stopped unless they are burned to ash. As you can imagine, their opposition does not fare well against them. And worse yet, those struck down by the infected are infected in turn. They rise shortly thereafter and join the rest on their trek. Master Delthar and others are in pursuit but I fear they will be hard pressed to stop them."

"I'd love to help," Raxe assured, "But the Hell Key…"

"It's not Demonsbane that we need against the walkers," Rionn explained. "The Hell Key must remain your priority. From what Delthar says the creatures are not demon spawn. I fear the demon was the architect of their transformation but Delthar says they do not possess a demonic aura, so they would not ignite your magic. He is learned and has been more than dependable to me and my father before me, so I doubt that he would be mistaken in this."

"What you describe sounds like a virus," Raxe mused. "A magic virus, but still a virus."

"Virus?" Rionn Lorr asked. "I'm not familiar with that term. Our healers have never mentioned it to me."

"I'm not a doctor so I can only give you the layman's explanation. A virus is like a bug, or group of bugs. They're too small for the human eye to detect without the use of special machinery to magnify them. The little bugs live in the body and have different affects on it. Most of them are bad. Those bugs can be passed on from one body to another in different ways. Some can travel through the air while others depend on physical contact."

"Interesting," said the Head Mage as he stroked his chin thoughtfully. "You mentioned the need for special machinery to see these bugs. What kind of machinery?"

"It's called a microscope," Raxe answered. "It's like a telescope, but instead of making distant objects appear closer, it uses light and curved lenses to make very small objects seem larger. They can be used to view individual particles of blood and flesh. In our world we call those particles cells."

"I wish you could work with our healers and alchemists to solve this dilemma," Lorr said.

"I wouldn't be much help. I just told you everything I know about viruses and microscopes."

"Still, it could be very useful," Rionn said, making a mental note to revisit this new information. "Now, about Shanderah's memories…"

"How can they help?" Raxe asked.

"Unless there is a change of direction," Rionn explained, "the walkers' path will take them right through the city of Ridgeland and then into the northern regions of the Runestone Mountains. I'd like to know why."

"That's Jon's stomping ground, right?" Raxe asked, referring to Jon the Firemaster, a powerful elemental whose name accurately described his power.

"Yes," Rionn confirmed. "I've tried to contact him to give warning but I have not been successful in locating him. As an honorary member of the Conjurer's Alliance, he possesses a speaking stone as do all of the other members. He does not participate on a regular basis and he often leaves his speaking stone behind, hidden safely, when he travels. It appears he has done so again, for I traced the speaking stone to its secure hiding place and it remains unmoved. I've used other methods to find Jon but they have been fruitless."

Rionn Lorr, Raxe knew, had at his command all kinds of magic that he could use to find someone. So when he said he could not locate Jon, the significance of the statement did not escape Raxe. "Do you think he's alright?" he asked.

"I assume so," answered Rionn Lorr. "He and his wife travel often, and when they do not want to be disturbed, Jon can be very resourceful about making sure they are not."

"That's not very dependable," Raxe observed.

"As I said, he is an honorary member," Rionn explained. "Any assistance he provides is voluntary. He has never failed to heed our call when we've needed him. However, he is not bound to Alliance service by the Solemn Oath, so he is not required to carry his speaking stone at all times as are official Alliance members. When he goes away for an extended period, though, or when he leaves the kingdom, he usually notifies us. We have messengers on the lookout for him and his wife all over the kingdom. He should be found soon and notified before returning to his home in Bluethorn."

"I hope so," Raxe said. "That would be one hell of a surprise to come home to."

"Indeed," Rionn concurred.

"Is there anything special about that area?" Raxe asked.

"Not as far as I know," Rionn answered. "Ridgeland and Bluethorn are moderate sized towns that hold no strategic value that I can think of. The southern half of the Runestones is rich with precious stones and metals, which is why they are mined them so heavily. The northern expanses are not. The men of Bluethorn and Ridgeland mine fire rocks from the north Runestones. They process them into blasting sand that they either sell in its powdered form or use to manufacture explosives. It's not a lucrative enough business to merit this kind of attention from an attacking force."

"Maybe the Dierglyorr wants the fire rocks," Raxe offered. "He could use them for weapons."

Rionn nodded his head thoughtfully. "It's possible. We cannot rule it out. But I do not see the logic. The rocks are useless before processing, which is an incredibly time consuming, skilled, and dangerous undertaking. It seems the Dierglyorr would find a quicker and more subtle way to outfit his army."

Rionn paused as if continuing an internal debate before continuing. "No, these locations do not hold any substantial military or monetary significance. Fort Bastion, on the other hand, is a military stronghold. But they are moving away from it. Silverleaf is closer than either Ridgeland or the Runestones and it has a large store of military supplies and weaponry. They're moving away from it, as well. They're even bypassing the capital city."

"There has to be a reason," Raxe said.

Rionn nodded. "Exactly. Knowing why they're going in their present direction might help us figure out a way to stop them as quickly as possible without losing too many more of our soldiers." Both were silent for a moment before Rionn spoke again. "The only thing that is out of the ordinary about that area is its history."

Raxe raised an eyebrow. “History?”

“That is the area where my great, great grandmother, Daniatiae Lorr, died during Heaven’s War. The story was passed down verbally but I’ve been able to piece together the written record from old volumes in the royal libraries as well as texts found in the temple beneath Infinity Isle.

“In the text, the Protectors foresaw that the war would mean the end of the Old Ones. They wanted their Children to continue to protect the Kingdom of Lorr. Daniatiae Lorr was appointed as this kingdom’s first Head Mage before the war began. The account speaks of her death at the hands of the Leaders and their demons in the northern Runestones, but it doesn’t reveal anything of significance about the area itself. I was hoping Shanderah might have had some historical knowledge that could help us.”

Raxe paused as he searched his thoughts. He tried to will Shanderah’s transferred memories to the forefront of his mind but nothing Rionn Lorr said triggered any of them.

“I’m sorry man,” he apologized. “I’m not getting anything. Can you quote any passages from the texts? That might spark something.”

Rionn Lorr shook his head. “No. I’ve not memorized the story. I will be returning to Greenglenn in the morning. I can get the readings and relay to you the text word for word.”

“Cool,” Raxe said. “But we’re leaving in the morning. How will you contact me from so far away?”

The Head Mage reached into his cloak and produced two dark brown boxes, each about the size of Raxe’s palm. He gave each box four firm shakes before handing one to Raxe. He undid a small latch on the lid of the box he kept and pulled it open. The box was half filled with light brown sand. A thin wooden stick, almost as long as the rectangular box was wide, rested atop the sand.

“Reflection sand,” Rionn told him. “Yet another magical tool recovered from Infinity Isle. What is written in one box using the stylus within shows up in the other box. “I will show you how to use it.”

Rionn Lorr used the stylus in the small box to trace a strange symbol in the sand. The symbol was composed of three parallel lines. They were vertically oriented relative to the way he held box. The two outside lines were the same length and spaced about a half of an inch apart. The third, longer line was in the middle. The top point of the middle line was level with the same spot on the lines to either side, but it was longer by about a third at the bottom. A horizontal line was then drawn across the top of all three, extending past the outside left and right lines by about a quarter inch.

Rionn then drew a circle at the bottom of the middle line and added a horizontal line that spanned the width of the box and was tangent to the bottom of the circle. He allowed the symbol to stay in the stand for a few moments, approximately five seconds by Raxe's count, and then used his index finger to stir the sand and brush away the symbol.

"At this point," Rionn informed, "the reflection sand is ready for the writing or reception of messages. It won't work now because the boxes are too close together. If the box holders are within listening range of each other, the magic is not needed, but I assure you it will work once there is greater distance between us."

"I'll take your word for it," Raxe said.

"Take care of it," Rionn warned. "The sand is imbued with ancient magic. If it is somehow lost, it cannot be replaced by ordinary sand."

Raxe nodded. "Will do."

Rionn nodded in return. "The box will tremor lightly when a message is sent," he said. "However, there is a chance that you might not notice the tremor, so you should check it periodically for messages. I'll do the same."

"Understood," Raxe replied.

"That is all, for now," Rionn said. "Sleep well, Raxe."

12.4

As he walked back to his quarters, Raxe looked to the west at the Hells. The view sent a chill down his spine. From this distance and in the suns' eerie half-light, the Hells seemed more sinister than they had during the height of the day. The crown of the northernmost sun struggled to stay above the rapacious peaks, extending shadows that swept over the rise and fall of the foothills like gargantuan tentacles creeping slowly and silently eastward after unwary prey. Raxe shook away his apprehension and turned his mind to the previous night's meeting with Sabrina and Azhju'lestra.

His daughter.

He was not sure he would ever be able to wrap his mind around that one. It was easier to believe those creeping shadows actually were giant tentacles coming to attack the town. The girl looked so much older than she should have. At three years of age, he kept thinking that she should have been a toddler. He had to remind himself again that she was not entirely human. The gills on her neck made that obvious, which made the whole situation even weirder. And craziest of all was that Sabrina insisted that the girl accompany them on their search for the Hell Key.

He did not know whether to be flattered that Sabrina, the Mistress of the Sea and last of the water fairies, would choose him to be the father of her child, or to be incensed that she would do such a thing without his knowledge or permission. As he entered his rented room and latched the door, he wavered back and forth on what to make of his predicament. By the time he stripped out of his tunic and breeches, pulled on the cotton sleeping leggings thoughtfully provided to him by the inn staff, and climbed into bed, he had decided to reserve judgment until a little more time passed. He was tired. He would think a lot better after a good rest.

The down-filled mattress was too soft, but Raxe was too mentally exhausted to care. He tried to clear his mind of the storm of questions and concerns and tossed and turned in an attempt to find a comfortable sleeping position. He finally found it face down, right leg bent, and arms wrapped around his lumpy feather pillow. But still he could not sleep. The excitement of once again crossing the WorldGate would not let his mind rest. He marveled at the power it must have taken to create such magic, and wondered what other worlds were out there.

Shanderah told him about how the Old Ones and the early generations of Children would cross the WorldGate often to look upon the many Great Works of the Lord Ascendant. The tale was similar to a few of the ones his grandfather told him when he was a boy. Raxe tried his best to tune the old woman out back then. But when she put the contents of her mind into his, the stories became more than just dimensionless words.

On the sporadic occasions when they would come to him, usually in dreams but sometimes even while he was awake, the words often became the vivid pictures, sounds, smells and tastes of memory. He could even feel the interest and excitement Shanderah felt when she was told the tales conveyed to her by her parents more than two centuries earlier. It was as if the original memories of people who experienced those stories were passed to Shanderah over the years the way she had passed her memories to him.

And maybe they had, for all Raxe knew. A Child of the Old Ones could project thoughts and, if powerful enough, images into the minds of their offspring. There was no doubt that at least one of her parents would have been powerful enough. Shanderah was able to pass her memories to Raxe. Her divine parent and ancestors would have been even more powerful and capable than she.

She was told the story about Raxe's direct ancestor, The Gatekeeper, and how he stood guard over the WorldGate and regulated its use at the Lord Ascendant's behest. At the start of Heaven's War, the Gatekeeper sealed off the Gate to at least keep any of the Children of the Old Ones from using the WorldGate Key to recruit help, voluntary or otherwise, for the war. The Leader Old Ones later countered this move by giving the Dierglyorr the ability to cross the WorldGate without the use of a talisman.

Such a wonderful gift lost, and for what? To keep the Leaders from controlling mankind? When Raxe considered the abominable things people did to each other during the history of man he could almost understand the Leaders' desire to subjugate and control human beings. He thought about the atrocities of war and slavery; of the dehumanization of oppressed people by those with more physical, financial, or technological might; and of other perversions resulting from the gift the free will. It was hard to disagree with the assertion that someone or something was needed to protect mankind from itself.

12.5

Rionn Lorr dreamt the same dream he always dreamt. The circumstances, people and places often varied, but the theme never changed. From the time he became Head Mage and took on the responsibilities that came with such a lofty station, his dreams had been filled with worry, with the dire consequences facing the Kingdom that Bore His Name should he fail in his duties.

Hundreds of terrible scenarios played themselves out over the years. Disastrous results of poor decisions made in the past as well as the possible fallout from future mistakes swirled relentlessly in his mind. He saw thousands dying from plague and war, by fire and flood. He watched helplessly as mountains were brought low and oceans were scorched dry. Every death and every catastrophe was caused by his poor judgment. Sometimes he failed to act when action was necessary; sometimes he acted too soon. And at other times his actions were just plain wrong.

Tavin Lorr, his father, warned him that these dreams were the legacy of a true Head Mage of Lorr, one who cared about kingdom, continent, and the world beyond. The dreams were not premonitions of the type experienced by those with the gift of foresight. They were not a legacy in the sense of something passed down from generation to generation. The dreams were a product of human nature. It was only natural that when people thought about a particular subject all day, they were likely to think about it in their sleep. The things that worried them when they were awake would more likely than not re-visit them in their dreams.

His father told him to be more concerned if he ever *stopped* having the bad dreams, for the nightmares were a product of his worry and his worry was a result of how much he cared. To stop dreaming was to stop worrying. To stop worrying was to stop caring. If he ever occupied the position of Head Mage for any reason other than care and concern for the land and its people, then his nightmares would no longer be visions of what *might* happen. They would instead be portents of what was destined to happen.

But the warnings did nothing to prepare him for the torturous nighttime imaginings. When he was younger and still new to the position of Head Mage, the dreams kept him awake almost every night. The only thing that kept the dreams from sinking him into a madness of despair and hopelessness was his ever-present magic.

Once he was selected to be his father's successor as Head Mage, his father taught him how to use his magic to form ethereal tendrils of power that would provide a constant connection between him and the places he held dear. Rionn used those tendrils to bind himself to his home on the Island of Cartha and to Lorr Palace so that he would always feel the comfort and strength of home; and so he would always know whether or not those places were threatened, no matter how far he traveled. He also used those tendrils to weave a mesh of magic around the places he occupied to serve as an early-warning alarm system.

He could feel those tendrils of magic when he was asleep and awake, but he needed them the most while he slept. The warmth of their energy soothed him when his dreams threatened to engulf him. Their strength anchored him to reality and reassured him that he was only dreaming.

It took close to a decade before he was finally able to sleep through the night despite his ominous dreams. He would still toss and turn in his sleep and all too often wake up more tired than refreshed, but as time passed he found that he needed less and less of his magic to keep him anchored to the real world and his sanity. Eventually he grew to accept his legacy and recognize the grim dreams for what they really were: a manifestation of his love for his world and a source of motivation for him to keep it safe.

By the time he married Catherine he was sleeping soundly through his dreams and through the night, at least on the outside. With his magic to keep him buoyed in the ocean of worry that were his dreams, he taught himself to analyze the dreams even while he dreamt them.

The dreams helped him visualize possible consequences of his decisions. They helped him to winnow out bad ideas and narrow his choices down to those most likely to have a favorable outcome. He wondered if his father had developed the same ability. Rionn believed he had, and that Tavin Lorr had decided to let his son discover and develop the ability on his own. That was his father's way.

His wife never knew about his nightmares. If Rionn could help it, she never would. That was the only secret he kept from her. There was really no point in her knowing. There was nothing to be done about it and the knowledge would only worry her needlessly. But he would have to tell little Shanderah, he knew. When his daughter became a woman and neared the time when she would take his place as Head Mage, assuming that was her destiny, he would warn his daughter as his father had warned him. If the gods chose to bless her so, it would take her less time than it took him to master the magic used to remain grounded through the nightmares, to make them fade to a dull hum in the background of her consciousness so she could sleep soundly.

And then that dull hum suddenly went silent. Even though it had long since retreated to the deep corners of his perception, the abrupt silence struck him with the force of an explosion. The snapping of those tendrils of magic sent him hurtling out of his dreams and tumbling through a vacuum of nothingness. Rionn Lorr woke with a start, sitting up so quickly that his head spun. He could feel goose bumps rising on his skin. His heart hammered in his chest. Something was terribly wrong and he had no idea what it was.

Chapter 13: Interruptions

13.1

Raxe slept so soundly that he nearly missed the soft shift of air in the room. The stir was softer than a whisper, and had it not been for his years of training and experience, he would have never felt it. He rolled over onto his back just in time to see the moons' light reflect off of a silver blade slashing down at his neck.

Raxe rolled under the arc of a short sword and kicked his right foot out with all of his strength. The blow was struck with the intention of breaking ribs but the heel of his bare foot struck an abdomen so heavily muscled that he could not even feel the other's ribcage. It did drive the attacker back, but not before the tip of the blade he saw – as well as the knife he did not see in his attacker's other hand – slid across his right triceps and calf. The stabbing motions became slicing ones when the assassin was thrown backward by Raxe's kick.

Raxe continued his roll out of bed and to the floor. He tried to get a glimpse of his attacker but the room was too dark and the intruder was moving too fast. As the attacker regained his balance, Raxe snatched Demonsbane from the straps that cradled it beneath the elevated bed frame. He had just enough time to raise it horizontally over his head in a wide, two-handed grip to block the next quick attack. If it were not for the pale moons' light filtering into his room and bouncing off of the knife blades, he would never have seen it coming.

The metal axe handle cross-blocked the knife slashing down from his left while the wide axe blades shielded his face from the stabbing long knife on his right. The sharp tolling of metal striking metal helped to clear some of the cobwebs from Raxe's mind. He swung the blade at what he assumed was his attacker's midsection based on the angle of the incoming knives. The offworlder eagerly visualized the spurting blood, guts and shards of bone. The whistling axe blades, however, cut through empty air as the dark figure leapt away with amazing speed. Raxe barely had a chance to shoot to his feet before the attacker was on him again.

His drowsiness was finally gone, washed away by the adrenaline and endorphins rushing through his system. Now that he was more alert the moons' light began to reveal more details. Raxe lifted his battle-axe with his left hand to block a slash coming in high from his left. The other knife came in low from the right in narrow sideways sweep. Raxe's right hand caught a thick wrist but the thrust was so powerful that he could not stop the tip of the blade from digging into his right abdominal muscle.

He braced himself for the kick he saw coming for his left thigh, but the heavy blow still sent him stumbling back toward his bed. Raxe regained his balance quickly and threw himself low and to the left to avoid the lightning fast kick aimed at the right side of his head. The would-be assassin, who Raxe could tell was at least six feet six inches tall and incredibly broad across the shoulders, rushed him again.

Raxe was ready this time. He dropped into a tiger stance and waited for his attacker to reach him. His hands grew warm in anticipation of battle. The short sword arced in from the left. Raxe brought up Demonsbane in a close, two-handed grip so that the razor's edge of the crescent axe blade caught the edge of the sword. Demonsbane bit through the short sword all the way to the ridge, assisted by the momentum of the attacker's great strength.

Before the axe blade could slice all the way through the blade, the assassin twisted it in a way that halted Demonsbane's momentum. The big man yanked powerfully to the left, pulling Raxe off balance and toward both a rising knee and knife blade. Raxe's left hand released his battle-axe so that he could block the knee with his forearm and with his right, he pivoted Demonsbane's handle down to deflect the stabbing blade. But Raxe was not in a position to do anything about the other's foot sweeping in from the left and kicking his legs out from under him.

Falling back first, Raxe snapped his left foot up as high as he could and caught his attacker in the temple. The kick sent the stranger staggering back toward the open front door as

Raxe fell. But as the assassin fell back, he twisted the short-sword sharply enough to wrench Demonsbane free of Raxe's one-handed grip.

The breath was driven from Raxe's lungs when he hit the floor. He took a moment to gasp for air and was afraid the pause would mean his death, but he had forgotten about the inherent magical properties of his enchanted weapon. Its weight was massive when anyone not of his direct bloodline tried to lift it. And if anyone outside of his bloodline so much as laid a finger on the bare metal of the weapon, its magic would unleash a fatally explosive surge of energy. The agent outside of the Harvey's Chicago apartment learned that lesson the hard way.

The stranger's strength was obviously greater than Raxe's, but because of the magical nature of the battle-axe, Raxe knew Demonsbane would become unbearably heavy the moment it left his grip. Back in Chicago, when he had first wielded Demonsbane, it had taken two fully-grown, physically fit men to lift the enchanted weapon. Even then it had to be in a box or sack.

Raxe waited for the battle-axe to pull the assassin off balance when it dropped like a stone to the floor. But it did not drop. In fact, the massive intruder lifted both weapons – the short sword with the battle-axe still hooked to it – in only one hand without difficulty. The a narrow swath of moons' light fell across the top half of the assassin's face and glinted against cold, steel-gray eyes that regarded Raxe with something that resembled disappointment.

"*You* are the great Child Raxe?" he asked, the words dripping with contempt. Raxe noticed the deep voice was thick with an unfamiliar accent. "I have had greater challenges from our younglings in training."

Raxe flipped to his feet and could only stare in disbelief. The stranger hefted the battle-axe as if it weighed next to nothing. *How strong is this guy?*

The offworlder continued to watch as the assassin sheathed his knife somewhere behind his back and reached up to Demonsbane's handle. Raxe smiled in anticipation, knowing the fight was over.

The assassin's big, calloused fingers wrapped firmly around the enchanted blade's handle and pulled it free of the short sword. There was no explosion, no violent reaction at all to Demonsbane's magic. Raxe's heart skipped a beat. This stranger had done something to Raxe that had not happened since the early stages of his weapons training under his mother and grandfather. He had taken Raxe's weapon away.

And then the assassin charged, wielding the short sword in one hand and Demonsbane in the other. Raxe shook away his astonishment and confusion to focus on staying alive.

Raxe ducked, backpedaled and labored to stay outside the range of the cutting edges and powerful kicks. Raxe was amazed at how quick and limber this man was for his size. The precise attacks were clearly some sort of martial art. His fighting style was reminiscent of Muay Thai and Capoeira, Raxe noted, as the assassin attacked with quick, sweeping blows of his knees and elbows – as well as his weapons and feet – at various unconventional angles that were increasingly difficult to dodge.

The assassin swung Demonsbane low. Raxe avoided the curved deadly edge of his own weapon by jumping quickly, pulling his legs up and then flattening his body as he fell. Before he hit the floor he scissor-kicked his legs and locked them on the shin and ankle of his opponent's forward leg. The assassin's footing was solid though, so while the tripping attack made him stumble he did not fall. But the maneuver did manage to give Raxe enough time to spring back to his feet and regroup.

He used the brief respite to get a good look at his adversary. The assassin wore a long cloak that was pulled back behind his shoulders and tucked into the broad sash tied tightly around his slim waist. Multiple knives of varying sizes were tucked securely into the sash. A long scarf was tied around his head in a way that concealed every part of his face with the exception of his eyes. The sleeveless tunic and long breeches he wore were loose fitting, but Raxe could still see the impression of a huge chest and muscular thighs. He wore soft-soled, knee-high boots made of animal hide.

The man's bare arms, long and muscular but not bulky, looked like they were carved from stone. In the dim light Raxe could not tell what color his clothes were, but they blended in very well with the shadows. This was an experienced assassin.

Raxe dropped into a right lead ready stance and gave a wry smile. He had been longing for a good hand-to-hand fight for years. This, however, was a bit more than he wanted. *Be careful what you wish for*, he chuckled to himself. The stranger saw the smile and thought he was being mocked. His cool eyes suddenly blazed as he advanced.

The attacker only took two steps before he faltered, stumbled forward and fell on his face. An arrow protruded from his back, right through his heart.

Rell Kallen stood in the darkened doorway and was lowering his bow. He was in full gear. A long hooded cloak was pulled back to reveal an unadorned brigandine vest – which Raxe thought of as a medieval flak jacket – over a woolen tunic. He wore loose fitting leather trousers and shin-high hiking boots. His longsword hung ready in the baldric strapped to his back and his quiver, full of arrows, was strapped securely to his thigh. Had he slept in his full gear...or had he been sleeping at all?

Raxe scowled. He had been trained to always keep one man breathing for interrogation. "If we had taken him alive," he chided, "We could've found out who sent him."

And then he felt the stinging realization that during the fight, that part of his training had been completely forgotten or ignored. And so had his oath not to kill. He had tried to kill this man as surely as Rell Kallen had. The Ranger Elf just happened to be successful.

Rell Kallen was shrugging. "No need to worry. This one did not come alone."

Raxe inhaled sharply. "Joel!"

13.2

Raxe scooped up Demonsbane and brushed past the Ranger Elf as he rushed across the hallway. The corridor was lit with small candle lamps spaced ten feet apart lining both walls. Glancing to his right, he could see the open door to Rell's room and a large, lean but muscular man dressed in the same way as his own would-be assassin. The man was lying dead in the threshold with a stab wound in his chest. Raxe spared a moment to consider how formidable the elf must be to dispatch the warrior on his own and so quietly, especially if the dead man was as tough as the man Raxe fought.

The other things he noticed were the several still bodies strewn about the hall. These men were dressed in the light armor of the Royal Guard. The Royal Guard was almost as formidable as the King's personal warriors, the Home Guard. Raxe could not believe so many had been killed just outside of his door without rousing him. It was a testament to how terribly talented these assassins really were.

Raxe kicked in Joel's door and found Joel in his bed, but Joel was not sleeping. He was tied securely to his bed and struggling without success against ropes that secured him to the mattress. A gag consisting of a wad of course cloth was stuffed in his mouth and held there with a twisted kerchief that was tied in a tight knot at the base of his skull. Raxe went to cut Joel lose but paused when he heard a loud crash from the adjacent room. Rionn Lorr's room. Raxe continued on to Joel while Rell Kallen ran to the window and threw open the wooden shutters.

Demonsbane cut quickly through the rope and then Raxe joined the elf at the window. Joel was right behind him, working at the difficult knot of his gag. He could hear the sounds of fighting before he got to the window, and when he did, he saw Ethan, Quick, and Rionn Lorr battling two incredibly tall, chiseled men dressed in the same fashion as the two dead assassins inside the inn. One of them used a broadsword and the other a large spiked iron mace.

Rionn battled valiantly with his twisted staff. The way he blocked arcing swings and deflected thrusts demonstrated that he had some weapons training. Raxe was impressed and somewhat surprised. He had always thought of Rionn Lorr as a powerful wizard and a scholar, not a trained fighter.

Ethan expertly wielded his broadsword, his skill approaching his late father's even at such a young age. Raxe thought Ethan might have even been a little quicker than Meldrick. Quick used his long sword like he was born to it. He parried, dodged and attacked like a seasoned warrior. Raxe was amazed that the gangly, almost clumsy adolescent he remembered from his first visit had become so accomplished in just a few years. But as impressive as the three men were, the ultra-athletic, incredibly strong, and highly skilled warriors relentlessly pressed the attack.

"Why aren't they using their magic?" Raxe asked the Ranger Elf. "Rionn and Quick can end this in seconds." And then he remembered how the magic of Demonsbane failed to harm his would-be assassin.

It was clear that neither Rionn, Ethan or Quick were a match for the men on their own, but Rionn Lorr went from one duel to the other, giving just enough support to keep the young warriors from falling. Raxe and Rell both knew the battle could not last very much longer. The wizard, soldier and changeling were being overwhelmed.

"I know not why they ignore their magic," Rell said as he raised his bow and cocked an arrow. "But I'll end it now."

The bowstring thrummed when it was released, sending the arrow zipping toward the taller of the two assailants. The Ranger Elf's eyes grew wide when his target swung his iron mace with amazing quickness and batted the arrow right out of the air.

The distraction of the arrow was just enough for Ethan to get past the mace wielder's guard. His long sword nicked the assassin's left shoulder as the taller man pivoted away from the blade. When the towering man stepped back, Rionn Lorr hooked his staff behind his knees to trip him before returning his attention to the shorter, broadsword-wielding assassin that was busy pushing back Quick with blow after heavy blow.

As the taller one stumbled backward, Ethan feinted to draw the man's guard. Already fighting to keep his balance, the assassin was fooled by the feint and brought his mace to the left to block, leaving his right side open. Ethan thrust his broadsword between the assassin's ribs before he could regain his balance or finish bringing his mace around to defend himself.

The broadsword assassin saw his companion go down. He also saw the offworlder Raxe and the Ranger Elf jump through the window to charge into the fray, leaping over the corpses of the fallen men of the Royal Guard who had been standing watch outside of the inn. Five against one were odds too great even for a warrior of his caste, especially when two of the five had been able to get past his brothers-in-arms. He wasted no time in turning and sprinting away.

The others gave chase but the muscular, long legged assassin easily distanced himself from Quick, Rionn, and Ethan. Rell Kallen, however, pulled away from Raxe, ran right past the other three and gained on his quarry.

"I'll take this one alive," he promised the others as he darted past.

Raxe watched in disbelief as the Ranger Elf closed the distance between himself and the fleet-footed assassin with amazing speed. Within a matter of seconds only a few yards separated them. The larger man stopped abruptly and turned, whipping his broadsword around to decapitate his pursuer.

Without slowing, Rell Kallen brought his long sword up not to block, but to attack the oncoming blade. The broadsword was much heavier than the elf's long sword, but the elf's weapon was obviously made of a denser metal than any Raxe had ever seen other than Demonsbane. And the elf was clearly even stronger than he was fast. His long sword batted the bigger sword away with enough force to send the huge assassin spinning.

Rell followed the sword strike with a powerful jabbing heel kick that, coupled with his forward momentum, sent the assassin flying nearly ten yards. The assassin hit the ground rolling with enough force to kick up a plume of dust. In the dim firelight of the street lamps, Raxe barely noticed four small throwing daggers shoot out from the dust cloud.

The Ranger Elf saw them clearly enough. He leapt in the air and turned his body parallel to the ground. His long sword flashed once again, deflecting two of the daggers while the other two sailed harmlessly above and below his horizontally oriented body. Rell Kallen performed a pirouette as he fell and broke his fall by catching himself with his free hand. By the time he popped back up, the assassin was already up and running. The elf took off in pursuit once again.

And then a massive six-legged horned lizard, so large that its thick shoulders were five feet high, sprung from between buildings and ran alongside the assassin. The lizard was nearly ten feet long. Sinewy muscles flexed beneath dark green scales that reflected the yellow-orange glow of the blazing street lamps. The creature was sleek, its underbelly was low to the ground and its mid and hind legs were long and articulated similar to grasshopper legs. The fore legs, however, were much broader and more heavily muscled.

The most amazing thing about this fearsome creature was the fact that a weathered hide saddle was strapped around its midsection. The assassin jumped onto the lizard's back and snatched up a set of reins. With a powerful leap, the creature sailed away from the swift elf as if he were standing still. Rell Kallen stopped and raised his bow, but before he could even knock an arrow the lizard steed turned abruptly to the right and disappeared behind a one-story building.

The arm holding the bow shook with his frustration as Rell Kallen lowered it. He thrust the arrow back into the quiver strapped to his thigh and turned to the other four as they approached him.

"Where is Joel?" Rionn Lorr asked breathlessly.

They all turned to the inn to see Joel stepping out of the front entrance almost seventy yards away. He was still working on the knotted kerchief tied around his face. The five of them began walking back to the inn.

"Who was the welcoming committee?" Raxe asked.

"S'Zan Rho," Rionn Lorr answered. "They are a warrior nation from the southwestern shores of the Westin continent, just outside of the Kingdom of S'Zan. The men we saw here are about the average size of their kind. The women are nearly the same height. Every man and woman in the S'Zan Rho nation learns to fight from childhood."

"These were not just S'Zan Rho," Rell Kallen added. "They're *Ken d'Zanir,* which in your language means Blade of the Divine. The *Ken* are elite assassins of the S'Zan Rho."

"They ride land dragons?" Ethan asked. "I've never seen such a thing."

"That's what that monster's called?" Raxe asked. "Do they spit flames or something?"

"Almost," Quick confirmed. "They spray a corrosive, paralyzing liquid from their mouths that they use to subdue their prey."

"As big and fast as they are," Raxe observed, "Acid-spit seems like overkill."

"It's also for its defense," Rell added. "They come from the fringes of the Known Lands, where there are creatures that hunt even them."

"Damn," Raxe swore before turning to the Head Mage. "It would've been a little easier if you and Quick had used your magic, don't you think?"

Rionn Lorr sneered. "Yes, if it had been available to us."

Raxe stopped in mid-stride and turned to the Head Mage with a raised eyebrow. "What happened to *your* magic?"

"I wish I knew," Lorr said, his voice edged with frustration. "I would not have even known it was gone if I had not noticed the sudden dissipation of my sentry spell."

"Sentry spell?" Raxe asked.

"Yes," Rionn said. "It's a web of magic that I cast around and within the hotel. I occupy the center of the web, and similar to a spider's web, I can feel the vibrations of anything that contacts or passes through it."

He purposely neglected to mention how far the web of magic really reached. As Head Mage, there was some information he had to keep secret, lest his enemies use it against him.

"I'm always aware of it, on both a conscious and subconscious level," he continued. "So when the web vanished I awoke. I got up to check on Quick and Ethan next door and they were already outside fighting."

"If Ethan and I had not been up talking," Quick chimed in, "they would have taken us in our sleep. We went out of the open window to give ourselves more room to maneuver. When I tried to transform, though, nothing happened. Even now I cannot change forms. What sort of trickery is this?"

"The magic that keeps Demonsbane from being handled by others failed, too," Raxe shared. He turned to the Head Mage. "Rionn, you've never seen this before?"

"No," the Head Mage admitted.

The men were interrupted by the sound of Joel's voice. He had finally freed himself of the gag.

"Who the hell were those guys?" he called from down the street. "And why'd you let two of them get away?"

"Two?" Ethan asked. "Only one escaped, the one who just fled on the land dragon."

Joel shook his head. "No, there was another guy on the roof back there." He pointed to an empty rooftop. "He's not up there now, but he was when I first came outside."

Quick stopped abruptly and threw up his hand to halt the other four men.

"Rell Kallen," the changeling began, "what do you sense?"

Raxe knew he asked Rell this question because the elf would be the only individual in the group with heightened senses approaching the changeling's. The Ranger Elf's nose wrinkled as he sniffed the air. His pointed ears twitched as he strained them.

"Nothing out the ordinary," the elf answered. The wind shifted, and the elf's arching eyebrows rose and he sniffed once more. "The dead assassins' steeds," he realized.

"They stalk us from the shadows," Quick revealed. "When the beasts are born, their riders form a bond with them that domesticates the land dragons. But when their riders die that bond is severed and the beasts revert to their natural instincts. They hunt."

"By the gods," Rionn Lorr swore as he stared worriedly in Joel's direction.

The other four men looked and their eyes widened.

Even from a distance of over thirty yards, Joel could see their expressions in the streetlight. He slowed to a stop.

"What?"

The hair on the back of his neck stood on end when he realized that they were not staring at him, but past him. He turned around slowly, and less than fifteen yards away were the two most horrific creatures he had ever seen.

13.3

The first thing Joel thought of when he looked at the hissing reptiles was that they were giant six-legged chameleons. However, these monsters' eyes were not bulbous protrusions, but hooded slits similar to a desert horned lizard. Their snouts were proportionately longer. A small cluster of horns sprouted from high on the creatures' flat brows. One foot-long, blunt-tipped horn stood out among the other ones. The smaller horns were of varying lengths but none longer than half the length of the dominant horn. The land dragons' short, razor-sharp teeth were bared, a dense and chaotic pattern of yellowish knife tips thrusting out of black gums. Those teeth were made for shredding, and from the ravenous look in their eyes, they preferred live prey.

The lizards were poised to strike. Their scaled bellies touched the ground as they crouched. Sharp knees on disproportionately long hind legs pointed high in the air. Taut muscles rippled so violently that the creatures seemed to be shivering from excitement.

Joel was shivering as well, but from the icy clutch of fear. He could feel his heart beating in his throat.

Without their magic, there was nothing Rionn or Quick could do. The offworlder was too far away to protect Joel. Joel was unarmed and unskilled in combat, and even if he were a seasoned fighter he would be no match for one land dragon, let alone three.

Raxe started to sprint to Joel's aid but he stopped short when another land dragon bounded from the shadows halfway between Joel and the others. The land dragon immediately turned towards Raxe and assumed the same threatening posture as his mates.

"And there is the third steed," Rell observed needlessly. His hand slowly reached into his quiver and clutched two arrows between his fingers.

"So what do we do now?" Raxe asked, straining to speak in a calm voice so as not to startle the lizards. He turned to Quick. "Well? Is there any way out of this? If we stay real still, think they'll leave us alone?"

Quick shook his head. "No." He slowly reached for and gripped the hilt of his sheathed sword. "They will attack."

"And our magic still eludes us," Rionn Lorr added.

The giant trembling lizards began to hiss louder. Their shuddering torsos expanded as if they were being inflated with air. Joel grew even more terrified and awed as the lizards puffed out to nearly twice their original bulk. Raxe held Demonsbane in a white-knuckled grip and wondered how he would get past the land dragon in front of him to get to Joel before it was too late.

"What are they doing?" he whispered to Quick.

"They prepare to spit," was the changeling's answer.

Raxe wondered why none of them looked particularly worried about getting sprayed with acidic saliva. He turned to the elf and looked at the bow in his hand. "You gonna use that or what?"

"He'll miss," Quick explained. "The land dragon is set and alert. He would see the arrow coming and evade it. They are incredibly fast. He has to wait until it's airborne."

Just when it seemed the hissing, expanding reptiles were going to burst, they exhaled sharply and sent blasts of fine mist into the air in front of them. Both Raxe and Joel threw themselves to the ground as the mist dissipated into thin clouds of steam only a few feet in front the land dragons' snouts before dissolving completely and disappearing.

Raxe looked up at the others with relieved confusion. They all remained standing and were not in the least bit moved by the attempted spray.

"The S'Zan Rho remove the land dragons' acid sacs when they are young," Quick responded to the unasked question. "But your relief is ill founded."

Raxe turned back to the lizard just in time to see it pounce. He heard and felt two arrows zip over his head as he threw himself to the side. The land dragon soared past him and crashed heavily into the ground with an explosion of dust. Its back rose and fell with shallow breathing but it was otherwise still. Raxe stood up to see an arrow embedded deeply into each of its eyes.

"You're welcome," the Ranger Elf said, lowering his bow, "For this and the assassin in your bedroom. Repay me by retrieving my arrows when the beast stops breathing."

Joel heard the commotion but was afraid to look away from the two monsters before him. His head pounded severely, echoing in time to his thunderous heartbeat. He instinctively knew the weird blast of mist was only the beginning, and his fearful suspicions were confirmed when his red-rimmed vision locked in on the creatures as they leapt at him.

"Joel!" Raxe roared and sprinted in Joel's direction.

Raxe felt as if he was moving in slow motion when he saw the other offworlder completely engulfed within the bulk of the land dragons' long, lean bodies. The creatures went into a frenzy. Their snapping maws, jerking torsos, and slashing claws stirred up a dust cloud around them so heavy that they disappeared within it. The others heard the land dragons hiss and shriek as blood sprayed out of the dust cloud in every direction.

Raxe raised Demonsbane as he approached the melee, but by the time he reached them the land dragons had gone still. He slowed as the dust settled upon the giant lizards. They laid flat on their stomachs side by side, facing in opposite directions, eyes staring blankly. Raxe took another cautious step forward and then jumped back as an explosion of blood, bone, and chunks of scaly hide erupted from where the lizards lay. Joel emerged screaming from the spray of gore and ran past Raxe as if he did not see him standing there.

Joel was soaked in crimson slime that flew out to the sides as he flailed his arms madly, wielding what looked like knives in both of his hands. He ran about twenty feet before he stumbled and fell to his knees. Except for his panting and wheezing, he went completely silent.

As Raxe walked toward him he could see that Joel was struggling for breath. He reached into his pocket – with normal human hands – and pulled out his inhaler. The small device was not only covered with blood, it was crushed. Joel dropped the ruined device into a puddle of blood, his eyes bulging with fear and his wheezing growing louder.

"Rionn!" Raxe called to the Head Mage. "He can't breathe!"

Rionn Lorr sprinted back to the inn. "The medicine is in my cloak!" he yelled as he ran.

Joel looked at his bloody hands and arms. He looked down at the growing puddle of blood beneath him being fed by the dripping mess that covered him from head to toe.

"What…did I…do?" he gasped between wheezes.

"Save your breath, man," Raxe advised.

Joel turned to look back at the bloody corpses of the land dragons and looked back at his hands. They were normal now, except for the thick, red wetness that coated them. He looked up and around at people coming out onto the streets. Shopkeepers living above their stores and innkeepers and other guests of the two inns on the block filtered out of the buildings. Lights began to blink on in windows.

And then the whispering started. They all had no doubt been watching the entire spectacle from darkened windows and now they marveled openly at the bloody carnage on the street.

"You killed them," Rell Kallen said as he and the others approached. His tone betrayed that he was fairly impressed. "Why so glum?"

"And what happened to the knives you wielded?" Ethan asked. "Those must be formidable weapons indeed."

Joel cocked his head at the question as if he did not understand and took another labored breath. Confusion mixed with the fear and discomfort that darkened his countenance. "Knives?" he asked.

"Those weren't knives," Raxe said.

Rionn Lorr returned with an open pouch. He took a pinch of dried herbs out and held them to Joel's lips. The doubt in Joel's eyes was clear but his ever-shortening breath was more than enough encouragement for him to give it a try. He opened his mouth and accepted the bitter herbs.

"Don't swallow the leaves right away," Rionn instructed. "Chew it and swallow the juices until the bitterness fades."

Joel did as he was told. A few seconds later the wheezing started to audibly subside.

"How did you manage that feat?" Rionn Lorr asked Joel, marveling at the land dragon corpses. "Our magic has been cut off from us somehow. Yours seems to be unaffected."

"How did I *manage* it?" Joel asked bitterly. "Hell, I can't even *remember* it."

"Why do you seem so upset after such an incredible feat?" Ethan asked. "Is it the lung sickness?"

"This is all new to him," Raxe explained. "He doesn't quite know what to make of it."

"Sounds familiar," Quick said, giving Raxe a knowing look.

"I can speak for myself," Joel snapped when he finally regained his breath. "I'm upset because this is all bullshit."

He stood up and looked at the mess on and around him. "This is a nightmare. I shouldn't even be here. I should be in Chicago with my wife." He stormed off, striding back to the inn. He pulled off his bloody shirt and dropped it to the ground as he passed men pulling the bodies of the dead *Ken* out of the inn. The men stared at him curiously while he stomped up the stairs and through the entrance.

"A bit pouty, that one," Rell observed. He turned to Rionn Lorr, who was staring intensely at the rooftops. "No magic, eh?" The Ranger Elf reached up and behind his back to grasp the grip of the longsword in his baldric. "You did a passable job of fighting with that staff of yours, but without your magic you'd be no match for me. I could kill you right now and you'd be powerless to stop me."

Rionn Lorr did not even look toward the elf. He continued to spy the rooftops and responded without passion or concern. "You could try."

Raxe, Ethan and Quick all tensed. Rell Kallen seriously considered striking, but the mage would still be useful if he ever got his magic back. Besides, he was not in the mood to fight all four of them, especially the offworlder with the battle-axe that was indestructible and could cut through anything. Those were natural properties, not magical ones.

"Another time," Rell said with a smug smirk.

Rionn turned an icy blue stare in the elf's direction. "This might be your best opportunity."

"Fellas," Raxe interjected. "I don't know what you two got going on over there, but we've got more pressing things to worry about."

"No doubt," Rionn replied, turning his gaze to Quick. "Joel said there was another. Can you detect his scent?"

"Not from here," Quick admitted. "But if I can just…"

His body wavered and he morphed into an owl. He looked up and gave an excited "hoot" before flapping his broad wings and shooting off into the darkness.

Raxe looked curiously at the Ranger Elf and the Head Mage. Rionn Lorr had goaded Rell, all but daring him to attack, something that was completely out of character for the usually humble and composed man. It occurred to Raxe that Rionn knew his magic had just returned. He wanted an excuse for engaging Rell in battle. Their short, sharp exchange revealed something between them, something more than philosophical differences and mutual distrust.

"Ok," Raxe began, deciding to think upon their animosity another time. "Am I the only one scared to damn death here? If the demon knows how to squelch our magic, what chance do we stand against it?"

"We stand a very good chance," Rionn Lorr answered. "If it was just a matter of taking our powers away the demon would come to kill us itself. That makes me believe that whatever took our magic did so indiscriminately. It likely covered an area, like a net, wide enough to extinguish all magic within its range. A demon is a creature entirely of malevolent magical energies. A complete absence of magic would likely be harmful, if not fatal, to a demon."

"But it would not hesitate to allow others to use such a weapon to destroy its enemies," Rell Kallen offered.

"I must speak to the innkeeper," Rionn Lorr said. "Recompenses must be made for the damages to the inn."

Raxe scanned the rooftops while Rell Kallen made his way to the fallen assassins. The three bodies had been laid side by side and Rell Kallen began to search them. Raxe frowned at the sight of the elf taking and pocketing the *Kens'* knives and ceremonial jewelry.

The sound of flapping wings took his attention away from the elf and to the owl that was landing next to him. Within moments, the human form of Quick was standing before him.

"The one from the rooftops also fled on a land dragon," Quick informed. "I have no doubt that we could track them, but it would take time –"

"Time that we do not have," the Ranger Elf interjected. "Our sky sleigh leaves at first light. And in any case, I know where the assassins are going."

"Where?" Ethan asked.

"To join with the rest of their detachment," Rell explained. "When the *Ken d'Zanir* are contracted, they travel in detachments two-hundred strong. They set up camp miles away from their targets' location. A group of four is sent in to carry out the assassinations."

"Why do they travel in such large groups?" Ethan questioned.

"In case the first four fail," Rell told him. "They can send more. They will send as many as necessary until they complete their mission or until none of them are left."

Raxe imagined facing one hundred and ninety-seven warriors with the size, speed, and skill of these three and had to stifle a shudder. He was starting to miss is guns. "I guess we don't want to follow them."

"But they'll send more," Ethan realized aloud. "Will we be safe until first light?"

"Yes," Rionn Lorr answered as he rejoined the others. "The larger detachment usually camps close to a day's ride away from large cities like Port Lorrian. In case they are discovered, they want enough distance between themselves and any possible attacking force to either flee successfully or prepare their defense. I'll send for a force large enough to make them flee."

"Whoever sent them after us obviously knows why we're here," Raxe added. "Which means they also know our plans. Those ones that escaped will expect us to be gone by the time they reach their camp. I doubt they'll be sending anyone back to the inn."

"He's right," Rionn Lorr agreed. "But I'll send a force after them anyway. I want those assassins driven out of the kingdom. And we are leaving tonight. Who knows what else the demon may send against us? Anyone who can still sleep after all of this can sleep on the sky sleigh."

13.4

Moments after the Head Mage announced the change of schedule, Raxe began to worry about how he would contact Sabrina to let her know.

As he made his way back to his room, he considered asking Rionn if he could use his magic to contact the Mistress of the Sea of Spirits. And then he remembered that he had an ability of his own to call upon. He was not sure if it was a trace of Shanderah reminding him or if it was a burgeoning awareness of his newfound sensitivity to magic, but his grandfather's words came back to him clearly.

> *"I can read your mind. I could read your mother's too. And your mother could read yours...*
>
> *"Parents can read the kid's mind, but not vice-versa...the parent can also project thoughts into their kid's mind. And that's not the half of it..."*

Raxe reached his room and, thankfully, the blood had been cleaned up. He locked his door, not wanting to be distracted by anyone, and then sat on the bed. He regulated his breathing, taking deep, slow breaths. Within moments he could detect with crystal clarity the auras of his daughter, Rionn Lorr and Rionn's Child Shandie. He even thought he felt a faint pulse of a fourth, unfamiliar presence.

Raxe reasoned it had to be his grandfather. He had never felt his grandfather's aura from across the WorldGate before, but apparently his heightened awareness was allowing it to happen. The WorldGate had to have been distorting it so that it was not recognizable.

He focused on his daughter's aura. It was easy to do because her presence was so dominant in his consciousness. Not knowing exactly what to do next, he wondered how his grandfather projected thoughts to him and how Dan and old Shanderah were able to project and receive to and from one another across the WorldGate. No answers came to him. Nothing came to him from the old sorceress's memories.

None of his conversations with his grandfather ever touched upon the mechanics of their shared telepathy.

Instead of looking for explanations that would not come, Raxe decided to do what he could. He focused again on Azhju'lestra's essence and used it as a canvas to reconstruct her image from his memory.

Once again Raxe was watching her standing beside her seductive mother on the shores of Lake Onyx. He zoomed in on his daughter's beautiful little face until it was framed with the moonlight and the gray, glassy surface of the great lake behind her.

Azhju'lestra

He said the word aloud as he thought it. The resulting sound reminded of him of speaking into a microphone while standing right next to the speakers that were projecting his voice, but without the feedback. That had never happened when he spoke aloud while communicating telepathically with his grandfather.

The moment after the echo of his voice faded, the image of his daughter's face responded. Her thin eyebrows rose slightly in mild surprise as if recognition brightened her features. Unlike earlier that evening, when the moons' illumination was behind her, the soft light bathed her face with a pale silvery glow. The girl's eyes were a very light shade of brown shot through randomly with a series of dark and pale streaks of brown. The moons' light glittered in the streaks to add indescribable hues that formed a prism effect. For lack of a better comparison, her eyes reminded Raxe of frozen cola, an intriguing and beautiful mix of colors. The background that framed her face dissolved and was whisked away on a gust of wind and replaced by a sight from a more recent memory.

Raxe zoomed out, pulling back his focus to take in more of Azhju'lestra's surroundings, and saw that Sabrina was no longer beside her. The sky sleigh field was now behind her. It was not, however, the bright daylight scene from yesterday morning. It was nighttime. Giant sleigh birds lounged quietly in the field. The three moons shined down upon the field in the exact same position they were in when he was outside just moments earlier.

Worry not, Raxe, his daughter's soft voice drifted to him. *I am already here. Mother said you would leave early after tonight's attack and she sent me here to await you.*

Cool, Raxe thought. This time, though, he did not speak aloud and noticed that his psychic voice sounded like his normal speaking voice. It felt a little strange to be the one initiating such communication but it felt natural.

A question about how Sabrina found out about their attack so soon flitted through his mind, followed quickly by the memory that she was faerie. She was the Mistress of the Sea of Spirits. She most certainly knew lots of things.

See you in a few minutes, Raxe thought to his daughter.

His daughter.

The very idea of it freaked him out.

13.5

The lower of the two suns had barely risen clear of the eastern horizon when a contemplative Master Mage Delthar rode several horses back from the leading edge of the company of royal cavalry. He started at the sudden feel of a warm and soft vibration against his third rib and then quickly gathered himself, realizing what it was and surprised that it had startled him at all.

Until that moment he had not realized how distracted he was by his thoughts of the terrible occurrences at the Warriors' Rest and Fort Bastion: The graves, dug up from the inside; Captain Johnican transforming into a murderous caricature of a human being.

Delthar reached deep into his cloak and wrapped his long, bony fingers around one of the small, rough, dull stones suspended from a thin loop of braided leather tied around his neck. The placement of this stone amid the others let him know it was the blue one, the one attuned to the Head Mage. The rhythm of the seeing stone's vibration conveyed that this was a conference among several members of the Conjurer's Alliance. The warmth it gave off spoke to the importance of the conference.

"General Ramos," Delthar called to the warrior riding near the lead of the company. When the High General turned Delthar continued. "I have an urgent communication from the Head Mage. Ride ahead, I'll rejoin you when I can."

Ramos nodded in acknowledgement as Delthar slowed his horse's pace and led it to the side of the trail. If it had been a one-on-one personal communication Delthar would have continued to ride. Conferences through seeing stones, however, could be disorienting while riding. The use of seeing stones required a moderately complex spell for a one-on-one communication. Conferences were even more complex because the users had to divide their consciousness among several mental images and voices. This sometimes resulted in vertigo, headaches or nausea for experienced conjurers even when they were perfectly still. The discomfort was twice as bad if one was in motion during a conference.

Delthar reined his horse to a halt, dismounted, spread his robes and sat on the damp grass. He pressed the speaking stone against his forehead while mentally reciting the necessary spell. After adding a small pulse of his own magic, the stone cooled and in his mind's eye the images of three familiar faces materialized. From his right to his left he saw Master Mage and Head Alchemist Lauren Nyla, Echelon One Mage Jonathan Markus, and finally, the Head Mage Rionn Lorr. Delthar could not see their surroundings, only ghostlike images of their faces against a background of gray space.

"Lady Nyla," Rionn Lorr began, not bothering with formalities. Their crisis did not allow time for such trivialities. "What news do you have?"

"Good news," Nyla reported. "Our scientists have used the information you gave them to develop a functional equivalent of what the offworlder called a microscope. They've employed the most noted craftsmen and spectacle makers in the capital city to assist them. I employed conjurers who are particularly gifted in the manipulation of solid matter to work with our best alchemists to develop light stones that burn bright and cold enough for our purposes. They have already constructed a working model. They are now experimenting with different levels of light and lens curvatures to increase magnification and clarity. We hope that in another two days or so we will be able to examine the samples provided to us by Master Mage Delthar."

"Good news, indeed," Rionn praised. "I have seen the expedition safely away, so I can and will be there before midday tomorrow to assist in any way I can."

Delthar watched his mental image of the Head Mage turn its attention to the Echelon One mage. "And you, Mage Markus?"

"We have confirmed that the infected, shortly after their initial transformation, as well as the reanimated corpses, will not attack unless provoked. They will trudge peacefully – almost blindly – past citizens as long as they are not disturbed. But as Master Mage Delthar can confirm, they are murderously violent with or without provocation in the brief moments just after their transformation."

"Indeed," Delthar agreed.

"As a result," Jonathan continued, "we've cleared a path for them all the way to Ridgeland. All of the settlements, from small villages to larger cities to the rural counties, have been instructed to let the walkers pass without interference. There were some dicey moments in the beginning but there have not been any incidents for a day or so. Colonel Strong has requested reinforcements and we await word from General Kinney."

Delthar chimed in. "That request has been granted by the *High* General. Inform the colonel that a full regiment is in route to Ridgeland. General Ramos and I are less than a day behind you and the battalion. We will probably join you before you reach Ridgeland."

"Master Mage Delthar," Rionn Lorr said, turning his full attention to his friend and mentor. "Are you certain you would not be of more use to our cause here with me at the castle? Minister Geoffrey asks the same of General Ramos. Your wisdom and knowledge would aid us greatly in finding a cure to this infection. Ramos's strategic cunning might be put to better use in our war room than in the field."

"You assume a cure even exists," Delthar returned. "But no, Rionn, I believe my assistance is more critical in Ridgeland. If and when we have to do battle with the infected, the soldiers and the Echelon mages will need all of the help they can get. And unless Minister Geoffrey sends Ramos a direct order to return, the bull-headed general would see this enemy with his own eyes in order to best formulate a strategy to stop them. I know you both fear for our safety at our advanced ages, and your concern is appreciated. But believe me, we are both far more formidable than our years would indicate."

"It was not my intention to imply – "

"I know, Rionn," Delthar assured. "You've just witnessed my best attempt at wit. I sometimes forget how difficult it is to convey humor across these seeing stones."

"Just be careful, Master Delthar," Rionn implored. "And you as well, Jonathan. I have full confidence that you will hold our enemies at bay until we find an acceptable solution."

When the communication ended, Master Mage Delthar pursed his lips beneath his thick white mustache. He wished he shared his old student's confidence.

13.6

Shara Dune's frustration was starting to get the best of her as she made her way through the long halls of the baron's stronghold. Anger quickened her pace so much that even the long-legged sand creatures serving as her personal guard had to hasten to keep up with her. The three creatures took care not to accidentally step on the hem of the flowing gown that trailed in their queen's wake, knowing full well that her wrath would be severe if they did so.

The baron's soldiers, six men serving as Queen Shara Dune's would-be escorts, trailed even further behind. They were not willing to get any closer to the massive sand creatures than they absolutely had to. Each of the four long tentacles protruding from the monsters, from both shoulders and just below their ribcage on either side, swung back and forth much like human arms while they walked, and each tentacle carried its own deadly weapon. None of the soldiers wanted to get "accidentally" nicked by one of those weapons.

"Queen Shara Dune," one of the escorts called. "I really don't think it's a good idea to go to the baron's personal chambers unannounced."

"I heard you the first time you voiced that opinion," the Desert Queen reminded. "If I hear your voice again, I'll have one of my charges rip your tongue from your mouth."

Shara Dune wanted to be gone from this place. She had grown tired of playing errand girl for Mage Stratham Glund. He bade her to stay for a little while longer after she had secured Baron Tauran's continued assistance, hinting that she might be needed for one more task. Shara grudgingly agreed, even though she hated the county of Eastedge even more than the Kingdom of Cartha.

Eastedge was a hole. Literally. It was a county built in a deep valley in the southwestern foothills of Hell's Mountains that was, according to the histories, the desiccated remains of a once great mountain spring that fed a winding river that snaked through the Hells. After Heaven's War, all that was left was a dusty, hardscrabble, irregularly shaped earthen bowl with walls that sloped slowly but steadily over the course of several miles.

As much as she loathed agreeing to this task, she saw an opportunity. Mage Glund and whomever he worked for had no confidence that Tauran would follow orders without someone right there to prod him. So Shara agreed to persuade the crooked baron, making certain that Glund understood that her price would be double for the next task, whatever that might be, and would increase with each addendum to their original agreement.

As they wished, she would tend to Baron Tauran. And she would do it in a way that would convince him to do as he was told whether she was there to oversee him or not.

They rounded the corner and started down a long corridor with no doors other than the one at the far end of the hall. Six men stood outside the door. Presumably they were guards but they did not look like guards to Shara Dune. They were armed but they were just milling about, talking and laughing instead of guarding the safety of their baron. They looked like thugs loitering outside of a tavern or whorehouse.

The men snapped to moderate attention when they noticed the stunning redhead and her monstrous entourage striding purposefully down the hall. They looked worried at first, but when they saw only three sand creatures and then the half dozen of the baron's men trailing them, their advantage in numbers turned their concern into smugness. One of them, a man with ruddy skin, coarse short hair, of medium height and muscular build, stepped forward. His dark and beady eyes and slightly upturned nose reminded the Desert Queen of an evil pig. The expensive shoes, the neatly pressed shirt under a polished leather jerkin and the ankle-length breeches he wore stood out in stark contrast to the ragged stubble on his jaw and chin.

A pig in nobleman's clothing, Shara thought dryly.

"I have to ask you to halt, Shara Dune," the fancy-dressed swine began, holding out an open hand. "The baron doesn't wish to be disturbed."

From the muffled sounds coming from the behind the thick wooden door, Shara knew why. The grunts, whimpers, and lewd laughter were all too familiar to her. Her irritation grew exponentially.

"That is *Queen* Shara Dune to you, Heath. And the baron's wishes mean nothing to me."

Heath did not know whether to be flattered or frightened by the fact that the Desert Witch knew his name. Confusion flashed across his eyes for an instant before he sneered and gave her what he thought was an intimidating gaze.

"I'm sorry, *Queen*," Heath said with a mocking bow. "But you do not rule here, and the baron has asked not to be disturbed for a time."

Shara Dune frowned. This fool had no idea with whom he was dealing. She locked her strange, sand-brown eyes onto his, exerted a bit of her magic and said:

"Open the door, Heath."

"Of course, my queen," Heath said, his mood abruptly changing from flippant to reverent. He turned and reached for the door handle. Another guard, his face flush with confusion, grabbed Heath's shoulder and turned him roughly.

"Have you lost your mind, man? Tauran will flail you if you open – "

His words were cut short by a flashing blade that cut into his neck so deeply that it nearly beheaded him. Blood splashed on the tentacle that wielded the sword and the fatally wounded guard toppled to the floor.

Heath stood motionless with a blank expression while the other four guards panicked and foolishly drew their swords. Four of the rear escort rushed up from behind while the remaining two brought up their small crossbows.

Amid the sudden human cries of combat and the clanging of metal, Shara heard the low-pitch thrum of crossbow shots. With a wave of her hand, the bolts vanished in mid flight. The shooters looked on in disbelief, having no idea that the streaking bolts had reappeared right behind them, still in flight, until they were pierced through from their backs to their chests.

The four-tentacled sand creatures whipped their weapons this way and that. The blows came at the hapless humans from impossible angles with frightful quickness and power.

Shara could see that the baron's men were well-trained fighters despite their crude social skills. But even though the remaining guards outnumbered the Desert Queen and her guard nine to four, the baron's men never had a chance.

Within seven seconds all was silent. Wild streaks of blood stained the walls, floors, and ceilings. The crimson fluid dripped from the tentacles and weapons of the sand creatures and splattered across their barrel chests and broad paunches. Shara, however, remained incredibly unblemished.

The only surviving guard was Heath. His eyes never left Shara's during the confrontation. His blank expression never changed. The only difference in his countenance was the blood splashed across his face and jerkin. Shara looked at him and nodded.

"You may open the door now."

Heath nodded deeply and opened the door to the spacious room. As Shara suspected, it was an obscenely large bedchamber. Baron Dirk Tauran was standing beside the bed, naked, facing the Queen of the Forsaken Desert without embarrassment or fear. His thick, dark brown hair was tossed wildly about his head. His wide shoulders, broad chest, and round belly were covered with long brown hairs that laid flat against his pale, reddened skin under a slick sheen of sweat.

The man she knew as Leesil at least hid his shame with the corner of the bed sheet, which he held nervously with both hands. The tall, muscled *Ken* foreigner stood several feet away from the bed, still dressed in his full gear, facing the opposite direction. Shara saw him reach into his cloak as if he was going for a weapon but he pulled an empty hand out instead and let it rest at his side. She thought she saw something akin to relief on his face, as if he was glad for the interruption. The raven-haired, golden skinned young beauty Shara brought with her from the *E'Strahil Vah* House lay breathless under the covers, fear and disgust twisting her pretty features. Ugly dark bruises marred the otherwise flawless skin of her shoulders and left cheek.

Tauran glanced at the bloody mess outside of his door, sighed, and shook his head.

"I see they tried to stop you," he noted with disinterest.

"Did you tell them to stop me?" Shara questioned.

"I told them not to let anyone in. I never expected *you* to come. If I thought you would visit my bedchamber I would have been sure to tell them to make an exception."

Shara glanced at the misused girl and turned a disapproving glare at the baron. "I see you have no idea how to appreciate a gift, Tauran."

"She was not a gift," Tauran countered. "She was payment to use as I please." He gave the girl a lingering, wolfish gaze. "She's not as sweet as the dark cherry I have stored in my dungeons but she is almost as tasty."

"If I may interrupt," Leesil joined in. "May I ask the meaning of this intrusion so that we may…continue?"

"Your bodyguard's kin," Shara began, pointing at T'cheln, "have failed miserably in their task at Port Lorrian."

T'cheln bristled. "They did not account for the presence of the Ranger Elf Rell Kallen," he rumbled. "If your benefactors had informed us that our targets included a Ranger Elf, our *Au Sho*, what you call squad leaders, would have sent in the appropriate – "

"What matters is that the Children and their companions still live," Shara cut him off. "They will soon travel by sky sleigh to the south. Tauran, you know what has to be done."

Tauran gave a dismissive wave. "Find someone else to do it. I've tired of these games. I have a county to rule. And T'cheln is my retainer, *not* my bodyguard. I have no need of a bodyguard."

That statement alone told her how foolish Tauran really was. A ruler as inept as he, in a county as lawless as this one, would have countless people trying to assassinate him. But of course, a ruler as inept as he with more ego than common sense would never even consider the possibility of someone stealing his barony just as he stole it from the previous baron. The Queen of the Forsaken Desert fixed Tauran with her gaze, willing her persuasive magic at him.

"This girl was a trade for your *continued* assistance. This newest task represents that continued assistance."

"Your magic doesn't work here, girl," Tauran said with a smug grin.

Shara's alluring gaze turned furious. Somehow either Tauran, or more likely his *Ken d'Zanir* retainer, managed to dampen her magic. "You would dare use your quaint little tricks on me, Tauran? Well, I can assure that my attendants are not affected by your efforts."

Everyone in the room knew it was true. Sand creatures evolved from demons created during Heaven's War, and while they retained a bit of that demonic magic, their frightful strength, speed and savagery were purely physical traits. The effect of the loss of their magic was largely negligible.

The sand creatures advanced. T'cheln pulled his short sword free of its sheath with his left hand and produced and long bladed, sword-breaker dagger from the folds of his cloak. Its hooked metal teeth gleamed menacingly in the soft torchlight as the *Ken d'Zanir* dropped into a fighting stance. The young girl under the jumbled bed sheets whimpered in terror. Leesil cringed and pulled the sheet tighter around him as if it could provide him some sort of protection. Tauran darted his hand behind his large, ornate headboard and snatched out the broken, jagged-edged Dragon-fang.

Shara sneered and gave a grunt in command to her charges, stopping them halfway across the room. As badly as she wanted these men dead, especially the impudent Tauran, she had to think of the larger plan. It would be delightful to kill the baron and his men and take the magic foolishly entrusted to them by their benefactors, but she feared it might strain her relationship with them and delay her ultimate goal.

Besides, there was no telling what other weapons that damned *S'Zan Rho* had hidden beneath his cloak. Shara knew of the notorious warriors from her travels. She knew that in the Known Lands their fighting prowess was second only to Ranger Elves. Tauran had Dragon-fang. With the corrosive properties of that blade he could get lucky enough to cause injury. There was no doubt that she and her sand creatures would slaughter these fools, but Shara could lose one or more of her sand creatures in the process. Tauran's charges were obviously expendable but Shara's were not. The insolent baron's death – as satisfying as it would be – was not worth the effort at the moment.

When Tauran noticed that there would be no attack, the false defiance on his countenance gave way to very real relief. Leesil made no attempt to hide the happiness brought about by this unexpected reprieve. He nearly giggled. The girl continued to sob, but this time with a relieved sigh. T'cheln sheathed his weapons, his expression unreadable but his body language relaxed.

"I will spare you," Shara declared. "But I do so on the condition that you will honor your agreement."

The Desert Queen strode to Tauran. Under any other circumstances, the approach of a woman with captivating pale brown eyes, fire-red hair, and such a hypnotically perfect figure would have him at full attention. But her sandy eyes never left his as she completely ignored his nakedness. And magic was not needed to project the fury and deadly threat that radiated from her in waves. She walked toward Tauran until her forehead was almost touching his nose.

"If we are sent back here again to induce you to follow orders," she said in a low, icy tone, "we will decorate this vast bedchamber with every drop of your blood." Her eyes bored deeper into his while Tauran's eyes suddenly bulged with pain and surprise.

Leesil had to stifle a chuckle when he saw Shara's hand strike out and grab the baron's crotch. He could see from Tauran's pained, teary-eyed expression that the Desert Witch was putting her long fingernails to good use. With her other hand, she pulled the golden, bejeweled, decorative comb from the back of hair, letting thick locks of her fire-red tresses tumble down around her sun-gilded shoulders.

The comb had a long, narrow handle that ended in a fierce needlepoint, which she thrust to within a quarter inch from Tauran's manhood.

"But before I kill you, I will take these as a memento of your stupidity and ineptitude. Do we understand one another, *baron*?"

"Yes," Tauran said in a harsh whisper. "I assure you, witch, that I will give you no reason to return."

Shara released his manhood and turned her back to him in one motion. She deftly fixed her hair into its original style and slid the comb back into place as she strode past her sand creatures. They turned and fell into step behind her and filed out of the chamber.

The young girl had to scramble out of the way when Tauran collapsed onto the bed moaning in agony.

"Why did you just stand there?" he said weakly to Leesil and T'cheln. He coughed for a moment before continuing. "How could you let that whore witch do this to me?"

T'cheln shrugged. "If I had interfered, her creatures would have interfered and we would all be dead. My job as your retainer is to train you in our fighting arts and to keep you safe from harm, even if that means protecting you from yourself. No matter how difficult you make it."

Leesil looked down at the bed and smiled. "So…I guess you're done for tonight, eh, Tauran? Since T'cheln apparently does not like women, this young temptress and I might as well –"

"Get out of here, you bastard!" Tauran barked. "T'cheln, see him out and guard my door. No one enters. No one! And the girl stays."

"I do like women," T'cheln grumbled as he and Leesil left the room. "Respectable women. And *S'Zan Rho* men do not share."

13.7

Lisa stood rigidly in the middle of the musty, claustrophobic hotel lobby, hugging her coat tightly against her chest to conceal the cleavage that her low-cut tank top did not. She wanted to put her coat back on but the lobby was oppressively hot. The hotel was so low scale that she was surprised the heat worked at all. The duffle bag hanging from her right shoulder was growing heavy and causing her to sweat even more.

Since she was sweating profusely without the coat, she chose comfort over modesty and left the coat off. To make matters worse, an icy breeze cut through the lobby every time the outside door opened, which was not frequently enough to make her put her coat back on but frequently enough to make her abandon any hope of comfort. Despite its ratty conditions, the hotel was fairly busy with clientele of the hourly variety.

The intermittent icy breeze caused her tired legs to shiver involuntarily within the thin pantyhose she wore beneath her mini-skirt. They had been to several clothing stores over the last couple of days in less than stellar neighborhoods in order to find just the right outfit. This would be the third cash-only hotel that they stayed in in as many nights so that they did not have to use a credit card. Dan had several credit cards under several different names, but for all he knew, the organization might be aware of all of them. Dan insisted that their best cover in a place like this would be as a hooker and a john.

Their disguises consisted of more than mere costumes. Since Dan knew they were being actively hunted by a clandestine agency, he insisted that they wear facial disguises. Lisa found to her amazement that the old man was rather skilled with professional grade theatrical makeup. Dan told her earlier that day that if he had more time and access to more supplies, he could make them look like completely different people. But as it was, his main concern was making them harder to spot by anyone monitoring the various public video systems. Red-light cameras, speed monitoring cameras, gas station surveillance system and other low-resolution devices that were most prevalent on the street would add enough extra distortion to make them that much more difficult to identify.

For their current disguises he used prosthetics and adhesive glue to effectively give himself larger ears and a rounder nose. He gave Lisa slightly fuller cheeks and a longer nose. Contacts made his eyes darker and he gave Lisa what she thought were silly green eyes. Expert application of a cream base altered her skin color from its natural light-brown caramel to a darker nutmeg. He used another cream base to make himself a shade lighter.

The changes were not drastic and she had to admit that she did not look bad…slutty, yes, but not unattractive to those who liked that kind of woman. Lisa drew the line, however, at the blush and eye shadow and eyeliner. She conceded to his unexpected expertise with the special effects makeup but no way was a two hundred year old man about to apply makeup to make her look like his idea of a hooker. She added the makeup herself, going a little heavier than usual on the blush and mascara and a little brighter than usual on the lipstick, but she made it a point not look garish or overdone.

Lisa initially resisted the disguises. She remembered that other than fake badges and names, neither Dan nor Ryan wore disguises as far as she knew. Dan explained that Ryan's new dreadlocks effectively served a dual purpose of altering *and* hiding his facial appearance, and he would never let Dan put that stuff on him anyway. And because Ryan rarely gave his "poor old grandfather" (Dan's words) a chance to get out of the damn car except to rush in and out of extended stay hotels, the chances of them getting spotted were minimal.

Dan convinced her that he and she were being actively sought after and the enemy had a pretty good idea of where they were, or at least their general whereabouts. This allowed them to narrow their search and concentrate their efforts on one city and its surrounding area rather than an entire country. They were being hunted more closely than he and Ryan ever were.

Dan wanted to work his way out of state but he knew airports, commercial waterway ports, buses and trains were out of the question no matter how well they changed their appearances. The organization would have those places locked down. Even the highways were dangerous, but with effective disguises, they might be able to slip by on a small road somewhere. Dan was just waiting for the right time, which he said was coming soon, for them to cross over to Indiana from Chicago's southeast side and then go south or further east.

Lisa accepted Dan's reasoning but still wondered why she had to disguise herself as a hooker. Dan explained that in a cash-only establishment like this, people were less likely to pay attention to a younger working girl with an old client, whereas a more respectable-looking couple would raise eyebrows as well as the curiosity of potential thieves and grifters. In short, they would stand out more if they looked decent. They needed to keep as low a profile as possible.

Lisa wondered if Dan was really trying to disguise the two of them or if he just wanted to see her dressed like a slut. She did not yet know him well enough to tell.

She reluctantly agreed to go along with the act and was starting to regret the decision. She was self-conscious about her revealing outfit and alternating between shivering from the cold and sweating in the sweltering heat as she waited for Dan to finish haggling with the desk clerk. When they finally finished, the balding, heavyset, middle-aged man behind the counter leaned over and whispered something to Dan while looking over at Lisa. Both men smirked deviously. Dan pulled his duffle bag off of the desk and walked over to her.

"What was that all about?" she asked suspiciously.

"Just guy talk," Dan answered as they made their way to the stairwell. He stopped at the foot of the stairs and made a motion for her to continue.

"Ladies first," he offered graciously.

Lisa looked down at her short skirt and imagined the old man would love to follow her up a flight of stairs.

"No thanks," she said dryly. "Age before beauty."

"If you insist," Dan chuckled. He held out his arm. "A little help, please?"

"I guess," she conceded, taking his arm but making sure to stay a step behind. She could feel the desk clerk staring at her posterior and hoped he could not see up her skirt.

The two of them went up to the second floor of the four-story building and took a left. Their room was at the end of the hall. Dan unlocked the door and ushered Lisa in, locking the deadbolt and the knob latch behind them and flipping the light switch to turn on the ceiling-mounted light.

The room was even hotter than the lobby and way too small. One twin bed consisting of a rickety frame, box spring, and a mattress occupied the far corner. A small dresser with an old lime-green lamp, circa 1975, resting on its worn top and a wooden chair pushed up against it were the only other pieces of furniture in the room. There was an old television sitting atop a wire-frame stand. There was no phone. The stuffy room was permeated with the smell of mold and a faint, sour smell that Lisa chose not to even wonder about. The bathroom was on the right. Its door was halfway open and the little of the bathroom that Lisa could see was spotted with all manner of stains on the floor and walls.

Dan set his duffle bag down beside the bed and commenced an inspection of the room while Lisa set her duffle bag on the floor and walked over to the television. She was frustrated, but not surprised, that there was no remote control. She reached down and switched on the set, which was showing the local news, and noticed that the little box on top of the TV set was an analog-to-digital converter box.

"No cable," she said. "Why am I not surprised?"

She stood up and watched the newscast, which was just transitioning to a follow-up story about an explosion at a downtown hotel a few nights earlier. She gasped when they mentioned that it was the Drake, the hotel that she, her husband, and the other Children of the Old Ones had occupied before going their separate ways. According to the report, the explosion took out a few rooms but the rest of the building withstood the blast. The authorities were still investigating but had not found the source of the explosion.

Dan grunted. "Yeah, and guess which room was included in the blast."

Lisa recalled her husband's actions shortly before he crossed the WorldGate. He had sniffed a couple of times and then his doubt and fear immediately turned into anxious resolve. He knew danger was on the way.

The rough sound of the dresser sliding across the thin, worn carpet made her look up. The old man had moved the small wooden chest of drawers to search behind it.

"You did that at the other places," Lisa noted. "What are you looking for?"

Dan looked up at her and smiled. "This."

His long, wrinkled fingers gripped the small green lamp and lifted it from the desk. With his other hand he gripped the base of the lamp and twisted. The round, flat, fake wooden base unscrewed with a few turns. To Lisa's surprise, a small globe-shaped webcam was set inside the base. Dan turned the hollow lamp upside down to look inside the cavity.

"It looks like ugly green glass from the outside," he said. "But it's like a two-way mirror with a tinted outer surface. The power cord doesn't go to the lamp. It goes to the camera. Anybody who tries to turn it on will just think the bulb's blown." Dan lifted the tiny webcam to his face. "No peep show tonight, assholes," he said before yanking the cord out of the back of the camera.

Lisa shook her head in disgust. "That son of a bitch," she swore, thinking about the leering desk clerk.

When the newscast on the television was replaced by a commercial, Lisa took her duffle bag into the bathroom. She could hear Dan talking to her while she checked the small bathroom window.

"This is a good room," he said.

"Good room?" Lisa called back in disbelief. "It's bugged. And it's filthy! No way am I sleeping in that bed."

"I still have some clean sheets that I lifted from the Drake." Dan assured her. "And I'm not talking about how clean the room is."

"What *are* you talking about, then?"

"It's strategic," Dan answered. "From this corner room we can see the front of the building through one window and the side of the building from the other. Those are sides with the only two exits. No one can come in or out without being seen, at least not from the street, anyway. There were no corner rooms available in the other places. We lucked out."

"Lucked out, sure," Lisa deadpanned.

"Are you changing?" Dan asked. "I hope you're not putting on a show for someone."

"Don't worry, I checked for cameras before I changed," Lisa assured. She stepped out of the bathroom dressed in loose sweat pants, t-shirt, running shoes, and no makeup. She had applied the remover for the spirit gum used to secure the prosthetics on her face and washed all of it, the makeup and the base off. Her face could breathe again and it felt good. "You were saying no one can come in from the *street* without being seen. Where else would someone come in?"

"There's roof access," Dan explained. "But the fire escape has been torn down and there are no other buildings around that are tall enough or close enough for someone to get up there from another rooftop. They would have to parachute in or be dropped off by a chopper, both of which would be too conspicuous for a covert group like the organization."

"Sounds like you've done this before," Lisa noted.

"It's been a while, but yeah, I have," Dan revealed.

"How long do we have to stay here?"

"Not long," Dan promised. "We won't stay in any one place longer than a day or so."

"Clean sheets or not," Lisa continued, "I'm not sleeping in that bed unless you pull a clean mattress out of thin air. You can have it. I'll use some of those clean sheets to make a pallet on the floor."

"No argument here," Dan assured. "I've slept in nastier places."

He fell onto the creaky bed. Instead of bouncing he sunk heavily down into the worn mattress. He pulled off his prosthetic ears and nose. The spirit gum was not needed because they were pieces that he had created, colored, and fitted long ago; whereas Lisa's had to be made on the fly. His nose and ears looked strange in contrast to the lighter complexion of the rest of his face. Lisa could clearly see the relief he felt from getting off of his feet despite his attempts to hide his exhaustion.

"I hope you're a heavy sleeper, girl, 'cause you might be joined by vermin during the night on that floor."

Lisa frowned. She was usually a light sleeper so she had to consider which would be worse: sleeping on a mattress that was undoubtedly rank with bodily fluids of all types; or risking harassment by rats and roaches skittering across the floor. With a disgusted and frustrated sigh she still chose the floor. She would just have to wrap herself up tightly in the blanket from head to toe and pray that her exhaustion would allow her to sleep through the night. She pulled up the one chair, sat down, and looked over at Dan.

"What do we do now?" she asked.

"For starters," Dan answered, "Move that chair over to the left, away from the windows." He watched her move her chair and shook his head in the negative to let her know she was not in a good spot. After two more shifts, he finally nodded in the affirmative.

"Why not just close the blinds?" Lisa wondered aloud.

"What blinds?" Dan asked.

Lisa looked over and noticed that there were no blinds, only transparently sheer, stained curtains. "Great."

"Do you know how to shoot?" Dan asked.

Lisa looked at him as if he had just spoken in another language. The question surprised her.

"A gun? No." She started to rub her forehead nervously, wiping away invisible sweat. "Where did that question come from?"

"You'll have to learn," Dan said sympathetically. "You do realize that, don't you?"

Lisa's initial look of frustration betrayed her desire to argue, but the expression turned quickly to hopelessness as she realized Dan was right. "I can't do this," she said softly.

Dan's tone remained sympathetic even as an edge of sternness crept into it. "We've already been through this…"

"I know I don't have a choice," she cut him off. "I know who's after me, what's after me…after us. That's not what I'm talking about."

Dan waited patiently as she searched her thoughts.

"I mean I *can't* do this," she explained. "I'm a veterinarian. I've never even held a gun, much less fired one. What the hell do I know about secret agents? About magic?"

"Lisa – "

"I'm going to get us killed," she continued, rubbing her forehead even faster. "I'm scared out of my damn mind."

Dan reached out and wrapped his knobby fingers around the hand she was using to rub her forehead.

"You think I'm not?" he asked. "I know I put on a fearless front, but I'm scared to damn death, too. I've been old for a long time, now. The last time I was on any kind of mission was probably before your parents were born." He cocked his head. "How old *are* you anyway?"

Lisa forced a weak smile and gave him a playful swat on the shoulder. Dan rubbed it in mock pain before continuing.

"The thing is you can't ever let fear stop you from doing what you have to do." When Lisa hoisted a defeated shrug and lowered her chin to her chest, Dan gave her hand a soft squeeze. "Tell me, how do you feel about Joel?"

"I love him," Lisa said in a "no duh" tone. "What kind of question is that?"

Dan rolled his eyes. "I know you love him. I'm asking how do you *feel* about him? Describe it."

"Well, love," she repeated. She paused to think of more words to put to it. "I think he's strong, passionate, smart – "

"Would you die for him?" Dan asked bluntly.

Lisa looked up in surprise. She took a deep breath and said: "Yes. To save his life, I would."

"Does he feel the same way about you?"

Lisa thought it presumptuous at first to just assume he would. Then she thought about the things he had done for her in the past, the sacrifices he made voluntarily – eagerly, in fact – for the things she wanted or needed but would never even think to ask for. She thought about the way he looked at her, the way his eyes sometimes held a glint of awe as if she were the most beautiful of God's creations. She had to answer honestly.

"Yes. I think he would," she said.

"I guess that's an easy one," Dan said. "How about this: Would you kill for him?"

The knit of her brow told him that the question was indeed a tougher one. "If his life was danger…"

"I don't mean if someone had a gun to his head and you had to shoot them to save Joel's life," Dan qualified. "I mean if he was nowhere around, and you knew that the only way you could ever see him again was if you killed someone. If you knew that someone would kill him in the future if you didn't kill that someone in the present. Could you do it?"

She thought for a long moment. "I don't know," Lisa answered honestly. "I really don't know."

"Under the same circumstances," Dan pressed. "Do you think he would kill for you?"

Lisa faltered, so Dan went on. "I'm not trying to mess with your head or upset you. I don't expect you to know the answers right now. I'm asking these questions because they're very likely to come up in the near future. We both have good reasons to be afraid, no doubt about it. We're about to go through some serious shit, and so is Joel. We'll all be changed people when this is over. But you have to realize that if you want to see him again you may have to make some hard decisions. You can't let fear keep you from doing what has to be done."

"So what have *you* done?" Lisa questioned. "How many people have you killed?"

Dan paused and smiled sadly. He did not like to talk about that part of his past. But she answered his questions so he would answer hers.

"Never counted," he said. "Never wanted to remember."

"Do you remember the places?" Lisa went on.

"China, Germany, Italy, Japan, Austria," Dan recounted. "I was one of the few black soldiers allowed in the elite divisions of the military back in the thirties and forties. I personally knew only one other besides me."

"What did you do you in the elite divisions?" Lisa asked.

Dan frowned. "I'd rather not get into that."

"I'm trusting you with my life," Lisa countered. "I think I'm entitled to have some idea of your expertise."

Dan frowned again. "POW extractions during and after the wars," he relented. "I was part of a few squads that went against some sensitive, high-priority targets. I'm not too proud of many of the things I did, but I did what I had to do."

"You're a patriot, then," Lisa assumed.

"Not in the traditional way," Dan admitted. "This country is probably the best in the world when it comes to personal freedoms and opportunity, but there's too much wrong with it, too much bad history for me to be 'patriotic' in the general sense. I love the ideals this country claims to represent, but claiming and being are two different things."

"So why fight for this country?"

"I fought in both World Wars because I felt they were just," Dan explained. "I tolerated the racism and ignorance that polluted this country and the military because those wars were about stopping an evil that threatened to dominate the world. They weren't just about political or financial interests poorly disguised as morality and patriotism."

"I don't think I've ever heard anything so…so virtuous," Lisa said. "You don't strike me as that type."

"I'm not, usually," Dan confirmed with a sly smile. "Most of the time I'm just a dirty old man. I take magic seriously, though, and the magic passed down to me as a Child of the Old Ones carries with it a responsibility to use it for the good of the world."

"That's what Joel is doing now," Lisa said with sad longing softening her voice.

"Exactly," Dan agreed. "Even if he doesn't accept it yet, that's exactly what he's doing, and what he must do. And so should you."

"And so should I what?" Lisa asked.

"You should use your magic for the good of this world and others," Dan answered seriously.

"What magic?" Lisa questioned. She remembered what he and Rionn Lorr mentioned about the magic of conception and touched her stomach. "You mean my baby?"

Dan shook his head. "No, not your baby."

"Then what?" Lisa pressed.

"Let me give you a quick lesson about magic," Dan began. "There are two primary groups of magic workers: Conjurers and Constrained Focus mages. Conjurers manipulate magical energy, whether it's internal or external, and in some cases both. There are three categories of conjurers: wizards, witches – or warlocks if they're men – and sorcerers."

"What's the difference between wizards, witches, and sorcerers?" Lisa asked. "I always thought they were just different words describing the same thing."

"Not at all," Dan informed. "It's kind of hard to explain the differences without something to compare them to." He scratched his chin as he thought for a moment. "Do you like music?" He gave her an appraising up-and-down look. "You look like a dancer."

"Stop flirting," Lisa chastised. "Yes, I like music."

"OK," Dan continued. "In music you have singers, songwriters, and musicians. Singers create music with their voice. Musicians use instruments. Songwriters, well, they write songs for themselves or for singers and musicians so that they can create music through instrument or voice. You have people who have to study for years to be proficient at their craft and you have prodigies, people born with an inclination to create music by one of those methods."

"Right," Lisa agreed.

"Think of magic like music. A wizard is like a singer, a real singer, someone with a genuinely nice voice, I mean. A singer does not need an instrument to create music. A singer makes music with his or her voice. In this way they're like wizards. A wizard doesn't need tools or spells to manipulate magic. They can use those things if they want, but they don't necessarily have to. They have magic within them. They just have to learn how to call it forth and control it the same way singers have to learn how to manipulate their voices.

"A witch or a warlock is like a prodigy musician or composer. Witches can't draw magic from within themselves because they don't have it within themselves the way wizards do. But they do have a natural affinity for, and sensitivity to, magical energies. They can instinctively use instruments or spells the way a prodigy pianist can play by ear or a gifted composer can compose with very little training. Like wizards, they can study spells and instruments to hone and expand their ability.

"A sorcerer or sorceress is like a musician that isn't born with any musical talent. They often turn out to be better musicians or songwriters than those who were born with natural talent. 'Naturals' can sometimes get lazy and depend solely on their intuitive or natural abilities. But those not so blessed tend to work and study harder out of necessity.

"Sorcerers have an interest in magic, but no internal magic to call upon and no natural affinity to it. They have to train and study and learn to use spells and instruments of magic. They may never have the same potential, but with enough determination and effort they can become better conjurers than some wizards and witches."

"What about the Constrained Focus mages?" Lisa asked.

"Constrained Focus mages are people who have very limited, very specific magic," Dan told her. "Elementals are one kind of Constrained Focus mage. They're individuals born with the ability to manipulate one of nature's elemental forces.

Lisa smiled, in both interest and amusement. "What about you and Raxe? Are you two Constrained Focus mages?"

Dan nodded. "We grow stronger in the presence of demonic energy and we have the ability to create weapons of magic. We were born with those traits and they're the only internal magic we have. They're a part of us."

"Any other types?" Lisa asked.

Dan thought back to some of the experiences his grandson had in the Kingdom of Lorr. He envied Ryan despite their dire circumstances. Dan could only relay tales that were passed down from generation to generation. Ryan could tell the stories firsthand.

"Sure, there are other types," Dan said. "Ryan told me about a young man – or male, I should say – named Quick, who lives across the WorldGate. He's a changeling. He can transform into any type of animal. That's the only internal magic he has. But he, or anyone with the inclination, can manipulate magic if they put in the work."

"So that means anyone can be a sorcerer or sorceress," Lisa surmised.

"Yeah," Dan agreed. "Anyone can. But that's like saying anyone can be a musician. They can if they put in the work, but they have to have an interest. Not everyone does."

"What about me?" Lisa asked incredulously. "You said *I* have magic. Which category am I in?"

"I can only assume Constrained Focus."

"Why can you only assume?" Her dubious tone made it clear that she was challenging him more than she was curious. Dan had heard that tone before from his grandson.

"I can sense the presence of magic but I can't always identify it," Dan explained.

"You analyzed my pregnancy pretty well."

Dan grinned. She was persistent. "I've experienced it before," he said. "The first time I sensed that kind of magic I didn't know what it was. My mother was pregnant with my little sister and my father told me what it was I was sensing. It's a very unique type of energy, so I've been able to recognize it ever since."

"You have a younger sister?"

"Had," Dan corrected. "I had two younger sisters, actually. Cecilia was the older of the two and Virginia was the youngest. Virginia died a little over ninety two years ago, Cecilia about twenty years earlier."

"How did they die?"

"Old age," Dan said softly. "Virginia lived to be ninety-five."

"But why didn't they… I mean, if you're…"

"Why did they die so 'young' if they're *my* sisters?" Dan finished for her. When Lisa nodded, Dan continued. "No matter how many children a Child of the Old Ones has, only one is born with the longevity of the Old Ones. It's usually the firstborn but not always. That's why I only had one kid. I watched my little sisters grow old and die while I just..." Dan paused for a few deep, silent breaths. "I just lingered. I stayed relatively young. It didn't seem fair."

Lisa was beginning to feel bad about asking that last question. She would have told Dan that he did not have to continue but he seemed to want to share now. She got the impression that he had not talked about this in a long time and that he needed to.

"When Ryan's mom, my baby, was born, I felt the magic in her right away. I knew I would stop right there. I didn't want to put my daughter through what I went through with my sisters. As selfish as it sounds, there was no way I was willing to watch any of my children grow old and then pass me in age – at least physically. I stopped because I didn't want to have to bury any of my children." He paused again and then scoffed bitterly. "As it turned out, I had to, anyway. She would've outlived me if not for that car wreck, though. Fate is a bitch that way."

He took another long pause and a short sniff. "That's why Ryan doesn't have any siblings. His mom didn't want him to go through what I did. Hell, neither did I, for that matter."

Lisa wondered what it meant for their family if Joel really was a Child of the Old Ones. She kept using the qualifier 'if,' not quite willing to believe what she was hearing. Even after all she had witnessed just days earlier, she still could not believe the man sitting in front of her was over two hundred years old. But what if it was true? When would she start to pass her husband in physical aging? She could not imagine being a doddering old woman with a husband that looked young enough to be her son or grandson. Would he still want her? Why would he? The implications began to worry her.

"You let me wander off, girl," Dan said. "That's more than enough about me. Let's get back to *your* magic."

"Oh, yeah," Lisa said, relieved to be distracted her from her own troublesome thoughts. "So why do you assume I'm Constrained Focus?"

"Remember, witches and sorceresses don't have internal magic. Only wizards and Constrained Focus mages have the internal magic I feel in you. Wizards in general have such sensitivity to internal and external magic that they would recognize it within themselves at a pretty early age.

"They sense the magic in everything, living and inanimate, in a way that others can't. They feel things that others don't. Even if they don't realize it as magic, they know it's *something*. It's pretty hard to miss. Have you experienced anything like that?"

"No," Lisa admitted.

"I didn't think so. So the magic I feel in you must be very specific. It's constrained, if you will."

"What kind of magic?" Lisa asked. Dan noticed the challenging tone had shifted to one of genuine curiosity.

"I have no idea."

Lisa was crestfallen. "You know all of that other stuff but you don't know that?"

"Like I said, I can feel magic, but I can't identify it if I've never felt it before. But I can help *you* identify it."

Her dubious frown returned. "How?"

"Well," Dan started, glancing out of the window while gathering his thoughts. He stopped abruptly and knitted his gray, wispy eyebrows.

"What –" Lisa started. Dan stopped her with a raised finger.

"Someone's coming into the building," he revealed. "And I don't think he's friendly."

"How can you tell?" Lisa asked.

"Spooks have a certain demeanor," Dan told her. "They have a certain body language that's hard to hide. Freelancers blend in a little better but if you look hard enough you can spot them, too."

"What do we do?" Lisa asked nervously.

"We wait."

13.8

So they waited. And waited.

After a half hour of tense silence, Dan suggested that the two of them take turns on watch so they could get some sleep. Lisa agreed. She was no stranger to sleeping short hours and keeping late hours. As a veterinary student in Alabama she spent many a late night on foal or calf watch, waiting for a pregnant mare or cow to give birth. It had been several years since she had graduated but she believed the experience would serve her well in this instance.

"Do you want first watch or second?" Dan asked in a voice just above a whisper.

"It doesn't matter," Lisa answered in the same low tone. "With all of the things I have on my mind I doubt I'll be able to sleep, anyway."

"Don't count on it," Dan warned. "You didn't get much sleep the last couple nights. Eventually your body will take the rest it needs whether you want to or not. Tonight may be the night you crash."

"I won't crash," Lisa said stubbornly.

"Are you one of those early to bed, early to rise types, or do you go to sleep late and sleep as long as possible?"

"When I don't have to work the next day, I guess I stay up pretty late. Midnight or a little later."

"Good," Dan said. "I'm an early-bird."

"Really? I figured a dirty old man like you would be a real night-owl," Lisa teased.

Dan chuckled. "Only with the right kind of inspiration," he said with a wink. "But with you being married and all, I doubt you'd provide that kind of inspiration."

"Damn right."

"Then you take first watch," Dan said. "It's almost midnight now, so give me three hours, and then I'll take watch until six."

"Is that going to be enough sleep for you, Dan?"

"I'm a light sleeper," Dan said. "If you feel exhaustion getting the best of you, don't hesitate to wake me up."

"I won't," Lisa assured. "I just wish I thought about bringing something to read. Staying awake shouldn't be a problem, but with no cable I'm gonna be bored out of my mind."

"Maybe I can help you with that," Dan said. He leaned over to retrieve his duffle bag and rummaged through it. He pulled out two small, dark blue ring boxes. He handed one of the boxes to Lisa. When she took the box and opened it, her eyebrows rose in surprise.

"Earrings?" she asked. "Why are you giving me jewelry?"

"Just a little gift to cement our partnership," Dan said seriously. And then he laughed at the doubtful expression on the young woman's face. "Just joking, girl. They're earpiece communicators, like Bluetooth devices, only more sensitive. They can pick up and transmit the slightest whisper. They're synched to this," Dan popped open his ring-box to reveal what looked like a hearing aid.

"I don't really need a hearing aid," Dan bragged. "But it's a great disguise for a communicator, just like your earrings."

Lisa watched curiously as he reached back into the bag and pulled strange pieces of what appeared to be metal out the bag. Among the many objects he pulled out were cylinders of differing lengths, a fist-sized sphere with a small hole on one side and larger hole on the opposite side, and something that she could have sworn was a rectangular, palm-sized computer monitor, like a smart phone, but flatter and smaller. A couple of short lengths of black wire, a long, narrow leather strap, and a shorter, narrow leather strap came out next.

He put all the pieces together with practiced ease and speed with a series of snaps and clicks, never once having to re-connect any of the components. When he was done, he held something that resembled a sawed-off double-barreled shotgun with a long scope mounted at the midpoint of the stunted barrels. The rear of the scope was attached to a small plasma display. The nose-ends of the barrels were fitted into the wider hole of the sphere.

The gun did not have the type of stock that she had seen on regular shotguns. Instead, the short side of a four by eight inch rectangle of dark, dense wood was snapped into the underside of the two barrels. A U-shaped, three-by-five inch hole was cut out of the top of the square where it attached to the barrels to house the trigger and serve as a handle.

The smaller strap Lisa had noticed was wrapped and looped around the double barrels at the midpoint of the scope to hoist the barrels and balance the weight of the weapon. It looked like a toy, or, at best, a prop from a sci-fi movie.

Dan stood and held out the customized weapon to Lisa. Lisa raised her eyebrows in mild surprise and rose to her feet. Her hands came up slowly, but instead of holding them palm up to accept the weapon, she held them palms out in a pushing gesture.

"Why are you giving that to me?" she asked defensively.

"So you can get a feel for it," Dan said, as if the answer was obvious.

"I've never shot a regular gun," Lisa protested. "I sure won't be able to use that complicated-looking thing."

"Don't let its looks fool you," Dan said proudly. "This is perfect for people with shaky hands and people who have never shot a gun before."

"How so?" Lisa asked.

"It's lighter than it looks," Dan told her. "The barrels look like they're made of metal but they're actually a hard plastic alloy. The kickback is barely a twitch, and the plasma display shows the view from the scope. There's a chip in there that controls a target-lock function. Once the target is engaged, that little sphere up there rotates to keep it locked on target even if the target moves a little or the shooter is twitchy. As long as the target is isn't quick enough to dodge a speeding bullet, you'd have to make a conscious effort to miss once you've got a lock."

"Are you bragging?" Lisa questioned. "What, did your grandson give it to you?"

"Hell no," Dan said. "I designed it myself and had some people I know put it together. Ryan doesn't even know I have it." He lifted the weapon higher, urging Lisa to take it. "Go ahead. Put the long strap over your shoulder. That automatically powers it up. Grasping the handle activates the targeting functions."

Lisa leaned away, still refusing to take it. Dan gave up trying to hand it to her and instead moved the weapon around to show each element as he explained its operation.

"There's a button high on the handle that you can press with your thumb. That locks in the target. If you hold it down while pulling the trigger it goes from single shot mode to auto-fire mode. I call it 'spray' mode. Pretty nice, huh?"

Dan grinned mischievously while Lisa only stared.

"It's in simulation mode, now. And it's not loaded," Dan continued. "You can pull the trigger to get a feel for that, too. The magazine is still in the bag. When you're ready to load it, it snaps into a slot on the base of the handle."

Lisa stared at the weird modified weapon for a long time. She was no stranger to guns, having grown up around them. Her father and older brothers hunted deer and small game in Alabama and her uncle was a deputy. She had never shot a gun though; had never even so much as held one. No matter how much the men in her family insisted on her learning how to shoot, she always refused. Even her mother knew how to shoot. Lisa, however, remained adamant in her refusal.

As a small animal veterinarian, she had treated animals with different types of gunshot wounds so she had witnessed the kind of damage they could do to flesh and bone. That merely reinforced her aversion to guns. She never had a desire to and she had no intention of ever shooting one. She knew this situation was different, though. She doubted a gun would do any good against a demonic attack but men were after them, too. As much as she dreaded it, she knew her life might depend on the use of a firearm.

"OK," Lisa surrendered. With some trepidation she finally took the weapon. Dan told her it was light but she was still surprised at how easily she could hoist it. She put the long strap over her right shoulder and flinched in surprise when the modified shotgun began to vibrate softly.

"Good," Dan said as he helped her adjust her hold on the weapon. "Grab the handle with your right hand and rest the stock against your right biceps… There you go. Now take the small strap up front with your left hand to help support the nose-end. OK. Is that comfortable?"

"No."

"Not yet, anyway," Dan said patiently. "But it will be. Practice with it while you're on watch but don't get too distracted. Remember, the whole purpose of 'watch' is to keep anything or anyone from sneaking up on us."

"I will," Lisa promised, thinking about the "spook" Dan claimed to have seen. "But you said you saw an agent. Do you think it's safe to go to sleep?"

"I saw him," Dan agreed, "But that doesn't mean he's coming for us."

"Who else would he be coming for?"

"A hooker, maybe," Dan offered. "Agents need love, too…or sex, anyway. He could be after another target. Or maybe he's lying low like we are. This could be where he crashes while he's on another mission. We don't know, and that's why you need to keep watch. Are you up to it?"

"I guess," Lisa conceded. "Go ahead and get some sleep."

"Thanks," Dan said. "And remember, don't hesitate to wake me up if you hear or see anything. And I mean *anything*. If you hear a noise you don't recognize, too many shadows pass through the hall under the doorway, let me know. Don't shrug off anything and don't try to convince yourself that you're being too paranoid. Understand?"

"I understand. Goodnight, Dan."

Dan's gaze lingered heavily on her for a moment. His dark brown eyes, despite the wrinkles around them, burned intensely as he studied her. Just when he was starting to unnerve her, his gaze lightened and he smiled and nodded.

"Good night," he finally responded. "I'm gonna sleep like a frigging log." He kicked off his shoes and crawled under the covers. Within moments he was snoring.

"Sleep well, old guy," she said. "With the way you snore, I *definitely* won't have any trouble staying awake while I'm on watch."

Lisa turned her attention to the strange shotgun. Just as Dan said, the plasma display lit up when she wrapped her right hand around the handle. The image was surprisingly sharp. A transparent "X" inside a rectangle constructed of dashed lines shone in neon cyan and hovered in the middle of the screen. Lisa centered the "X" on the lamp and used her thumb to depress the small button on the handle. The gun beeped and the cyan crosshairs turned a bright shade of green. Lisa was already tense, and the sudden sound caused her to jump.

She pivoted the shotgun up an inch or so, causing the image in the display to pan, but she noticed that the crosshairs stayed trained on the lamp. Lisa moved it a couple of inches to the right and left and noted how the image in the plasma display moved in response, but the crosshairs moved as necessary to stay frozen on the target. It reminded her of a video game. She then moved the nose of the shotgun a few inches up and down, this time keeping an eye on the sphere connected to the double-nosed end of the barrel. If she listened hard enough, she could hear a faint buzz as the sphere rotated in order to keep the nose on target. She continued to move the shotgun around, targeting the few objects in the room, Dan included.

Even though she remembered what Dan said about the gun not being loaded, her heart rate still picked up when she considered pulling the trigger. Loaded or not, she had never done anything like this before and the thought of it made her nervous. Just to be sure, she turned the shotgun over carefully and inspected the slot Dan told her was at the bottom of the handle. Sure enough, the slot was empty. Lisa swallowed hard brought the modified shotgun to bear, aiming it once again at the lamp. She took a deep breath, held it, and exhaled as she pulled the trigger.

The trigger emitted a sharp click and the green cross became a bright shade of red. The crosshairs blinked and alternated with the word "HIT" in red letters. The sequence lasted about two seconds before the crosshairs stopped blinking and reset to its original cyan.

"Hmmmm," she said to herself, at last intrigued. She pulled the trigger again, intentionally jerking the barrel hard to the left. The crosshairs turned yellow and the word "miss" flashed. She did it a few more times, each time moving the barrel at a smaller angle. After a time, she could tell just how far she could veer while remaining locked on target.

13.9

Lisa glanced at her watch and was surprised to see that almost an hour had passed. She then decided to get a feel for the spray mode Dan spoke of. She depressed the target-lock button and held it down while she pulled the trigger. The sphere mounted at the nose of the double barrels made a whirring sound and rapid clicks marked every shot. The sound reminded her of the time she stuck a drinking straw in the spokes of spinning bicycle tire. She could feel the gun tremor slightly in time with the clicks.

She released the trigger and the sound immediately stopped except for one last click that did not sound quite the same as the others. The last click was somewhat muffled and was deeper in tone. Her head cocked to the side when she heard it again. And then she realized that the sound was not coming from the gun.

It came from the door.

Lisa turned toward the door just in time to see the latch turning as it was being unlocked from the outside. Her eyes bulged and fear seized her voice. Before she could draw a breath to cry out, the door swung open and a man stepped through the door. His skin was pale, almost white, his eyes were wide and bloodshot, and he could not stop them from shifting maniacally around the room. The windbreaker he wore was far too thin for the cold weather and his corduroy pants were ripped in several places. He was obviously amped up on drugs, though, so Lisa doubted the weather bothered him. He held a revolver in one hand and used the other to put his finger over his lips to shush Lisa.

"Make a sound and I'll blow your fucking brains out," he whispered harshly.

Lisa looked down at Dan as he continued to snore. She glanced over at the duffle bag on the floor on her side of the bed, out of the intruder's view. To her surprise, she actually considered diving for the bag and the ammunition within it. That thought was quickly swept away by the intruder's next whispered words.

"Put down the toy and step back, bitch. Now!"

Shocked and afraid, Lisa did as commanded. The man stepped closer, eyeing her warily. After she put the gun down the intruder visibly relaxed and the nervousness in his eyes turned into confidence. He looked down at the snoring old man and smiled, showing off his thin cracked lips and brown cracked teeth.

"Wore the old man out, eh?" he taunted. "Well you just be still and quiet and maybe he'll wake up in the morning."

Lisa heard the words, but the crazy look in his hazy eyes made her doubt that he intended to leave either of them alive. She saw the same look she had seen in the eyes of the men Joel killed downstate. She wished her husband was with her. Instead, she was with a sleeping old man that looked as if he was not about to wake up for anything.

The intruder crept over to the bed and stood over Dan. "Yeah," he said as he studied the snoring form curled up beneath the covers. "You wore him out, all right." He looked over at Lisa. "You might have to give me a sample."

Lisa took a step back, fighting panic.

"What? I'm not good enough for a freebie?" the man flashed a wolfish grin. "Too bad for you, slut, cause I'm takin' what I –"

His words were cut short when Dan's left hand shot up to his throat. Dan used his right hand to grab the intruder's right hand, slipping his finger behind the trigger to keep the gun from firing. The intruder used his left hand to clutch at Dan's wrist in an attempt to remove the old man's grip from his throat. The effort was useless.

Lisa gasped at the would-be robber's eyes. They opened even wider than they had been and the confidence in them turned to fear. They bulged so much that Lisa thought they would pop out of his skull. The gun fell onto the bed as Dan flicked his wrist and pulled. With a violent yank, Dan tore the man's throat open, causing blood to gush out of the wound and run onto the sheets.

Lisa could no longer contain her panic. She was still too afraid to scream but not too afraid to move. Dan looked up at her in surprise when she raced out of the room.

"Lisa!" he snapped. "What the hell are you doing?"

She never heard him. All she heard was her heart pounding in her ears and her running shoes hitting the wooden floor. The hallway flashed by her in a blur and within seconds she was running down the stairs. The desk clerk looked up when she came dashing through the lobby.

"Hey!" the clerk called. "What's wrong?"

"Call the police!" Lisa managed between ragged breaths as she went to the closed entrance. She pulled at the door but it would not budge. There was no latch available. The door had to be unlocked with a key. "Unlock the door!" she cried, yanking frantically on the handle.

"I'm afraid I can't do that, darlin'," the clerk sneered. He eased a small gun from under the counter. "Just sit still for a moment. As soon as Charlie's done with the old man he'll come on down and we'll figure out what to do with you."

"Charlie ain't comin'," floated Dan's voice from the stairway. The clerk turned to see the old man standing at the halfway point of the stairs.

Lisa saw that Dan was hefting his modified shotgun with the strap slung diagonally across his torso. The clerk saw it, too, and smiled.

"Is that even real?" he chuckled.

"Drop the gun unless you want to find out."

"Nice bluff, pops."

The clerk brought the gun around quickly, but not before the modified shotgun made a muffled, metallic thump reminiscent of a soft knock on a thick metal door. A small explosion of red mist plumed above the clerk's shoulders an instant before he flew back and down with violent swiftness, disappearing behind the counter with a loud crash.

Lisa leaned back against the door and slid slowly to a sitting position on the floor. Dan came down the stairs. She brought her violently shaking hands up to the both sides of her head and her breathing became a series of halting gasps.

"What if there were more of them in the hallway or the lobby?" Dan chastised. He was careful to control the volume of his voice but his anger was acute. "Don't you *ever* run unless I tell you to! Ever! Do you understand?"

"I...can't...breathe," Lisa choked out. She was shaking uncontrollably and tears streamed down her face.

"You're hyperventilating," Dan noted. He shifted the shotgun behind his back, walked over to her, went to one knee and put a thin, wrinkled hand on her shoulder. "Take a deep breath and hold it."

"But..." Lisa gasped, "I...can't...breathe..."

"If you couldn't breathe you wouldn't be able to talk, sweetheart. Now just take a deep breath, hold it for a couple of seconds and then let it out."

Lisa tried but was only able to gulp a quick breath and hold it for a fraction of a second.

"Again," Dan commanded gently. Lisa did. That time, she was able to take a deeper breath and hold it a bit longer.

"Again."

Lisa repeated the process three more times before her breathing returned to something a little closer to normal. But her hands still fluttered nervously as she used both of them to rub her forehead.

"Thanks," she said quietly.

"Don't mention it," Dan said with a dismissive wave. "I'm sorry I snapped at you. I know I shouldn't expect you to take all this in stride so soon but you gotta understand. I can't protect you if you leave me like that, OK?"

When Lisa nodded her understanding, Dan stood and made his way over to the counter.

"What are you doing?" Lisa asked.

"Gotta clean this mess up," Dan informed. "You're welcome to help."

"Y-you're kidding, right?"

"It's just a little blood. Aren't you a vet?"

"I can't believe you're asking me to –"

"Never mind," Dan said as he ducked behind the counter. "I imagine that's a bit much to ask under the circumstances."

Even he had to flinch when he saw the damage his shotgun had done. The top half of the clerk's head was gone, transformed into a gory, bloody mess that pooled beneath him.

"I'll get it cleaned up as best I can, but you've got to pull yourself together. I have to have your help to move this guy. He's too heavy for me to move alone."

Lisa waited and tried unsuccessfully to slow her shaking hands. She wondered why she did not panic this way when Joel defended her against the assassins. She imagined it was because those killings had not been as messy. Those men were further away and everything had happened so quickly that the events barely registered with her until it was all over.

But not this time. Her anxiety started to rise again when she recalled the blood from the robber's torn throat and the way the clerk's head exploded from the shotgun blast.

A thought occurred to her. "Dan," she began. "How did you know to bring the shotgun with you?"

Dan peeked over the counter. "The guy upstairs used a key to get into our room. I figured it was a scam they worked together. A feeble-looking old man and a nervous hooker make for easy marks. No telling how many people they've run that scam on. I knew that if I was right, he wouldn't let you leave." Dan ducked below the counter to continue his gruesome task.

"Where are we going once we're done here?" Lisa asked.

"Nowhere," Dan revealed. "This is probably the safest place for us now that Frick and Frack are neutralized. After we sterilize the room upstairs, you and I will get our bags and spend the rest of the night locked up in the break room. I'll bet he has a couch and TV with cable back there. He probably has a bed, too."

"Sterilize the room?" Lisa questioned. "I doubt there's enough bleach in this whole building to clean the blood up there."

"Not that kind of sterile," Dan corrected. "I mean sterilize any traces of us. I'm talking about fingerprints, loose hairs and other forensic traces."

"But they already know who we are," Lisa said. "What's the point?"

"I'm not worried about them using those traces to identify us, Lisa. Those types of physical traces can be used in tracking spells. Remember, we have more to worry about than just mortal men."

Lisa was not ready to think about that "more" yet. The thought was too unbelievable and terrifying. She preferred to worry about the more mundane threats to their wellbeing.

"What about the agent you said you saw earlier tonight?" she asked. "You think he could still be around?"

"Oh, yeah," Dan said as if he had just remembered something. "That was a little lie I told you to keep you alert."

Lisa's first reaction was to snap, to give him the dressing down of his long life, but she took a moment and suppressed that urge. After taking a deep, calming breath, she spoke. "With the way you were sleeping how would you have known how alert I was?"

Dan peeked over the counter again and leveled a stern glare that made Lisa feel like an elementary school student being chastised by a teacher.

"Is that why you didn't wake me up when you heard him unlocking the door, because I was sleeping so soundly? You knew that noise wasn't the shotgun. You should have woken me up right then."

"I was –" Lisa stammered. "Wait. How do you know what I heard? You were awake!"

"Of course," Dan said to her as if she were a dimwit. "You were alert enough, but you doubted yourself and you didn't follow orders and then you froze. If I had really been asleep we'd both be dead right now."

Lisa dropped her head and studied a spot on the floor. "I'm sorry…" she said softly.

"Don't apologize," Dan ordered, ducking out of view again. "I'm not fussing. I'm teaching. You're gonna make mistakes. I expect that. Just don't make the same ones more than once. I made a promise that I wouldn't let anything happen to you and I intend to keep it. But you have to help me keep it."

"I will," Lisa replied. "*I* promise."

"I'm holding you to that," Dan warned with exaggerated menace. "And for starters, you're getting in some target practice tomorrow with live ammo. Got it?"

"Yes, Dan," Lisa managed.

"Good," Dan stood up and stretched. "Now get over here and help me move this fat bastard."

Lisa gulped and rose shakily to her feet, wiping tears from her eyes and face. She tried to erase the image of the clerk's exploding skull as she walked over to where Dan waited behind the counter. She had to stop for a moment to compose herself. Her legs continued to tremor, though not as violently as before.

After steadying herself, barely, she continued on to the back of the counter. Dan had used the clerk's shirt to wipe up much of the surrounding mess and wrapped the bloody shirt around what was left of the man's head. Even though the worst of it was concealed, Lisa still had to stifle a scream when she saw the blood soaked shirt. Dan saw her jump and was expecting her to bolt again, but this time she did not. Instead, she took a deep breath and took yet another moment to calm herself.

"I'll grab his legs," she said softly.

Chapter 14: Sleigh Ride

14.1

Joel was glued to his seat at the starboard aft of the sky sleigh's passenger compartment, well away from any windows. The thin air and the physical strain of violent bouts of airsickness left him exhausted. The ride, though not as rough as he expected, was rough enough.

The fear was worst of all. Its cold weight sat like a stone in his gut, compounding the discomfort of his nausea. His heart had not stopped pounding since he boarded the sleigh. He never had a fear of heights or airplanes but he could find no comfort knowing giant birds were towing the sky sleigh.

He noticed the pitching and swaying of the vessel bothered Raxe too, at first. After a few hours, however, Raxe seemed to overcome his initial discomfort and left Joel to suffer alone. He noticed that Azhju'lestra had no problem at all. A glance at the gills on her neck reminded him that she had spent most of her life under water. She was used to the constant motion of the sea so it was not surprising that airsickness was not a problem for her. Joel thought that her natural environment would make her afraid of heights. That was obviously not the case. In her own quiet way she seemed to be enjoying herself.

The contents of Joel's half-full sick bucket sloshed around with a sickening sound that threatened to make him fill it even further. He was struggling to hold it back when he heard the sound of footsteps and looked up to see his fellow offworlder – fully armored – and his strange daughter step into the doorway. As she had been since they met her at the sky sleigh field, she was as close to her father as she could get without actually making physical contact. Her unique light brown eyes furtively darted this way and that. A casual glance would make someone think she had a short attention span or was simply too shy to make eye contact. When Joel looked closely he could tell that she was making a quick but thorough appraisal of everything her gaze touched.

"You need me to dump that bucket?" Raxe teased.

"Yeah," Joel said. "The smell is making me sick."

Raxe chuckled. "Dump it yourself, man. You need to stretch those legs and get some fresh air."

"Fresh air?" Joel asked. He stood shakily with the sick bucket in his hands and took slow, measured steps to the waste chute behind a tall wooden partition at the rear of the compartment. "How? By sticking my head out a porthole? You must be crazy."

Raxe heard the chute open and then close before calling back, "You gotta get your air legs under you, J."

"*Joel*," Joel corrected, stepping from behind the partition. "All I gotta get is the hell off of this damn sleigh."

Joel's negativity was starting to annoy Raxe. Now he knew how Rionn Lorr and the others felt when he arrived in the Kingdom of Lorr for the first time with his contrary attitude and confrontational manner. Knowing how Joel felt let him to empathize with, and more importantly, tolerate the other's pessimism. It was still really getting annoying.

He and Azhju'lestra followed Joel back to his seat. Raxe realized that was the same spot he occupied on his trip to Infinity Isle: the corner of an interior cabin with no outside view. He smiled to himself and took a seat on the bench to Joel's left. Azhju'lestra sat at Raxe's left elbow. Raxe put a comforting hand on Joel's shoulder.

"I know there's nothing I can say that will make you feel any better about all of this –"

"Then why say anything?" Joel cut him off.

"The sooner you accept this, the better off you'll be," Raxe finished. "Sometimes you gotta just let the current take you where it will. This place can even grow on you a little bit if you let it."

"Let it grow on *you*, then."

Raxe's raspy voice took on a colder tone. His hand on Joel's shoulder tightened. "Look, man, I wasn't given a choice when I came here last, so I had a reason to be bitchy. You had a choice, so what's your excuse?"

"You call what I had a choice?" Joel snapped.

"What you had, Joel, was a reason," Raxe reminded. "Like I did, even though I was never given the opportunity to choose. Once I stopped crying about being here and concentrated on why I was here, it was that much easier to do what had to be done."

"Thanks for the words of wisdom, master *Raxe*," Joel said sarcastically. "Now will you leave me the hell alone?"

Raxe stood, removing his hand from Joel's shoulder.

"Worry can drain you emotionally and physically," Raxe warned. "And it distracts you even more. That combination can get you and the people around you killed in this business. And you're in this business now whether you like it or not." He turned and took a few steps toward the entrance.

"Ryan," Joel sighed loudly. "Or is it Raxe?"

"They call me Raxe here," Raxe said, looking over his shoulder. "Either is fine. What's up?"

"Look," Joel began. "I'm not usually such an ass. It's just that this whole thing is crazy. I don't know what I'm supposed to be doing here. I've been scared to death since I stepped into the WorldGate." He frowned and chuckled darkly. "A *WorldGate*, man! Do you hear how that sounds?"

"Believe me, I do," Raxe assured.

"I kill people," Joel confessed, staring blankly at the floor. "I'm a killer, and I don't even know it when I do it."

It was Raxe's turn for a dark chuckle. "That's probably a blessing."

"A blessing?" Joel asked incredulously. "Waking up surrounded by corpses? With blood on my hands? I'd hate to see your idea of a curse."

"A curse would be remembering it," Raxe said. "Take my word for it. Be thankful that our magic works the way it has to work."

Joel turned to Raxe and cocked his head. "What the hell does that mean?"

"When my magic and this battle-axe were new to me, it took over my body. It was hell, not being able to control my actions. But that was what kept me alive. It controlled me because it *had* to until I understood how to work with it."

"So you learned to control it?" Joel asked hopefully.

Raxe shook his head. "I said work with it. I realized that it wasn't about control. Opening myself up to it made it work more effectively and it was easier on me, both physically and psychologically."

"But why do I have to kill people?" Joel argued. "If I'm that powerful, why not just, shit, I don't know, incapacitate people, you know? Why can't I just knock people out or break legs or something?"

Raxe looked at him for a time. "You're asking that question to the wrong guy. I used to be an assassin."

"You think I *should've* killed them?" Joel asked.

"Incapacitating organization agents won't work," Raxe told him. "They won't stop until they kill you; or until you do something to stop them permanently. I'm sure your magic, like mine, makes you do what you have to. It knows those guys have to die to ensure your safety. And maybe it's best for you psychologically to not remember when you do it."

"Magic," Joel said. His voice was quiet but it dripped with uncertainty.

He looked down at his hands, wondering with dread how many more men and beasts he would kill in this godforsaken world. Forcing the anxiety away with a shake of the head, he turned his gaze back to his fellow offworlder.

"How many people have you killed, Ryan?"

"More than I care to say," Raxe rasped after a short pause. "But I'm done with that now."

"Really?" Joel asked, genuinely surprised. "You know I've never done anything like this, but it seems like it'll be pretty tough to get through it without killing someone."

Raxe scoffed. "I know."

Joel exhaled sharply. "You really think we can do this?"

"I don't think we have a choice," Raxe answered, his voice and expression cold and rough like slate rubbing against slate. "Enough about that. Go find a porthole. You'd be surprised at how good some fresh air can make you feel. Just don't look down."

Raxe walked out into the main corridor. Azhju'lestra, walking at his side, looked over her shoulder with curious eyes at Joel. Father and daughter hesitated when they heard stomping and neighing coming from the rear of the sky sleigh. The horses were restless. Hell, Raxe knew he would be restless, too, if he were cooped up in the musty rear cabin of a flying termite trap.

He also thought he heard the avicaws screeching at a more intense pitch than usual. It was his fear of heights creeping up on him, he knew. He had done everything he could think of to conquer that fear. From skydiving to flying fighter jets in the Air Force, to bungee jumping, he had done it all. And he was still afraid. He believed his exploits during his last visit to Lorr had cured his fear, but apparently they had not. A quick walk to the pilot's box would set him at ease, he decided. He continued to the fore of the vessel, his daughter by side, and reached the set of rungs that led to the upper compartment and called up.

"How is everything, gentlemen?" he asked.

"The 'caws are of a mind to bear east," was the reply. "Happens from time to time. Nothing we can't handle."

Raxe did not know anything about giant flying birds or how they were controlled. If the crew was not concerned he figured there was no reason he should be. He glanced down at Azhju'lestra.

"What do you think, Azh?"

The girl's darting eyes settled on Raxe's, a shroud of worry darkening her soft brow. "The horses and birds are worried," she said bluntly. "So I am, too."

Raxe stared thoughtfully at his young daughter, thinking how crazy it was that she was even on this mission. She was a little girl. It did not matter that one glance was more than enough reminder that she was no ordinary little girl. With his blood flowing through her veins, the divine blood of the Old One ancestor that was his namesake in this world, combined with the enchanted blood of her water faerie mother, there was no telling how powerful she was.

But she was still a little girl. How would handle herself in a crisis? Would she be a distraction? How could she *not* be a distraction? He started to second-guess his decision to bring this girl, who appeared to be about six years old but was really only *three.* It was bad enough when he found out Ethan, a sixteen year old boy, was a part of this quest.

Almost on cue, the Sureblade teen stepped out into the corridor as Raxe and Azh walked by his cabin.

"Raxe, sir," Ethan called.

"No 'sir,' kid," Raxe said. "What's up?"

Ethan glanced up for a moment, unfamiliar with the colloquialism, before realizing what the offworlder meant.

"With my own eyes, I have never seen you fight," the teen began. "But I have heard many tales from Quick as well as soldiers who fought alongside you during the Cursed Opening. They say your style of fighting is similar to the *Ken d'Zanir*, only more precise."

"I'd agree with that description," Raxe concurred.

"Could you teach me?" Ethan asked hopefully.

Raxe hesitated, surprised by the question. He never thought of himself as a teacher.

"Why do you need to learn that stuff, kid? I've seen you in action. You're a helluva fighter already."

"I'm not good enough," Ethan said earnestly. "At least not for this mission. I've bested two and three men at a time in swordplay in the past but I would not be able to best one *S'Zan Rho* warrior. I could not even best that clown Tauran because of his training in the *Ken d'Zanir* fighting style. If you taught me your style of fighting I would be more useful."

"I could teach you a few moves," Raxe began. "But it takes years to really learn to fight the way I fight. You have to prepare your body to be strong and flexible in ways it has never been before you can even begin to be really effective."

A crestfallen look shadowed Ethan's face. "Well, then, could you show me those few moves?"

"Sure," Raxe said.

Ethan's face brightened a bit.

14.2

Joel sat and stared at the doorway after Raxe left. He took several deep breaths of the stuffy air in the cabin and decided that Raxe might have been right. Keeping a hand on the wall to steady himself, Joel stood and walked slowly out of the interior rear compartment. Once he was in the main hall he quickly found a safety lead attached to a three-foot high rail on his right that spanned the length of the short corridor. He fastened the lead to his belt.

The lead slid smoothly along the rail as Joel shuffled along the hall, surprised at how well it helped to steady him against the slight pitching of the sleigh. At the opening of another small compartment in the middle of the sky sleigh on the starboard side, he unhooked the safety lead and stepped into the compartment. A two-foot wide circular porthole about five feet high was set into the far wall of the small space. He swung the glass porthole cover inward, bent over and stuck his head out of the window.

One deep breath – without looking down, of course – proved Raxe right. Joel took another deep breath and then another. He had apparently grown more accustomed to the thin air than he realized. He marveled at how easily he could breathe. The herbs given to him by the Head Mage seemed to strengthen his lungs as well as clear them. Joel could not remember the last time he was able to breathe so deeply.

Joel could see the *Sundance* flying behind his sky sleigh. The sight was surreal. Three massive avicaws soared in perfect synchronicity, towing the sleigh smoothly beneath and behind them. He took a chance and looked down at Hell's Mountains to the west. They reminded him of the McCullough Range in Nevada. The Hell's were, for the most part, arid and dusty, with sparse plant life barely visible from this high in the sky. The sleigh was not flying high enough to allow him to see across the entire width of the north-south trailing wall of mountains, but it was high enough to reveal a narrow valley that snaked through the length of the range for as far the eye could see.

"Are you looking at the valley?" asked someone from behind him.

Joel turned with a start and saw the gangly youngster named Quick.

"Yeah," he answered.

"It's called the Serpent's Way," Quick shared. "They say it was once filled with water, that it was a deep river that ran through Hell's Mountains. Before Heaven's war, Lake Onyx was much higher than it is now. It encompassed much of the southern portion the Wyrm Mountains and the northern part of the Hell's and fed the river.

"The valley is all that remains of the river. It ran from Lake Onyx, through the Bountiful Forest, which was transformed to the Forsaken Desert during the War, through the southern central band of the Demon's Spine Mountains and into the Gulf of Cartha. Before sky sleighs it was the fastest route to the Carthan Kingdom from the northern regions of Lorr."

"Thanks for the history and geography lessons, kid," Joel said dryly, turning back to stare out of the window. "But you should save it for someone who's interested."

Quick stared at his back for a moment. He suppressed a rude rejoinder, reminding himself that this new offworlder's predicament undoubtedly placed him in not the friendliest of moods. He wondered how many more times he would have to remind himself of this before he had his fill.

When the sound of the teen's footsteps faded, Joel turned his attention from the mountains below to the sky above. It was beautiful and bright despite a thin blanket of powder-white wisps of cloud. The feathery cloud cover was too light to contain the brightness of the suns, but it was vast. It began miles ahead of them to the south in a sharp line and stretched out to the north and west. Beyond the line where the cloud cover ended in the south was an eternity of deep, beautiful azure. Patches of it teased him through multiple cracks in the shallow cloud ceiling overhead.

A strange sensation crept upon him.

The sensation was like a scent, or a faint aftertaste in the back of his throat, so insubstantial it was almost a memory.

He craned his neck up to look in the direction from where he thought the sensation originated. He peered higher in the western skies and saw columns of bright suns' light beaming through various breaks in the clouds. It was as if God himself was shining countless spotlights onto the earth.

And then he did a double take when a couple of the rays of light seemed to flicker in the distance. Joel squinted to focus and waited to see the flicker again. He did, only this time it was closer. The clouds grew a bit darker as a barely visible shroud moved swiftly in *Cloud Chaser*'s direction. Joel was startled by a sudden call from the pilot's box.

"Something approaches from the northwest!" called the navigator. Apparently he had seen what Joel was seeing.

Rell Kallen came running into the compartment and shouldered Joel aside to look out of the porthole. His sharp elven eyesight studied the clouds. The usually unflappable Ranger Elf gasped.

"By the Old One Ahn'Lorah," Rell swore. "Those are Scythe-wings."

"Scythe-wings?" Joel asked.

"SCYTHE-WINGS!" Rell yelled at the top of his lungs.

The words echoed as the crew relayed the message throughout *Cloud Chaser*. Men and women began to scramble up and down the corridor and commands were called out from every direction.

"What are scythe-wings?" Joel asked nervously.

Rell turned to Joel. "I suggest you strap in, offworlder." He absently fingered a small lump suspended from the barely visible imprint of a string hanging around his neck tucked inside of his tunic just below the collar. "This ride is about to get rough." He hurried from the compartment.

Joel forgot about his discomfort in the commotion and rushed to fasten himself into the nearest harness. His heart beat so furiously it caused the harness to vibrate. Quick and two soldiers came in and secured themselves to the remaining three seats and harnesses in the compartment. Quick sat next to Joel.

"Uh, Quick?" Joel uttered. "What's a scythe-wing?"

"A predatory hawk," Quick answered without turning to look at Joel.

Joel waited for more but nothing was forthcoming. The hawks of his world came to mind. But that did not seem enough to cause the near panic he was witnessing. He was almost too afraid to ask his next question.

"If they're just hawks, why is everyone so spooked?"

Quick turned and gave him a serious look. "They're about half the size of avicaws," Quick explained. Joel's eyes bulged. Quick continued. "They fly in flocks…or swarms, and they attack anything in their path that is not a dragon."

Joel fell silent, but his left eyebrow twitched with worry. He hooked his thumbs through his harness strap and gripped it tightly. *How am I able to* smell *them?* he wondered.

The noise outside of the cabin grew. Cries of "Ready the spars!" and "Unlatch the foils!" could be heard along with assorted expletives that would have been amusing to Joel if this had not been such a dire situation. He could hear trap doors banging open and closed and hinges squealing as well as the sounds of cranks turning and the thumping of heavy boot falls upon the decking. The horses in the back were stomping around wildly. Their hooves pounding on the wooden planks and their worried neighing almost drowned out the panicked cries of the avicaws.

Among all those sounds, he heard something else. It started out as a constant static background to the clamor aboard the sky sleigh. The static was soon accompanied by what sounded to Joel like a drawn-out wailing in the distance. A shadow fell over the right side of the sky sleigh.

"Hard to starboard!" someone yelled frantically.

The vessel lurched to the right and picked up speed, pressing Joel's back firmly against the wall. Quick said the birds of prey were half the size of avicaws, which made them half again as long as Joel was tall and at least twice his weight. And there were a flock of them. His heart beat faster and his chest tightened.

"Starboard?" Joel asked. "The hawks are coming from that direction!"

"They're trying to make it below the peaks of the Hells," Quick told him. "We can't outrun them, and scythe-wings only attack in open areas of sky, land, and water. The mountains will provide safe cover."

The background noise grew louder and louder until it began to separate into individual, more recognizable sounds. The background static turned into the sounds of multiple flapping wings. The wailing clarified into high-pitched avian screeches that chills creeping up Joel's spine.

"It's the avicaws they want," Quick said so suddenly that Joel jumped in his seat.

"What?" Joel asked.

"The scythe-wings are hungry," Quick told him. "I can hear it in their cries...and something else as well..." Quick trailed off, rubbing his chin in thought while listening.

"What?" Joel asked. "What else?"

"I'm not sure, but I *am* sure that they mean to feed on the avicaws."

Joel could hear himself wheezing, so he released the white-knuckled grip his left hand had on his harness and dug frantically into his pocket for the little pouch of herbs given to him by Catherine. He put a pinch of the mixture into his mouth and chewed it thoroughly. As his breathing started to come easier for him, he wondered where Raxe was and what he was thinking about their predicament.

14.3

"Scythe-wings?" Raxe asked Ethan, who was strapped in to his right. He had to yell above the cacophony of the crew, horses, and the approaching swarm. "What the hell are scythe-wings?"

Ethan's fear was evident. His eyebrows were drawn down tightly and he pressed his back against the wall so firmly that Raxe thought the teen might break through. "They're hawks," Ethan answered. "Only bigger. They're larger than men, in fact. I've never seen one but I've heard of them. They are from the western fringes of the Known Lands, very near the natural barrier to the Unknown Lands. I've never heard of any being seen this far east."

"Mother has spoken to me of scythe-wings," Azhju'lestra added from where she was seated and strapped in to Raxe's left. "She said that back before the First Children called forth the barriers that separated the Known and Unknown lands, she had seen them many times in the far western world. She did not like them because they often fed on her creatures."

"Aye," interjected lieutenant Lawrence Windermere. "I've seen them myself in the northwestern fringes of the Troll Lands, over the skies of the Earth's Blood Ocean. I watched them pull a fully-grown blood whale from the ocean and pick its bones clean in mid air. Until now, that was recorded as the furthest away from the Unknown Lands they had ever been."

Raxe did not know exactly what a blood whale was, but it sounded pretty damned big. "They didn't come after you?" he wondered aloud.

"Our battalion retreated to the cover of the forest," Windermere said. "It is said that they may attack on broad, open areas of land and sea but they avoid mountainous and forest terrain. It worked for us, anyway."

"Do you think we can make it to the Hell's range before the scythe-wings catch us?" Raxe asked.

"Not likely," Windermere said. "You can hear how close the winged beasts are now."

Azhju'lestra leaned in a little closer to Raxe but stopped short of leaning on his arm. She gazed worriedly at the blue sky and white clouds through the porthole.

Harl Timson had been a sky sleigh pilot for almost a quarter of a century. He was seventeen when he received his first job as a pilot – which was much younger than usual – and being older than forty made him much older than the average pilot. It was a hard life, and most pilots did not last much longer than ten years. Injuries, close brushes with death and the rigorous physical demands of the job made the attrition rate of sky sleigh pilots higher than most other professions. Harl, however, was tougher than most other men, sleigh pilots included. He was proud of his longevity.

Over the years he had flown over hurricanes, through blizzards, and even managed to evade a young rouge dragon in one particularly harrowing case, but he had never been as frightened as he was at this moment. The dragon that chased him was large, and Harl was able to guide his one-bird racing sleigh into a stand of tall monolith oak trees that were packed too densely for the large golden dragon to follow. Besides, Harl half-believed the immature dragon had been toying with him and had no real intention of harming him. He had no doubt, however, about the intention of this threat.

Dozens of the big brown hawks dropped from the cover of the clouds and raced after *Cloud Chaser* and *Sundance* in a wide but orderly arc. The broad line of birds seemed to have no end. They continued to stream out of the clouds even as the lead birds closed on the trailing *Sundance*. Primal fear gripped his faithful sleigh birds. The usually predatory avicaws realized that they had become the prey. In all of his years, Harl had never seen a swarm of scythe-wings. He had heard of them, so he made it a point never to journey far enough west to come anywhere near their territory. But here they were, chasing him.

It took all of Harl's skill as a driver and all of his physical strength to keep the avicaws under some semblance of control. Coortahn, the copilot and navigator, yelled commands at the crew and coordinates at Harl as authoritatively as he could muster, but his fear was evident in the high pitch and occasional cracking of his voice. Every thirty seconds, the rear lookouts called out the proximity of the pursuing swarm of scythe-wings. Neither Harl nor Coortahn needed the alerts. Both men could hear the screeching and heavy wing beats of the approaching birds, and so could the well-trained but terrified sleigh birds.

Both pilot and copilot started at the loud thump of the floor hatch being thrown open. Coortahn looked down at the braided, dusky blonde hair of the Ranger Elf Rell Kallen. Before either man could speak, Rell shouted:

"It's the sleigh birds they're after! Cut them loose!"

Harl started to argue. He had raised and trained these birds from hatchlings and could not bear to lose them. But he knew the avicaws had a chance of out flying the scythe-wings without the burden of the sleigh.

"Free them *now*, human!" Rell exhorted. "Lest this sleigh is torn apart in the scythe-wings' wake!"

Harl cursed and spat and then gave the command.

"CUTTING LOOSE!" the sky sleigh captain yelled.

"Cutting loose?" Joel asked Quick nervously. He heard the two frightening words repeat and resonate throughout *Cloud Chaser*, followed once again by the sounds of boots stomping and hinges squeaking and cranks cranking. "Cutting *what* loose?"

"The avicaws," Ethan replied to Raxe.

The young Sureblade wondered anxiously about Nicolette and the rest of the Keeper's Hounds in the *Sundance*. The scythe-wings would reach *Sundance* before *Cloud Chaser*. Instead of riding with his team, Ethan chose to ride in the lead sleigh so he could talk to Quick and the offworlder. He should have been back there with them. He should have been back there with Nicolette.

"The avicaws?" Raxe echoed, startling Ethan. "What the hell do you mean they're cutting loose the avicaws?"

"The sleigh is equipped with gliders," Ethan assured, "like wings. They will allow us to descend at a safe speed.

The sounds you hear now are the wing masts being extended and the tail fins being deployed."

"The rigging is there in case of emergency," Quick said to Joel. "And this is most definitely an emergency."

Joel did not look in the least bit relieved as Quick continued. "I suggest you tighten your harness as snug as possible…and don't worry about your sick bucket. It will be all over the place with or without the bucket."

The seven-person sky sleigh crew, not counting the pilot and copilot, expertly went about their tasks. They opened the foils; the spars, thin and pliable but strong, were extended from the top and underside of *Cloud Chaser* by a complex system of levers. They used a small set of pulleys to unreel the foils along the spars. The foils, or glider wings, were canopies woven from the strong, silky thread of solluhs plants and did an excellent job of holding the sleigh aloft. The crew awaited the command to release the lines that held the canopies fast to the spars, thus opening the foils fully to catch the air and begin the gliding process for the sky sleigh. Cries of "Wings ready!" echoed through the sleigh until they reached the ears of the pilot.

Harl took a deep breath and looked over to his copilot, who was looking back at him. Each man unlatched vertically fastened metal bars that swung down from opposite sides of the pilot box. Each bar was hinged to another that fed up the short wall and through the roof, where it was hinged to yet another bar in the space between the ceiling and the roof of the pilot box. From there it was attached to a network of bars and hinges and lines that finally attached to the spars to allow the pilots to steer. Controlling the sleigh was the easy part. The hard part was releasing the wings.

Their timing had to be perfect. If they opened up too long after releasing the sleigh birds, the canopies could tangle instead of opening to catch the wind and *Cloud Chaser* could spiral out of control. If the wings were opened while the avicaws were still attached, the sudden diverging forces could either snap the sleigh's glider wings or strangle the avicaws. The glider wings were designed to work after the avicaws were released. They were not strong enough to support both the sky sleigh and the weight of three crippled or dead avicaws.

With simultaneous nods to one another, Harl flipped the toggle that triggered the release of the lines fastening the avicaw harnesses to the sleigh and then he released the reigns. The sleigh birds raced away, instantly yanking the reigns through the smooth piping that allowed the strong leather straps to pass from the birds' harnesses to the inside of the pilot box.

"AWAY!" Harl yelled at the top of his lungs. Then he held his breath and braced himself as *Cloud Chaser* dropped.

He listened for the low-pitched whoosh of the opening foils catching the wind. If he heard flapping, they were doomed. The captain exhaled when he heard the *whoosh* then turned to watch his avicaws fly at a southeast angle while the sleigh continued due west toward the Hell's. The avicaws took a sharper turn to the east, racing away from the much more numerous predators. The avicaws towing the *Sundance* flew right behind them.

As expected, the scythe-wings followed the fleeing sleigh birds. *Cloud Chaser* shook violently when several of the large birds brushed the sleigh while banking to the left to follow the avicaws. Harl and Coortahn held on to the steering bars for dear life and kept the bucking vessel under some semblance of control. The shuddering lasted several seconds but to Harl it seemed like an eternity. When the sleigh was at last gliding undisturbed, Harl thanked the gods that none of the hawks had struck the vessel's canopy wings. Coortahn turned to him and offered a weak smile of nervous relief.

Moments later, one of the crewmembers came to give a damage report. He relayed that the foils were blessedly intact, but some harm had been done to the rear compartments. The crew was still assessing the extent of damage.

14.4

Raxe's stomach lurched when *Cloud Chaser* went into free fall. It lurched again when the wings opened successfully, abruptly halting the free fall and changing the trajectory from straight down to forward. Then came the crashing and bucking from the scythe-wings, and Raxe thought he was about to spew more violently than Joel had earlier. Azhju'lestra had a firm grip on his arm. There was a worried look on her face and her wide eyes flicked back and forth even quicker than usual, but she otherwise remained amazingly calm under the circumstances.

He thought he heard wood tearing loose and metal creaking amid all of the other sounds, but once all of that ended the glide was smoother than expected. Whatever the damage, it was not bad enough to affect the flight of the sky sleigh. There was still the occasional lurch but Raxe expected it to be worse. It was comparable to the motion of a small, twin-engine plane caught in turbulent skies.

The hungry cries of the scythe-wings faded somewhat as the flock of giant hawks went off to pursue the sleigh birds. Out of morbid curiosity Raxe unfastened his harness, left his cabin and stepped across the hall to the cabin facing his to look out of the port side window of the cabin. Azhju'lestra followed, but she was not tall enough to see out of the porthole and seemed to have no desire to do so anyway. Raxe got a good look at a few of the giant hawks and immediately saw where their name came from. Their black beaks were huge even in proportion to their already imposing size. The beaks started as foot-long inverted arcs that came to a sharp apex before hooking downward much more severely than even the avicaws', and ended in a tapered wicked point that looked ideal for snagging and ripping flesh.

Raxe saw that the larger avicaws were flying at wide angles away from one another, but he could still in the distance. If the avicaws were supposed to be faster than scythe-wings Raxe could only assume they were indeed exhausted from flying so hard and fast with the sky sleigh in tow. He saw the swarming hawks branch off in six different directions to converge on each of the birds.

Joel came shuffling into the room. He was not hooked to the safety line this time, but he braced his arm against the wall for balance. He came up behind Raxe and looked over his shoulder out of the porthole just in time to see the fierce hawks tear into the larger avicaws.

Six small clouds of dark red mist and blue-black feathers erupted at the end of six lines of streaking scythe-wings. The giant hawks swarmed amidst the spraying blood, darting in and out, fighting one another to snag a piece of flesh from a competing set of hungry claws. Some managed to cling to the body and beat their wings frantically to keep their prey airborne while their wicked beaks pecked over and over until they were forced away and replaced by a more aggressive or less exhausted hawk. The slaughter seemed to grow smaller as the gliding sky sleigh pulled further away.

Soon after, their angle of flight took the spectacle out of their line of sight. The carnage was behind them now, and since the rear compartments of the main body of the vessel contained cargo and animals, there were no windows in the rear passenger compartments. Even if there were a rear view, the group would not have gone to the rear of the sleigh to use it. They were no longer interested in the ghastly sight.

Raxe and Joel sat heavily upon wooden benches built into the wall below the porthole. Rell and Ethan entered the room. Rell, as usual, wore an unreadable expression while a pale Ethan wore a look of disgust.

"I take it you just watched the feeding," Raxe said.

Rell stepped forward. His arching eyebrows set in a serious knit. "What is your plan for when we set down in Hell's Mountains?"

"Arrange for transportation so the sleigh crews can go home," Raxe said. "We'll continue south. By horseback, I figure we'll be about four days from Hargathall's Cleft. If we can't find any sign of the missing soldiers from the previous expedition at the canyon, we'll go north to Shaddiston and look for them there."

"We can't waste time searching for dead men," Rell argued. "Mar-dah's keep is of paramount importance."

"Exactly. And they can help us –" Raxe stopped when the elf turned sharply away. Raxe initially took the action as a slight, but when he noticed the pointed ears twitching, he knew something had caught the elf's attention.

"What is it?" Raxe asked.

Quick ran into the room holding an armful of cloth sacks with leather straps looping from them. The look in his eyes drew Raxe's attention completely away from Rell Kallen.

"Everyone take a uniwing!" Quick called. "The scythe-wings are returning! We have to evacuate!"

Raxe rushed over and snatched two of the sacks from Quick's arms. Raxe recognized the sacks as the equivalent of parachutes from his first trip in a sky sleigh. He had gotten brief instructions on their use before the trip to Infinity Isle. This time, however, they had been so rushed that no such training was given to Joel or Azh. Raxe went over to his daughter to help her put on the uniwing.

"Won't we be sitting ducks out there in the open the sky?" Joel asked as he took a sack from Quick's arms, trying hard to suppress his panic. He was already terrified, having never been sky-diving in his life. His hands trembled as he fumbled with the straps of the uniwing.

"Our only other choice is to be 'sitting ducks' in this sleigh while they tear *Cloud Chaser* to splinters," Quick answered.

"If you survive that," Ethan added, "You'd fall to your death or get ravaged by the scythe-wings on the way down. At least this way we'll have a fighting chance."

"Again with the double-edged choices," Joel muttered.

The young Sureblade buckled the last strap on his uniwing and scooped up his crossbow and quiver from where he set them on the floor. Both had been strapped to him but he had to remove them to make room for his uniwing. He quickly fastened them back to his weapons belt and then cut a length of rope from the lasso looped around his shoulder. He used it to lash his long javelin to his back. He then checked to make sure the small thong of leather was fastened securely to the opening of his sheath to keep his father's broadsword from sliding free.

"Don't you think all that gear will be a little obtrusive?" Raxe asked.

"I'll not leave my father's weapons," Ethan snapped.

"Just asking," Raxe said before turning to the other offworlder, who was still worrying with his uniwing. "Joel, try not to think. Just jump, count to five and then pull the release cord."

"Try not to think." Joel echoed. "That'll work."

Raxe ignored Joel and turned to Quick. "You said they wanted the avicaws."

"Their cries were cries of hunger," Quick explained as a female crewmember took a uniwing from him.

"But you said there was something else," Joel recalled. He imitated Raxe stepping through one of the loops and fastening it to his upper thigh.

"Yes," Quick confirmed, handing out the last uniwing. "It had to be magic. The trace of it was so faint that I could not quite recognize it, but scythe-wings would not fly this far to the east out of natural instinct. There are spells that can plant suggestions into creatures that remain long after the magic has faded. Once they got here, their natural instinct to feed took over and magic would no longer be needed."

"And now that they've finished the avicaws…" Raxe mumbled.

He did not have to finish his sentence. Everyone knew the scythe-wings were returning for another course. Instead of talking he pulled the strap of his small travel pack diagonally over his shoulder and tightened it as much as the metal buckle would allow. He then concentrated on securing his uniwing. When that was done, he checked his left hip to be sure Questblade was securely fastened into its scabbard and then kneeled so that he and his daughter were eye to eye.

"Quick lesson," he said to her, pointing out the three looped cords. Each cord was a different color and each hung from a small, tightly packed pouch where the straps converged at her stomach.

"The green cord releases the glide wing canopy if you need to move parallel to the ground, the blue releases the canopy that will let you descend, the red one detaches both canopies in case you need to fall fast. With both wings, the brown cords on the right and left are used to steer."

The little girl listened closely but did not reply.

"Can you do this, Azh?" Raxe asked.

She gave him a puzzled look, as if she did not understand the question. "I suppose I must."

"I mean do you know *how* to do it? Do you understand?"

"It seems a simple apparatus," Azh observed as she mimicked the men donning the uniwings. She seemed to have no trouble cinching the straps and buckles. A mischievous smile brightened her face.

"It looks like fun."

14.5

The horses grew restless again and even wilder than before. Their neighs and whinnies grew more panicked as they stomped and kicked against the floor and walls so hard that they sent shudders all through the sleigh. Even in the pilot box at the opposite side of the sky sleigh, Harl and Coortahn could hear the snapping of wood and the metallic ping of bolts giving way.

"The rear compartments were already damaged by the scythe-wings," Coortahn said needlessly, "The panicking horses are causing even more damage!"

"I know," Harl snarled. "To ground! Full ahead!"

"Full ahead!" Coortahn called to the crew. The crewmen within the sleigh adjusted the tail rudder and wings to achieve maximum speed. Their downward angle allowed gravity to hasten their acceleration, but the giant hawks continued to gain.

"Secure your steering lever and get to your uniwing," Harl ordered his copilot/navigator.

"What about you, captain?" Coortahn implored. "Won't you be doing the same?"

"I'll be holding her steady," Harl grunted. "You know as well as I what the captain's responsibility is. You'll be faced with the same choices when get your own sleigh. Now go! We're approaching cloud cover, that's where I want everyone to dive. We can only pray that the hawks will continue after the sleigh."

Coortahn gave Harl a firm pat on the shoulder and a heartfelt salute and followed his captain's order.

Any hope Joel had of avoiding the inevitable died when he saw *Cloud Chaser*'s co-pilot step into the main cabin. The horses were in full panic. Their bucking, stomping and kicking sounded like muffled thunder. Each strike reverberated through the main cabin and Joel's knees quaked with every one. The sound of wood rattling and the whistle of wind through fractures in the walls drifted up to them from the rear compartment. The whole time, the whipping of flapping wings and hungry cries of the scythe-wings provided a constant, terrifying background resonance. Amid all of that pandemonium, however, the loudest noise in his ears was the beating of his own heart.

Joel started at every sharp snap of breaking wood and metallic clang. And then he literally jumped when the rear compartment lurched with a jolt that sent a violent tremor throughout the sky sleigh. The lurch was followed by a prolonged, echoing creak. He saw Coortahn's eyes go wide with dreaded realization. It was time.

"Drop the hatch!" he commanded.

The crewman on the aft side of the wide port hatch pulled a heavy lever. There was a screech of metal sliding upon metal followed by a loud clank and the heavy port hatch swung down and open. A cold wind whooshed into the main compartment just as an ominous groan of straining wood echoed from the rear compartment.

Azhju'lestra yelped when a booming snap rocked the vessel. In the next instant the rear compartment fell away and took the rear wall of the main cabin with it.

Sudden shifting winds roared through the ruined sky sleigh and threatened to sweep them all away. The beautiful blue sky with the white blanket of cloud had suddenly become terrifying. In fact, it was barely visible behind the terrible scene before the startled crew and passengers. The jagged edges of wooden planks framed a dreadful portrait of flailing, frothing, wide-eyed horses dropping out of view and swarms of mammoth brown hawks plummeting after them.

They could also see *Sundance,* the trailing sky sleigh that had also released its avicaws, gliding into the clouds, followed closely by a huge detachment of the giant birds. Ethan gasped at the thought of his fellow Hounds.

Nicolette.

"Dive! Now! Dive!" Coortahn screamed.

The port hatch was wide enough for four people to stand side by side with over a foot between them. Quick was the first one out. He leapt out of the hatch and seemed to hover for a fraction of a second before the speeding sky sleigh caused the illusion of some invisible force snatching him out of view. He was not wearing a uniwing, so Joel thought the young man was committing suicide before he remembered Quick was a changeling.

The sky sleigh dipped into a dense sheet of clouds. Two female crewmembers and a male one, joined by Ethan, immediately dropped out of the open hatch. Rell jumped with the next three crewmen. Raxe noticed the elf tucking into the collar of his tunic a small pouch at the end of the thin loop of string that always hung around his neck. The elf's bow was strung and hanging snugly over his right shoulder and his quiver was strapped securely to his thigh. Raxe thought he caught a hint of sulfur as the Ranger Elf hurried past.

Cloud Chaser dropped out of the cloud cover and was again surrounded by bright blue sky. Raxe could see the ground far below. It was rising quickly.

"C'mon!" he yelled to Joel and Azhju'lestra.

Raxe and his daughter started forward but Joel was frozen in fear. He could not bring himself to step to the threshold and he could not take his eyes off of the swarm of scythe-wings still diving after the doomed horses. The image grew smaller as the pitching sky sleigh pulled away from the distracted giant predator birds.

"GO!" Coortahn admonished, urging Joel forward with a firm grasp of his shoulder.

Joel's reaction was like lightning. His frightened eyes remained locked on the giant hawks even as he knocked Coortahn's arm roughly away, grasped the copilot's wrist, and slung him easily out of the open port hatch, all in one motion.

Raxe saw Joel's eyes glaze over an instant before he tossed Coortahn. It was as if he was not even aware of his actions. The blank expression turned to fear once again when the stream of hawks suddenly broke off from their diving flock mates to resume their pursuit of *Cloud Chaser*.

Raxe stepped so close that the two men were almost nose-to-nose.

"Live or die, cuz," Raxe grated. "We're outta here." He turned to Azhju'lestra, kneeled and took her hand. "Go with him," he said calmly, nodding toward the lone remaining crewman. "Daddy will be right behind you." He kissed her on the forehead before walking her away from Joel and transferring her hand to the crewman.

The offworlder gave the man a glare that promised strong retribution if his daughter was not taken care of. The crewman gave a nervous nod of understanding before the two of them turned and jumped out into the sky. Raxe turned toward Joel but stayed out of arm's reach.

"You coming?" he asked.

Joel finally wrenched his gaze slowly away and turned it to his fellow offworlder. The look of hopeless fear in his eyes was all the answer Raxe needed. He had seen that look in the military, as well as with the Cutters and in his service to the organization. It was the irrational, paralyzing terror of someone who knew they were about to die.

"One way or another, man," Raxe promised. "Let's see what you do when all your choices are taken away."

He raised Demonsbane over his head and with a grunt brought the flat side of the blades slamming down onto the wooden plank floor. Joel's eyes went white and he crouched to lunge at Raxe. The straining wood cracked and splintered beneath his feet and gave way just as Joel pushed off.

Both men dropped into the blue void.

14.5

Quick transformed into an avicaw the moment he was clear of the disintegrating sleigh. He had to ignore his natural instinct to immediately flee the swarm of scythe-wings so that he could keep pace with the sleigh as the other passengers bailed out. A few years ago, when he was much more ignorant to the dangers of the world and had no real perception of death, he probably would have found these circumstances fun. But the things he had seen during his travels with Raxe, Meldrick, and Shanderah had tempered his enthusiasm about perilous situations. All thoughts of enjoyment were swept aside by the knowledge that there were many lives besides his at stake. He did not know how many people he could save but he was determined to save as many of them as he could.

When he saw the two offworlders crash through the bottom of the sky sleigh he knew all except the captain were off of the vessel. Harl was doing an incredible job of controlling what was left of the sleigh, keeping it airborne in an attempt to draw the predator birds away from the escapees. A handful of scythe-wings continued to pursue the crumbling but swift-moving sky sleigh. They converged on it just as it reached the peaks of Hell's Mountains. Quick saw large planks of wood and streamers of cloth spray in every direction from the ripping claws and beaks of the giant hawks as the metal oval skeleton of the cockpit went down and out of view into the mountains.

Quick said a prayer for Harl Timson and banked hard toward the descending passengers of the doomed *Cloud Chaser*. He saw no sign of anyone from the *Sundance*, so he said a prayer for them, too. Three of the first four people to bail out of *Cloud Chaser* just after him must have been experienced sleigh flyers, because the way they handled their uniwings showed that they were certainly experienced divers. Both women and the man were only scant seconds away from the safety of the mountain range. They had already disengaged their glide wings and released their chutes.

Ethan, however, was having a bit of trouble. His flight was erratic, and at the speed he was moving, he was at least ten seconds away from cover. Fortunately he was still able to maintain a safe distance from the pursuing scythe-wings. The same could not be said for the rest, though.

Rell Kallen and the three crew members with whom he jumped had spread to safe enough distances away from one another during their free-fall to open their glide wings if they chose, but the speed at which the pursuing predator birds gained on them was disheartening. Their uniwings would slow their descent enough for the giant hawks to catch them, so the men and the elf remained in free-fall.

Coortahn, also an obviously skilled diver, maneuvered his body to force the wind to veer him sharply to the right at a northwestern angle, momentarily avoiding the attention of the scythe-wings. The giant hawks were locked in on the sky sleigh and the rest of the escapees. All of them were angling to the southwest toward the closest peaks. Unfortunately it did not take long for the scythe-wings to notice Coortahn. A thin stream of the predator birds broke away from the larger flock to go after the copilot. Coortahn's heroic effort meant a few more scythe-wings were distracted from the rest, but not nearly enough.

Raxe and Joel were also beyond his help. The scythe-wings dived after them moments after they fell from *Cloud Chaser's* belly. The speed of their free-fall was the only reason the scythe-wings had not already captured them. They were adult Children of the Ones, Quick told himself. He hoped they would be able to take care of themselves. The youngest Child was his concern.

The changeling avicaw made a tight arc as he turned toward the still-freefalling Azh. The young Child perfectly imitated the crewmate that accompanied her out of the sleigh, gliding parallel to him and mimicking his movements as they slowly put distance between one another in order to safely release their glide wings. From Quick's approach, he would reach the crewmate first. Because they were coming in his direction, Quick would be able to get to both of them before the closing predators, but only if he reached them before they released the glide wings. The wings would slow them down enough for the scythe-wings to reach them before Quick could. He knew it would be very close either way.

The changeling's intention was to get close enough for the crewmate to grasp him and mount his feathered back. The crewmate, however, had no way of knowing the giant bird's intentions. He did not even know Quick was a changeling. When he saw the teen jump without a uniwing he thought the youngster had simply panicked. All he knew was that the trained sleigh birds were dead, so to him the approaching avicaw was just a wild newcomer that intended to beat the scythe-wings to an easy meal.

Too ashamed and too frightened to spare the girl as much as an apologetic glance, the crewmate twisted his body and veered away from the approaching avicaw. Azh's eyes grew wide, but not in fear for herself. She was concerned for the crewmate. Quick's hypersensitive hearing heard her yelling at the crewmate not to flee. To Quick's amazement the little girl immediately understood what was happening even in the middle of such a harrowing predicament. The man's panic, however, as well as the wind whistling past his ears, kept him from hearing her words. He shot away as Quick continued on to Azh.

The changeling took an arc that brought him around to match her direction and speed. He turned his back to her and drifted in so closely that he almost nudged her. A small hand grasped the big feathers on his back, and then another, and then her tiny legs pressed tightly against him.

"I wanted to fly the uniwing," she pouted, "but this will be fun, too!"

Quick squawked a short admonishment and pulled away, putting more distance between himself and their pursuers while heading for the Ranger Elf and the three crewmembers that dived with him. He said a small prayer for the panicked crewmate that refused his help as the man released his glide wing and headed to the mountain range. Several scythe-wings converged on him only seconds later.

That was one instance where Quick cursed his acute hearing. The sounds of rending flesh and snapping bones and screams of agony drifted to him through the rushing wind and hungry cries of the predatory birds.

Rell Kallen would not go down without a fight. He stayed in free-fall, needing the speed to keep as much distance as possible between himself and the scythe-wings. Even as he angled towards the mountain range he knew that he would never the reach the mountains without opening the glide wing. But he also knew that the cluster of scythe-wings that broke away from the main flock to come after him would have him in mere seconds after he pulled either of his cords, and long before the changeling avicaw approaching from the right could rescue him. The one thing he knew to be truer than any other, though, was that he would not go down without a fight.

He spun himself around until his back was to the ground and he was facing the pursuing scythe-wings. As disconcerting as it was to see the sky rushing away from him and not being able to tell how close he was to the ground, he knew the predator birds would reach him long before the earth would, and he had to see them approaching for what he had planned.

The Ranger Elf pulled his bow from his shoulder with his left hand and with his right hand he slid three slender arrows out through the small seam in his tightly fastened quiver, holding them tightly between his four fingers. He knocked the arrows and took aim at the approaching flock. Narrowing his canted elven eyes, he instantly zeroed in on the three scythe-wings closest to him. He adjusted his aim for the rushing air and the giant hawks' angles of approach. He pulled back the taught bowstring and let the arrows fly. The arrows found their marks. Before they struck their killing blows, sending feathers and blood spraying into air, Rell had already knocked three more arrows. He loosed them and knocked three more even as the next three stricken hawks began to plummet to the ground.

The other scythe-wings would be upon him before he could send any more than three additional volleys, but Rell Kallen was not worried. From his left, he saw a spot of light that, within a fraction of a second, had grown to a bright, yellow-orange flare as it streaked toward him. The Ranger Elf sent one more trio of arrows into the closing group of predator hawks before pulling back the bow in his left hand and grasping out at the air with an open right hand. The instant his arm and fingers were fully extended, the flame-colored streak was upon him. Rell closed his hand into a tight fist, clutching a handful of warm, glowing down and was whisked away from the approaching scythe-wings.

Quick pulled up sharply as the fiery streak, with Rell Kallen in tow, tore past him. He was immediately concerned about Azh but the centrifugal force of his sudden change of direction kept her pinned to his back. The changeling's keen vision saw clearly what was to the others only a flash of light. It was yet another bird, but nothing like his current avicaw form nor the scythe-wings. This brilliant red-and-yellow avian was half again as long as an avicaw but not as broad. The head was short and blunt, and a flaming yellow comb protruded from its crown. Its wings were disproportionately long and seemingly too narrow to support the bird's slender but lengthy frame.

Quick, however, knew that the bird's flight was powered not by the physical strength of its wings but by its magic. It was the magic that caused the fiery glow that left a long red-orange contrail and the smell of burning air in its wake. He had heard stories about the creature that had just streaked past but he had never seen one. He had always believed the legendary bird was either extinct or just a myth. He heard the little Child's gasp of astonishment.

Apparently she, like him, had never seen a Phoenix.

The startling passing of the Phoenix gave even the scythe-wings pause, but not for long. In moments they were once again in full pursuit of their freefalling meals. Quick turned his attention to the three men still in free-fall. They were experienced divers, Quick could tell.

They twisted and stroked in the air to angle their free-fall in the direction of the mountain range. They would straighten their bodies like arrows to momentarily pull away from the pursuing birds and then spread their arms and legs to create drag and influence their direction. But the changeling knew it could not last. The ground was closing fast and the men would have to open their wings if they had any real hope of reaching Hell's Mountains. And worse, the scythe-wings closed more and more air between them each time they increased drag.

The changeling avicaw banked deliberately to bring himself parallel to the crewmen. They were less panicked than their dead mate and his sharp avicaw eyes could see the relief in their faces as they beckoned to him excitedly. They opened their bodies to slow themselves just enough for Quick to catch up to them. Within a few seconds made excruciating by the steadily gaining scythe-wings, two of the crewmen had skillfully joined Azh on the giant bird's back.

The scythe-wings were almost on them and the third diver was still falling. Both Quick and he knew there was not enough time for the man to mount. The lead hawk was already nipping at Quick's tail feathers. The avicaw put on a sudden burst of speed and snatched the diver out of the air with a huge right claw around his waist and then he put real distance between himself and the enthralled scythe-wings. The diver wrapped his arms in a death grip around the powerful talons and howled his relief.

Quick went all out, not concerned about exhausting himself the way the doomed sleigh birds had. While he could not tow so much extra weight indefinitely, he had more than enough energy left to beat the scythe-wings to the peaks of the Hell's.

He hoped.

14.6

In his air force days Raxe learned to skydive as part of his training. He thought that would be the best way to face and conquer his fear of heights. It put him in a situation where he had to act or die, and he rose to the challenge every time. But not even that was able to completely banish his fear.

Riding on sky sleighs and gryphons and dragons and magic clouds had also helped him acclimate to his fear, but only somewhat. And now, with a swarm of giant man-eating hawks pursuing him, he was fighting panic. Fortunately he had years ago learned how to maintain focus in terrifying predicaments. Experience had taught him to use the negative energy of fear to fuel his strength, his focus, and most importantly, his resolve.

Raxe's plan was to angle his way to Joel and hold onto him as they fell. If necessary, he was prepared to use himself, specifically his enchanted armor, to shield Joel from the scythe-wings' razor sharp edges. Unfortunately, Joel did not cooperate. The man dropped like a stone, not making any attempt to control his fall. Once Raxe gathered himself and looked over, he could see that Joel had fainted.

Oh hell, Raxe thought. His frustration was quickly tempered when he recalled that until a few weeks ago, this guy was a computer-aided drafter. A pang of sorrow at how unfair this all must seem to Joel pushed Raxe's frustration completely away and galvanized his determination to get Joel through this safely. He had just turned his body and was attempting to straighten it so that he would streak towards his fellow offworlder when something slammed heavily into his hip and sent him tumbling through the air uncontrollably.

His airborne tumble took him into the sunrays of a cloud break, where he was able to finally control his free fall. Before he could get his bearings, a large shadow engulfed him. Instinctively he snatched Demonsbane from his hip and spun around at the same time. All he saw was his axe blades cut through dull brown feathers. In the next instant he saw the headless body of a scythe-wing plummeting away. The spraying blood from the neck stump formed a crimson spiral in the sky as it fell.

Raxe had just enough time to get his bearings before two more scythe-wings, followed by several more, could reach him. He had been knocked eastward, away from the Hell's range. He took a quick look at the plight to the west.

The sky sleigh was crumbling to pieces on the far side of the easternmost mountains while countless scythe-wings dived after the sky sleigh escapees or zigzagged after a lone avicaw that could only be Quick. He looked to where Joel should have been, but his heart sank when all he saw was a broad line of scythe-wings streaming further westward, carrying Joel away from the rest of the crew. The front of the line of giant hawks was swollen with activity. The attacking scythe-wings twirled and darted in and out erratically as they took Joel over the mountaintops. Even though he did not see the splash of blood that was visible when the hawks fell upon the avicaws, they were flying in the same frenzy he had seen them in when they attacked the sleigh birds. It was a feeding frenzy and Joel was the main course. Raxe strained to find any sign of Joel but all he saw was the savaging flock of deadly birds.

And then his own group of scythe-wings was upon him.

Powerful, hooked beaks slammed over and over into his armored torso and thighs, tossing him this way and that. He could hear sharp talons scraping against his armor as well, but far too many times he could feel the sting of razors cutting the exposed parts of his flailing arms and legs. As much as his appendages whirled, however, they were not out of control. His armor-booted feet, gauntleted fists, the greaves on his forearms, and especially Demonsbane's large blades, made the birds pay dearly for entering the circumference of his defense.

The salty, coppery taste of blood filled his mouth. The sound of angry and pain-filled avian shrieks stung his ears and the loud pings and high-pitched screech of talons and beaks scraping against metal set his nerves on end. Crimson spray and loose, scattering feathers blinded him, but Raxe swung, kicked, and punched on. The shock of impact let him know that every one of his strikes connected, so numerous and unrelenting were his attackers.

He lost track of how long he had been falling and fighting, but the scythe-wings finally relented. His vision cleared and he oriented himself to see the sky rising away from him. The few scythe-wings that survived his manic defense were flying away from his field of vision. He ringed Demonsbane, grabbed a ripcord and turned his body face down to release his glide wing.

The ground was not much more than few yards away.

Raxe had only enough time to curl his body into a fetal position. A horrible jolt and a deafening crash were the only things he was aware of just before everything abruptly went quiet and dark.

14.7

Quick easily pulled away from the pursuing scythe-wings but he knew they would not relent. His first responsibility was to get his charges to safety. Ethan and three of the crewmembers had found safety among the densely-packed cliff faces and narrow passes of the mountain range. Quick intended to deliver his passengers to their comrades.

The changeling avicaw swooped into the mountain range, staying close to the mountainsides while weaving smoothly through narrow canyons and rocky cliff walls. Within minutes he spotted Ethan and the crewmembers huddled in a shallow grotto nestled among huge boulders. The changeling avicaw settled down to unload the rest of the survivors.

He knew scythe-wings hunted by swarming their prey and overwhelming it with numbers. The closeness of the mountainous terrain would not allow the scythe-wings to maneuver and attack in their accustomed fashion. They would have to approach in smaller numbers, making them more vulnerable to counter attack. Ordinarily, that type of cover would be enough to discourage a flock of the predatory hawks and send them after easier prey.

This, however, was no ordinary situation. Quick's instincts told him that the magic driving the savage birds, as subtle as it was, might compel them to work their way around the cliffs and crags to get at their prey.

He was correct. When Azh climbed down from his back to join the rest, Quick could hear the approach of the pursuing scythe-wings. They were filtering their way through the maze of mountains with magic-induced resolution. The oversized hawks would be less formidable among the slopes and overhangs of the rough mountains, but they would still be deadly. The fact that they were determined enough to come this far was evidence of their murderous determination. Quick would have to draw them away from the humans and devise a plan for driving them away permanently.

Quick morphed into his human form and turned to the sky sleigh survivors.

"The hawks' hunger is not natural," he said. "The cover of these mountains will slow them but it won't stop them."

One of the scythe-wings sailed into view from around a high cliff and spotted them. As it shot toward them, several others followed.

"Get into that cave," Quick instructed, pointing to a narrow fissure in the mountainside less than twenty yards away. "I will block it and draw the scythe-wings away."

Ethan hurriedly ushered the sky sleigh crew and Azh to the mouth of the cave. Quick rushed behind them, morphing as he did so. He leapt high into the air, stretched out parallel to the ground, and landed in the form of a trigargan.

A twelve-foot tall, twenty-foot long bulky herbivore with natural armor, it resembled a colossal blunt-snouted armadillo. Its shell was gray and short fur of the same color covered the few places not protected by its armor plates. The unarmored tail, however, was proportionately longer than an armadillo tail, and from the beasts' narrow head protruded three curving horns. Two horns protruded symmetrically from the sides of its head. The middle horn curved up from the base of the skull and over the top of its head to end in a dull tip that pointed forward and slightly down.

Once the eight others were safely in the cave, the trigargan nudged a massive boulder in front of the opening. The boulder did not completely cover the cave mouth but the small openings were too narrow to allow the giant hawks through. The boulder had barely settled when a scythe-wing swept down and pecked at the hardened plates on the changeling trigargan's back. Quick barely felt the strike. Another predator hawk fell upon him and tried unsuccessfully to gouge his flesh with wickedly sharp talons but failed to do more than scratch the tough hide.

The trigargan erupted into a fit of bucking and kicking. It turned and swung its head as much and as quickly as his lumbering form would allow, clipping any scythe-wing not fast enough to avoid him. Within minutes, though, the trigargan was swarmed. More and more of the giant hawks made their way to the mammoth beast.

The predator hawks tried to peck at the trigargan's eyes while evading the deadly horns. Others scrambled along the ground like waddling vultures and tried to get at his softer underbelly. Their wings fluttered madly as they skipped forward and back and from side to side, darting in to nip at his belly and skittering away to avoid the trigargan's clawed stomping feet. The careless ones had their necks or backs broken or their skulls pulverized.

Ethan, Azh, and the rest watched in fearful awe through the spaces between the boulder and cave opening. Azh's wide eyes mirrored the worry of the surrounding men and women. Every so often, a scythe-wing would peer back at them and reach a talon or hooked beak through the opening. Each attempt was met with a blow from a sword or dagger that discouraged the scythe-wing, but another would soon take its place.

Quick knew he could not keep this up indefinitely. The number of giant hawks attacking him grew every few seconds. Some of the scythe-wings were able to hook the tight seams between his plates of natural armor and worry at them painfully before he could drive them away. Their razor sharp beaks eventually started to penetrate the thick skin on his legs and tail, causing blood to seep from the multiple scars. It was getting more and more difficult to protect his eyes. Quick wanted to attract as many of them as he could before carrying out the next phase of the plan he was still forming but he was beginning to tire.

The changeling trigargan lowered its horned head and retracted it into the plates protecting his shoulders. The beast looked like a giant sectioned battering ram with three curled horns jutting from its tip. The mammoth creature aimed those horns at a cliff that fell sharply away from the mild slope fifty yards away from the cave sheltering his companions. The short, thick legs burst into motion and carried the trigargan toward the cliff with surprising speed. The sound of his passing sounded and felt like a slow roll of thunder.

The sky sleigh survivors gasped almost in unison as they watched the trigargan plunge over the cliff. A stream of scythe-wings followed, shrieking excitedly.

Quick did not allow himself to free-fall in his trigargan form for long. He turned end over end as he fell and emerged from his third turn in his avicaw form. He leveled off and flew as fast as he could, tilting and twisting around narrow cliff walls and dipping in and out of valleys while the relentless scythe-wings followed. What he really wanted to do was fly up and over the peaks of the mountains, but too many scythe-wings paced him from above and were close enough to catch him if he flew that way. Instead, he flew parallel to the ground at a slow descent to keep as much distance between him and his pursuers as he could.

Avicaws' larger, more powerful wings made them among the fastest birds in the world in open spaces where they could fly straight and full out. Scythe-wings, however, were smaller and individually they could maneuver through small spaces better than the larger avicaw. Quick did not have a chance to give himself as much of a lead as he did when entered the mountain range, so the hawks quickly gained on him as the rocky mountainsides whipped by in a blur. He could hear their hungry cries only yards behind him. There was no more time to waste trying to outrun them among the mountains.

Quick changed his angle of flight to a steep climb. The scythe-wings that were coming down on him cried out and attacked. The razor-tipped beaks and the evil points of the scythe-wings' claws drew blood as they raked across his hide, but the changeling's size, speed, and momentum allowed him to burst through the assault. He ignored the pain and struck out at them with his own formidable beak and talons as he went by.

A long, wide line of scythe-wings followed him skyward, into the thick sheet of clouds and then above them. Quick took them on a long, wide arc that looped slowly around until he was headed east. But then the thin air and the day's exertion began to take their toll. If the hawks had not been enthralled they would have grown exhausted and given up long ago, but the magic drove them beyond their natural physical limits and savagery.

Quick flew parallel to the clouds for as long as he could. He wanted to get all of the pursuing hawks to fly through the clouds before he descended, but there was no way he could be sure they had. With fatigue setting in, he had no choice but to go down. He zipped back through the clouds and went into a diving spiral. The scythe-wings followed.

He then morphed back into his human form. A human mouth and hands were needed for what he planned next.

Master Mage Delthar told him many times that the only magic he should meddle with was his transforming magic. He warned the young changeling that he was far from prepared to use his apprentice training anywhere other than the practice halls and yards of the *Chronicai Tul Myst*. Quick actually agreed, but there were some very simple spells that he had mastered and perfected in the early days of his schooling. He also remembered something that Rionn Lorr had told him during one of their lessons:

When you absolutely must use your magic, always cast the simplest spell necessary to achieve your aims.

There was no spell any simpler than a phase change, particularly turning water into ice. Instead of focusing on an individual hawk, Quick widened his focus to the entire flock. As he plummeted toward the ground he made some hurried hand movements and, being sure to use the exact inflections and tones taught to him, he murmured:

"From sun's fire to chill of night, breath of the gods, turn water to ice."

The droplets of moisture that attached to the scythe-wings' feathers when they flew through the clouds started to harden into clinging pebbles of ice. Quick repeated the gestures and words over and over as quickly as he could. In a matter of seconds, the chill from the ice on the hawks' wing feathers spread to the surface of their skin. Their rapid wing beats began to falter as the cold leached their energy away. By the time the ice and cold spread to the chests of the scythe-wings, they were already plummeting to the ground.

Quick, as exhausted as he was, was not quite out of danger. The scythe-wings dropped from the sky like feathered stones. The changeling transformed once again, this time into a hummingbird. The quick little bird flitted this way and that, narrowly avoiding ice-hardened falling bodies. He made a beeline toward the foot of the mountains while the giant falling hawks crashed to the hard ground around him with sickeningly heavy thuds accented by the loud crunch of shattering ice and breaking bones.

A pang of sorrow pierced his heart for having to kill so many of the Lord Ascendant's creatures, but the magic driving the scythe-wings left him no choice. The spell cast on the deadly birds was a subtle one, a slight boosting of their naturally voracious hunger and relentlessness to devastating effect. The spell was as simple as the one he cast to stop them, and it was as effective as it was simplistic. And Quick had no idea how to remove it.

When he returned to the mouth of the cave he saw that the boulder he had used to block the opening was gone. The surviving crewmembers and Ethan were standing several yards up the slope of the mountainside and watched him return with expressions of awe.

Azh stood a few feet away from the mouth of the cave next to her father, who was seated on one of the large chunks of the boulder that had been neatly sliced into fourths and lay sprawled around the close packed earth. His helmet and travel pack rested next to him on the large stone as Raxe brushed dust from the cloven boulder off of the sides of the axe blades. His hands were shaking and he had a dazed look in his eyes.

Raxe had seen Quick transform so many times that he was able to do a much better job of masking the awe he felt. This time was no exception when he watched the hummingbird grow and stretch and shed its feathers. The featherless wings folded onto themselves and the folds merged into soft, flesh colored tentacles that flowed into the shape of thin arms. The feathers on his legs and torso retracted and changed into the same clothing he was wearing on the sky sleigh. In a moment, Quick's human form stood before them.

"I thought you might be injured," Quick said to Raxe.

"What can I say?" Raxe shrugged weakly. "I tucked into a ball and let the back of the cuirass absorb the impact. This is some damn good armor. My ears are still ringing, though. How are you, kid?"

Quick could see through Raxe's show of bravado and knew the man was more shaken than he was willing to admit.

"Winded," Quick understated. The adrenaline-charged incident having past, fatigue settled onto him like a heavy, wet blanket. He could barely keep his knees from quaking.

"I see you managed to keep your travel pack," Ethan noted, pointing at the small dun colored pack at Raxe's side.

"Yeah," Raxe said. "I was lucky. I had it tucked into my mid-section when I touched down. The strap broke, though."

"At least you still have it," Ethan said, disappointment clouding his eyes. "I lost mine while I was airborne."

"That's understandable," Raxe said.

Ethan shook his head. "But it's not acceptable. The shard of Sollustre's Eye was in that pack."

That gave Raxe pause. They needed the Eye as an early warning of a demon presence. The Dierglyorr had managed to elude it somehow, but it was much better to have it and not need it than need it and not have it.

"It couldn't be helped," Raxe finally said. "Don't beat yourself up about it."

Ethan nodded, yet the shadow of his disappointment continued to darken his face.

Raxe turned to Quick. "What'd you do?" he asked. "I saw you morph into human form for a second before those birds started raining to the ground. You were too far away for me to tell what happened."

"A freezing spell," Azh said with a smile of wonderment as she stared wide-eyed at Quick.

The changeling had never had someone look at him with the type of admiration he saw in Azh's expression. He was used to surprised awe and breathless shock and even fear when humans saw firsthand what he could do. Azh's beaming appreciation made him blush slightly in spite of himself. His moment of flattery disappeared in an instant when he thought about the missing offworlder.

"Joel," Quick said, leaving the rest unspoken.

Raxe looked up at the high, jagged earthen wall that was Hell's Mountains. The sky above the peaks not hidden by the low blanket of clouds revealed nothing but blue sky. The sight of the berserk giant hawks engulfing Joel and disappearing into the western skies was still painfully sharp in his mind.

"He's gone," Raxe said softly.

"He can't be," Quick argued. "He's a Child of the Old Ones. Surely –"

"He's gone!" Raxe roared. A strange, almost maniacal look came to his eye and all of the survivors saw it.

When Raxe spoke again his voice was tense and angry, but his volume was subdued and the strange look was gone. "The scythe-wings took him," he continued. "The same way they took the horses and all the other poor bastards who were too slow or too stupid to get away."

For a time, no one spoke. Raxe's sudden flash of anger had startled them to the point where they were all too uneasy to respond. Then again, they did not have to. All eyes were on him. As the appointed leader of this expedition he knew that they all waited for him to decide their next move but he had no idea what to do next. He rested his elbows on his knees and buried his face in hands.

Ethan hurried over to Quick with a worried look. "Did you see any survivors from the *Sundance?*"

Quick dropped his head. "I'm sorry my friend. I did not."

Ethan fell silent. He closed his eyes and all he could see was Nicolette's beautiful face. All he could hear was her voice. Just days ago they had expressed their true feelings for one another for the first time. Now she was gone.

"What do we do now?" Ethan asked.

Raxe only sighed. What *could* they do?

This was why he chose the life of a solo agent with the organization. He never wanted to be responsible for other's lives. He had failed to keep the Cutters together, but at least no one died on his watch as interim commander. But now…

What would he tell Joel's wife? Joel promised Lisa that he would return. Raxe helped to convince both of them that

Joel had to come across the WorldGate and then failed to protect him. Rionn Lorr believed that Joel was the key to their success and apparently so did the demon.

And now Joel was gone.

Raxe thought about Dan and Lisa on the other side of the WorldGate, fighting for their lives against the demon and its minions with no one to help them.

He had to remind himself that this was a mission, and most missions had casualties. That reminder did nothing to ease his anger and frustration but it did make him realize that the only way he could help his grandfather and Joel's widow was to complete his mission on this side of the WorldGate and then return home.

Rell Kallen had fled. Joel and over half of their company had been devoured by the scythe-wings. And none of that mattered now. Raxe forced himself to accept of the only thing that did matter. He lifted his head from his hands. His gaze found Ethan, Quick, and the other survivors in turn.

"What do we do?" Raxe echoed. "What we went on the mission to do. We find the Hell Key before the Dierglyorr does and we send that demon back to hell."

Epilogue

A dark blue sedan sped south on Chicago's Dan Ryan expressway. Two men sat inside. Other than their different hair colors – one dark brown and the other pale blonde – they could have almost passed for twins. Both sported short, neat haircuts. Both wore dark slacks and blazers, both of which concealed multiple compact but powerful firearms. One kept a sharp eye on the road as he weaved through the late evening traffic while the other talked on a cell phone.

"Yes, sir," he said. "The hotel owner, who has to play clerk since the old clerk literally lost his head, tried to tell us the cops took everything that could be considered evidence. We assumed old man Franklin took any video and computer storage devices he could find but we suspected the owner had a stash of hidden backups from his surveillance cams and the hidden room-cams. We convinced him to show us and got what we needed."

The driver smiled fondly at the memory. The owner/clerk chipped more than a few teeth on the Glock that he was forced to chew during the interrogation. The driver wished they had been given permission to kill the smart-mouthed bastard, but since they were not, he had to be content with giving the fat wiseass a good beating.

"The resolution was better than I'd expect for such a cheap motel," the passenger continued. "There were only a couple of minutes of footage from the room before Franklin broke the connection. They wore some pretty good disguises. We might not have made them at all if we hadn't found the backup lobby footage that showed them after they'd taken their makeup off. There's no question that it was Franklin and the Harvey woman."

There were a few seconds of silence before he continued.

"Yes. We've picked up the package and we're almost back at the hotel. We're coming to the exit now." He listened for a few more seconds before saying "Yes, sir," and pressing a button on the small phone to turn on the speaker function.

"About this package," the supervisor's voice said from the phone. "I know this is unusual for us, but these are unusual circumstances. And because these are such unusual circumstances, from here on out you are not to mention the package to anyone. There's a possibility that outside entities may soon attempt to monitor our lines of communication, so in future conversations, don't even mention the package to *me* unless I bring it up first. Do you understand, gentlemen?"

"Yes, sir," said the driver and passenger nearly in unison.

"Good," said the supervisor. There was a click and the line went dead.

The passenger clicked the phone off and turned to his partner. "The supervisor is chattier than usual on this one."

"Yeah," the driver acknowledged. "He's taking a more active role in this case. But this is an investigation of one of our own…and one of our best. I'd imagine the supervisor's ass will be in an even bigger sling than ours if we can't find Axe and the people working with him."

"I still don't get why the hell we have to take this 'package' back to the hotel," the passenger said to the driver as he jabbed his thumb at the back seat. "No way can that thing track them from there. Does the supervisor think they're walking or something? This is the city, not the woods. They're either in a car or bus."

"No shit," the driver replied. He glanced quickly over his shoulder at the portable kennel in the shadows of the back seat and the weird animal within. "And what kind of dog *is* that, anyway?"

The agent in the passenger seat shook his head. "The supervisor called it a 'retriever' but that doesn't look like any retriever I've ever seen."

"I know," he driver said. "It looks more like a hairless, oversized Chihuahua."

The passenger frowned and shook his head as he studied the lounging canine. "The head does, a little," he granted. "Only meaner, and the snout is too long. Its body is more like a young greyhound than a Chihuahua."

"Yeah," the driver agreed. "But it's huskier than a greyhound. And those teeth…those fangs look evil."

The upper and lower canine teeth were so long that the animal had to perpetually bare its fangs to keep them from piercing its own lips. Even though it was lying still, oversized head resting on its forepaws, it looked like it was silently growling at them.

"Everything about it looks evil," the driver said before changing the subject. "So do we get to kill the clerk this time or what?" he asked.

"The supervisor didn't say," the passenger answered. "And you know as well as I do that if he doesn't give the order, we don't do the deed. That's why Axe is in the shit."

The canine in the back seat suddenly jumped to all fours so quickly and forcefully that the kennel bounced.

"Whoa!" the passenger yelped, reflexively reaching for the gun in his left shoulder holster beneath his blazer.

The dog's eyes narrowed to slits and started to glow with a strange lavender shimmer. Its head began to dart excitedly from side to side.

"What the hell's wrong with that thing?" the passenger asked nervously.

The driver shrugged. "No idea…but we're just down the street from the hotel. You think that's a coincidence?"

By the time they stopped at the front of the hotel, the dog was standing erect and leaning forward slightly. It was as still as a statue and might have been mistaken for one if not for the rapid rise and fall of its broad chest. Its lips pulled back even farther to reveal black gums and more wicked teeth.

A look of disbelief shrouded the passenger's face. "No way," he said. "Do you see that?"

"Are you talking about his eyes?" the driver asked, catching a glimpse of the beast in his rear view mirror and then quickly looking away. "Scary,"

"Scary as hell," the passenger concurred. "But that's not the only thing freaking me out. The supervisor told me that would happen. What's freaking me out is that the dog's already picked up their scent. From *inside* this car. With the damn windows rolled up. I guess we don't get to rough up the clerk again. Drive to the corner."

The driver did, and when they reached the corner, the dog quickly turned to the right and assumed its earlier attentive pose. A barely audible growl began to rumble from deep within the beast's chest.

"OK," the driver said. "I guess we go right."

"What the hell kind of dog *is* that?" the passenger asked.

"Damned if I know," the driver said. "But I'd hate to be one of the rabbits he's hunting."

END

Keep reading for a preview of the next book in the Kingdom of Lorr Chronicles:

DEMON OF LORR

A Kingdom of Lorr Novel

M.J. Stewart

Chapter 1: Forced Detour

1.1

Colonel Rheingold Strong watched the fully armed and armored company of Gryphon Ryders approach from the gray southern skies and wondered if this was overkill. His superiors sent only a squad a few days earlier when the colonel led his battalion against the horrible walking dead. This time they sent a full company. Strong could make out one platoon of lance, one of longbow, one of spear, and one of crossbow. He knew they pursued a formidable foe, but his mounted battalion already more than doubled the number of men they were pursuing.

The company of Ryders glided down smoothly in a tight arrowhead formation of ten columns of ten Ryders. They flew almost wingtip-to-wingtip in a wide, staggered pattern. The head of the two middle columns flew a length and a half ahead of the column leaders to the left and right and a full three lengths ahead of the Ryders just behind them. That pattern continued along the span of the company's lines to form a flying wedge or chevron. The bird-cats were in perfect synchronicity, flapping their huge wings in unison, wings that spanned anywhere from fifteen to twenty feet. The large bird-cats canted at the same angles at the same time, effortlessly maintaining the same distance from their flock mates no matter what maneuver they performed.

Just ahead of the two middle columns, the colonel noticed two men wearing wizard's robes. Long staffs hung from both of their saddles. One of the robed men wore the dark brown of an Echelon One mage and the other, a younger man, wore the lighter tan robe of an Echelon Two mage. Mentor and student. As they descended, the tan robed mage and his gryphon turned west and darted away. Strong assumed the younger wizard had gone ahead to scout.

Colonel Strong tallied the head count. High General Ramos had already dispatched Strong's mounted light battalion of five hundred, which consisted of five companies: one hundred sword and shield one hundred full arms, one hundred lance, one hundred spear and ninety eight archers, with Strong and his second to lead them. The Minister of War decided to fortify Strong's battalion with a company of Gryphon Ryders one hundred strong and two powerful Echelon wizards. How could all of this be needed to subdue fewer than two hundred mortal men that did not even employ magic?

Lieutenant Colonel Caleb Godson sat upon his steed a few feet to the colonel's left. He paid no mind to the impressive spectacle descending from the sky. His attention was focused in the opposite direction. He studied the ground curiously. Strong knew the longtime soldier well enough to recognize that he was searching for something.

"Let me know what you find, Caleb," Strong said before turning his attention to the Ryders, who were now earthbound.

With their oversized eagle's wings folded in against their flanks, the gryphons' wide padded cat's paws and muscular feline legs carried them across the sparsely grassed terrain as smoothly as their wings carried them across the skies. The colonel recognized the commanding officer riding at the head of the middle right column.

"Captain Zedek!" Strong called.

The captain heeled his mount to a stop right next to the right flank of Strong's cavalry horse. The two men locked wrists.

"It's been three years, yes?" Captain Zedek greeted.

"Yes," Strong confirmed. "The Cursed Opening."

"Aye," the captain nodded. "We only see each other in dire times." The captain nodded toward the brown-robed mage. "This is Mage Gilder Raynard, an Echelon One mage sent by Rionn Lorr himself."

The mage and colonel nodded and grasped forearms. "Well met," they said to each other.

"'T'is good to see you, Strong," Zedek continued. "But these bein' the only circumstances when that happens, I'd rather not see you at all."

"I have to say I wasn't expecting to see you," Strong admitted. "They only sent us a mere squad of Ryders when we faced those walking dead back east. Now we're pursuing a company of only two hundred normal human men. Does this seem a bit much to you?"

"I hope it *is* a bit much," Zedek said. "That way we'd be done with this all the quicker so that we can go back east to help defend against those walking dead monsters."

"I would not be in such a rush to face those creatures if I were you," Strong advised. "We've just come from there, and as taxing as it was to have been called back across the kingdom when we were less than two days away from Ridgeland, I was more than relieved to hear a regiment had been stationed there. That meant we could come west to fight men instead of those walking dead…things."

"Surely they were no worse than the demons we faced during the Cursed Opening?" Zedek asked.

"Not in might, no," Strong agreed.

He thought about the poor soldier that spotted his son traveling with the walking dead. Strong could still remember, more clearly than he would have liked, the fear and confusion and heartbreaking sadness burned into the soldier's eyes when his own child attacked him. He could still hear the savage screams of rage and anguish of the men under his command as they were attacked and then transformed into the dreadful creatures.

"But in other ways," the colonel concluded, "they were much worse than the demons."

Mage Gilder leaned forward. "Do not underestimate the men we pursue," he warned. "They are *S'Zan Rho* and *Ken d'Zanir*. With their fighting prowess it would take every last man in your battalion to give you a slim chance to best one company of *Ken* in traditional combat. But the *Ken* are not engaging us in traditional combat. We fear they may have some… assistance."

"Since you and your junior Echelon mage are here, I assume they have assistance of a magical nature," Strong said. The confrontation suddenly became less appealing.

"Something like that," the mage muttered.

"What the bloody hell does that mean?" Strong demanded.

"We fear they have found a way to block magic," the mage said.

Strong thought about that for a moment and frowned. "Then what good are you and your protégé going to be?"

Zedek chuckled darkly. "I asked the same question, my friend."

"We don't have to engage them directly," the Echelon One mage began. "With our magic, we can scout much further and faster than your men. As we speak, Mage Kenth is off to cast probes to pinpoint their location."

Strong nodded. "Of course it would be an advantage to know their exact location at all times. But we already know they are running from us and in what direction." The wily soldier raised an eyebrow. "What would be really nice would be if you wizards could use your magic to transport us right on top of them."

Mage Gilder scoffed. "If only it were that easy."

"Then all we can do is follow their trail," Strong said. "From what I've heard of their lizard mounts, we won't run them down. By all accounts those land dragons can run almost as fast as gryphons can fly. But their trail is clearly heading west, where they will have to either enter the Hells to cross into Darshay or meet a ship somewhere on Lake Onyx to ferry them west."

Zedek nodded and added: "It would be foolish for them to travel south, for it would take too long to flee the kingdom. If they do continue south we will have a regiment circling around to wait for them, will we not? All we would have to do is trail them and cut off their retreat."

"You assume they are running," the mage pointed out. "What if they are not?"

"They may be tough," Strong said. "But surely they are not stupid. They must know a superior force would have been sent after them."

"Yes," the mage agreed. "But they are *Ken*. It is not in their nature to flee unless there is no other alternative. Their extra assistance could very well be providing them more than just the ability to block magic, and they are formidable enough without assistance."

"Aye," said Zedek. "I've not seen them fight, but I've heard tales of them when I've visited the western regions of Derr'Shan. If they be as tough as they're made to sound, I'd not expect them to turn tail and run."

"When Mage Kenth casts his probes," Mage Gilder added, "he will spot any ambush the *Ken* may have set. If at any time the probe is snuffed against his will from their ability to neutralize magic, he will immediately know their general location and then pull back to send word to me."

Lieutenant Colonel Godson rode to them at a brisk trot from further along the *Ken d'Zanir*'s trail. The colonel saw the hard set of his Lieutenant Colonel's square jaw, the dark look in his eyes, and knew something was bothering him.

"What is it, Lieutenant Colonel?" Colonel Strong asked as Godson approached.

Godson shook his head with uncertainty. "There is something strange about these tracks, sir. It's been bothering me since we found their abandoned camp north of Port Lorrian. It appears that they are all staying near the shoreline as they head west."

"What do you mean it 'appears' they're staying along the shoreline?" asked the colonel. "Their tracks are easy enough to follow."

"Yes," Godson conceded. "And if these were hoof prints I would have spotted it earlier. These oversized, six-legged lizard tracks are a bit harder to read. But I'm convinced now that there are nowhere near two hundred sets of tracks. At the most, there is half that amount."

Without a word, Mage Raynard gave a small tug to his mount's reins. The mage and the gryphon shot into the sky, racing eastward and parallel to the battalion's path. The two warriors watched the wizard and gryphon shrink out of view as they sped away.

1.2

Mage Paulus Kenth sat astride his gryphon at the top of a steep rise and looked west. He would have preferred to go east. The horror that was making its way to the Bluethorn and Ridgeland region was a much greater threat to the Kingdom of Lorr than a fleeing enemy. However, the Head Mage Rionn Lorr had ordered them to go west. Kenth would fulfill his duty as thoroughly and quickly as possible.

He was no fool, though. Mage Kenth knew he was sent here because he was an inexperienced Echelon Two mage. This threat was the less dangerous of the two. Kenth had distinguished himself during the excavation of Infinity Isle. He was an Echelon Three mage at the time, but his ability to locate even the smallest enchanted talismans and artifacts had impressed Master Mage Delthar enough to recommend his promotion to the Head Mage. Upon his promotion, the Master Mage requested that Kenth be a part of the team that monitored Soullustre's Eye for the presence of demons in the Known Lands. As the second-ranking conjurer in the Kingdom of Lorr, behind only the Head Mage, Delthar's recommendation was highly sought by all Echelon mages.

Kenth appreciated the endorsement. It was a prestigious and important assignment that would have put him in regular communication with the Mage Delthar, but Kenth preferred a more mobile assignment. The Head Mage granted his request and sent him on this mission. Even though it was little more than a dull scouting expedition, it was better than sitting in a dark room staring at tiny yellow lights in a big ruby ball for hours on end.

His sharp eyes followed the curve of the great lake until it disappeared behind the rising foothills of the Northern Hells and then he whispered a spell to summon his farsight. The spell caused a stirring of energy behind his eyes. Into that compressed swirl of magic he lent a bit of his sight, his hearing, his senses of smell and touch.

When the swirling magic was properly saturated with his senses, he pushed down from behind his eyes and moved it through his neck and left shoulder, down his left arm and into his open palm.

A more conservative wizard would have sent it down his right arm and through the long, straight, tapered staff clutched in his right fist. The staff was carved from hard pale wood and was nearly as long as the mage was tall. Runes were carved neatly, if sporadically, along its polished surface and a loop was cut into the wide, broader high end of the staff. Within the loop was secured a large, clear crystal. The staff would have helped to focus and filter the magic, to expend it more efficiently than releasing it through flesh, but Mage Kenth did not want to focus his magic this time. He wanted the broad, unfocused burst that rushed warmly from his left hand because it would cover a wider area.

His magic filled the earth, sky and the southern edge of Lake Onyx as it rushed westward. It moved like the wind, searching nearly thirty square miles for any scent, sight, or sound to relay back to its master. It eventually picked up the familiar sounds of an armed march. The rhythmic sound of heavy footfalls – not the sharp *thump-thump* of hoof beats and more like the muffled *whumph whumph* of wide paws – was clear enough to let him know that there were many large animals on the move. Mage Kenth's magic relayed to him the vibration of the earth in time with the sound. He could hear the clink of metal upon metal. Through his magic, he gauged the sound had traveled nearly a half mile before reaching his extended hearing. Although he could not yet see them, he had a good idea why.

There was a small dale just beyond the higher elevation of the foothills, the north edge of which ended at the steep cliffs of Hell's Bluff. His extended sight had not quite reached the bluffs and could not yet see down into the dale. He was sure the enemy was crossing through the dale at that moment. Mage Kenth eagerly anticipated the visual. He had never seen a land dragon, the fabled and fierce lizard that served as the *Ken d'Zanir*'s steeds. He was eager to do so.

But the magical breeze dissipated just shy of Hell's Bluff. Mage Kenth suspected it would, knowing that thirty miles was just about the range of that particular spell when dissipated in so wide a pattern. The Echelon mage whispered the spell once more and sent the magic down his right arm and into his staff this time. The broad casting of his sight gave him their general location. He could now focus on them.

Using the staff to concentrate the breeze of magic, he held it high to cast a horizontal beam of power that followed the same general path as the broader instance of his farsight. He had a general idea of where they were, but he wanted to be sure. The compressed beam would allow his extended sight to travel nearly three times as far so that he could get a visual confirmation of their precise location. The magic would also convey the exact distance.

The magic beam cut west for a time and then, to the Echelon mage's dismay, it ended abruptly.

This time, though, it ended well shy of the bluffs.

"They're coming back this way," he realized aloud.

Mage Kenth whipped the reins and gave a couple of short tugs to his right, compelling his gryphon to dart into the sky, dip its right wing and bank around sharply clockwise until it was flying back east the way they had come. The wizard leaned in close and dug his heels into the bristly fur on the bird cat's leonine flanks. Its feathered head and neck dipped lower and its long cat ears folded back as they gained speed and altitude.

As the mighty wings beat furiously, the mage tossed one more concentrated farsight spell from his staff. This time it was a sheet of magic that would linger and give him an idea of how fast the enemy was approaching. The blanket of magic ended sharply less than fifteen miles away and shrank back toward him with frightening speed.

A wave of what Mage Kenth could only describe as nothingness swept eastward. It was like a hungrily expanding void that devoured his extended senses and threatened to devour him as well.

He knew of the land dragons' renowned speed, and instantly regretted not having mastered the *myst* spell, which created a cloud-like mist on which the spell's caster could ride through the air at incredible speeds.

Only Echelon One mages, Master Mages, and the most adroit sorcerers were powerful enough to cast the spell and maintain it for great distances.

But he knew that he and his gryphon had enough of a head start to beat them back to royal battalion. From the sounds of the approaching enemy that floated to his magic just ahead of the ravenous void, Mage Kenth estimated the distance from the edge of the void to the Ken was roughly a half-mile.

Not nearly far enough for the Echelon Two Mage.

As the minutes passed and the gryphon streaked across the sky, Mage Kenth closed his eyes and concentrated, calling upon his magic to form a mental warning that he sent out ahead of him to his mentor. An instant later he tossed yet another blanket farsight spell behind him.

The magic detected a host of loud and horribly familiar *thwack*ing sounds just before his magic came racing back at him. The void rushed eastward even faster than before, *much* faster. So fast, in fact, that Mage Kenth was compelled to look over his shoulder with his normal vision.

A host of large, sharp wooden bolts, as thick as an average-sized man's arm, tore through the sky and came right for him. There was a moment of confusion as he recognized the bolts as smaller versions of the ammunition used in bolt-firing ballistae mounted on seafaring warships. That was why the sound was so familiar.

He got over his confusion quickly and yanked the reins down while kicking his left heel into the gryphon's flank. The command sent his mount into a sharp bank that caused the lead bolt – which for some reason was wobbling as it flew toward him – to sail just to the right and above the bird-cat and rider at the apex of its arc.

Mage Kenth mentally recited a spell to cast a protective barrier around him and his mount.

But there was no longer any magic within him.

With a frightened start, he whipped the gryphon into a steep dive that he hoped would take him below the path of the whistling bolts. He hoped in vain.

One bolt ripped through the gryphon's left wing. The bird-cat let loose an ear piercing screech and went into a spiraling plummet that threw his rider from the saddle.

The wizard desperately recited every spell he could think of as he fell. He had to recite them mentally because the rushing air around him sucked his voice away. He waved his hands frantically in an attempt to weave a web of magic that would use the very air to stop his fall, or at least slow his descent to a non-lethal speed.

But there was no more magic to weave. Not a trace of it remained within him or without.

As he fell, a strange serenity overcame him. He knew he was about to die and there was nothing he could do about it.

Echelon Two Mage Paulus Kenth closed his eyes, let the wind roar past his ears, and took the time to wonder just how the magic-devouring void had been able to catch up to him so quickly.

He recalled the wobbling lead bolt that he had barely managed to avoid. He thought it strange that the missile had a small, dark red ribbon attached its flat end. And then he realized why it had flown so erratically. There was something strapped to it...a dark fist-sized object that he vaguely remembered seeing somewhere else.

Before he could remember where he had seen that object before, he struck the earth with a deadly jolt and was no more.

1.3

Raxe stood only inches away from the edge of a high cliff among the vast and barren mountain range, anger clouding his thoughts. He knew he should have been traveling with the rest of his team, which was made up of him, the six surviving members of the sky sleigh crew, Quick, Ethan and Raxe's daughter, Azh.

More importantly, though, he knew he would be no good to any of them until he could get his temper under control. An irrational anger smoldered inside of him and he was having a hard time dampening it.

Joel was gone, stolen away by a swarming flock of scythe wings. Even though Joel's power was unpredictable and uncontrollable, it had proven to be impressive. They needed that power for this mission. Joel was finally starting to open up, too. Just when he had begun to move past the fear and worry that distracted him to the point of being more of a liability than an asset, he was torn away from the group. That sparked frustration within Raxe that was almost too much for him to bear.

It had been years since he had been so angry that he thought he might lose control. In fact, it had not happened since his pre-teen years just after his mother died. It took a while, but to his grandfather's great relief, Raxe finally learned to control his anger. He first taught himself to become numb to it. And then he found a way to transform it into the calm, cold resolve that made him such an effective soldier and assassin.

His anger had been mastered, or so he thought, so he was surprised when it began to erode his calm and resolve. Why would it happen now after so many years of effectively controlling it? Joel was barely related to him, a cousin almost as distant as Shanderah and Rionn Lorr. In fact, until a few days ago Joel was a complete stranger to him. Raxe would not expect Joel's loss to have such a profound effect on him. Did he feel a greater love and sense of duty for the Kingdom of Lorr than he realized?

If anything, that should have strengthened his calm and

resolve the way it had on his first visit to Lorr, when the sorceress Shanderah died and he made up his mind to confront the King of the Dragons for the first time. But now he was anything but calm and resolved. All he wanted was smash something, to use his enchanted battle-axe to tear into the mountain until he reached the other side or died trying.

He knew he would not be any good to his team in this psychological state, so he sent them on without him with the promise that he would catch up with them when he felt he was ready. Azh was much more hesitant to leave without him than the others but he eventually convinced his daughter to leave with the rest of them.

If he bothered to look down he would have been able to see the group making its way carefully down the steep, rocky, switchback trail on the face of the mountain. His attention, however, was directed skyward. He peered over the peaks of Hell's Mountains into the western skies, frustration causing his hands to clinch into tight fists.

Raxe was not accustomed to failure. Every mission he had ever undertaken – whether it was with the Air Force, Special Forces, the Cutters, or the organization – ended in success. He had experienced setbacks on countless occasions but outright failure was something with which he had very little experience…until he lost Joel.

The Head Mage believed Joel was not only the key to this mission to retrieve the Hell Key; he believed Joel was the key to their primary goal of defeating the Dierglyorr. The demon apparently believed the same thing. It had pursued Joel in two worlds before it finally got to him.

And it got to him on Raxe's watch.

The image of the giant birds swarming Joel and carrying him into the western skies was still agonizingly sharp in his mind. That image served to add fuel to his anger and once again Raxe had to struggle to keep it together for the sake of their primary objective. If for no other reason than revenge, he had to press on and make this mission a success no matter how unlikely success might be after the all of their losses.

But there were plenty of other reasons to press on, not the least of which was his grandfather's safety. The demon continued to hunt his grandfather and Lisa on the other side of the WorldGate. Stopping the Dierglyorr on this side of the WorldGate would go a long way toward ensuring their safety. Another reason to complete his mission was the safety of both this world and his. As badly as the Dierglyorr wanted to destroy the Children of the Old Ones, that was merely the first step in its overall goal of dominating all of mankind on both sides of the WorldGate.

And then there was the promise he made to Ethan's mother. Raxe vowed to Annastace that he would do everything within his power to return her first born home to her safely. Raxe had to keep it together to keep his promise to her. He thought about Annastace's hazel eyes and the way they so earnestly reflected her emotions. The look in her eyes at her fallen husband's memorial three years earlier had almost brought tears to his eyes when he had not cried since his mother's funeral nearly twenty years before.

Meldrick Sureblade had been on a mission with Raxe when he was struck down, and now Meldrick and Annastace's son was accompanying Raxe on a mission. He knew that he could not bear to see Annastace's eyes filled with that sadness again.

Raxe's frustration eased a bit at the thought of Annastace. The anger that sought to overtake him shrank away like some supernatural nocturnal beast slinking away from the dawning sun. His resolve began to solidify and he started to feel more like himself. The anger and frustration were still there, but their intensity finally receded to a more manageable level.

A glance down the mountainside revealed that the team was several hundred feet almost directly below him. They had reached a part of the mountain that was not as steep and treacherous as the stretch of the mountain face they had to negotiate moments earlier. They were only a few dozen yards from the foot of the mountain. Raxe was about to follow their path when he thought better of taking the same route that they had taken.

It took more than two hours for them reach their current location. In the interest of time and relieving a little more frustration, Raxe decided to take a different route.

He backed away from the ledge about thirty feet. He checked to make sure the strap holding his small travel pack to his side was tight and that the strap that held Questblade within its sheath was secure. After a deep breath he broke into a sprint. He ran to the edge of the cliff and leapt, sailing in a long arc that abruptly turned into an intimidating drop.

The rest of the team saw him jump. All of them, with the exception of Azhju'lestra, started to panic. Their first thought was that the frustrated offworlder had gone mad and decided to take his own life. The little girl simply watched her father and smiled.

As Raxe tucked himself into a tight ball and plummeted to the base of the mountain, the others recalled that he had survived a much higher fall just hours earlier. He was a Child of the Old Ones, after all, a descendant of fabled god-like beings. He wore the enchanted armor of his divine ancestor and namesake. By the time he landed with a loud crash of stone and metal, the rest of the group was chuckling at their fearful reactions.

Raxe stood up and stepped out of the dust cloud caused by his impact, shaking dirt from his long dreadlocks and brushing it from the brown skin of his exposed biceps and elbows. Quick, Ethan, and the surviving sky sleigh crew approached him warily. While he did not look as maniacally outraged as he had a couple of hours ago, frustration was still clearly etched into his face.

Azhju'lestra ignored his expression and walked over quickly to resume her usual place at his right hand. A strange instinct tempted him to put his arm around the adorable youngster's small shoulders but he stopped short. It was still too awkward for such shows of fatherly affection.

They had not spent enough time in each other's presence for him to develop any kind of genuine paternal feelings for the girl. If not for the fact that he could feel their familial bond through her aura and their shared heritage as Children of the Old Ones, Raxe would never have believed she was his daughter.

Kids made him uncomfortable. There was no room in his violent world for children. They were too fragile and unpredictable. On top of everything else, Azhju'lestra was just plain weird.

She looked six or seven years old even though she was barely three. She rarely talked and she showed virtually no emotion except for a flash of excitement when she leapt from the doomed sky sleigh with the rest of the crew and passengers. Raxe was not sure if she stayed so close to him out of affection or because her mother, a water faerie even more mysterious than Azhju'lestra, ordered her to. Until Raxe had a better idea of her feelings about him he thought it best to hold back on showing even a small bit of affection.

Quick saw the uneasy expression and lingering anger on Raxe's countenance and hesitated for a moment. But what he had to say was too important. He risked a step toward the offworlder.

"About Joel…" Quick began. "I saw no – " he stopped short of saying "pieces" and sought a better word. "I saw no evidence that the scythe wings had savaged him. He may yet live. Can you not you feel his presence through the connection shared by the Children of the Old Ones?"

"No," Raxe said. His damaged, deep, sandpaper voice rumbled. "But I never could feel Joel's aura. Neither can Rionn Lorr or Gramps."

"Should we not try to discover evidence of Joel's fate, whatever it may be?" Quick asked.

"No!" came a familiar voice from around a large outcropping. All heads turned as the Ranger Elf Rell Kallen stepped into the open. His long braided hair was windblown but otherwise the elf was none the worse for wear.

Raxe rasped, "If my bones weren't still rattling I'd break your legs." His rough, gravelly voice took on a sinister tone. The site of the relatively unscathed Ranger Elf brought the irrational anger creeping back. He took a deep breath and managed to keep it at bay.

As everyone else who had escaped from the sky sleigh battled the deadly scythe wings, the Ranger Elf was whisked to safety by a flaming winged creature that streaked through the sky almost too fast for the human eye to follow.

"That little trick of yours comes in real handy for a

coward," Raxe growled.

"It was magic, not a trick," Rell corrected. "But then I would not expect an ignorant offworlder to know the difference."

"You have a Phoenix stone," Quick observed. "Not exactly standard gear for a Ranger Elf, is it?"

"This is not a standard mission," Rell returned. "My queen has charged me with the retrieval of the Hell Key and I mean to fulfill that charge. That is something I cannot do from the afterlife." He raised an eyebrow. "You know of the Phoenix stone? You're rather learned for such a young one."

Quick's pride urged him to boast of his training at the Kingdom of Lorr's *Chronichai Tul Myst* academy of magic. His instinct urged against it. Instinct won out. He changed the topic of discussion back to the matter at hand.

"How should we find out what happened to Joel?" Quick asked Raxe.

"We *don't*," Rell interjected. "If he survived he'll live or die by his own wits. The Hell Key must remain our priority."

"Rionn didn't bring him here to die," Raxe reminded. "I know he hasn't been much help but we'll need him before this is over. There's a good chance he's alive. Back at Port Lorrian, when the *Ken* attacked, they tied him up but tried to kill everyone else. That could mean the demon needs him and I damn sure don't wanna find out why. If he's not dead we have to get him back."

It was at that moment that Raxe realized why Rionn Lorr brought Joel to the Kingdom of Lorr, even if the Head Mage himself did not know exactly why at the time. Joel's power was not affected by whatever it was that neutralized the others' magic at Port Lorrian.

While everyone else was powerless, Joel managed to kill two fierce land dragons with his bare hands…or what passed for his hands at the time. If Joel's power could not be dampened, he could be an invaluable weapon for their cause.

But then again, Raxe knew, Joel could be just as dangerous a weapon *against* their cause if the Dierglyorr found a way to use Joel against them.

"And if he *is* dead?" Rell challenged. "How long do we

search? The demon won't wait for us to find his corpse. It will do what it must to gain control of the Hell Key. We must do the same."

"The Ranger Elf has a point," Ethan mumbled, his head hung low.

Raxe was surprised Ethan was talking at all. He had been brooding silently since the sky sleighs were brought down, and with good reason. The young tracker lost his fellow Keeper's Hounds in that attack, including a couple that he held in particularly high regard. Ethan was no stranger to combat, but he was still only sixteen years old. Raxe wondered if Ethan was really that strong or if he was just a damn good actor.

"There is no doubt that Rionn Lorr brought Joel here for good reasons," Ethan continued. "However, we all are charged with the task of retrieving the Hell Key. I think we should locate Mar-dah's keep as soon as possible."

"I know a talisman as powerful as the Hell Key should never be in the possession of a demon," Quick agreed. "But even if the Dierglyorr does find it first, it can't use it. The WorldGate and Hell Keys can only be used by Children of the Old Ones."

"If I must," Rell added impatiently, "I will continue on to Hargathall's Cleft alone. If there are any clues there to the location of Mar-dah's keep, who's to say the demon won't find them if we dally?"

The surviving sky sleigh crew looked on with keen interest while the elf, offworlder, changeling and Keeper's Hound considered their options. They also wondered what their role would be now that the sky sleighs were gone.

Raxe was the leader of this expedition and he could command all save the elf to do as he wished, and what he wished was to go after Joel. Rionn Lorr had earned Raxe's trust, which was not an easy thing to do.

It seemed to him that Rionn's efforts to bring them both across the WorldGate would be wasted if they did not at least try to find the other offworlder.

At the same time, however, he could not discount the concerns of the elf and the young Sureblade. What would they do if the demon found Mar-dah's keep and the Hell Key within it while they searched for Joel? That could not be allowed. Quick was right in his assertion that the Keys could only be used by Children of the Old Ones. However, Rionn Lorr and Raxe knew something the others did not, not even the crafty Ranger Elf.

There was another Child of the Old Ones out there.

The Child was likely the offspring of Mar-dah and the desert witch Shara Dune. They knew of the Child's presence but had been unable to pinpoint his or her location, nor Shara Dune's, for that matter. If the Dierglyorr, an ancient and immensely powerful sixth level demon, gained possession of both the Hell Key and the hidden Child, it would have complete control of the gates of hell.

With an army of demons at its command, its ability to cross the WorldGate at will, and its knowledge of magic long forgotten by any other living being save the King of the Dragons, it could do far more damage than Mar-dah had during the Cursed Opening. But then again, what would happen if they abandoned Joel? They could later find themselves in another situation where their magic failed. Joel would be the only one that could help them. Without Joel's help, or even worse, if the demon found a way to use Joel, they might not find the Hell Key anyway.

On a whim, Raxe turned to Azhju'lestra. The little half-water faerie girl tugged on a long aqua-blue lock of her silky hair. Raxe squatted down so that his eyes were level with his daughter's.

He marveled yet again at her resemblance to his mother. Only her hair, complexion and eyes resembled Sabrina's. The sparkling of those multi-hued coral-colored eyes in the fading sunlight, along with her tiny, curious smile, extinguished the last bits of frustration still smoldering within him.

"What do you think, Azh?" Raxe asked playfully.

"Ask Questblade," she answered without hesitation.

She said it as if it were the most obvious thing in the world. Raxe wondered how she even knew what Questblade was, and then remembered that the enchanted short sword was one of many topics of conversation he had with Quick on the sky sleigh before everything went wrong. He had to chuckle at his absent-mindedness. Even though magic was no longer brand new to him, it was far from second nature.

His own internal magic was involuntary so he never had to think about it to invoke it. He knew the enchanted short sword was on his hip but it never occurred to him to use it. Azh, on the other hand, to whom magic was as common as breathing, probably thought her father was a dunce.

"Good thinking, girl," Raxe said. He gave her a quick kiss on the forehead without even thinking about it. Azh flashed a surprised smile at the peck.

So much for not showing affection, Raxe thought.

He unsheathed Questblade and held it with the blade resting on his open left palm and the pommel gripped firmly in his right hand, just as his grandfather showed him. Clearing his mind of everything but the question, he thought:

What path should I take?

Having used the enchanted blade before, it was easier for him to invoke its magic a second time. The people standing around were silent. He could not even hear them breathing and he wondered briefly if they were holding their breath. A moment later he forgot about them altogether. He forgot about the warming blade in his hands. He forgot about everything else. There was only the question.

What path should I take?

And then there was the heat pulsing through his bones and muscles like warm blood through veins and arteries. White light filled his mind for a moment before it shrank into a vision of his grandfather's short sword floating against an ocean of black, pointing toward the heavens.

Quick could have sworn he saw a flash of light. It was so fleeting that he could not be sure if it was real or imagined. He did, however, feel the magic.

A glance at the curious expressions on the faces of the Ranger Elf and Azhju'lestra revealed that their sensitivity to magic had picked up something as well. Ethan and the sky sleigh crew, while very interested, did not show any signs that they had noticed the burst of magic.

A moment later Raxe was placing the short sword,

pommel down, onto the rough sloping earth.

Amazingly, the sword stood straight up the flat base of its otherwise spherical pommel, impossibly balancing on the sloping and uneven ground. *This* drew the attention of Ethan and the crewmembers. They now wore the expressions that Quick and the other two magic folk wore when they felt the magic of Questblade as it pulsed from Raxe.

The blade stood for a moment longer before dropping onto its flat side. The tip of the short sword pointed southeast.

"South," Rell Kallen said with a smug half-smile. "The blade points in the direction of the Demon's Spine and Hargathall's Cleft. It is settled, then. The magic of the Children of the Old Ones has spoken."

Raxe caught the sarcasm in that last part but he knew he could not argue. The magic of Questblade *had* spoken. While it did point towards the Demon's Spine, Raxe knew he could not abandon Joel. His gut told him if there was any chance his fellow offworlder was alive, they had to find him.

"Questblade speaks only for me," Raxe declared. "It doesn't speak for the rest of you. The blade says *I* go south. The elf chooses to go south. The rest of you don't have to."

"Of course we will," Ethan assured. "We are warriors charged by the King and the Head Mage to accompany you on this quest, not frightened children seeking an excuse to abandon the mission."

"We will follow you into the heart of Mar-dah's dark stronghold and beyond, if need be," Quick added.

"No, you won't," Raxe returned.

He looked at the mountaintops. The cool shadow of Hell's Mountains had fallen over the group. The wicked peaks of the foreboding mountain range seemed to devour the setting suns. Raxe turned back to Ethan.

"Tonight, we rest," Raxe began. "In the morning you and Quick will go west into the mountains, into Darshay if you have to, and find out what happened to Joel.

"When you find him, do whatever you have to do to bring him back and meet us at Hargathall's Cleft." Raxe paused as he considered the alternative. "If you find evidence that he's dead, catch up with us as fast as you can."

The offworlder turned a cold warning glance to the Ranger Elf and continued. "Azh, Rell Kallen and I will go to Southborough with the sky sleigh crew. We'll re-supply and arrange transportation for the crew to get back to Greenglenn. From there we'll continue on to the Demon's Spine."

Rell Kallen said nothing and nodded his agreement. The elf was fully prepared to go after the Hell Key alone but he could not deny that Raxe's presence could be useful.

Ethan started to protest. The set of Raxe's jaw, however, and the seriousness of his glare silenced the young soldier before he uttered a word. The expression of hurt on the young man's face said more than any words could.

Raxe knew how dedicated Ethan was to completing the mission assigned to him. He also knew how proud the young Sureblade was to follow in his father's footsteps by defending his kingdom alongside a Child of the Old Ones.

Though Ethan made a valiant effort of hiding it, he was crushed by the fate of the other Keeper's Hounds. The loss of his follow demon hunters made him even more determined to see this mission through to the end. But they had to find Joel…or at least find out if he was dead, even if Questblade told him to do otherwise.

Ordinarily, the fact that he had been named leader of this expedition would compel his charges to follow his orders without him having to offer any explanations. Raxe, however, had to be sure that Ethan would perform his task without the distraction of constantly wishing he were a part of the search for the Hell Key.

The young man needed to be encouraged. Ethan needed to be challenged if he was going to put forth maximum effort to find the other offworlder.

"If you trust the Head Mage," Raxe began, "trust me. He named me leader for a reason." He placed his right hand on Ethan's shoulder. "Don't think I'm just sending you two away to protect you. I'd be better off with all of the swords and magic I can get, and those scythe wings are probably just the beginning of the danger we'll all face.

"But Joel is as important to this mission as I am. Rionn

understood that. You have to understand how important it is for you to find him. Both of our worlds could depend on it."

Ethan felt a warm blush of shame for his momentary doubt. His resolve solidified as he lifted his chin and his shoulders.

"Then we *will* find him," Ethan Sureblade vowed.

Raxe almost felt guilty for not being completely honest with the teen. In truth, he believed Ethan would be much safer searching for Joel than he would be searching for the Hell Key. He had been uneasy about bringing Ethan in the first place and only did so at the insistence of Rionn Lorr. Raxe did not care if Ethan did have his father's lasso, crossbow, javelin and broadsword – as well as what the Head Mage had called the Gifted Sight. Sixteen was too freaking young for a job this dangerous. This was Raxe's chance to keep his promise to Ethan's mother. He was afraid that if he missed this opportunity he might not get another.

1.4

Lieutenant Colonel Caleb Godson was the first to spot the return of the Echelon One mage. Gilder Raynard streaked high through the air atop a thick cloud of mist, which not only puzzled but also worried the Lieutenant Colonel. He reached over to grasp the shoulder of his superior officer, who was engaged in a discussion of strategy with one of his captains. Colonel Strong looked up at the Lieutenant Colonel and then looked to where Godson was pointing. Strong's steel-gray eyes narrowed to watch the mage approach at great speed, as if he were an arrow shot from the golden bow of the Old One Lorr Himself.

"Why is he returning on a myst and not his gryphon?" the Lieutenant Colonel asked.

"His myst is faster," Strong noted grimly.

Less than two seconds later the thick, white, mist swirling around the wizard's legs and feet settled him gently to the ground and then dissolved into nothingness. The grim set of the wizard's thin lips and narrow jaw, along with the cold dread in his dark blue eyes, worried Colonel Strong. Before he could ask what was wrong, the Echelon One mage began shouting commands.

"Shields to the front, Strong! Quickly! Bring both the front and rear in to me as tightly as they can manage! And prepare to ride north!"

"North?" Strong asked. "There's nothing north of here but Lake Onyx!" He had to call out the last part because the wizard was already streaking to the great lake on his myst.

The Colonel turned to his Lieutenant Colonel, who looked just as confused as Strong felt. He paused for only the briefest moment.

"You heard the man!" Strong barked. Echelon One mages were both powerful and battle tested. Strong may not have understood their art but he respected their abilities and he trusted them. "Shields to the front!" The Colonel looked north at the quickly shrinking form of the wizard as men scrambled and orders were shouted.

A shadow fell over the hazy sky. Strong turned quickly,

his back to the lake, and looked left to see the eastern skies blocked from view by a thick hail of sharpened black bolts flying at them in a high, horribly slow-moving arc. His eyes widened and he quickly looked to his right.

To his horror, against the faint glow of the two suns through overcast skies above the peaks of the Northern Hells, another hail of deadly bolts sailed skyward toward them in the same inexorable arc.

Both of the assaults spanned too wide a distance for the battalion to clear if they tried to ride south to avoid them. And Strong was certain that their enemy was prepared for – and likely counting on – just such a reaction.

The sounds of startled swears could be heard among the rising volume of shouted orders, heavy hoof beats, the clanging of metal, and the sound of heavy wings beating as the Gryphon Ryders launched into the air. Every sound was strained with urgency. They moved with fear-fueled haste yet well-rehearsed precision. As the wizard had commanded, all of the shield men settled in at the front, overlapping and locking their shields to form a steel wall over the western edge of their broad column.

Strong started when he thought about the soldiers at the rear, where there were no shields to protect them from the bolts sailing in from the east. Even while afraid, the seasoned warrior was calm and calculating, estimating how far the bolts would penetrate into his battalion.

The bolts approaching from the east would arrive first. From the trajectory of the deadly missiles and the speed at which his men funneled inward at a tight northwestern angle, the bolts would land almost a quarter of the way inside of the back end of the retreating column.

The Colonel looked to the west and calculated that the hail of bolts would cut just slightly less deep into the front lines, just beyond the three rows of shield men that protected it. He held his breath as the deadly sharp blackwood bolts falling from the east began their downward arc, picking up speed as they descended.

All his men could do was hasten their already frenetic pace. Some looked over their shoulders as they spurred their mounts to breakneck speeds. Others dared not look, leaning just above bobbing manes and keeping their faces rigidly forward, pushing their cavalry horses with both shouted commands and heels to muscle-sheathed ribs.

Colonel Strong said a prayer for his soldiers as the bolts were nearly upon them. He wanted to turn away but he refused to, believing that turning away would be a betrayal of the men about to die for him and their kingdom.

But the lead bolts abruptly changed direction, and so did all of the rest, as if hitting an impenetrable wall. And when Strong squinted, he could indeed see the faintest glimmer of light, an almost invisible red glow at the tip of the bolts just as they bounced astray and flipped away end over end in every direction but straight down.

It was as if the bolts were hitting an invisible roof and then sliding down the sides until they fell safely away, eventually either tumbling out into Lake Onyx or landing just outside the lines of the southernmost edge of their collapsing column. Strong looked north again and saw the wizard more than a dozen yards out in the suddenly churning lake water.

Mage Gilder's face was a mask of fierce determination and focus. His plain, long, dark brown staff – which resembled a straight bow staff – was held high in his right hand while his left was thrust beneath the dark surface of the lake. The great flock of gryphons, with their massive wings beating and gliding in turn, cast dark silhouettes behind the mage as they circled the stark gray skies in the distance. The staff glowed the same pale magenta as the transparent glimmer that turned away the hard blackwood bolts.

"The wizard is shielding the rear lines," Strong breathed. "Thanks be to the old ones."

"Colonel!" Godson called as he rode back to Strong's side, pulling the commander's attention away. "The wizard would have our men ride out into the lake? That isn't a shallow river we can ford. They'll drown if they go out there. We outnumber the attackers. We should stand and fight!"

The Colonel felt the same way, but despite his doubt, he trusted the wizard. When he turned north yet again and noticed that the pace of the churning water surrounding Mage

Gilder was beginning to slow, and when he saw light ribbons of vapor wafting up from the water's surface, his doubt turned into confidence.

He had seen that phenomenon before. It was just south of the capital city of Greenglenn at the Tyne River when the Head Mage had performed the same enchantment to allow them to cross the swollen river. He wanted to sigh in relief but he did not have time.

"To the lake!" Strong roared, his deep voice booming above the din. "As quickly as your mounts can carry you! Don't stop running until your horses are swimming!"

Without hesitation, but with more than a few curious glances, his soldiers launched their steeds toward the lakeshore. Lieutenant Colonel Godson threw a stunned glare at his superior and opened his mouth to object, but he stopped cold when he saw Strong's dark glare of warning.

"There's a reason they sent a battalion and two Echelon mages against a company of mere men," Rheingold Strong said in an intensely even tone. "I trust Mage Gilder, and even if you don't, you *will* follow orders."

The colonel looked over at the mass of bolts falling from the western skies. The front had retreated, but not enough. Strong narrowed his sharp eyes again as he looked for the faint glow of the magical shield being cast by the Echelon mage. When he found it, he was anything but relieved.

The shield was beyond where the bolts would strike, and to his dismay, it was shrinking all the time, retreating almost as if it was fleeing from the threat it was created to counter.

And then it was completely gone.

Strong cringed when the heavy bolts poured violently down onto the front line. The deep clang of the hard wooden bolts striking steel boomed across the foothills like thunder. The sound of screams from men and horses followed closely behind as the lead bolts extended just beyond the shield line, far too many of them finding flesh and bone.

The weight and force and sheer number of the arm-length bolts drove the shield men to their knees. Other bolts found their way through the seams in the wall of shields. As shield men fell to the onslaught, the wall collapsed inward in quick and disciplined movements to close the gaps and keep the wall as solid as possible. The wall shrank quickly but drifted steadily backward, and after a few agonizingly long seconds the battalion was finally out of range.

But in their wake was a horrific scene. Dozens of impaled bodies, both human and equine, were pinned to ground in grizzly positions. As the last bolt fell, a small army of fiercely muscled, leather-armored warriors riding monstrous, six-legged reptilian mounts came pouring over the foothills from the east and west. Both groups fanned out as they came on, prepared to intercept any attempt to flee to the south.

The strategy was fully expected, but the nightmarish sight of the snarling, slavering, snapping land dragons still caught the colonel utterly unprepared. The beasts' terrible size and speed, their rows of needle-pointed teeth, and their crowns of horn clusters gave them look of a horde loosed from the very depths of hell. Even Lieutenant Colonel Godson, so eager to fight, was momentarily struck dumb at the sight.

The monstrous steeds and their intimidating masters closed on the front line at a fearful pace. The colonel was prepared to give the order for the battalion to reverse their retreat and attack their pursuers in full force, knowing in his heart that they could not win but preferring to die in battle, not dying while fleeing. But he changed his mind when he turned his worried gaze north once more to check the wizard's progress.

The muddy shoreline had been transformed into white slush. The frontrunners of his retreating battalion leapt over the slush and landed not in the lake, but on it. A rectangular sheet of ice expanded along the surface of the water, forming a white island almost a half-mile in area. Strong was reminded of the battle of Silverleaf, the opening skirmish in what would become the short but ruinous campaign known as the Cursed Opening.

The Head Mage created a bridge of ice across the Tyne when Glynhalla the Rainmaker, a rain elemental and agent of the evil Child Mar-dah, flooded it. And like that ice bridge, this island of ice was not smooth and slippery, which would have been a hazard to their cavalry horses. It was rough and slushy, firm enough to hold them but giving just enough to grant secure purchase to the hooves of the charging steeds.

He thanked the Lord Ascendant that the wizard was able to finish his work before their enemy's mysterious magic vacuum finished its work.

Colonel Rheingold Strong changed his command.

"Arc Thorndevil formation, soldiers! To the south! Archers' Greeting and Raxe's Anvil! Hold those *Ken* bastards! Everyone else, keep moving to the lake!"

Within a matter of seconds the remaining shield men formed another wall, this one curved and bowed outward toward the onrushing *Ken.* This time they left just enough space between their shields to allow their wall of steel to be complimented by the company of lance men, who fitted their pointed polearms between the seams.

The formation resembled the long side of a thorndevil, a heavily muscled, three-foot long weasel-like animal found in the Badlands and southern regions of the continent. The animal had a thick hide and was armed with strong needle pointed quills that it used for defense against larger predators and offense against its prey.

The companies of archers and spears swiftly lined up just behind them along the length of the front, their spears and crossbows and longbows leveled. Raxe's Anvil – a formation named for the Old One Raxe who, like his father, was both warrior and blacksmith to his fellow Old Ones – fell in behind the archers.

Raxe's Anvil was comprised of the full arms company, strong and fierce warriors wearing the heaviest armor they could while still riding in relative comfort atop their massive warhorses. They carried oversized war hammers, spiked clubs, bronze maces, long-handled battleaxes, spiked flails and two-handed greatswords.

The five companies easily outnumbered the attacking warriors, but the lizard-riders came on without pause, shouting war cries sounding eerily like the collective roar of a pride of enraged tygras. The instant the formations were complete, the archers and spearmen greeted their attackers with a devastating volley of crossbow bolts and longbow arrows and spears. Another volley darted in from overhead as the Gryphon Ryders swooped in to assist.

Many of the *Ken d'Zanir* fell from blows to vital areas, but not nearly enough of them. Far more were able to protect their vital areas with shields, buckles, and the broad-headed heavy weapons that they hoisted with such ease.

The arrows that got through to pierce their muscular arms, legs and even outer pectorals were brushed away with little or no regard as the warriors charged on. Most of the land dragon steeds completely ignored the bolts that bounced off of their green-scaled hides and the bony horn clusters atop their heads. A few missiles brought a very small number of the great beasts down when they were lucky enough to find their eyes or the back of a throat when they found an open pair of jaws that could not snap shut fast enough.

The *Ken d'Zanir* was on them before the archers could launch a second volley. The archers retreated as the *Ken* crashed into the front line with an explosion of metal almost as thunderous as the arrival of the hail of blackwood bolts. This explosion, however, was not accompanied by only the screams and roars of men and horses. It was made even more terrible by the shrieking and hissing of the monsters upon which the *Ken d'Zanir* rode.

Colonel Strong and his lieutenant colonel looked on in dismay while soldiers continued to race pass them on their way to the frozen island on the lake. Strong felt helpless as the front line crumbled under the assault of the *Ken*. In less than a minute they had torn through the Thorndevil Arc and were met by Raxe's Anvil. Surprisingly, the *Ken* actually dismounted and charged the full-arms company on foot. It was then that Godson fully understood why his commander had called for a retreat.

The *Ken*, impossibly nimble and quick for their size, dodged the furious hooves and snapping teeth of the royal army's warhorses to snatch soldiers from their mounts. The huge men from the western fringes of the Westin Continent, the western edge of the Known Lands, were easily equal to at least two of the Kingdom of Lorr's elite warriors. The difference between the Lorrian soldiers' and the *Ken*'s size, strength, quickness and fighting skill brought to the Lieutenant Colonel's mind the image of a group of seasoned warriors fighting against green adolescents.

And as if the *Ken* themselves were not bad enough, their steeds were exponentially worse.

The smallest of land dragons were longer and heavier than the biggest warhorses. They were lower to the ground, which gave them even more of an advantage. The sleek, six-legged reptiles savagely attacked the horses and the soldiers with their long curved claws and rows of razor-sharp teeth. The beasts' speed was incredible. Their long bodies had the flexibility of a snake. And they did not die easily.

It took several soldiers to bring down one of the land dragons and most of them died in the effort. Tooth and claw bit through holes in chain mail and penetrated leather and weak points in metal armor. The sheer weight and strength of the monstrous lizards broke necks and backs.

The Gryphon Ryders lent support where they could. They shot arrows and launched wicked javelins down into the *Ken*. Many of them even swooped down to strike at them with blades and polearms. But the *Ken* also had bows, slings, and javelins. Both gryphons and Ryders fell from the sky. High-leaping land dragons brought down Ryders who dared to swoop too low.

Lieutenant Colonel Godson looked on as the number of defending soldiers diminished with frightening speed and almost missed Strong's order for retreat. He wheeled his mount around and sent it dashing for the lake. He did not look back until he was more than two-dozen yards onto the island of ice.

When he did look back, he swore aloud.

Nearly a quarter of the attacking company had already penetrated Raxe's Anvil and was bearing down on the retreating, mounted archers. The archers turned and fired as their cavalry horses charged onto the frozen lake. The leading *Ken* warriors fell to the hail of concentrated arrows and crossbow bolts but their steeds continued on, pointed tongues lolling hungrily as they closed the distance between them even faster without their riders' weight to slow them down.

The rider-less land dragons were the first of the enemy to leap easily across the slushy shoreline onto the wide sheet of ice. Their weight and the force with which they landed sent a shudder through the sheet of ice, causing it to tilt. Colonel Strong, who had retreated as far back as he could on the crowded ice island, looked on in horror.

They were trapped. There was nothing to slow the approach of the *Ken* and their steeds and there was nowhere left to go.

"What now, Mage?" he called over to Mage Gilder, who stood a few yards away and looked to the west across the Great Lake Onyx. The mage turned and raised a hand for patience, looking much too untroubled in Strong's opinion.

Strong was about to lay into the mage when he heard a loud rumble and then an explosive crack coming from the direction of the shore. To his slight relief, the island had broken almost straight across the quarter-mile wide sheet of ice, about ten yards away from the shore. The momentum of the rushing land dragons pushed the frigid island further out into the lake. The chasm between the sheets of ice only grew as more land dragons, many with riders and many without, leapt across the water from the smaller piece of ice to the larger one.

Within the span of ten seconds, the larger island was too far away for even the powerful bounds of the land dragons to clear the distance. But by then there were more than enough of them on the island to do a considerable amount of damage.

The Colonel would minimize their opportunity.

"Into the lake with these bloody whoresons!" Strong cried. "Attack! Attack! Attack!"

The royal battalion was only too happy to obey. They swarmed the stranded *Ken* and their mounts. This time their numbers was too great for even the awesome warriors and land dragons. The Lorrian forces savagely struck down both man and beast while driving them to, and over, the edge of the island and into the ice-chilled lake water.

The heavy land dragons were obviously not amphibious reptiles. This was evident in the way they immediately flailed and then sank after falling into the deep water. The men, as powerful and confident as they were, were not stupid enough to attempt to regain the drifting sheet of ice and swam for the shore. More than a few of the royal soldiers died during the assault, but with assistance from the Gryphon Ryders it did not take long to clear their little frosted island of the enemy.

"Colonel!" Lieutenant Colonel Godson cried in alarm as the last sounds of battle faded to silence. "Look to the shore!"

The slight relief Strong felt when the small island broke away was dismissed by yet more concern.

"I was waiting for this," he growled.

Back at the shoreline, long rows of land dragons came trotting over the foothills hauling what initially appeared to be wagons carrying large mechanical devices. But Strong knew they were not wagons. They were small wheel-mounted ballistae, the projectile war machines reminiscent of giant crossbows. Those were the devices that had launched the deadly blackwood bolts to start this one-sided battle.

As the land dragons were steered into several lines just beyond the shore, the *Ken* warriors hastily loaded and aimed the oversized slings.

"The battalion is an easy target," Godson whispered.

"May the Old Ones protect us," Strong prayed.

"Not the Old Ones," came Mage Gilder's strong voice from the colonel's right. "An Elemental, maybe."

Strong looked further into the distance to his right and saw a wave approaching from the western waters of the great lake. He knitted his brow in curiosity and wonder at the sight. The natural tide came in and out of this side of Lake Onyx from the north and south.

How in the seven hells could the steadily growing wave come in from the west?

The leading ripples of the oncoming wave slowly spun the ice island and carried it even further away from shore, but not quickly enough to take them out of the range of the ballistae's sharpened blackwood shafts. The ice island began to turn even faster as the growing wave approached, so fast, in fact, that the horses and the men had to brace themselves. The horses widened their four-legged stance while the men sat on their haunches. Those who carried long polearms jabbed them into the icy surface and held tight. Strong spun nimbly in the opposite direction to keep the *Ken* in sight.

The *Ken d'Zanir* saw the wave approaching and realized that it grew exponentially as it came on. Many of them retreated as far away and as swiftly as they could from the shoreline. The ballista operators, though, stubbornly continued their work. Before they could trigger their several rows of ballistae, the wave roared onto the shore at its weird angle and completely engulfed the machines, men and animals that were not quick enough to escape.

By the time the water settled, the ice island had spun over a half-mile out into the lake. Only stray pieces of water-soaked wood and metal remained on the shore. There was no sign of the *Ken d'Zanir* who manned the ballista. Mage Gilder's last remark finally registered with the colonel.

"An Elemental," he echoed. "The Sea Mistress is here?"

His answer was a stirring of water in the distance out west. He caught a glimpse of beautiful flowing hair as the stunning Sabrina, Mistress of the Sea of Spirits, disappeared beneath the surface of the Great Lake Onyx.

"How could she help us?" Strong asked. "Is she immune to the *Ken's* ability to neutralize magic?"

"She's beyond the circumference of the *Ken*'s void," the Echelon One mage explained. "Once she used her magic to set the wave in motion from beyond their reach, the physical properties of wave took over. Like pushing a cart down a hill, after the initial push, gravity does the rest."

"What do we do about the *Ken*?" Godson asked.

"Their projectile weapons were either destroyed or swept out into the lake," Strong answered. "I don't expect they will try to wait us out. They will surely understand that the Sea Mistress can attack them from a distance."

"Their weapons," Lieutenant Colonel Godson said uneasily. "They were hauling wheeled ballista weapons. How could they have accomplished that without us seeing the telltale tracks?"

Strong stroked his wide, stubbly chin. "The ballista had to be waiting for them out west," he surmised. "And the group that hid so well from us and then attacked from the east after we passed had to have had the ballistae delivered to them."

"Yes," Mage Gilder agreed. "The question is who delivered it to them, and who placed them there for the *Ken* who attacked from the west?"

"And another critical question," Strong began, "Where are the *Ken* going now?"

"I fear their destination is south," Mage Gilder answered. "They were never fleeing from us. This was a planned attack. If not for Mage Kenth's warning to me, their attack could very well have wiped us all out."

"Mage Kenth?" Strong had almost forgotten about the lower ranking mage. "Where is he?"

The grave look on the mage's face was answer enough.

After a brief moment of silence, Lieutenant Colonel Caleb Godson spoke. "Why would the *Ken* be going south?"

"From what the Head Mage has told us," Mage Gilder explained, "their primary mission is to stop the Child Raxe and his party from recovering the Hell Key from the Demon's Spine Mountains. The *Ken* will follow them until they catch them and kill them. Attacking us was a bonus. The *Ken* will resume their pursuit of the Child. They'll keep to the eastern fringes of the Hells in order to remain concealed as they make their way south."

A dark look fell over the colonel's face. "And *we* will follow the *Ken* until we catch and kill *them*."

"Yes!" added Captain Zedek with fierce determination as he settled his gryphon down alongside Mage Gilder. "All we need to do is send for more men. Just one more battalion would – "

"Take too long to arrive," Mage Gilder finished. "We must track them ourselves."

"I appreciate your ferocity, mage," Strong admitted. "But that would be a fool's errand. We'll be lucky to have half of our original number, and we obviously did not have enough men to begin with. What's worse, you'll have no magic to use against them."

"But we will have the element of surprise," Mage Gilder returned, a devious gleam in his dark blue eyes. "They will not expect us to hunt them after this loss. And though my magic will not work against them directly, there is much I can do with my magic in preparation for our next meeting. They are not the only warriors who can use trickery."

Colonel Strong turned a questioning gaze to Godson. The grim determination he saw in the faces of his Lieutenant Colonel and the captain of the diminished Gryphon Ryder company encouraged him. All of them knew it was virtually suicide to pursue the *Ken*. They were all soldiers, though, fierce and proud. They were all hungry to redeem themselves after such a crushing defeat. The only question was how.

"Wizard Gilder, I'll need you to contact the palace to send for reinforcements," Strong said. "You wizards can communicate much faster than we can using scouts or pigeons, if had pigeons. We will follow the *Ken* at a safe distance while we make our preparations. We may or may not engage them. Whether or not we do will depend on how ready I think we are. If nothing else, we should be able to provide a clearer trail for our reinforcements to follow.

"But if at any time I feel we have an advantage," the colonel concluded, "we will attack with even more savagery than they displayed when they ambushed us."

1.5

Two of the *Ken d'Zanir* stood atop a grassy rise overlooking the shores of Lake Onyx. They were just under a hundred yards out of reach of the wave that had swept away the ballistae, the land dragons that transported them, and the men that worked them.

Both men, like the rest of the *Ken d'Zanir,* were well over six feet tall, broad of shoulder and narrow of waist, their long limbs lean and chiseled with muscle. The taller of the two was taller by roughly three inches, which made him close to seven feet tall. The top of his large head was adorned with a coiled headdress made of short, stubbly, azure-furred tygra hide. The hide was wrapped several times around his head with tightly braided strips trailing down his back.

They stood among a litter of blackwood bolts that protruded from the earth, many of them still pinning dead and dying men and horses to the ground. The taller warrior snatched one of the bolts from the ground. The bolt had a small red ribbon bound to its flat end. After pulling it out of the ground he flipped it so that the pointed end was facing up.

A dark fist-sized object was bound securely to the staff a few inches from its deadly point. The object had a rough surface that was such a dark reddish-brown it could easily be mistaken for black. It was somewhat round but not a perfect sphere. It was tied to the staff by a thin but tough leather thong that was fitted through a small hole drilled through the object. The *Ken's* long, thick fingers worked on the knot for a few seconds until it was undone. He handed the bolt to his companion and then tied the ends of the thong around his broad neck.

All the while, both men looked out at the ice island as it continued to float slowly out onto the great lake. The shorter of the two spoke first.

"It was the water witch, High *Ken* Lonos. I saw her just as she submerged."

"Of *course* it was the water witch, *Ken* L'Atir," replied High *Ken* Rkam Lonos in an irritated tone.

He did not see the Mistress of the Sea as his second had and he had no idea where the wave had come from, but as commander of this detachment of *S'Zan Rho* warriors, he would never admit it to an underling.

"I smelled her foul presence well before I saw her," Rkam Lonos lied. "These weak easterners could never have survived an assault from the *Ken d'Zanir* without the help of foul magic."

"Do you think she was successful by mere chance?" L'Atir asked. "Or do you think she knows the limits of our ability to extinguish magic?"

The *Ken* commander gave a dismissive wave with a big hand. "It matters not. She will not interfere again. Our benefactor has declared that she will be dealt with in short order, as will the rest of the unholy magic wielders in these eastern lands…especially the so-called Children of the Old Ones. Our *truly* divine assistance will assure their fate."

L'Atir smiled deviously. "Yes, for the Leader God S'Zan guides us."

"As always," Rkam Lonos agreed. "For now we will resume our pursuit of those who seek the Hell Key. On the way, we will pass through Port Lorrian to re-supply and sate our appetites. *All* of our appetites. And upon our exit we will tear that cursed city and its denizens to the ground. No one will be spared."

L'Atir's sly smiled faltered for a moment. "No one?" He asked. "Including the women and children? Prince T'Cheln may greatly object to such mass slaughter."

"T'Cheln is *not* the commander of this unit," Lonos reminded. "*I* am. As long as he is babysitting that ridiculous baron while we do the real work of imposing the will of the grim God S'Zan on these accursed easterners, his opinion and his parentage mean nothing to me. And you would do well to *never* question my judgment again."

The shorter man nodded and gave a quick bow of acquiescence. "Of course, commander. I apologize for my insolence. It would be my great pleasure to strike three fingers from my right hand for my indiscretion."

"No need for that," Rkam Lonos said, apparently satisfied

with the offer. He stood tall and surveyed his force.

"We lost three men at Port Lorrian," he continued, "and several more here. We will make the entire city of Port Lorrian pay for our losses. Our benefactors want us to make a 'grand statement' of our faith in the course of hunting the Child Raxe, and we will do just that.

"The people in this kingdom are followers of the weakling gods Lorr and the Ascendant One. It will be an honor for them to fall by our hands. And then we will make the Child Raxe pay just as dearly. Gather our men, L'Atir. We ride to Port Lorrian. No man, woman, or child will be left alive when we leave!"

www.ingramcontent.com/pod-product-compliance
Lightning Source LLC
Chambersburg PA
CBHW071628260626
47170CB00001B/2

9780988915824